Shere Khan   Tabaqui   Father Wolf

Akela   Mowgli   Baloo

Sahi, the Porcupine   Bagheera   Mother Wolf

Wolf Family   Red Flower   Mor, the Peacock

RUDYARD KIPLING

MOWGLI'S Brothers

CHRISTOPHER WORMELL

Collins

An Imprint of HarperCollins*Publishers*

First published in Great Britain in 1992 by
HarperCollins Publishers Ltd in association with
Creative Education Inc, 123 South Broad Street,
Mankato, Minnesota 56001. Designed by Rita
Marshall. Illustrations © 1992 Christopher Wormell

The text of this edition of Mowgli's
Brothers is taken from the first
English edition of The Jungle Book,
published in London in 1894.

Printed in the United States of America

A CIP record for this title is available from the British
Library. ISBN 0 00 193839 8. The illustrator asserts
the moral right to be identified as the illustrator of
the work.

Now Chil the Kite brings home the night

That Mang the Bat sets free—

The herds are shut in byre and hut

For loosed till dawn are we.

This is the hour of pride and power,

Talon and tush and claw.

Oh hear the call!—Good hunting all

That keep the Jungle Law!

It was seven o'clock of a very warm evening in the Seeonee hills when Father Wolf woke up from his day's rest, scratched himself, yawned, and spread out his paws one after the other to get rid of the sleepy feeling in their tips. Mother Wolf lay with her big gray nose dropped across her four tumbling, squealing cubs, and the moon shone into the mouth of the cave where they all lived. "Augrh!" said Father Wolf, "it is time to hunt again"; and he was going to spring down hill when a little shadow with a bushy tail crossed the threshold and whined: "Good luck go with you, O Chief of the Wolves; and good luck and strong white teeth go with the noble children, that they may never forget the hungry in this world."

It was the jackal—Tabaqui, the Dish-licker—and the wolves of India despise Tabaqui because he runs about making mischief, and telling tales, and eating rags and pieces of leather from the village rubbish-heaps. But they are afraid of him too, because Tabaqui, more than anyone else in the jungle, is apt to go mad, and then he forgets that he was ever afraid of anyone, and runs through the forest biting everything in his way.

Even the tiger runs and hides when little Tabaqui goes mad, for madness is the most disgraceful thing that can overtake a wild creature. We call it hydrophobia, but they call it *dewanee*—the madness—and run.

"Enter, then, and look," said Father Wolf, stiffly; "but there is no food here."

"For a wolf, no," said Tabaqui; "but for so mean a person as myself a dry bone is a good feast. Who are we, the Gidur-log [the jackal people], to pick and choose?" He scuttled to the back of the cave, where he found the bone of a buck with some meat on it, and sat cracking the end merrily.

"All thanks for this good meal," he said, licking his lips. "How beautiful are the noble children! How large are their eyes! And so young too! Indeed, indeed, I might have remembered that the children of kings are men from the beginning."

Now, Tabaqui knew as well as anyone else that there is nothing so unlucky as to compliment children to their faces; and it pleased him to see Mother and Father Wolf look uncomfortable.

Tabaqui sat still, rejoicing in the mischief that he had made, and then he said spitefully:

"Shere Khan, the Big One, has shifted his hunting-grounds. He will hunt among these hills for the next moon, so he has told me."

Shere Khan was the tiger who lived near the Waingunga River, twenty miles away.

"He has no right!" Father Wolf began angrily—"By the Law of the Jungle he has no right to change his quarters without due warning. He will frighten every head of game within ten miles, and I—I have to kill for two, these days."

"His mother did not call him Lungri [the Lame One] for nothing," said Mother Wolf, quietly. "He has been lame in one foot from his birth. That is why he has only killed cattle. Now the villagers of the Waingunga are angry with him, and he has come here to make *our* villagers angry. They will scour the jungle for him when he is far away, and we and our children must run when the grass is set alight. Indeed, we are very grateful to Shere Khan!"

"Shall I tell him of your gratitude?" said Tabaqui.

"Out!" snapped Father Wolf. "Out and hunt with thy master. Thou hast done harm enough for one night."

"I go," said Tabaqui, quietly. "Ye can hear Shere Khan below in the thickets. I might have saved myself the message."

Father Wolf listened, and below in the valley that ran down to a little river, he heard the dry, angry, snarly, sing-song whine of a tiger who has caught nothing and does not care if all the jungle knows it.

"The fool!" said Father Wolf. "To begin a night's work with that noise! Does he think that our buck are like his fat Waingunga bullocks?"

"H'sh. It is neither bullock nor buck he hunts tonight," said Mother Wolf. "It is Man." The whine had changed to a sort of humming purr that seemed to come from every quarter of the compass. It was the noise that bewilders woodcutters and gipsies sleeping in the open, and makes them run sometimes into the very mouth of the tiger.

"Man!" said Father Wolf, showing all his white teeth. "Faugh! Are there not enough beetles and frogs in the tanks that he must eat Man, and on our ground too!"

The Law of the Jungle, which never orders anything without a reason, forbids every beast to eat Man except when he is killing to show his children how to kill, and then he must hunt outside the hunting-grounds of his pack or tribe. The real reason for this is that man-killing means, sooner or later, the arrival of white men on elephants, with guns, and hundreds of brown men with gongs and rockets and torches. Then everybody in the jungle suffers. The reason the beasts give among themselves is that Man is the weakest and most defenceless of all living things, and it is unsportsmanlike to touch him. They say too—

and it is true—that man-eaters become mangy, and lose their teeth.

The purr grew louder, and ended in the full-throated "Aaarh!" of the tiger's charge.

Then there was a howl—an untigerish howl—from Shere Khan. "He has missed," said Mother Wolf. "What is it?"

Father Wolf ran out a few paces and heard Shere Khan muttering and mumbling savagely, as he tumbled about in the scrub.

"The fool has had no more sense than to jump at a woodcutter's camp-fire, and has burned his feet," said Father Wolf, with a grunt. "Tabaqui is with him."

"Something is coming uphill," said Mother Wolf, twitching one ear. "Get ready."

The bushes rustled a little in the thicket, and Father Wolf dropped with his haunches under him, ready for his leap. Then, if you had been watching, you would have seen the most wonderful thing in the world—the wolf checked in mid-spring. He made his bound before he saw what it was he was jumping at, and then he tried to stop himself. The result was that he shot up straight into the air for four or five feet, landing almost where he left ground.

"Man!" he snapped. "A man's cub. Look!"

Directly in front of him, holding on by a low branch, stood a naked brown baby who could just walk—as soft and as dimpled a little atom as ever came to a wolf's cave at night. He looked up into Father Wolf's face, and laughed.

"Is that a man's cub?" said Mother Wolf. "I have never seen one. Bring it here."

A wolf accustomed to moving his own cubs can, if necessary, mouth an egg without breaking it, and though Father Wolf's jaws closed right on the child's back not a tooth even scratched the skin, as he laid it down among the cubs.

"How little! How naked, and—how bold!" said Mother Wolf, softly. The baby was pushing his way between the cubs to get close to the warm hide. "Ahai! He is taking his meal with the others. And so this is a man's cub. Now, was there ever a wolf that could boast of a man's cub among her children?"

"I have heard now and again of such a thing, but never in our Pack or in my time," said Father Wolf. "He is altogether without hair, and I could kill him with a touch of my foot. But see, he looks up and is not afraid."

The moonlight was blocked out of the mouth of the cave, for Shere Khan's great square head and shoulders were thrust into the entrance. Tabaqui, behind him, was squeaking: "My lord, my lord, it went in here!"

"Shere Khan does us great honour," said Father Wolf, but his eyes were very angry. "What does Shere Khan need?"

"My quarry. A man's cub went this way," said Shere Khan. "Its parents have run off. Give it to me."

Shere Khan had jumped at a wood-cutter's camp-fire, as Father Wolf had said, and was furious from the pain of his burned feet. But Father Wolf knew that the mouth of the cave was too narrow for a tiger to come in by. Even where he was, Shere Khan's shoulders and fore paws were cramped for want of room, as a man's would be if he tried to fight in a barrel.

"The Wolves are a free people," said Father Wolf. "They take orders from the Head of the Pack, and not from any striped cattle-killer. The man's cub is ours—to kill if we choose."

"Ye choose and ye do not choose! What talk is this of choosing? By the bull that I killed, am I to stand nosing into your dog's den for my fair dues? It is I, Shere Khan, who speak!"

The tiger's roar filled the cave with thunder. Mother Wolf shook herself clear of the cubs and sprang forward, her eyes, like two green moons in the darkness, facing the blazing eyes of Shere Khan.

"And it is I, Raksha [The Demon], who answer. The man's cub is mine, Lungri—mine to me! He shall not be killed. He shall live to run with the Pack and to hunt with the Pack; and in the end, look you, hunter of little naked cubs —frog-eater—fish-killer—he shall hunt *thee!* Now get hence, or by the Sambhur that I killed (*I* eat no starved cattle), back thou goest to thy mother, burned beast of the jungle, lamer than ever thou camest into the world! Go!"

Father Wolf looked on amazed. He had almost forgotten the days when he won Mother Wolf in fair fight from five other wolves, when she ran in the Pack and was not called The Demon for compliment's sake. Shere Khan might have faced Father Wolf, but he could not stand up against Mother Wolf, for he knew that where he was she had all the advantage of the ground, and would fight to the death. So he backed out of the cave-mouth growling, and when he was clear he shouted:

"Each dog barks in his own yard! We will see what the Pack will say to this fostering of man-cubs. The cub is mine, and to my teeth he will come in the end, O bush-tailed thieves!"

Mother Wolf threw herself down panting among the cubs, and Father Wolf said to her gravely:

"Shere Khan speaks this much truth. The cub must be shown to the Pack. Wilt thou still keep him, Mother?"

"Keep him!" she gasped. "He came naked, by night, alone and very hungry; yet he was not afraid! Look, he has pushed one of my babes to one side already. And that lame butcher would have killed him and would have run off to the Waingunga while the villagers here hunted through all our lairs in revenge! Keep him? Assuredly I will keep him. Lie still, little frog. O thou Mowgli —for Mowgli the Frog I will call thee— the time will come when thou wilt hunt Shere Khan as he has hunted thee."

"But what will our Pack say?" said Father Wolf.

The Law of the Jungle lays down very clearly that any wolf may, when he marries, withdraw from the Pack he belongs to; but as soon as his cubs are old enough to stand on their feet he must bring them to the Pack Council, which is generally held once a month at full moon, in order that the other wolves may identify them. After that inspection the cubs are free to run where they please, and until they have killed their first buck no excuse is accepted if a grown wolf of the Pack kills one of them. The punishment is death where the murderer can be found; and if you think for a minute you will see that this must be so.

Father Wolf waited till his cubs could run a little, and then on the night of the Pack Meeting took them and Mowgli and Mother Wolf to the Council Rock —a hilltop covered with stones and boulders where a hundred wolves could hide. Akela, the great gray Lone Wolf, who led all the Pack by strength and cunning, lay out at full length on his rock, and below him sat forty or more wolves of every size and colour, from badger-coloured veterans who could handle a buck alone, to young black three-year-olds who thought they could. The Lone Wolf had led them for a year now. He had fallen twice into a wolf-trap in his youth, and once he had been beaten and left for dead; so he knew the manners and customs of men.

There was very little talking at the rock. The cubs tumbled over each other in the centre of the circle where their mothers and fathers sat, and now and again a senior wolf would go quietly up to a cub, look at him carefully, and return to his place on noiseless feet. Sometimes a mother would push her cub far out into the moonlight, to be sure that he had not been overlooked. Akela from his rock would cry: "Ye know the Law—ye know the Law. Look well, O Wolves!" and the anxious mothers would take up the call: "Look—look well, O Wolves!"

At last—and Mother Wolf's neck-bristles lifted as the time came—Father Wolf pushed "Mowgli the Frog", as they called him, into the centre, where he sat laughing and playing with some pebbles that glistened in the moonlight.

Akela never raised his head from his paws, but went on with the monotonous cry: "Look well!" A muffled roar came up from behind the rocks—the voice of Shere Khan crying, "The cub is mine. Give him to me. What have the Free People to do with a man's cub?"

Akela never even twitched his ears: all he said was: "Look well, O Wolves! What have the Free People to do with the orders of any save the Free People? Look well!"

There was a chorus of deep growls, and a young wolf in his fourth year flung back Shere Khan's question to Akela: "What have the Free People to do with a man's cub?"

Now the Law of the Jungle lays down that if there is any dispute as to the right of a cub to be accepted by the Pack, he must be spoken for by at least two members of the Pack who are not his father and mother.

"Who speaks for this cub?" said Akela. "Among the Free People who speaks?" There was no answer, and Mother Wolf got ready for what she knew would be her last fight, if things came to fighting.

Then the only other creature who is allowed at the Pack Council—Baloo, the sleepy brown bear who teaches the wolf cubs the Law of the Jungle: old Baloo, who can come and go where he pleases because he eats only nuts and roots and honey—rose up on his hind quarters and grunted.

"The man's cub—the man's cub?" he said. "*I* speak for the man's cub. There is no harm in a man's cub. I have no gift of words, but I speak the truth. Let him run with the Pack, and be entered with the others. I myself will teach him."

"We need yet another," said Akela. "Baloo has spoken, and he is our teacher for the young cubs. Who speaks besides Baloo?"

A black shadow dropped down into the circle. It was Bagheera the Black Panther, inky black all over, but with the panther markings showing up in certain lights like the pattern of watered silk.

Everybody knew Bagheera, and nobody cared to cross his path; for he was as cunning as Tabaqui, as bold as the wild buffalo, and as reckless as the wounded elephant. But he had a voice as soft as wild honey dripping from a tree, and a skin softer than down.

"O Akela, and ye the Free People," he purred, "I have no right in your assembly; but the Law of the Jungle says that if there is a doubt which is not a killing matter in regard to a new cub, the life of that cub may be bought at a price. And the Law does not say who may or may not pay that price. Am I right?"

"Good! good!" said the young wolves, who are always hungry. "Listen to Bagheera. The cub can be bought for a price. It is the Law."

"Knowing that I have no right to speak here, I ask your leave."

"Speak then," cried twenty voices.

"To kill a naked cub is shame. Besides, he may make better sport for you when he is grown. Baloo has spoken in his behalf. Now to Baloo's word I will add one bull, and a fat one, newly killed, not half a mile from here, if ye will accept the man's cub according to the Law. Is it difficult?"

There was a clamour of scores of voices, saying:

"What matter? He will die in the winter rains. He will scorch in the sun. What harm can a naked frog do us? Let him run with the Pack. Where is the bull, Bagheera? Let him be accepted." And then came Akela's deep bay, crying: "Look well—look well, O Wolves!"

Mowgli was still deeply interested in the pebbles, and he did not notice when the wolves came and looked at him one by one. At last they all went down the hill for the dead bull, and only Akela, Bagheera, Baloo, and Mowgli's own wolves were left. Shere Khan roared still in the night, for he was very angry that Mowgli had not been handed over to him.

"Ay, roar well," said Bagheera, under his whiskers; "for the time comes when this naked thing will make thee roar to another tune, or I know nothing of man."

"It was well done," said Akela. "Men and their cubs are very wise. He may be a help in time."

"Truly, a help in time of need; for none can hope to lead the Pack for ever," said Bagheera.

Akela said nothing. He was thinking of the time that comes to every leader of every pack when his strength goes from him and he gets feebler and feebler, till at last he is killed by the wolves and a new leader comes up—to be killed in his turn.

"Take him away," he said to Father Wolf, "and train him as befits one of the Free People."

And that is how Mowgli was entered into the Seeonee wolf-pack for the price of a bull and on Baloo's good word.

Now you must be content to skip ten or eleven whole years, and only guess at all the wonderful life that Mowgli led among the wolves, because if it were written out it would fill ever so many books. He grew up with the cubs, though they, of course, were grown wolves almost before he was a child, and Father Wolf taught him his business, and the meaning of things in the jungle, till every rustle in the grass, every breath of the warm night air, every note of the owls above his head, every scratch of a bat's claws as it roosted for a while in a tree, and every splash of every little fish jumping in a pool, meant just as much to him as the work of his office means to a business man. When he was not learning he sat out in the sun and slept, and ate and went to sleep again; when he felt dirty or hot he swam in the forest pools; and when he wanted honey (Baloo told him that honey and nuts were just as pleasant to eat as raw meat) he climbed up for it, and that Bagheera showed him how to do.

Bagheera would lie out on a branch and call, "Come along, Little Brother," and at first Mowgli would cling like the sloth, but afterward he would fling himself through the branches almost as boldly as the gray ape. He took his place at the Council Rock, too, when the Pack met, and there he discovered that if he stared hard at any wolf, the wolf would be forced to drop his eyes, and so he used to stare for fun.

At other times he would pick the long thorns out of the pads of his friends, for wolves suffer terribly from thorns and burs in their coats. He would go down the hillside into the cultivated lands by night, and look very curiously at the villagers in their huts, but he had a mistrust of men because Bagheera showed him a square box with a drop-gate so cunningly hidden in the jungle that he nearly walked into it, and told him that it was a trap.

He loved better than anything else to go with Bagheera into the dark warm heart of the forest, to sleep all through the drowsy day, and at night see how Bagheera did his killing. Bagheera killed right and left as he felt hungry, and so did Mowgli—with one exception. As soon as he was old enough to understand things, Bagheera told him that he must never touch cattle because he had been bought into the Pack at the price of a bull's life. "All the jungle is thine," said Bagheera, "and thou canst kill everything that thou art strong enough to kill; but for the sake of the bull that bought thee thou must never kill or eat any cattle young or old. That is the Law of the Jungle." Mowgli obeyed faithfully.

And he grew and grew strong as a boy must grow who does not know that he is learning any lessons, and who has nothing in the world to think of except things to eat.

Mother Wolf told him once or twice that Shere Khan was not a creature to be trusted, and that some day he must kill Shere Khan; but though a young wolf would have remembered that advice every hour, Mowgli forgot it because he was only a boy—though he would have called himself a wolf if he had been able to speak in any human tongue.

Shere Khan was always crossing his path in the jungle, for as Akela grew older and feebler the lame tiger had come to be great friends with the

younger wolves of the Pack, who followed him for scraps, a thing Akela
would never have allowed if he had
dared to push his authority to the proper
bounds. Then Shere Khan would flatter
them and wonder that such fine young
hunters were content to be led by a
dying wolf and a man's cub. "They tell
me," Shere Khan would say, "that at
Council ye dare not look him between
the eyes"; and the young wolves would
growl and bristle.

Bagheera, who had eyes and ears
everywhere, knew something of this,
and once or twice he told Mowgli in so
many words that Shere Khan would kill
him some day; and Mowgli would laugh
and answer: "I have the Pack and I have
thee; and Baloo, though he is so lazy,
might strike a blow or two for my sake.
Why should I be afraid?"

It was one very warm day that a new notion came to Bagheera—born of something that he had heard. Perhaps Sahi the Porcupine had told him; but he said to Mowgli when they were deep in the jungle, as the boy lay with his head on Bagheera's beautiful black skin: "Little Brother, how often have I told thee that Shere Khan is thy enemy?"

"As many times as there are nuts on that palm," said Mowgli, who, naturally, could not count. "What of it? I am sleepy, Bagheera, and Shere Khan is all long tail and loud talk—like Mor the Peacock."

"But this is no time for sleeping. Baloo knows it; I know it; the Pack know it; and even the foolish, foolish deer know. Tabaqui has told thee, too."

"Ho! ho!" said Mowgli. "Tabaqui came to me not long ago with some rude talk that I was a naked man's cub and not fit to dig pig-nuts; but I caught Tabaqui by the tail and swung him twice against a palm-tree to teach him better manners."

"That was foolishness; for though Tabaqui is a mischief-maker, he would have told thee of something that concerned thee closely. Open those eyes, Little Brother. Shere Khan dare not kill thee in the jungle; but remember, Akela is very old, and soon the day comes when he cannot kill his buck, and then he will be leader no more. Many of the wolves that looked thee over when thou wast brought to the Council first are old too, and the young wolves believe, as Shere Khan has taught them, that a man-cub has no place with the Pack. In a little time thou wilt be a man."

"And what is a man that he should not run with his brothers?" said Mowgli. "I was born in the jungle. I have obeyed the Law of the Jungle, and there is no wolf of ours from whose paws I have not pulled a thorn. Surely they are my brothers!"

Bagheera stretched himself at full length and half shut his eyes. "Little Brother," said he, "feel under my jaw."

Mowgli put up his strong brown hand, and just under Bagheera's silky chin, where the giant rolling muscles were all hid by the glossy hair, he came upon a little bald spot.

"There is no one in the jungle that knows that I, Bagheera, carry that mark —the mark of the collar; and yet, Little Brother, I was born among men, and it was among men that my mother died— in the cages of the King's Palace at Oodeypore. It was because of this that I paid the price for thee at the Council when thou wast a little naked cub. Yes, I too was born among men. I had never seen the jungle. They fed me behind bars from an iron pan till one night I felt that I was Bagheera—the Panther—and no man's plaything, and I broke the silly lock with one blow of my paw and came away; and because I had learned the ways of men, I became more terrible in the jungle than Shere Khan. Is it not so?""

"Yes," said Mowgli; "all the jungle
fear Bagheera—all except Mowgli."

"Oh, *thou* art a man's cub," said the
Black Panther, very tenderly; "and even
as I returned to my jungle, so thou must
go back to men at last—to the men who
are thy brothers—if thou art not killed
in the Council."

"But why—but why should any wish
to kill me?" said Mowgli.

"Look at me," said Bagheera; and
Mowgli looked at him steadily between
the eyes. The big panther turned his
head away in half a minute.

"*That* is why," he said, shifting his paw on the leaves. "Not even I can look thee between the eyes, and I was born among men, and I love thee, Little Brother. The others they hate thee because their eyes cannot meet thine; because thou art wise; because thou hast pulled out thorns from their feet— because thou art a man."

"I did not know these things," said Mowgli, sullenly; and he frowned under his heavy black eyebrows.

"What is the Law of the Jungle? Strike first and then give tongue. By thy very carelessness they know that thou art a man. But be wise. It is in my heart that when Akela misses his next kill— and at each hunt it costs him more to pin the buck—the Pack will turn against him and against thee. They will hold a jungle Council at the Rock, and then— and then—I have it!" said Bagheera, leaping up. "Go thou down quickly to the men's huts in the valley, and take some of the Red Flower which they grow there, so that when the time comes thou mayest have even a stronger friend than I or Baloo or those of the Pack that love thee. Get the Red Flower."

By Red Flower Bagheera meant fire, only no creature in the jungle will call fire by its proper name. Every beast lives in deadly fear of it, and invents a hundred ways of describing it.

"The Red Flower?" said Mowgli. "That grows outside their huts in the twilight. I will get some."

"There speaks the man's cub," said Bagheera, proudly. "Remember that it grows in little pots. Get one swiftly, and keep it by thee for time of need."

"Good!" said Mowgli. "I go. But art thou sure, O my Bagheera"—he slipped his arm round the splendid neck, and looked deep into the big eyes—"art thou sure that all this is Shere Khan's doing?"

"By the Broken Lock that freed me, I am sure, Little Brother."

"Then, by the Bull that bought me, I will pay Shere Khan full tale for this, and it may be a little over," said Mowgli; and he bounded away.

"That is a man. That is all a man," said Bagheera to himself, lying down again. "Oh, Shere Khan, never was a blacker hunting than that frog-hunt of thine ten years ago!"

Mowgli was far and far through the forest, running hard, and his heart was hot in him. He came to the cave as the evening mist rose, and drew breath, and looked down the valley. The cubs were out, but Mother Wolf, at the back of the cave, knew by his breathing that something was troubling her frog.

"What is it, Son?" she said.

"Some bat's chatter of Shere Khan," he called back. "I hunt among the ploughed fields tonight"; and he plunged downward through the bushes, to the stream at the bottom of the valley. There he checked, for he heard the yell of the Pack hunting, heard the bellow of a hunted Sambhur, and the snort as the buck turned at bay. Then there were wicked, bitter howls from the young wolves: "Akela! Akela! Let the Lone Wolf show his strength. Room for the leader of the Pack! Spring, Akela!"

The Lone Wolf must have sprung and missed his hold, for Mowgli heard the snap of his teeth and then a yelp as the Sambhur knocked him over with his fore foot.

He did not wait for anything more, but dashed on; and the yells grew fainter behind him as he ran into the crop-lands where the villagers lived.

"Bagheera spoke truth," he panted, as he nestled down in some cattle-fodder by the window of a hut. "Tomorrow is one day both for Akela and for me."

Then he pressed his face close to the window and watched the fire on the hearth. He saw the husbandman's wife get up and feed it in the night with black lumps; and when the morning came and mists were all white and cold, he saw the man's child pick up a wicker pot plastered inside with earth, fill it with lumps of red-hot charcoal, put it under his blanket, and go out to tend the cows in the byre.

"Is that all?" said Mowgli. "If a cub can do it, there is nothing to fear"; so he strode round the corner and met the boy, took the pot from his hand, and disappeared into the mist while the boy howled with fear.

"They are very like me," said Mowgli, blowing into the pot, as he had seen the woman do. "This thing will die if I do not give it things to eat"; and he dropped twigs and dried bark on the red stuff. Half-way up the hill he met Bagheera with the morning dew shining like moonstones on his coat.

"Akela has missed," said the Panther. "They would have killed him last night, but they needed thee also. They were looking for thee on the hill."

"I was among the ploughed lands. I am ready. See!" Mowgli held up the fire-pot.

"Good! Now, I have seen men thrust a dry branch into that stuff, and presently the Red Flower blossomed at the end of it. Art thou not afraid?"

"No. Why should I fear? I remember now—if it is not a dream—how, before I was a Wolf, I lay beside the Red Flower, and it was warm and pleasant."

All that day Mowgli sat in the cave tending his fire-pot and dipping dry branches into it to see how they looked. He found a branch that satisfied him, and in the evening when Tabaqui came to the cave and told him rudely enough that he was wanted at the Council Rock, he laughed till Tabaqui ran away. Then Mowgli went to the Council, still laughing.

Akela the Lone Wolf lay by the side of his rock as a sign that the leadership of the Pack was open, and Shere Khan with his following of scrap-fed wolves walked to and fro openly being flattered. Bagheera lay close to Mowgli, and the fire-pot was between Mowgli's knees. When they were all gathered together, Shere Khan began to speak—a thing he would never have dared to do when Akela was in his prime.

"He has no right," whispered Bagheera. "Say so. He is a dog's son. He will be frightened."

Mowgli sprang to his feet. "Free People," he cried, "does Shere Khan lead the Pack? What has a tiger to do with our leadership?"

"Seeing that the leadership is yet open, and being asked to speak—" Shere Khan began.

"By whom?" said Mowgli. "Are we *all* jackals, to fawn on this cattle-butcher? The leadership of the Pack is with the Pack alone."

There were yells of "Silence, thou man's cub!" "Let him speak. He has kept our Law"; and at last the seniors of the Pack thundered: "Let the Dead Wolf speak." When a leader of the Pack has missed his kill, he is called the Dead Wolf as long as he lives, which is not long.

Akela raised his old head wearily:

"Free People, and ye too, jackals of Shere Khan, for twelve seasons I have led ye to and from the kill, and in all that time not one has been trapped or maimed. Now I have missed my kill. Ye know how that plot was made. Ye know how ye brought me up to an untried buck to make my weakness known. It was cleverly done. Your right is to kill me here on the Council Rock, now. Therefore, I ask, who comes to make an end of the Lone Wolf? For it is my right, by the Law of the Jungle, that ye come one by one."

There was a long hush, for no single wolf cared to fight Akela to the death. Then Shere Khan roared: "Bah! What have we to do with this toothless fool? He is doomed to die! It is the man-cub who has lived too long. Free People, he was my meat from the first. Give him to me. I am weary of this man-wolf folly. He has troubled the jungle for ten seasons. Give me the man-cub, or I will hunt here always, and not give you one bone. He is a man, a man's child, and from the marrow of my bones I hate him!"

Then more than half the Pack yelled: "A man! a man! What has a man to do with us? Let him go to his own place."

"And turn all the people of the villages against us?" clamoured Shere Khan. "No; give him to me. He is a man, and none of us can look him between the eyes."

Akela lifted his head again, and said: "He has eaten our food. He has slept with us. He has driven game for us. He has broken no word of the Law of the Jungle."

"Also, I paid for him with a bull when he was accepted. The worth of a bull is little, but Bagheera's honour is something that he will perhaps fight for," said Bagheera, in his gentlest voice.

"A bull paid ten years ago!" the Pack snarled. "What do we care for bones ten years old?"

"Or for a pledge?" said Bagheera, his white teeth bared under his lip. "Well are ye called the Free People!"

"No man's cub can run with the people of the jungle," howled Shere Khan. "Give him to me!"

"He is our brother in all but blood," Akela went on; "and ye would kill him here! In truth, I have lived too long. Some of ye are eaters of cattle, and of others I have heard that, under Shere Khan's teaching, ye go by dark night and snatch children from the villager's door-step. Therefore I know ye to be cowards, and it is to cowards I speak. It is certain that I must die, and my life is of no worth, or I would offer that in the man-cub's place. But for the sake of the Honour of the Pack—a little matter that by being without a leader ye have forgotten—I promise that if ye let the man-cub go to his own place, I will not, when my time comes to die, bare one tooth against ye. I will die without fighting. That will at least save the Pack three lives. More I cannot do; but if ye will, I can save ye the shame that comes of killing a brother against whom there is no fault—a brother spoken for and bought into the Pack according to the Law of the Jungle."

"He is a man—a man—a man!" snarled the Pack; and most of the wolves began to gather round Shere Khan, whose tail was beginning to switch.

"Now the business is in thy hands," said Bagheera to Mowgli. "*We* can do no more except fight."

Mowgli stood upright—the fire-pot in his hands. Then he stretched out his arms, and yawned in the face of the Council; but he was furious with rage and sorrow, for, wolf-like, the wolves had never told him how they hated him.

"Listen you!" he cried. "There is no need for this dog's jabber. Ye have told me so often tonight that I am a man (and indeed I would have been a wolf with you to my life's end), that I feel your words are true. So I do not call ye my brothers any more, but *sag* [dogs], as a man should. What ye will do, and what ye will not do, is not yours to say. That matter is with *me;* and that we may see the matter more plainly, I, the man, have brought here a little of the Red Flower which ye, dogs, fear."

He flung the fire-pot on the ground, and some of the red coals lit a tuft of dried moss that flared up, as all the Council drew back in terror before the leaping flames.

Mowgli thrust his dead branch into the fire till the twigs lit and crackled, and whirled it above his head among the cowering wolves.

"Thou art the master," said Bagheera, in an undertone. "Save Akela from the death. He was ever thy friend."

Akela, the grim old wolf who had never asked for mercy in his life, gave one piteous look at Mowgli as the boy stood all naked, his long black hair tossing over his shoulders in the light of the blazing branch that made the shadows jump and quiver.

"Good!" said Mowgli, staring round slowly. "I see that ye are dogs. I go from you to my own people—if they be my own people. The Jungle is shut to me, and I must forget your talk and your companionship; but I will be more merciful than ye are. Because I was all but your brother in blood, I promise that when I am a man among men I will not betray ye to men as ye have betrayed

me." He kicked the fire with his foot, and the sparks flew up. "There shall be no war between any of us in the Pack. But here is a debt to pay before I go." He strode forward to where Shere Khan sat blinking stupidly at the flames, and caught him by the tuft on his chin. Bagheera followed in case of accidents. "Up, dog!" Mowgli cried. "Up, when a man speaks, or I will set that coat ablaze!"

Shere Khan's ears lay flat back on his head, and he shut his eyes, for the blazing branch was very near.

"This cattle-killer said he would kill me in the Council because he had not killed me when I was a cub. Thus and thus, then, do we beat dogs when we are men. Stir a whisker, Lungri, and I ram the Red Flower down thy gullet!" He beat Shere Khan over the head with the branch, and the tiger whimpered and whined in an agony of fear.

"Pah! Singed jungle-cat—go now! But remember when next I come to the Council Rock, as a man should come, it will be with Shere Khan's hide on my head. For the rest, Akela goes free to live as he pleases. Ye will *not* kill him, because that is not my will. Nor do I think that ye will sit here any longer, lolling out your tongues as though ye were somebodies, instead of dogs whom I drive out—thus! Go!"

The fire was burning furiously at the end of the branch, and Mowgli struck right and left round the circle, and the wolves ran howling with the sparks burning their fur. At last there were only Akela, Bagheera, and perhaps ten wolves that had taken Mowgli's part. Then something began to hurt Mowgli inside him, as he had never been hurt in his life before, and he caught his breath and sobbed, and the tears ran down his face.

"What is it? What is it?" he said. "I do not wish to leave the jungle, and I do not know what this is. Am I dying, Bagheera?"

"No, Little Brother. That is only tears such as men use," said Bagheera. "Now I know thou art a man, and a man's cub no longer. The Jungle is shut indeed to thee henceforward. Let them fall, Mowgli. They are only tears." So Mowgli sat and cried as though his heart would break; and he had never cried in all his life before.

"Now," he said, "I will go to men. But first I must say farewell to my mother"; and he went to the cave where she lived with Father Wolf, and he cried on her coat, while the four cubs howled miserably.

"Ye will not forget me?" said Mowgli.

"Never while we can follow a trail," said the cubs. "Come to the foot of the hill when thou art a man, and we will talk to thee; and we will come into the crop-lands to play with thee by night."

"Come soon!" said Father Wolf. "Oh, wise little Frog, come again soon; for we be old, thy mother and I."

"Come soon," said Mother Wolf, "little naked son of mine; for, listen, child of man, I loved thee more than ever I loved my cubs."

"I will surely come," said Mowgli; "and when I come it will be to lay out Shere Khan's hide upon the Council Rock. Do not forget me! Tell them in the jungle never to forget me!"

The dawn was beginning to break
when Mowgli went down the hillside
alone, to meet those mysterious things
that are called men.

As the dawn was breaking the Sambhur belled

Once, twice and again!

And a doe leaped up and a doe leaped up

From the pond in the wood where the wild deer sup.

This I, scouting alone, beheld,

Once, twice and again!

As the dawn was breaking the Sambhur belled

Once, twice and again!

And a wolf stole back and a wolf stole back

To carry the word to the waiting pack,

And we sought and we found and we bayed on his track

Once, twice and again!

As the dawn was breaking the Wolf Pack yelled

Once, twice and again!

Feet in the jungle that leave no mark!

Eyes that can see in the dark—the dark!

Tongue—give tongue to it! Hark! O hark!

Once, twice and again!

LISTS
OF NOTE

LISTS
OF NOTE

COMPILED BY
SHAUN USHER

CANONGATE

Edinburgh · London

First published in Great Britain in 2014 by Canongate Books Ltd in conjunction with Unbound

Canongate Books Ltd, 14 High Street, Edinburgh EH1 1TE
www.canongate.tv

Unbound, 4–7 Manchester Street, Marylebone, London W1U 2AE
www.unbound.co.uk

1

Cover design and typesetting by Here Design

British Library Cataloguing-in-Publication Data
A catalogue record for this book is available on request from the British Library

ISBN 978-1-78211-452-9
ISBN 978-1-78211-453-6 (ebook)

Printed in China by C&C Offset Printing Co., Ltd

This book is dedicated to my three favourite people:

1. Karina
2. Billy
3. Danny

CONTENTS

INTRODUCTION

Since we first began walking the earth, humans have been creating lists of one kind or another, calmly content in the knowledge that all Things are constantly being assigned, prioritised, ranked and streamlined to within an inch of their lives. It doesn't bear thinking about, but to live in a world without them would, I reluctantly imagine, be a chaotic existence: not a single to-do list, shopping list, wish list, dictionary, list of favourites, rulebook, list of predictions, list of resolutions, address book, list of advice, list of contents – just a world full of things, muddled and overflowing, without a sense of purpose or collective identity.

To further explain our reliance on lists, it seems only right to list the reasons:

1. Life is chaotic – often unbearably so. The ability to divide some of that chaos into lists, to make the onslaught manageable, can bring much-needed relief.

2. Human beings are fearful of the unknown and as such have a real need to label and group things, to assign them to comfortable lists.

3. Lists can make us more productive and can eradicate procrastination. Nothing on earth, resignation aside, cuts through the thick fog of a daunting workload as effectively as a to-do list.

4. Everyone is a critic. Ranking things – best to worst, biggest to smallest, fastest to slowest – can be strangely addictive, no doubt because it makes us feel knowledgeable.

5. Time is precious. Distilling huge swathes of monotonous information into easily digestible lists ensures that we have more time to enjoy ourselves and make lists.

The depth of mankind's obsession with lists became starkly apparent to me five years ago, at which point I was delving into various archives, museums and libraries around the world to research my first book, *Letters of Note*, a collection of notable correspondence from throughout the ages, written by all manner of people. At almost every juncture of that journey, I was also discovering intriguing lists written by those same characters – lists of varying lengths, some handwritten, others typed, most of which captivated me for differing reasons.

Five years on and you now hold a gorgeous book that contains 125 of the most compelling lists I have been able to find. A list of lists. They span thousands of years: the oldest is an eye-opening list of workmen's absences written in Ancient Egypt; the most recent are merely a few years old. In between we have:

•   a list of murder suspects, scribbled by the long-serving secretary to John F. Kennedy just hours after the president's assassination;

- French novelist George Perec's magnificent *Attempt at an Inventory of the Liquid and Solid Foodstuffs Ingurgitated by Me in the Course of the Year Nineteen Hundred and Seventy-Four*;

- a shopping list written by Galileo that mentions the pieces of equipment he needed to produce his ground-breaking telescope;

- a list of dream interpretations written around 1220 BC;

- a backup list of alternatives to the famous line, "Frankly, my dear, I don't give a damn", written shortly after Hollywood censors deemed the word "damn" to be offensive;

- …and many, many more.

Many of the lists offer advice that you will take to your grave. Some offer a snapshot of history previously unknown. Others are simply a joy to read. Each and every one, however, is certainly a list of note.

THINGS TO DO TODAY!

Date:_____

Urgent ✓			Done ✓
☐	1.	Not Smoke	☐
☐	2.	Kiss June	☐
☐	3.	Not Kiss anyone else	☐
☐	4.	Cough	☐
☐	5.	Pee	☐
☐	6.	Eat	☐
☐	7.	Not eat too Much	☐
☐	8.	Worry	☐
☐	9.	Go See Mama.	☐
☐	10.	Practice Piano	☐

NOTES:

Not write notes

KISS JUNE

—

JOHNNY CASH
Date Unknown

Legendary singer-songwriter Johnny Cash proposed to the love of his life, fellow country star June Carter, on stage in 1968, 13 years after first meeting her. Their relationship stood the test of time and they remained together until her death, 35 years later. Cash was a romantic man and wrote countless handwritten love notes for his wife during their marriage; even his to-do lists, such as the one seen here, were brimming with affection.

TERMES OF A KERVER

—

WYNKYN DE WORDE
1508

The carving of meat was considered a fine art in the late Middle Ages, at least in the affluent homes where such foods could be afforded, with whole animals routinely and precisely sliced on the dining table for all to see by household staff armed with specialist knowledge. In 1508, these rules of carving and general preparation of meat were collated by influential publisher Wynkyn de Worde in *The Boke of Kervynge* (*The Book of Carving*), a guide which began with a list of terms to be used when carving various cuts of meat.

Termes of a kerver.	Terms of a carver.
breke that dere	break that deer
lesche yt brawne	leach that brawn
rere that goose	rear that goose
lyfte that swanne	lift that swan
sauce that capon	sauce that capon
spoyle that henne	spoil that hen
fruche that chekyn	frust that chicken
bnbrace that malarde	unbrace that mallard
bnlace that conye	unlace that coney
dysmembre that heron	dismember that heron
dysplaye that crane	display that crane
dysfygure that pecocke	disfigure that peacock
vnioynt that bytture	unjoint that bittern
vntache that curlewe	untack that curlew
alaye that fesande	allay that pheasant
wynge that partryche	wing that partridge
wynge that quayle	wing that quail
mynce that plouer	mince that plover
thye that pegyon	thigh that pigeon
border that pasty	border that pasty
thye that woodcocke	thigh that woodcock
thye all maner of small byrdes	thigh all manner of small birds
tymbre that fyre	timber that fire
tyere that egge	tear that egg
chynne that samon	chine that salmon
strynge that lampraye	string that lamprey
splatte that pyke	splat that pike
sauce that place	sauce that plaice
sauce that tenche	sauce that tench
splaye that breme	splay that bream
syde that haddocke	side that haddock
tuske that barbell	tusk that barbell
culpon that troute	culpon that trout
fyne that cheuen	fin that chevin
transsene that ele	transon that eel
traunche that sturgyon	tranch that sturgeon
vndertraunche that purpos	undertranch that porpoise
tayme that crabbe	tame that crab
barbe that lopster	barb that lobster

Here endeth the goodly termes.

¶Here begynneth the boke of keruynge and sewyn¬
ge / and all the feestes in the yere for the seruyce of a
prynce or ony other estate as ye shall fynde eche offyce
the seruyce accordynge in this boke folowynge

¶Termes of a keruer.

Breke that dere
lesche ẏ brawne
rere that goose
lyfte that swanne
sauce that capon
spoyle that henne
fruche that chekyn
vnbrace that malarde
vnlace that conye
dysmembre that heron
dysplaye that crane
dysfygure that pecocke
vnioynt that bytture
vntache that curlewe
alaye that fesande
wynge that partryche
wynge that quayle
mynce that plouer
thye that pygyon
border that pasty
thye that woodcocke
thye all maner small byrdes
tymbre that fyre

tyere that egge
chynne that samon
strynge that lampraye
splatte that pyke
sauce that place
sauce that tenche
splaye that breme
syde that haddocke
tuske that berbell
culpon that troute
fynne that cheuen
trassene that ele
traunche that sturgyon
vndertraunche that purpos
tayme that crabbe
barbe that lopster

¶Here endeth the
goodly termes.

¶Here begynneth
Butteler and
Panter.

Thou shalte be butteler and panter all the fyrst
yere / and ye muste haue thre pantry knyues /
one knyfe to square trenchoure loues / an other to be a

ATTEMPT AT AN INVENTORY
—

GEORGES PEREC
1974

French novelist Georges Perec was an experimental writer whose affection for the trusty list is rivalled by very few. In 1974 he attempted to keep a record of every single thing he ate and drank for the duration of the year and then presented the results in a list which, having been translated to English by John Sturrock, is strangely compelling. It is titled, unambiguously, *Attempt at an Inventory of the Liquid and Solid Foodstuffs Ingurgitated by Me in the Course of the Year Nineteen Hundred and Seventy-Four.*

Nine beef broths, one iced cucumber soup, one mussel soup. Two *Guéméné andouilles*, one jellied *andouillette*, one Italian *charcuterie*, one saveloy, four mixed *charcuteries*, one *coppa*, three pork platters, one *figatelli*, one foie gras, one *fromage de tête*, one boar's head, five Parma hams, eight pâtés, one duck pâté, one liver pâté with truffles, one pâté *en croûte*, one pâté *grandmère*, one thrush pâté, six Landes pâtés, four brawns, one foie-gras mousse, one pig's trotters, seven *rillettes*, one salami, two *saucissons*, one hot *saucisson*, one duck terrine, one chicken-liver terrine.

One blini, one *empanada*, one dried beef. Three snails.

One Belon oysters, three scallops, one shrimps, one shrimp *croustade*, one *friture*, two baby eel *fritures*, one herring, two oysters, one mussels, one stuffed mussels, one sea urchins, two *quenelles au gratin*, three sardines in oil, five smoked salmons, one taramasalata, one eel terrine, six tunas, one anchovy toast, one crab.

Two haddock, one sea bass, one skate, one sole, one tuna.

Four artichokes, one asparagus, one aubergine, one mushroom salad, fourteen cucumber salads, four cucumbers à la crème, fourteen celery *rémoulades*, two Chinese cabbages, one palm hearts, eleven crudités, two green-bean salads, thirteen melons, two *salades niçoises*, two dandelion salads with bacon, fourteen radishes with butter, three black radishes, five rice salads, one Russian salad, seven tomato salads, one onion tart.

One Roquefort croquette, five *croque-monsieurs*, three quiche Lorraines, one *tarte aux maroilles*, one yogurt with cucumber and grapes, one Romanian yogurt.

One *torti* salad with crab and Roquefort.

One eggs with anchovy, two boiled eggs, two eggs *en meurette*, one ham and eggs, one bacon and eggs, one eggs *en cocotte* with spinach, two eggs in aspic, two scrambled eggs, four omelettes, one sort-of omelette, one bean-sprout omelette, one horn-of-plenty omelette, one duck-skin omelette, one *confit d'oie* omelette, one herb omelette, one Parmentier omelette.

One sirloin, three sirloins with shallots, ten steaks, two steak *au poivres*, three *complets*, one rump steak with mustard, five roast beefs, two ribs of beef, two top rump steaks, three beef *grillades*, two chateaubriands, one steak tartare, one *rosbif*, three cold *rosbifs*, fourteen entrecôtes, three entrecôtes à la *moelle*, one fillet of beef, three hamburgers, nine skirts of beef, one flank of beef.

Four *pot-au-feus*, one daube, one jellied daube, one braised beef, one beef mode, one beef *gros sel*, one beef in a thin baguette.

One braised veal with noodles, one sauté of veal, one veal chop, one veal chop with pasta shells, one 'veal entrecôte', six escalopes, six escalopes *milanaise*, three escalopes à la crème, one escalope with morels, four *blanquettes de veau*.

Five *audouillettes*, three black puddings, one black pudding with apples, one pork cutlet, two sauerkrauts, one Nancy sauerkraut, one pork chop, eleven pairs of frankfurters, two port *grillades*, seven pigs' trotters, one cold pork, three roast porks, one roast pork with pineapple and bananas, one pork sausage with haricots. One milk-fed lamb, three lamb cutlets, two curried lambs, twelve *gigots*, one saddle of lamb.

One mutton cutlet, one shoulder of mutton.

Five chickens, one chicken kebab, one lemon chicken, one chicken *en cocotte*, two chicken *basquaises*, three cold chickens, one stuffed chicken, one chicken with

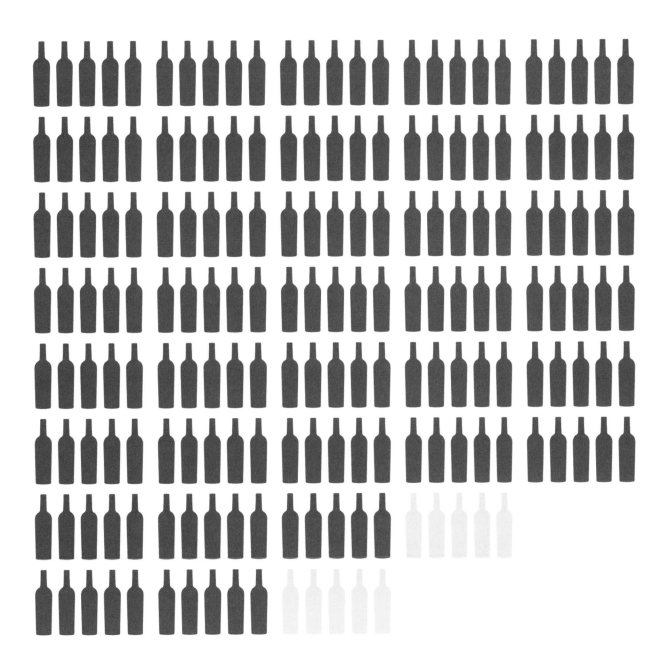

chestnuts, one chick with herbs, two jellied chickens.

Seven *poules au riz*, one *poule au pot*.

One pullet *au riz*.

One *coq au Riesling*, three *coq au vins*, one *coq au vinaigre*.

One duck with olives, one duck breast.

One guinea fowl casserole.

One guinea fowl with cabbage, one guinea fowl with noodles.

Five rabbits, two rabbits *en gibelotte*, one rabbit with noodles, one rabbit à la crème, three rabbits with mustard, one rabbit *chasseur*, one rabbit with tarragon, one rabbit *à la tourangelle*, three rabbits with plums.

Two young wild rabbits with plums.

One civet of hare *à l'alsacienne*, one daube of hare, one hare stew, one saddle of hare.

One wild-pigeon casserole.

One kidney kebab, three kebabs, one mixed grill, one kidneys with mustard, one calves' kidneys, three *têtes de veau*, eleven calves' livers, one calves' tongue, one calves' sweetbread with *pommes sarladaises*, one terrine of calves' sweetbreads, one lambs' brains, two fresh goose livers with grapes, one *confit* of goose gizzards, two chicken livers.

Twelve assorted cold meats, two *assiettes anglaises*, n cold cuts, two couscous, three 'Chinese', one *moulakhia*, one pizza, one *pan bagnat*, one *tajine*, six sandwiches, one ham sandwich, one *rillettes* sandwich, three cantal sandwiches.

One ceps, one kidney beans, seven green beans, one sweetcorn, one puréed cauliflower, one puréed spinach, one puréed fennel, two stuffed peppers, two *pommes frites*, nine *gratins dauphinois*, four mashed potatoes, one *pommes dauphines*, one *pommes boulangères*, one *pommes soufflées*, one roast potatoes, one sauté potatoes, four rice, one wild rice.

Four pasta, three noodles, one fettucine with cream, one macaroni cheese, one macaroni, fifteen fresh noodles, three *rigatoni*, two ravioli, four spaghetti, one tortellini, five tagliatelle *verde*.

Thirty-five green salads, one *mesclun* salad, one Treviso salad à la crème, two chicory salads.

Seventy-five cheese, one ewe's cheese, two Italian cheeses, one Auvergne cheese, one Boursin, two Brillat-Savarins, eleven Bries, one Cabécou, four goats' cheeses, two *crottins*, eight Camemberts, fifteen cantals, one Sicilian cheeses, one Sardinian cheeses, one Epoisses, one Murols, three fromages blancs, one goat's-milk fromage blanc, nine Fontainebleaus, five mozzarellas, five Munsters, one Reblochon, one Swiss raclette, one Stilton, one Saint-Marcellin, one Saint-Nectaire, one yogurt.

One fresh fruit, two strawberries, one gooseberries, one orange, three '*mendiants*' [a mixture of almonds, dried figs, hazelnuts and raisins].

One stuffed dates, one pears in syrup, three pears in wine, two peaches in wine, one vineyard peach in syrup, one peaches in Sancerre, one apples *normande*, one bananas *flambées*.

Four stewed fruit, two stewed apples, two stewed rhubarb and *quetsch*.

Five *clafoutis*, four pear *clafoutis*.

One figs in syrup.

Six fruit salads, one tropical fruit salad, two orange salads, two strawberry, raspberry and gooseberry salads.

One apple pie, four tarts, one hot tart, ten tart Tatins, seven pear tarts, one pear tart Tatin, one lemon tart, one apple and nut tart, two apple tarts, one apple tart with meringue, one strawberry tart.

Two crêpes.

Two charlottes, three chocolate charlottes.

Three babas.

One *crème renversée*.

One *galette des rois*.

Nine chocolate mousses.

Two *îles flotantes*.

One bilberry *Kugelhupf*.

Four chocolate gateaux, one cheesecake, two orange gateaux, one Italian gateau, one Viennese gateau, one Breton gateau, one gateau with fromage blanc, one *vatrushka*.

Three ice creams, one lime sorbet, two guava sorbets, two pear sorbets, one chocolate profiteroles, one raspberry melba, one pear *belle Hélène*.

Thirteen Beaujolais, four Beaujolais Nouveaux, three Brouillys, seven Chiroubles, four Chenas, two Fleuries, one Juliénas, three Saint-Amours.

Nine Côtes-de-Rhônes, nine Châteauneuf-du-Papes, one Châteauneuf-du-Pape '67, three Vacqueyras.

Nine Bordeaux, one Bordeaux Clairet, one Lamarzelle '64, three Saint-Emilions, one Saint-Emilion '61, seven Château-la Pelleterie '70s, one Château-Canon '62, five Château-Négrits, one Lalande-de-Pomerol, one Lalande-de-Pomerol '67, one Médoc '64, six Margaux '62s, one Margaux '68, one Margaux '69, one Saint-Estèphe '61, one Saint-Julien '59.

Seven Savigny-lès-Beaunes, three Aloxe-Cortons, one Aloxe-Corton '66, one Beaune '61, one white Chasagne-Montrachet '66, two Mercureys, one Pommard, one Pommard '66, two Santenay '62s, one Volnay '59.

One Chambolle-Musigny '70, one Chambolle-Musigny Les Amoureuses '70, one Chambertin '62, one Romanée-Conti, one Romanée-Conti '64.

One Bergerac, two red Bouzys, four Bourgueils, one Chalosse, one champagne, one Chablis, one red Côtes-de-Provence, twenty-six Cahors, one Chanteperdrix, four Gamays, two Madirans, one Madiran '70, one Pinot Noir, one Passetoutgrain, one Pécharmant, one Samumur, ten Tursans, one Traminer, one Sardinian wine, *n* sundry wines.

Nine beers, two Tuborgs, four Guinnesses.

Fifty-six Armagnacs, one bourbon, eight Calvadoses, one cherries in brandy, six Green Chartreuses, one Chivas, four cognacs, one Delamain cognac, two Grand Marniers, one pink gin, one Irish coffee, one Jack Daniel's, four marcs, three Bugey marcs, one marc de Provence, one plum liqueur, nine Souillac plums, one plums in brandy, two pear eaux-de-vie, one port, one slivovitz, one Suze, thiry-six vodkas, four whiskies.

N coffees, one tisane, three Vichy waters.

Lyndon -
KKK -
Dixiecrats -
Hoffa -
John Burch Society
Nixon
Diem
Rightist
CIA in Cuban fiasco
Dictators
Communists

WHO KILLED JFK?

WHO KILLED JFK?

—

EVELYN LINCOLN
November 22nd, 1963

On November 22nd, 1963, US President John F. Kennedy was shot and killed as he travelled in an open-top car through Dealey Plaza in Dallas, Texas, in one of history's most discussed murders. Also in the motorcade that fateful afternoon was his secretary of ten years, Evelyn Lincoln. Just hours after the assassination, as she flew back to Washington, DC, on Air Force One, Evelyn penned this list of suspects in the murder of her late-boss – a list that began with Vice President Lyndon B. Johnson and ended with "Communists". Some years later, Evelyn added the note seen on the list's reverse.

Lyndon –
KKK –
Dixiecrats –
Hoffa –
John Birch Society
Nixon
Diem
Rightist
CIA in Cuban fiasco
Dictators
Communists

There is no end to the list of suspected conspirators to Pres. Kennedy murder. Many factions had their reasons for wanting the young President dead. That fact alone illustrates how the world suffers from a congenital proclivity to violence.

EL. AF-1 11/22/63

THE ARMORY SHOW

—

PABLO PICASSO
1912

The 1913 International Exhibition of Modern Art, better known by most as The Armory Show, was a momentous occasion. It was the first modern art exhibition of any scale in the US and introduced the genre to a flummoxed and delighted public who until then had seen nothing like it. Organising the show was American painter Walter Kuhn, a man who was unsure of which European artists to invite; realising his weakness, he instead turned to Pablo Picasso for advice. Picasso responded with this handwritten list of recommendations. For the sake of clarity, I have appended the artists' full names.

Juan Gris

13 Rue Ravingon

Metzinger *[Jean Metzinger]*

Gleizes *[Albert Gleizes]*

Leger *[Fernand Leger]*

Ducham *[Marcel Duchamp]*

Delauney *[Robert Delauney]*

Le Fauconnier *[Henri Le Fauconnier]*

Marie Laurencin

DeLa Fresnay *[Roger de La Fresnaye]*

Braque *[Georges Braque – added by Walt Kuhn]*

Juan Gris
13 rue Ravignan

Metzinger
Gleizes

Leger

Duchamp

Delaunay

Le Fauconnier

Marie Laurencin

de la Fresnay

Braque -

ANTI-FLIRT CLUB

—

ALICE REIGHLY
1923

In the early 1920s, having been subjected to an unending stream of harassment from members of the opposite sex, a group of women in Washington, DC decided to form the Anti-Flirt Club, an organisation "composed of young women and girls who have been embarrassed by men in automobiles and on street corners", its aim being to protect such ladies from any further discomfort. As with all good clubs, a list of rules was issued to all members. It read as follows.

1. Don't flirt: those who flirt in haste oft repent in leisure.

2. Don't accept rides from flirting motorists—they don't all invite you in to save you a walk.

3. Don't use your eyes for ogling—they were made for worthier purposes.

4. Don't go out with men you don't know—they may be married, and you may be in for a hair-pulling match.

5. Don't wink—a flutter of one eye may cause a tear in the other.

6. Don't smile at flirtatious strangers—save them for people you know.

7. Don't annex all the men you can get—by flirting with many you may lose out on the one.

8. Don't fall for the slick, dandified cake eater—the unpolished gold of a real man is worth more than the gloss of a lounge lizard.

9. Don't let elderly men with an eye to a flirtation pat you on the shoulder and take a fatherly interest in you. Those are usually the kind who want to forget they are fathers.

10. Don't ignore the man you are sure of while you flirt with another. When you return to the first one you may find him gone.

DON'T SMILE *at* FLIRTATIOUS strangers SAVE THEM FOR *people* YOU KNOW

BOYLE'S WISH LIST

—

ROBERT BOYLE
1662

In 1662 a man often called the "Father of Modern Chemistry", Robert Boyle, wrote a remarkable and prophetic list of things that he hoped would one day be achieved by science – an eclectic selection of as yet unsolved problems he deemed the most pressing. The list was discovered shortly after his death, and in the 300-plus years since he penned it, many of these advances – GPS, light bulbs, organ transplants, cosmetic surgery – have been met.

The Prolongation of Life.

The Recovery of Youth, or at least some of the Marks of it, as new Teeth, new Hair colour'd as in youth.

The Art of Flying.

The Art of Continuing long under water, and exercising functions freely there.

The Cure of Wounds at a Distance.

The Cure of Diseases at a distance or at least by Transplantation.

The Attaining Gigantick Dimensions.

The Emulating of Fish without Engines by Custome & Education only.

The Acceleration of the Production of things out of Seed.

The Transmutation of Metalls.

The makeing of Glass Malleable.

The Transmutation of Species in Mineralls, Animals, and Vegetables.

The Liquid Alkaest and Other dissolving Menstruums.

The making of Parabolicall and Hyperbolicall Glasses.

The making Armor light and extremely hard.

The practicable and certain way of finding Longitudes.

The use of Pendulums at Sea and in Journeys, and the Application of it to watches.

Potent Druggs to alter or Exalt Imagination, Waking, Memory, and other functions, and appease pain, procure innocent sleep, harmless dreams, etc.

A Ship to saile with All Winds, and A Ship not to be Sunk.

Freedom from Necessity of much Sleeping exemplify'd by the Operations of Tea and what happens in Mad-Men.

Pleasing Dreams and physicall Exercises exemplify'd by the Egyptian Electuary and by the Fungus mentioned by the French Author.

Great Strength and Agility of Body exemplify'd by that of Frantick Epileptick and Hystericall persons.

A perpetuall Light.

Varnishes perfumable by Rubbing.

The Prolongation of Life.

The Recovery of Youth, or at least some of y Marks
of it, as new Teeth, new Hair colour'd as in youth.

The Art of Flying.

The Art of Continuing long under Water, and exercis-
-ing functions freely there.

The Cure of Wounds at a distance.

The Cure of Diseases at a distance, or at least by
Transplantaõn.

The Attaining Gigantick Dimensions.

The Emulating of Fish without Engines by Custome &
Education only.

The Acceleration of y Production of things out of
Seed.

The Transmutation of Metalls.

The makeing of Glass Malleable.

The Transmutation of Species in Mineralls, Animals, &   (Vegetably

The Liquõr Alkaest and other dissolving Menstrues.

The making of Parabolicall and Hyperbolicall Glasses.

The makeing Armõr light and extremely hard.

The practicable & certain way of findinɡ Longitudes.

The use of Pendulums at Sea and in Journeys, and the
    Applicaõn of it to watches

Potent Druggs to alter or Exalt Imagination, Wakinɡ,
    Memory and other functions, and appeas. pain,
    procure innocent sleep, harmless dreams &c.

A Ship to saile w:th All winds, and A Ship not to be
Sunk.

Freedom from Necessity of much Sleeping exemplify'd
by the Operaçons of Tea and w:^t happens in
Mad-men.

Pleasing Dreams & physicall Exercises exemplify'd
by ye Egiptian Electuary and by the Fungus
mentioned by the French Author.

Great Strength and Agility of Body exemplify'd by
that of Frantick, Epileptick and Hystericall
persons.

A perpetuall Light.

Varnishes perfumable by Rubbing.

SHOPPING TRIP TO DUNHUANG

—

RATNAVṚKṢA AND PRAKETU
10th Century

One morning in 10th-century China, two Tibetan monks named Ratnavṛkṣa and Praketu set off on a shopping trip to the ancient town of Dunhuang, a major stop on the Silk Road trade route, to buy a plethora of goods – mainly fabrics in the form of blankets and cloths – for their monastery. This shopping list is the record they kept of their numerous purchases, written in Khotanese and signed by witnesses; it is held at the British Library.

makala salya cvāvaja māśtä bistämye haḍai ṣa' khalavī cu ratanavaraikṣä āśī' u prrakaittu būrä ṣacu vāṣṭä bauḍä va herä nauda. gaḍā-hvasta thauracaihä bera śā u śaca prraiysge bira śā u kabalīja baysgyi hvāhyä kāmadä śe u hūḍaigä ysīḍai attaravāysä śau u hūḍaiga ysīḍai lahāpī śau u kāra kagä khau-ṣa thā‾racaihä pabanā śa u khaucīja khauśka śā u ījīnai hī-rāsä hvattarakīnai ūra-bada śau u gaḍā-hvastä śīyi haysänā-līkä thauracaihä dva u mījī jūna baysgyi kabala dvī u haija mai-stä kabala u pe u śīyi maistä kabala śā u aysūra-gūna da-jūna baimya kamaiśkä śā u nämāya śau baraka u ya.ma. hainai gaḍä hvastä baysgi thauracaihä śau u haysnālīka gaḍā hvastä thauracaihä dva u paha drau vī haysnālīkä śacī śau u haija baysgyi kabala dvī u hainai thauna śacī u haysnālīkä thauna śaca drāya u śīya baysgyi kabala tcaure u paima-vīstä kabalīnai draijsai śau u gahai śau u eysnaṃ śā maista u dairśvä khaucvä drauhye bitcä dairsa u tcaurrvä starrvä ñū-ṣtyelīka u śau barä khaucä pajsāsä sera u paima-vīstāva thauna śacä ha-darā śa u gaḍä hvastä thauracaihä jsa dā-gū baysgye paima jsa bira śā u kagīja ṣkaumaka vīlaka śā hatca ttrraba jsa u dā‾rmīnai ṣkā‾ma dale śau u habastä gahā śa : gahai va maistä śau u valaka gahai śau u hatca hasā‾ña jsa aiysna śā u nauṣtara śau u kabalījä bịrga kagyä karastä śe u kabalī-nai rūśkagä thūḍa-pa śau u kaimeja ysīḍä-mejanya kamaiśka śā u hai-ja baysgyä kabala pajse u hainä thauna : nā‾ u ysīra gū śacī śau u pai-mīnä thauna tcaura u phrramaina kabala śā u kā‾ra-kagä khauṣa śa hatca āvasakāṃ jsa u mījī jūna śadā kaimejä īśīma śa u {ysīcä spī-yi drai gūna mnan pa kamaiśka śā} u painajä śī nama śau u thauna śacī nūvarä {-e} parekṣi śau u chava nū kāṃhä parakṣa śau u hainä śadā damarāśī'nai maista kai-mejä śau u śe' āṣana śadā damarāśī'nai maistä kaimejä śau u dai-dä āṣana śadā śagīnai maistä kaimejä śau u paha drauvī sya-dai hvaradai thauracaihä śau u haysnālīka hūḍaigä śau baysgi u hadä naṣkūmāya namavīña thavalakañä khauca haudūsä sera pyaṣtalīka u hūḍaiga yā‾ma-bakä śau u thauracaihä śūkyainä dva u hūṇaugyä jsaiṇyāṃ hīrāṃ jsa habaḍa pyaṣtalīkya khadīrakya śe u pūstyāṇa tcairma tha valaka śā u mījījunä thauracaihä birä śā u maistä pū-stye śau u ejsīnai vasīyikä śau u nūvarä barä u vatsāvīśī'-nai hamauka śau pajūka śau u būśaunāṃ barakä śau habaḍa u ūla-ka-gä baraka śau u nvadāvaunä auramūṣa pajsa u gahā śa maistä gahai śau u valakä śau u thūra-ma śau u pūstyā‾nä : namavīja thavalakä śā pūstyāṃ jsa habaḍa u badana drāya u ṣkā‾mye herä nāsākä ranavarai-kṣä āśī' akṣärä ⌗ u prrakai akṣä'rä byaunä kvāṃ śī-thau āśī' akṣärä [signed] byauna būyunä śau-śū śvauñakā akṣärä [signed]

[Translation]

In the Year of the Monkey, the month of Cvātaja, the 20th day.

This is a record because the reverend Ratnav k a and Praketu rode to Shazhou and obtained things:

one … coat; one … coat of … silk; one pair of trousers of thick and wide blanket cloth; one undergarment of yellow … ; one … of yellow cloth; one pair of shoes of … leather with laces of … ; and one …; one lether belt of black … ; two white … ; two blankets … ; a red large blanket; one … and white large blanket; and one asura-colored flaming … ; one thick … of beaten red …; two … of beaten … for washing; one silk cloth for washing with … ; two thick red blankets; three silk red cloths and wash cloths; four thick white cloths; one … ; one large … ; one wool-.. … for blankets; thirty … in thirty … ; … in four …; one … of 15 ounces; one wool … silk … ; one smoke-colored coat of thick wool with … of beaten … ; one small … of leather; … one large … and one small … ; … … one skin of wolf hide for blankets; one sheep-skin fur for blankets; … … five thick red blankets; nine red cloths; one gold-colored silk; four woolen cloths; one silver-gilt blanket; one shoe of …-leather; one yellow-white three-color … ; one white … felt; one new … of cloth-silk; one large cover for a dharmar jika of red earth; a second large cover for a dharmarājika of dark earth; a third large cover for a … of dark earth; one left and right … of … hair; one thick … for washing; a … of 17 ounces … ; one … ; two … ; one … for book leather; … one silver cup; a new … ; one goblet made of vasaka wood; one … ; one full perfume purse; one purse of camel-skin; five … ; one … ; one large … and one small; one spoon; one … of felt, filled with … ; three ropes; and a container for … things.

The reverend Ratnavṛkṣa's akṣara. Praketu's akṣara. The witness Kvāṃ Ṣīthau's akṣara. The witness Būyunä Śauśū Śvaunaka's akṣara.

[signed]

THE DRINKER'S DICTIONARY

—

BENJAMIN FRANKLIN
January 13th, 1737

On January 13th, 1737, in his newspaper *The Pennsylvania Gazette*, the indefatigable Benjamin Franklin printed an extensive and thoroughly entertaining *Drinker's Dictionary* – essentially a list of 228 synonyms, all of which were then being used in local taverns to describe the act of being drunk.

Nothing more like a Fool than a drunken Man. Poor Richard.

'Tis an old Remark, that Vice always endeavours to assume the Appearance of Virtue: Thus Covetousness calls itself *Prudence*; *Prodigality* would be thought *Generosity;* and so of others. This perhaps arises hence, that, Mankind naturally and universally approve Virtue in their Hearts, and detest Vice; and therefore, whenever thro' Temptation they fall into a Practice of the latter, they would if possible conceal it from themselves as well as others, under some other Name than that which properly belongs to it.

But DRUNKENNESS is a very unfortunate Vice in this respect. It bears no kind of Similitude with any sort of Virtue, from which it might possibly borrow a Name; and is therefore reduc'd to the wretched Necessity of being express'd by distant round-about Phrases, and of perpetually varying those Phrases, as often as they come to be well understood to signify plainly that A MAN IS DRUNK.

Tho' every one may possibly recollect a Dozen at least of the Expressions us'd on this Occasion, yet I think no one who has not much frequented Taverns would imagine the number of them so great as it really is. It may therefore surprize as well as divert the sober Reader, to have the Sight of a new Piece, lately communicated to me, entitled

The DRINKERS DICTIONARY.

A

He is Addled,
He's casting up his Accounts,
He's Afflicted,
He's in his Airs.

B

He's Biggy,
    Bewitch'd,
    Block and Block,
    Boozy,
    Bowz'd,
    Been at Barbadoes,
    Piss'd in the Brook,
    Drunk as a Wheel-Barrow,
    Burdock'd,
    Buskey,
    Buzzey,
Has Stole a Manchet out of the Brewer's Basket,
His Head is full of Bees,
Has been in the Bibbing Plot,

Has drank more than he has bled,
He's Bungey,
	As Drunk as a Beggar,
He sees the Bears,
He's kiss'd black Betty,
He's had a Thump over the Head with Sampson's Jawbone,
He's Bridgey.

C

He's Cat,
	Cagrin'd,
	Capable,
	Cramp'd,
	Cherubimical,
	Cherry Merry,
	Wamble Crop'd,
	Crack'd,
	Concern'd,
	Half Way to Concord,
Has taken a Chirriping-Glass,
	Got Corns in his Head,
	A Cup too much,
	Coguy,
	Copey,
He's heat his Copper,
He's Crocus,
	Catch'd,
He cuts his Capers,
He's been in the Cellar,
He's in his Cups,
	Non Compos,
	Cock'd,
	Curv'd,
	Cut,
	Chipper,
	Chickery,
	Loaded his Cart,
He's been too free with the Creature,
Sir Richard has taken off his Considering Cap,
He's Chap-fallen.

D

He's Disguiz'd,
He's got a Dish,
	Kill'd his Dog,

Took his Drops,
It is a Dark Day with him,
He's a Dead Man,
Has Dipp'd his Bill,
He's Dagg'd,
He's seen the Devil.

E

He's Prince Eugene,
    Enter'd,
    Wet both Eyes,
    Cock Ey'd,
    Got the Pole Evil,
    Got a brass Eye,
    Made an Example,
He's Eat a Toad and half for Breakfast,
    In his Element.

F

He's Fishey,
    Fox'd,
    Fuddled,
    Sore Footed,
    Frozen,
    Well in for 't,
    Owes no Man a Farthing,
    Fears no Man,
    Crump Footed,
    Been to France,
    Flush'd,
    Froze his Mouth,
    Fetter'd,
    Been to a Funeral,
    His Flag is out,
    Fuzl'd,
    Spoke with his Friend,
    Been at an Indian Feast.

G

He's Glad,
    Groatable,
    Gold-headed,
    Glaiz'd,
    Generous,

Booz'd the Gage,
As Dizzy as a Goose,
Been before George,
Got the Gout,
Had a Kick in the Guts,
Been with Sir John Goa,
Been at Geneva,
Globular,
Got the Glanders.

H

Half and Half,
Hardy,
Top Heavy,
Got by the Head,
Hiddey,
Got on his little Hat,
Hammerish,
Loose in the Hilts,
Knows not the way Home,
Got the Hornson,
Haunted with Evil Spirits,
Has Taken Hippocrates grand Elixir.

I

He's Intoxicated,
     Jolly,
     Jagg'd,
     Jambled,
     Going to Jerusalem,
     Jocular,
     Been to Jerico,
     Juicy.

K

He's a King,
     Clips the King's English,
     Seen the French King,
     The King is his Cousin,
     Got Kib'd Heels,
     Knapt,
     Het his Kettle.

L

He's in Liquor,
    Lordly,
    He makes Indentures with his Leggs,
    Well to Live,
    Light,
    Lappy,
    Limber.

M

He sees two Moons,
    Merry,
    Middling,
    Moon-Ey'd,
    Muddled,
    Seen a Flock of Moons,
    Maudlin,
    Mountous,
    Muddy,
    Rais'd his Monuments,
    Mellow.

N

He's eat the Cocoa Nut,
    Nimptopsical,
    Got the Night Mare.

O

He's Oil'd,
    Eat Opium,
    Smelt of an Onion,
    Oxycrocium,
    Overset.

P

He drank till he gave up his Half-Penny,
    Pidgeon Ey'd,
    Pungey,
    Priddy,
    As good conditioned as a Puppy,
Has Scalt his Head Pan,
    Been among the Philistines,

In his Prosperity,
He's been among the Philippians,
He's contending with Pharaoh,
    Wasted his Paunch,
He's Polite,
    Eat a Pudding Bagg.

Q

He's Quarrelsome.

R

He's Rocky,
    Raddled,
    Rich,
    Religious,
    Lost his Rudder,
    Ragged,
    Rais'd,
    Been too free with Sir Richard,
    Like a Rat in Trouble.

S

He's Stitch'd,
    Seafaring,
    In the Sudds,
    Strong,
    Been in the Sun,
    As Drunk as David's Sow
    Swampt,
His Skin is full,
He's Steady,
He's Stiff,
He's burnt his Shoulder,
He's got his Top Gallant Sails out,
    Seen the yellow Star,
    As Stiff as a Ring-bolt,
    Half Seas over,
    His Shoe pinches him,
    Staggerish,
    It is Star-light with him,
    He carries too much Sail,
    Stew'd,
    Stubb'd,

Soak'd,
    Soft,
Been too free with Sir John Strawberry,
He's right before the Wind with all his Studding Sails out,
Has Sold his Senses.

T

He's Top'd,
    Tongue-ty'd,
    Tann'd,
    Tipium Grove,
    Double Tongu'd,
    Topsy Turvey,
    Tipsey,
Has Swallow'd a Tavern Token,
He's Thaw'd,
He's in a Trance,
He's Trammel'd.

V

He makes Virginia Fence, Valiant,
    Got the Indian Vapours.

W

The Malt is above the Water,
He's Wise,
He's Wet,
He's been to the Salt Water,
He's Water-soaken,
He's very Weary,
    Out of the Way.

The Phrases in this Dictionary are not (like most of our Terms of Art) borrow'd from Foreign Languages, neither are they collected from the Writings of the Learned in our own, but gather'd wholly from the modern Tavern-Conversation of Tiplers. I do not doubt but that there are many more in use; and I was even tempted to add a new one my self under the Letter B, to wit, *Brutify'd:* But upon Consideration, I fear'd being guilty of Injustice to the Brute Creation, if I represented Drunkenness as a beastly Vice, since, 'tis well-known, that the Brutes are in general a very sober sort of People.

THE LEXICON OF PROHIBITION
—
EDMUND WILSON
1927

In 1927, almost 200 years after Benjamin Franklin published *The Drinker's Dictionary* (see List No. 009), American literary critic Edmund Wilson followed suit by printing *The Lexicon of Prohibition*, a list of terms for drunkenness, arranged, he explained, "in order of the degrees of intensity of the conditions which they represent, beginning with the mildest stages and progressing to the more serious".

lit	potted	over the Bay	Commonwealth
squiffy	hooted	four sheets in the wind	lit up like a Christmas tree
oiled	slopped	crocked	lit up like a store window
lubricated	tanked	loaded	lit up like a church
owled	stinko	leaping	fried to the hat
edged	blind	screeching	slopped to the ears
jingled	stiff	lathered	stewed to the gills
piffed	under the table	plastered	boiled as an owl
piped	tight	soused	to have a bun on
sloppy	full	bloated	to have a slant on
woozy	wet	polluted	to have a skate on
happy	high	saturated	to have a snootfull
half-screwed	horseback	full as a tick	to have a skinful
half-cooked	liquored	loaded for bear	to draw a blank
half-shot	pickled	loaded to the muzzle	to pull a shut-eye
half seas over	ginned	loaded to the plimsoll	to pull a Daniel Boone
fried	shicker (Yiddish)	mark	to have a rubber drink
stewed	spifflicated	wapsed down	to have a hangover
boiled	primed	paralyzed	to have a head
zozzled	organized	ossifed	to have the jumps
sprung	featured	out like a light	to have the shakes
scrooched	pie-eyed	passed out cold	to have the zings
jazzed	cock-eyed	embalmed	to have the heeby-jeebies
jagged	wall-eyed	buried	to have the screaming-meemies
canned	glassy-eyed	blotto	to have the whoops and jingles
corked	bleary-eyed	lit up like the sky	to burn with a low blue flame
corned	hoary-eyed	lit up like the	

Some of these, such as loaded and full, are a little old-fashioned now; but they are still understood. Others, such as cock-eyed and oiled, which are included in the Drinker's Dictionary complied by Benjamin Franklin (and containing two hundred and twenty-eight terms) seem to be enjoying a new popularity. It is interesting to note that one hears nowadays comparatively rarely of people going on sprees, toots, tears, jags, bats, brannigans or benders. All these terms suggest, not merely extreme drunkenness, but also an exceptional occurrence, a violent breaking away by the drinker from the conditions for his normal life. It is possible that their partial disappearance is to be accounted for by the fact that this kind of fierce protracted drinking has now become universal, a familiar feature of social life, instead of a disreputable escapade. On the other hand, the vocabulary of social drinking, as exemplified by the above list, seems to have become particularly rich: one gets the impression that more nuances are nowadays discriminated than was the case before prohibition. Thus, fried, stewed and boiled all convey distinctly different ideas; and cock-eyed, plastered, owled, embalmed and ossified bring into play quite different images. Wapsed down is a rural expression, also used in connection with crops which have been ruined by a storm; featured is a theatrical word, which applies to a stage at which the drinker is stimulated to be believe strongly in his ability to sing a song, to tell a funny story or to execute a dance; organized is properly applied to a condition of thorough preparation for the efficient conduct of a formidable evening; and blotto, of English origin, denotes a condition of bland unconsciousness.

BILL OF MORTALITY

—

E. COTES
August 1665

In the summer of 1665, London residents began to drop like flies as the Great Plague swept across the city killing 68,596 people, young and old – in actual fact, that number covers only recorded deaths; the actual total is thought to be close to 100,000. At the time, weekly Bills of Mortality were circulated on which the last seven days' death toll was reported, broken down to show causes of death. The example seen here relates to the week beginning August 15th of that year as the plague's grip tightened, a period during which 3,880 people perished. A glossary is provided for the benefit of those who have never heard of such grimly named ailments as Kingsevil and Strangury.

Glossary:

Childbed: Mothers who died following childbirth, usually from infection

Chrisomes: Infants who died in their first month

Consumption: Those who died of tuberculosis

Dropsie: Enlargement of organs due to build-up of fluids

Flux: Dysentery

Imposthume: Abscess

Kingsevil: Lymphadenopathy of the neck

Rising of the Lights: Lung disease

Spotted fever and Purples: Meningitis

Stone: Gallstones

Strangury: Painful urination

Surfeit: Overeating

Teeth: Infants who have died during teething

Tiffick: Asthma/tuberculosis

The Diseases and Casualties this Week.

Abortive	6	Kingsevil	10
Aged	54	Lethargy	1
Apoplexie	1	Murthered at Stepney	1
Bedridden	1	Palsie	2
Cancer	2	Plague	3880
Childbed	23	Plurisie	1
Chrisomes	15	Quinsie	6
Collick	1	Rickets	23
Consumption	174	Rising of the Lights	19
Convulsion	88	Rupture	2
Dropsie	40	Sciatica	1
Drowned 2, one at St. Kath. Tower, and one at Lambeth	2	Scowring	13
Feaver	353	Scurvy	1
Fistula	1	Sore legge	1
Flox and Small-pox	10	Spotted Feaver and Purples	190
Flux	2	Starved at Nurse	1
Found dead in the Street at St. Bartholomew the Less	1	Stilborn	8
		Stone	2
Frighted	1	Stopping of the stomach	16
Gangrene	1	Strangury	1
Gowt	1	Suddenly	1
Grief	1	Surfeit	87
Griping in the Guts	74	Teeth	113
Jaundies	3	Thrush	3
Imposthume	18	Tissick	6
Infants	21	Ulcer	2
Kild by a fall down stairs at St. Thomas Apostle	1	Vomiting	7
		Winde	8
		Wormes	18

	Males	83			Males	2656		
Christned	Females	83		Buried	Females	2663		Plague—3880
	In all	166			In all	5319		

Increased in the Burials this Week————————1289

Parishes clear of the Plague————34. Parishes Infected————96.

The Assize of Bread set forth by Order of the Lord Maior and Court of Aldermen,
A penny Wheaten Loaf to contain Nine Ounces and a half, and three
half-penny White Loaves the like weight.

GEORGE WASHINGTON'S SLAVES

—

GEORGE WASHINGTON
April 1788

When he was 11 years old, future Founding Father and the first ever US President, George Washington, became the owner of ten slaves, whom he inherited from his father. When Washington died 56 years later, over 300 lived at his home, Mount Vernon. The list seen here was written in 1788 and details those "blacks [that he owned] above 12 years of age".

List of taxable property belonging to General Washington in Truro Parish.
April 1788

Blacks above 12 years of age.

Will	Simms	Billy – undr 16	Peg	Will
Frank	Joe	Joe ... "	Sackey	Paul
Auston	Jack	Christopher – "	Darcus	Abraham
Hercules	Bristol	Cyrus – "	Amy	Paschal
Nathan	Peter	Uriah – "	Nancy	Rose
Giles	Peter	Godferry – "	Molly undr 16	Sabeen
Joe	Scumburg	Sinah – "	Morris	Lucy
Paris	(past labor)	Mima – "	Robin	Delia
Gunner	Frank	Lylla – "	Adam	Daphne
Boatswain	Jack	Oney – "	Jack	Grace
Sam	Betty (past	Anna – "	Jack	Tom – undr 16
Anthony	service)	Beck – "	Dick	Moses "
Tom	Doll	Virgin – "	Ben	Isaac "
Will	Jenney	Patt – "	Matt	Sam Kit
Isaac	Charlotte	Will	Morris	London
James	Sall	Will	Brunswick	Cæsar
Sambo	Caroline	Charles	(past service)	Cupid
Tom Nookes	Sall Rass	Gabriel	Hannah	Paul
Nat	Dorchia	Jupiter	Lucy	Betty
George	Alice	Nanney	Moll	Doll
	Myrtilla	Kate	Jenny	Lucy
	Kitty	Sarah	Silla	Lucy
	Moll	Alice	Charity	Flora
		Nanny	Betty	Fanny
			Peg	Rachael
			Sail	Jenney
			Grace	Edy
			Sue	Daphne
			Agga Undr 16	

98 Horses
4 Mules
1 Covering Horse @ 2 Guineas
1 Chariot

List of taxable property belonging to
General Washington in Truro Parish.
April 1788.

Blacks above 12 years of age.

Will	Simms	Billy — ad 16	Peg	Will
Frank	Joe — 2	Joe — Do	Sackey	Paul
Ruston	Jack 5	Christopher Do	Darcus	Abraham
Hercules	Bristol	Cyrus — Do	Amy	Paschal
Nathan	Peter 6	Uriah — Do	Nancy	Rose
Giles	Peter 2	Godfrey Do	Molly — ad 16	Sabeen
Joe 5	Dumburg (stray lab)	Sinah — Do	Morris	Lucy
Paris	Frank	Mima — Do	Robin	Delia
Gunner	Jack 2	Lylla — Do	Adam	Daphne
Boatswain	Betty (per Swin)	Cracy — Do	Jack	Grace
Sam	Doll	Anna — Do	Jack	Tom — ad 16
Anthony	Jenney	Beck — Do	Dick	Moses — Do
Tom	Charlotte	Virgin — Do	Ben	Isaac — Do
Will	Sall	Bett — Do	Matt	Sam Kit
Isaac	Caroline	Will	Morris	London
James	Sall Wfs.	Will	Brunswick (per Swin)	Cæsar
Tombo	Dorehia	Charles	Hannah	Cupid
Tom Nokes	Alice	Gabriel	Lucy	Paul
Nat	Myrtilla	Jubiter	Moll	Betty
George	Kitty	Nanney	Jenny	Doll
	Moll	Kate	Silla	Lucy
		Sarah	Charity	Lucy
		Alice	Betty	Flora
		Nanny	Peg	Fanny
			Sall	Rachael
			Grace	Jenney
			Sue ( )	Edy
			Agga ad 16	Daphne.
				— 124 —

98 Horses.
4 Mules.
1 Covering Horse & 2 Guineas.
1 Chariot.

72

THE COWBOY CODE

—

GENE AUTRY
1948

For 30 years from the early 1930s, thanks to a hit CBS Radio show, numerous television and film appearances, and an illustrious country music career, American entertainer Gene Autry was known as the Singing Cowboy to millions of fans. In 1948, aware that many impressionable youngsters were keen to emulate his public persona, Autry came up with, and then promoted, the Cowboy Code – a list of ten rules which, if followed, would hopefully keep his admirers on the straight and narrow.

1. The Cowboy must never shoot first, hit a smaller man, or take unfair advantage.
2. He must never go back on his word, or a trust confided in him.
3. He must always tell the truth.
4. He must be gentle with children, the elderly, and animals.
5. He must not advocate or possess racially or religiously intolerant ideas.
6. He must help people in distress.
7. He must be a good worker.
8. He must keep himself clean in thought, speech, action, and personal habits.
9. He must respect women, parents, and his nation's laws.
10. The Cowboy is a patriot.

ADVICE TO CHICK ROCKERS

—

CHRISSIE HYNDE
1994

Having been frontwoman for a band as successful as the Pretenders since 1978, Chrissie Hynde is well placed to offer young women guidance on the subject of rock music. In 1994 she did exactly that by way of "Advice to Chick Rockers", a list which was subsequently printed in a teen magazine named *Mouth 2 Mouth*.

1. Don't moan about being a chick, refer to feminism or complain about sexist discrimination. We've all been thrown down stairs and fucked about, but no one wants to hear a whining female. Write a loosely disguised song about it instead and clean up ($).

2. Never pretend you know more than you do. If you don't know chord names, refer to the dots. Don't go near the desk unless you plan on becoming an engineer.

3. Make the other band members look and sound good. Bring out the best in them; that's your job. Oh, and you better sound good, too.

4. Do not insist on working with "females"; that's just more b.s. Get the best man for the job. If it happens to be a woman, great—you'll have someone to go to department stores with on tour instead of making one of the road crew go with you.

5. Try not to have a sexual relationship with the band. It always ends in tears.

6. Don't think that sticking your boobs out and trying to look fuckable will help. Remember you're in a rock and roll band. It's not "fuck me," it's "fuck you!"

7. Don't try to compete with the guys; it won't impress anybody. Remember, one of the reasons they like you is because you don't offer yet more competition to the already existing male egos.

8. If you sing, don't "belt" or "screech." No one wants to hear that shit; it sounds "hysterical."

9. Shave your legs, for chrissakes!

10. Don't take advice from people like me. Do your own thing always.

ROGET'S THESAURUS

—

PETER ROGET
1805

Born in 1779, British physician Peter Roget had a somewhat difficult childhood during which he was forced to deal with the deaths of close family members and the mental health problems of others in quick succession – indeed, it's possible that such a chaotic and challenging upbringing caused his obsession with an activity as neat and ordered as list-making. Around 1800, in part to fend off depression, he began to write the biggest list of all: his now legendary *Roget's Thesaurus*, and by 1805 the first draft, entirely handwritten and containing 15,000 words, was complete. It was finally published 47 years later and hasn't been out of print since. This page, headed "Existence", was the very first entry of that initial draft.

Existence

End, entity, being, exist.ce
Essence, quintess.ce, quidess.ce
Nature thing substance
  course World. fraoue
  position   constitution
Reality, (v. truth) actual,
  exist.ce – fact,
  course of things, under y sure
  extant, present

Nonentity, nullity, nihility
nonexist.ce noth.g nought
void, zero, cypher blank
empty

             unsubstantial
Unreal, ideal, imaginary
visionary, fabulous,
fictitious, supposititious
absent, shadow: dream
phantom, phantasm

Positive, affirmation absolute
  Intrisduic substantive
            inherent

Negation, virtual, extrinsic
  Potential. adjective

To be, exist, obtain, stand

pass, subsist, prevail, lie

– on foot, on y tapis

To constitute, form, compose, to consist of

            scope, habitude, temperament
State, mode of exist.ce condition, nature, constitut.n habit.

            place
Affection, predicament, situate.n posit.n posture contingency
Circumstances, case, plight, trisn, tune, – point, degree
Juncture, conjuncture, pass, emergency, exigency.

    Mode, manner, style, cast, fashion, form, shape
strain, way, degree. – tenure, terms,   tenor
forting, character, capacity
    ship
Relation, affinity, alliance, analogy, filiat.n (v. connect.n)

Reference, about, respect.g, regard.g, concerning, touching
  in point of, as to. – pertaining to, belong.g applicable to
  relatively, according to.
Comparable, commensurate incomp.ble income.te – ble,
  correspondent   – able, irricouciliable, disendant
  accordant

Ens, entity, being, exist^ce   Nonentity, nullity, nihility
Essence, quintess^ce quiddess^ce   nonexist^ce noth^g nought
Nature thing substance   void, zero, cypher blank
  course world frame   empty
  position constitution
Reality, (v. truth) actual   unsubstantial
  exist^ce — fact.   Unreal, ideal, imaginary
  course of things, under; sun   visionary, fabulous,
  extant, present   fictitious, supposititious
                                   absent, shadow. dream
                                   phantom, phantasm
Positive, affirmative absolute   Negative, virtual, extrinsic
  intrinsic, substantive   potential. adjective
              inherent
To be, exist, obtain, stand
  pass, subsist, prevail, lie
  — on foot, on ye tapis
to constitute, form, compose   to consist of
                                   scope, habitude, temperament
State, Mode of exist^ce condition, nature, constitut^n habit
Affection, predicament, situat^n point^n posture, contingency
                                            place
Circumstance, case, plight, train, tune, — point, degree
  juncture, conjuncture pass, emergency, exigency.

    Mode, manner, style, cast, fashion, form shape
Strain, way, degree. — tenure, terms,   tenor
footing, character, capacity
                -ship
  Relation, affinity, alliance, analogy, filiat^n (v. connect^n
Reference, about, respect^g regard^g concerning, touching
  in point of, as to — pertaining to, belong^g applicable to
  relatively, according to.
Comparable, commensurate   incomp^ble incom^te — ble,
  correspondent   — able. irreconcilable, discordant
  accordant

HEINLEIN'S PREDICTIONS

—

ROBERT HEINLEIN
1949

Robert Heinlein was one of the great science fiction novelists and author of numerous bestselling books. In 1975 he was named the first Science Fiction Writers Grand Master, and he was the recipient of many other awards during his career. In 1949 he compiled a list of predictions for the year 2000. They were eventually published in February 1952, in *Galaxy* magazine.

So let's have a few free-swinging predictions about the future. Some will be wrong—but cautious predictions are *sure* to be wrong.

1. Interplanetary travel is waiting at your front door, C.O.D. It's yours when you pay for it, which the government is doing at least on an experimental basis.

2. Contraception and control of disease is revising relations between sexes to an extent that will change our entire social and economic structure.

3. The most important military fact of this century is that there is no way to repel an attack from space.

4. It appears utterly impossible that the United States will start a "preventive war." We will fight when attacked, either directly or in a territory we have guaranteed to defend.

5. In fifteen years the housing shortage will be solved by a "breakthrough" into new technology which will make every house now standing as obsolete as outdoor privies. The housing is taken as a matter of course on the tenth day.

6. We'll all be getting a little hungry by and by.

7. The cult of the phony in art will disappear. So-called "modern art" will be discussed only by psychiatrists.

8. Freud will be classed as a pre-scientific, intuitive pioneer, and psychoanalysis will be replaced as a growing, changing "operational psychology" based on measurement and prediction.

9. Cancer, the common cold, and tooth decay will all be conquered. The revolutionary new problem in medical research will be to accomplish "regeneration," i.e., to enable a man to grow a new leg, rather than fit him with an artificial limb.

10. By the end of this century mankind will have explored this Solar System, and the first ship intended to reach the nearest star will be abuilding.

11. Your personal telephone will be small enough to carry in your handbag. Your house telephone will record messages, answer simple queries, and transmit vision.

12. Intelligent life of some sort will be found on Mars.

13. A thousand miles an hour at a cent a mile will be commonplace; short hauls will be made in evacuated subways at extreme speed.

14. A major objective of applied physics will be to control gravity.

15. We will not achieve a "world state" in the predictable future. Nevertheless, Communism will vanish from this planet.

16. Increasing mobility will disenfranchise a majority of the population. About 1990 a constitutional amendment will do away with state lines while retaining the semblance.

17. All aircraft will be controlled by a giant radar net run on a continentwide basis by a multiple electronic "brain."

18. Fish and yeast will become our principal sources of proteins. Beef will be a luxury; lamb and mutton will disappear, because sheep destroy grazing land.

19. Mankind will *not* destroy itself, nor will "civilization" be wiped out.
Here are things we *won't* get soon, if ever:
Travel through time.
Travel faster than the speed of light.
Control of telepathy and other E.S.P. phenomena.
 "Radio" transmission of matter.
Manlike robots with manlike reactions
Laboratory creation of life
Real understanding of what "thought" is and how it is related to matter.
Scientific proof of personal survival after death.
Nor a permanent end to war. (I don't like that prediction any better than you do.)

THE DREAM BOOK
—
AUTHOR UNKNOWN
Circa 1220 BC

Discovered in the ancient Egyptian village of Deir el-Medina and dating back to approximately 1220 BC, this intriguing papyrus document is particularly notable for a section known as The Dream Book – a list, written in Middle Egyptian hieratic by an unknown scribe, which offers interpretations for a wide variety of dream scenarios and classifies each as either good or bad. It is likely to have been copied from an earlier version and is now held at the British Museum.

Auspicious dreams:

IF A MAN SEES HIMSELF IN A DREAM:

sitting in a garden in the sun	GOOD: it means pleasure
demolishing a wall	GOOD: it means purification from evil
[eating] excrement	GOOD: consuming his property in his house
mating with a cow	GOOD: spending a happy day in his house
eating crocodile-[meat]	GOOD: [becoming] an official among his people
offering water (?)	GOOD: it means prosperity
drowning in the river	GOOD: it means purification from every evil
sleeping on the ground	GOOD: consuming his property
seeing carobs (?)	GOOD: finding a happy life
[seeing] the moon shining	GOOD: pardoning him by his god
veiling himself […]	GOOD: his enemies flee before him
falling […]	GOOD: it means prosperity
sawing wood	GOOD: his enemies are dead
burying an old man	GOOD: it means prosperity
cultivating vegetables	GOOD: it means finding victuals

Inauspicious dreams:

IF A MAN SEES HIMSELF IN A DREAM:

seizing one of his own legs	BAD: a report about him by those who are yonder (i.e. the dead)
seeing himself in a mirror	BAD: it means another wife
god has dispelled his weeping for him	BAD: it means fighting
while he sees himself suffering (in) his side	BAD: exrracting his property from him
eating hot meat	BAD: it means not being found innocent
shod with white sandals	BAD: it means roaming the earth
eating what he abominates	BAD: it means a man eating what he abominates in ignorance
copulating with a woman	BAD: it means mourning
he is bitten by a dog	BAD: he is touched by magic
he is bitten by a snake	BAD: it means the arising of words against him
measuring barley	BAD: it means the arising of words against him
writing on a papyrus	BAD: reckoning his wrongs by his god
stirring up his house	BAD: [it means] being ill
suffering through another's spell (?)	BAD: it means mourning
being a steersman in a ship	BAD: every time he is judged, he will not be found innocent
his bed catching fire	BAD: it means driving away his wife

THE DREAM BOOK

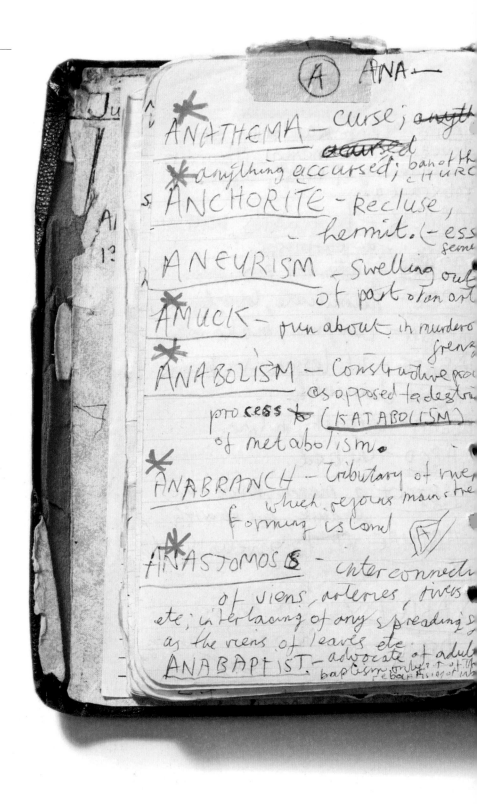

NICK CAVE'S HANDWRITTEN DICTIONARY

—
NICK CAVE
1984

The great Nick Cave is a lover of lists. He also, as someone who for decades has spent his time writing songs, screenplays and novels, has a mild obsession with language. It therefore makes perfect sense to learn that Cave sometimes writes, by hand, personal dictionaries filled with notable words – those words which for some reason need to be committed to paper, filed away for future use. Here is a page taken from just one magnificent example, penned in 1984 as he travelled in Berlin.

AVOCATION — vocation, employment

AVOUCH — v.t. affirm, maintain
attest, own. n. ~~avouch~~
n. — ment

AWN — head of cord, etc.

AWNING — canvas roof or shelter
to protect from sun

AWRY — crookedly, perversely — a. crooked
distorted
AVIDITY — eagerness wrong.
(AVID)

AVAUNT! — interj. — away!

AVAST! — interj. — stop!

AUTO

AUTOGENOUS — self generated

AUTOGAMY — self fertalisation

AUTO-EROTICISM — in psycho-analysis:
self produced erotic emotion

AUTOCRAT — absolute ruler

AUTOCHTHON (-ok-) primitive or original ~~inhab~~
inhabitant
AUTARCHY — despotism, absolute power
dictatorship

NECROPOLIS HO!

11

THE 50 DWARFS

—

DISNEY
1930s

In 1812, German storytellers the Brothers Grimm published *Snow White*, one of the most famous fairy tales in history and the basis for a wildly successful big-screen adaptation by Walt Disney Productions in 1937 over a century later. In 1934, as they began work on the animated version, the writing team at Disney compiled the following wonderful list of potential names for a group of characters whom the Brothers Grimm had chosen to leave nameless: the seven dwarfs. As we now know, Bashful, Grumpy, Happy, Sleepy and Sneezy were picked from this shortlist; Dopey and the name of their leader, Doc, were chosen at a later date.

Awful	Gabby	Sappy
Bashful	Gaspy	Scrappy
Biggo-Ego	Gloomy	Shifty
Biggy	Goopy	Silly
Biggy-Wiggy	Graveful	Sleepy
Blabby	Grumpy	Snappy
Busy	Happy	Sneezy
Chesty	Helpful	Sneezy-Wheezy
Crabby	Hoppy	Snoopy
Cranky	Hotsy	Soulful
Daffy	Hungry	Strutty
Dippy	Jaunty	Tearful
Dirty	Jumpy	Thrifty
Dizzy	Lazy	Weepy
Doleful	Neurtsy	Wistful
Dumpy	Nifty	Woeful
Flabby	Puffy	

WARTIME GOLF RULES

—

RICHMOND GOLF CLUB
1940

As the Battle of Britain tightened its grip in 1940, a bomb fell on an outbuilding belonging to Richmond Golf Club in Surrey, England, which luckily caused no deaths. As a result, the club's owners – rather than halt future rounds of golf – stiffened their upper lips and issued a rather unique list of temporary golf rules to all members that took into account the potentially life-threatening conditions on the course.

1. Players are asked to collect Bomb and Shrapnel splinters to save these causing damage to the Mowing Machines.

2. In Competitions, during gunfire or while bombs are falling, players may take cover without penalty for ceasing play.

3. The positions of known delayed action bombs are marked by red flags placed at a reasonably, but not guaranteed, safe distance therefrom.

4. Shrapnel and/or bomb splinters on the Fairways, or in Bunkers within a club's length of a ball, may be moved without penalty, and no penalty shall be incurred if a ball is thereby caused to move accidentally.

5. A ball moved by enemy action may be replaced, or if lost or destroyed, a ball may be dropped not nearer the hole without penalty.

6. A ball lying in a crater may be lifted and dropped not nearer the hole, preserving the line to the hole, without penalty.

7. A player whose stroke is affected by the simultaneous explosion of a bomb may play another ball from the same place. Penalty one stroke.

RULES OF PARENTING

—

SUSAN SONTAG
September 1959

Susan Sontag was one of the most important intellectuals of the last century – a critical essayist and celebrated author whose work never failed to stimulate debate. In September 1952, at 19 years of age, she had her first and only child, David, a son who went on to edit his mother's journals after her death in 2004. On a page of one of those journals can be found this list of parenting rules, written by Sontag seven years after she gave birth.

1. Be consistent.

2. Don't speak about him to others (e.g., tell funny things) in his presence. (Don't make him self-conscious.)

3. Don't praise him for something I wouldn't always accept as good.

4. Don't reprimand him harshly for something he's been allowed to do.

5. Daily routine: eating, homework, bath, teeth, room, story, bed.

6. Don't allow him to monopolize me when I am with other people.

7. Always speak well of his pop. (No faces, sighs, impatience, etc.)

8. Do not discourage childish fantasies.

9. Make him aware that there is a grown-up world that's none of his business.

10. Don't assume that what I don't like to do (bath, hairwash) he won't like either.

```
GONE WITH THE WIND                                    LEWTON

xxxxxxXnsthingxxanidxintxraxkxmaxiaxx

"---Frankly, my dear, nothing could xxxxx interest me less ----"  Bowie
                    , I don't care -----"   Anon.
                    , it leaves me cold -----" Ibid.
                    , it has become of no concern to me ----" Ibid.
                    , I don't give a Continental ----"      Ibid.
                    , I don't give a hoot!"               Ibid.
                    , I don't give a whoop!"              Ibid.
                    , I am completely indifferent ---"     Ibid.
                    , you can go to the devil, for all of me ---" Ibid.
                    , you can go to the devil for all I care ---" Ibid.
                    , I'm not even indifferent -- I just don't care --"  L
                    , I've come to the end---"   Millington
                    , I just don't care ---"    L.
                    , my indifference is boundless ---" Ibid.
                    , I don't give a straw
                    
                    ,It's all the same to me
                    ,it is of no consequence
                    
                    ,the devil may carem--- I don't!
                    
                    ,I've withdrawn from the battle
                    
                    ,the whole thing is a stench in my nostrils
                    
                    ,it makes my gorge rise
```

FRANKLY, MY DEAR...

—

SELZNICK INTERNATIONAL PICTURES
1939

Few lines in cinema history are as famous as *Gone with the Wind*'s "Frankly, my dear, I don't give a damn" – a response given by Rhett Butler to Scarlett O'Hara's question, "Where shall I go? What shall I do?" – and in 2005, the American Film Institute named it the Greatest Movie Quote of All Time. But, it could have been so different. Two months prior to the film's release, American censors deemed the word "damn" to be offensive and asked for it to be removed. The decision was only reversed weeks later due to a quick amendment to the Production Code by the board of the Motion Picture Association. Before that change was made, however, with the word "damn" temporarily banished, the film's producers prepared a list of alternatives.

DON SALTERO'S COFFEE HOUSE

—

DON SALTERO
Circa 1700

In 1695 a coffee house by the name of "Don Saltero's" opened in Chelsea, London which drew crowds from far and wide not for its refreshments, but for the hundreds of intriguing objects and oddities that lined its walls, shelves and ceiling: "cabinets of curiosities" filled with souvenirs from all corners of the globe that were sure to catch the attention of all who entered, collected as they were by the establishment's owner, James Salter. On entering Don Saltero's, visitors were handed a copy of *A Catalogue of the Rarities to be Seen at Don Saltero's Coffee-House in Chelsea*, a guide book of which 40 editions were printed over the years, all containing magnificent lists of objects such as this one.

On the Wainscot round the Room, beginning on the Piers between the Windows.

1   A Soland goose from the north of Scotland
2   A fine large hawk
3   A piece of the sugar cane, 8 feet long
4   A curious hydrometer, or weather gage
5   The bill and craw of a pelican
6   A curious skin of a snake, six feet and a half long
7   The claws of a lobster of a surprising largeness
8   A sea fan
9   Sea weeds
10 A maucauco from the East-Indies
11 The foal of a Zebra African wild ass
12 The skeleton of a cat
13 A Chinese idol
14 The pizzle of a whale
15 The head and paws of a Greenland bear
16 A sheet of paper made of silk, 12 feet long, 4 feet and a half wide, from China
17 A string of large Romish beads
18 A petrifies child
19 A Guiney deer
20 A wooden shoe that was put under the speaker's chair in the reign of K. James II.
21 The King of Widdaw's staff
22 The ear of an elephant
23 Pipes found in Gloucester
24 A print of the fly cap monkey
25 Ditto of a fine lizard, coloured from the life
26 Ditto of the dead warrant for the beheading of King Charles the First
27 Ditto of a flying squirrel, coloured from the life
28 Ditto of the Brasilian pye, or toucan, coloured from life
29 A sea horse's pizzle, of which cramp rings are made
30 A large otter
31 A surprising horn of an urus, or buffaloe
*31 The cobler's awl, plover
32 A fine horned owl
33 A Chinese pheasant
*34 Chinese instrument of wind music made of reeds
34 Two fine mussel shells, 2 foot long, from Portmahon
35 The rhinoceros's horn
36 The model of a mill with an overshot wheel, which works with sand (as the large ones do by water) most curiously contrived, and made in a bottle: the

stopper of the bottle is most wonderfully contrived in being fastened in the inside of the bottle with cross bars and spring bolts, with various things hanging to each end of every bolt, and yet so tight as not to admit of one grain of sand to escape.

37   The horns of a West-India stag

38   A Spanish apparatus, or belt to prevent cuckoldom, commonly called a Spanish padlock

39   A Romish bishop's crosier

40   The horn of a sea unicorn, 7 foot and a half long

41   A friar's discipline

42   A Staffordshire almanack, in use when the Danes were in England

43   A coffin of slate for a friar's bones, finely carved all over

44   A joint of the back bone of a whale

45   An iron bolt, shot red-hot at fort William by the rebels, 1745

46   The paws of a Russian bear

47   A large star fish

48   The paws of a seal

49   A piece of the keel of a ship eat by the worms

50   The head of a manatee, or sea-cow

51   The lance of Tow-How Sham, king of the Darien Indians, with which he killed six Spaniards, and took a tooth out of each head, and put it in his spear as a trophy of victory

52   The skin of a snake, ten feet and a half long, an excellent hydrometer

53   The foot of an elk

54   The head and tusks of a moss or sea lion

55   The head of a roe-buck from Scotland

56   The fin of a shark

57   A chopchin with which the Chinese cut their gold sympum, or Chinese board

58   A soull cap found in the hat of a French officer, when taken at the battle of Dettingen

*58   The grinder of an elephant

59   The tooth of a whale

60   Bastinadoe from China

61   An Indian sword of war, always left in the field of battle by the conqueror

62   An Indian leaf of the tree palmeta, used by the natives as a fan

63   An almanack for a blind man

64   A Moco fan

65   The head and horns of an antelope

66   The belt and pouches, shoe, and other ornaments of Tow How-Sham, king of the Darien Indians

67   A pair of Tartar lady's shoes

68   The coronation-shoes of King William III.

69   A pair of Tripoly stockings

70   A Turkish quiver for arrows

*71   A curious brass Cremona violin

71   A pair of maucasons or shoes from Hudson's Bay

72   A shirt of mail wore by the knights templars

73 A Chinese stocking

74 Queen Elizabeth's stirrup

75 A Chinese boot

76 The jaws of a shark with 280 teeth

77 A scaly coat of mail

78 A pair of Turkish women's shoes

79 A pair of Chinese women's shoes

80 Q. Catherine's wedding shoes, q. of Charles II.

81 A pair of Turkish men's shoes

82 A Turkish slipper

83 A pair of Chinese men's shoes

84 A pair of Spanish lady's shoes

85 A pair of brashalls to play at ballon, a game used in Italy

86 A curious wooden fan

87 A curious model of a church

88 A print of the maucauco, with some weeds from the gulph of Florida

89 The Lord's Prayer, the Creed, the ten Commandments, the prayers for the king and the royal family, and the 21st psalm; all wrote in the bust of king George

90 A very curious triform picture of king Charles I. and his two sons

91 A dried cat

92 A Turkish bow

93 The root of a tree in the shape of a hog

94 The head of a badger

95 The saw of a saw fish

96 King Henry the Eighth's coat of mail

97 A pair of gauntlets

98 Knives of the Cannibal Indians

99 An Indian bow and arrows

100 Two javelins

101 A Negro boy's cap made of rats skins

102 Snow shoes

103 A Chinese waistcoat, to prevent sweating

104 A Scots Highlander's target

105 A coat made of the bark of a tree

106 A whip from Archangel

107 A Mailay's hat

108 Queen Elizabeth's chambermaid's hat

109 The target of Tee-Yee-Neen-Ho-Ga-Row, Indian emperor of the Six Nations

110 Queen Elizabeth's work-basket

111 A Bohemian hat

112 A curious print, that changes, viz. from a man to a woman

113 A moving picture of Hudibras and the conjurer

114 Ditto of the bottle-conjurer

115 Ditto of a bashful widow

116 Two young tarapins, or land turtles

117 Two fine large ostrich-eggs

118 The shell sun fish

119 The egg of an ostrich, curiously carved

120 The star-fish

121 A bucaneer's staff

122 A Barbary spur

123 King Henry the Eighth's spurs

124 A print of the scarlet manakin from Surinam, coloured from life

125 Two Madagascar lances

126 An Indian bow

127 A Turkish pistol

128 A pistol with four barrels, taken from the French at the siege of Namur

129 Four Indian arrows, extraordinarily bearded

130 Two ancient broad arrows of Robin Hood

131 Two small poisoned arrows with bearded points

132 Oliver Cromwel's broad sword

133 A Spanish spadoe

134 King James's coronation sword

135 King William's ditto

136 A Scots dusk

137 Two poisoned daggers of great antiquity

138 A Mallay's Creese

139 A travelling clock, which is thirty-six hours going down. N. B. In common clocks the hand goes round, and the dial keeps its place; but in this the dial goes round and the hand keeps its direction

140 A spur of state from Mexico, taken in the Acapulco ship by admiral Anson

141 The flaming sword of William the Conqueror

142 A print of the Zebra, or African wild ass, coloured from life

143 A starved cat found between the walls of Westminster-abbey when repairing

144 The horns of an antelope

145 A fine large tarapin, or land-turtle

146 An antique chissel

147 A fine East-India bow and arrows, the arrows headed with poison, to shoot birds with

148 An Indian tomohawk, taken in the field of battle before Quebec

149 Fine lace imitated in paper

150 The head of the rhinoceros bird

151 The head of the spatula bird

152 The tooth of a sea-horse

NURSERY RHYME VIOLENCE

—

GEOFFREY HANDLEY-TAYLOR
1952

In 1952, having analysed 200 traditional nursery rhymes, British writer Geoffrey Handley-Taylor concluded in his book, *A Selected Bibliography of Literature Relating to Nursery Rhyme Reform*, that approximately half of those rhymes personified "all that is glorious and ideal for the child", but that the "remaining 100 rhymes harbour unsavoury elements". He then illustrated the latter point by way of this magnificent list, in which he tallied all instances of violence found in said nursery rhymes.

8 allusions to murder (unclassified)
2 cases of choking to death
1 case of death by devouring
1 case of cutting a human being in half
1 case of decapitation
1 case of death by squeezing
1 case of death by shriveling
1 case of death by starvation
1 case of boiling to death
1 case of death by hanging
1 case of death by drowning
4 cases of killing domestic animals
1 case of body snatching
21 cases of death (unclassified)
7 cases relating to the severing of limbs
1 case of the desire to have a limb severed
2 cases of self-inflicted injury
4 cases relating to the breaking of limbs
1 allusion to a bleeding heart
1 case of devouring human flesh
5 threats of death
1 case of kidnapping
12 cases of torment and cruelty to human beings and animals
8 cases of whipping and lashing
3 allusions to blood
14 cases of stealing and general dishonesty
15 allusions to maimed human beings and animals
1 allusion to undertakers
2 allusions to graves
23 cases of physical violence (unclassified)
1 case of lunacy
16 allusions to misery and sorrow
1 case of drunkenness
4 cases of cursing
1 allusion to marriage as a form of death
1 case of scorning the blind
1 case of scorning prayer
9 cases of children being lost or abandoned
2 cases of house burning
9 allusions to poverty and want
5 allusions to quarreling
2 cases of unlawful imprisonment
2 cases of racial discrimination

Diddlty, diddlty, dumpty,
The cat ran up the plum tree ;
Give her a plum, and down she'll come,
Diddlty, diddlty. dumpty.

THE MAFIA DECALOGUE

—

THE MAFIA
Date Unknown

Salvatore Lo Piccolo was on the run for 24 long years. When finally arrested in 2007 it is believed he was head of the Sicilian Mafia, the world's most famous criminal organisation and his "family" for decades. As with most families, the Mafia has rules. However, it wasn't until Piccolo's capture, after which Italian police discovered in his hideout, a document now known as the Mafia Decalogue, that these rules were unveiled for the world to see.

I SWEAR TO BE FAITHFUL TO THE COSA NOSTRA. IF I BETRAY MY FLESH MUST BURN — AS THIS IMAGE BURNS.

RIGHTS AND DUTIES

NO ONE CAN PRESENT HIMSELF DIRECTLY TO ANOTHER OF OUR FRIENDS. THERE MUST BE A THIRD PERSON TO DO IT.

NEVER LOOK AT THE WIVES OF FRIENDS.

NEVER BE SEEN WITH COPS.

DON'T GO TO PUBS AND CLUBS.

ALWAYS BEING AVAILABLE FOR COSA NOSTRA IS A DUTY — EVEN IF YOUR WIFE IS ABOUT TO GIVE BIRTH.

APPOINTMENTS MUST ABSOLUTELY BE RESPECTED.

WIVES MUST BE TREATED WITH RESPECT.

WHEN ASKED FOR ANY INFORMATION THE ANSWER MUST BE THE TRUTH.

MONEY CANNOT BE APPROPRIATED IF IT BELONGS TO OTHERS OR TO OTHER FAMILIES.

INDIVIDUALS WHO CANNOT BE PART OF THE COSA NOSTRA

ANYONE WHO HAS A CLOSE RELATIVE IN THE POLICE.
ANYONE WITH A TWO-TIMING RELATIVE IN THE FAMILY.
ANYONE WHO BEHAVES BADLY AND DOESN'T HOLD TO MORAL VALUES

WALT DISNEY PICTURES

INTER-OFFICE COMMUNICATION
P-4118

TO _____ANIMATION DEPARTMENT_____   DATE ____February 13, 1986____

FROM ____Peter Schneider____ EXT. __2630__   SUBJECT _____

Along with the new title for "Basil of Baker Street" it
has been decided to re-name the entire library of animated
classics. The new titles are as follows...

"SEVEN LITTLE MEN HELP A GIRL"

"THE WOODEN BOY WHO BECAME REAL"

"COLOR AND MUSIC"

"THE WONDERFUL ELEPHANT WHO COULD
 REALLY FLY"

"THE LITTLE DEER WHO GREW UP"

"THE GIRL WITH THE SEE-THROUGH SHOES"

"THE GIRL IN THE IMAGINARY WORLD"

"THE AMAZING FLYING CHILDREN"

"TWO DOGS FALL IN LOVE"

"THE GIRL WHO SEEMED TO DIE"

"PUPPIES TAKEN AWAY"

"THE BOY WHO WOULD BE KING"

"A BOY, A BEAR AND A BIG BLACK CAT"

"ARISTOCATS"

"ROBIN HOOD WITH ANIMALS"

"TWO MICE SAVE A GIRL"

"A FOX AND A HOUND ARE FRIENDS"

"THE EVIL BONEHEAD"

And of course our latest classic destined to win the
hearts of the american public...

"THE GREAT MOUSE DETECTIVE"

SEVEN LITTLE MEN HELP A GIRL

—

ED GOMBERT
February 13th, 1986

When, in early 1986, Disney executives decided to change the title of their upcoming animated feature from *Basil of Baker Street* to the less ambiguous *The Great Mouse Detective*, its production team were less than pleased. One animator in particular, Ed Gombert, harnessed his displeasure to comical effect by creating, and circulating, this fake memo purportedly from then head of department, Peter Schneider. On it, a list of Disney's back catalogue, renamed in a similarly bland style. The list was so popular that it soon reached a very unimpressed Jeffrey Katzenberg, then CEO of Disney, who, after questioning an entirely innocent Schneider, tried and failed to uncover the identity of its creator. To make matters worse, a copy then found its way to the *LA Times*. To Disney's dismay the movie's name was suddenly on everyone's lips, albeit for the wrong reasons.

For Characters Who Don't Dig Jive Talk:

A Really In There Solid Chick	An Attractive Young Girl
A Shape In A Drape	Looks Good In Clothes
Ball All Night	An All Night Party
Bring Him	Embarrass Him
Cat	A Jive Fan
Clipster	A Confidence Man
Cut on Down, Cut Out	To Leave
Dig Those Mellow Kicks	Knows How To Live
Dig What I'm Puttin' Down	Pay Attention
Drifter	Floater
Fall In On That Mess	Play That Thing
Fall On Down	Meander
Freakish High	To Get High As A Kite
Get Straight	Work It Out, Make A Deal
Good For Nothin' Mop	No Good Woman
Groovy Little Stash	Cozy Spot
Hipsters	Characters Who Like Hot Jazz
Hold Back The Dawn	Go On This Way Forever
Hype You For Your Gold	Take You For The Bank Roll
I'm Hippn' You Man	Putting You Wise
Joint Is Jumpin'	Place Full Of Customers
Juices	Liquor
Layin' It On You Straight	Telling You The Truth
Like A Motherless Child	Sedate
Lush Yourself To All Ends	Get Very Drunk
Out Of The World Mellow Stage	To Get Ecstatically Drunk
Pitch A Ball	Have A Good Time
Really In There	Knows The Answers
Same Beat Groove	Bored
A Square	Cornfed
Solid Blew My Top	Went Crazy
Solid Give Me My Kicks	Had Lots of Fun
Solid Stud	Influential man in the entertainment field
His Story Is Great	A Successful Man About Town
Take It Slow	Be Careful
Your Stickin'	Flush, Carrying A Bankroll

Made in U. S. A.

FOR CHARACTERS WHO DON'T DIG JIVE TALK

—

HARRY GIBSON
1944

Jazz pianist Harry Gibson was something of an anomaly of his time: an eccentric and frantic musician wowing audiences in the clubs of Manhattan with energetic music that was, in some ways, ahead of its time. His constant use of jive talk was the icing on the cake; he also, in 1944, coined the word "hipster". The list seen here – a beginner's guide to his dialect of choice – was printed that same year on the inside cover of his album, *Boogie Woogie in Blue*.

EINSTEIN'S DEMANDS

—

ALBERT EINSTEIN
1914

By 1914, theoretical physicist Albert Einstein's marriage to his wife of 11 years, Mileva Marić, was fast deteriorating. Upon the realisation that there was no hope for their relationship on a romantic level, Einstein proposed that they remain together for the sake of their two young sons, Hans and Eduard, but only if she agree to the following list of conditions. Mileva accepted them, but to no avail. A few months later she left her husband in Berlin and moved, with their children, to Zurich. They eventually divorced in 1919, having lived apart for five years.

Conditions.

A. You will make sure
1. that my clothes and laundry are kept in good order;
2. that I will receive my three meals regularly *in my room*;
3. that my bedroom and study are kept neat, and especially that my desk is left for *my use only*.

B. You will renounce all personal relations with me insofar as they are not completely necessary for social reasons. Specifically, you will forego
1. my sitting at home with you;
2. my going out or traveling with you.

C. You will obey the following points in your relations with me:
1. you will not expect any intimacy from me, nor will you reproach me in any way;
2. you will stop talking to me if I request it;
3. you will leave my bedroom or study immediately without protest if I request it.

D. You will undertake not to belittle me in front of our children, either through words or behavior.

A. Du sorgst dafür

~~Du sorgst dafür~~ 1) dass meine
ordentlich
Kleider und Wäsche (im Stand
gehalten werden

2) dass ich die drei Mahlzeiten
im Zimmer ordnungsgemäß
vorgesetzt bekomme.

3) Das mein Schlafzimmer
und Arbeitszimmer stets
in guter Ordnung gehalten
sind, insbesondere, dass
der Schreibtisch mir
allein zur Verfügung steht.

B. Du verzichtest auf alle
persönlichen Beziehungen
zu mir, soweit deren Auf-
rechterhaltung ~~nicht zur~~
~~Wahrung~~ aus gesellschaft-
lichen Gründen nicht
unbedingt geboten
ist. Insbesondere verzichtest
Du darauf
1) dass ich zuhause bei Dir
sitze
2) dass ich zusammen mit
Dir ausgehe oder verreise

...chtest Dich aus-
...ch, im Verkehr mit
...gende Punkte
...ten

...t weder Zärtlich-
... mir
...erwarten noch
...ndwelche Vorwürfe
...ben.

...st eine an mich
...ete Rede sofort
...eren, wenn ich
...ersuche.

...st mein Schlaf-
...beitszimmer sofort
...errede zu verlassen,
...en darum ersuche.

...flichtest Dich,
...urch Worte noch
...Handlungen in den
...Augen meiner
...herabzusetzen.

Hoffsjef Lövenskioldsvei 26
Ovre Ullern, Oslo
October 31, 1960

Mrs. Judith B. Jones, Editor
Alfred A. Knopf Inc.
501 Madison Avenue
New York City, NY

Dear Mrs. Jones:

    TITLES: I don't think the title should scare people, or that the
sub-title should sound too puffy. I think a welcoming, friendly approach
(with professional overtones) would be right. And I can see that
xomething like "French Cooking" is not good as people might come into
a bookstore and ask for "that book on French cooking", and that would
not necessarily mean us. However, it might be said in French:

        LA BONNE CUISINE FRANÇAISE

As a matter of fact, I quite like that.

Subtitle: "The fundamental book on French cooking for everyone whose
            hobby is cooking, and who wants to master the authentic French
            Techniques.
                    American ingredients. American measurements.
                            American terminology "

Other title suggestions:

IN LOVE WITH FRENCH COOKING	COOKING IS MY HOBBY
LOVE AND FRENCH COOKING	THE HOBBY OF FRENCH COOKING
THE LOVE OF FRENCH COOKING	FRENCH COOKING AS A HOBBY
COOKING FOR LOVE	SCHOOL FOR FRENCH COOKS
THE FRENCH COOKING MASTER	SCHOOL FOR FRENCH COOKERY
COOKING MASTERY	A COURSE ON FRENCH COOKING
MASTERY OF FRENCH COOKING (NO "the")	THE PASSIONATE COOK
THE FRENCH KITCHEN	THE PASSIONATE FRENCH COOK
FOOD FROM FRANCE	FRENCH COOKING FOR FUN
FRANCE'S FOOD	FRENCH COOKING FOR LOVE
THE NOBLE ART OF FRENCH COOKING	FRENCH COOKING FOR EVERYONE
THE MASTER FRENCH COOKBOOK	COOK FOR YOUR SELF À LA FRANCAISE
GREAT FRENCH COOKING	
THE COMPULSIVE COOK	

MASTERING THE ART of FRENCH CUISINE COOKING / COOKERY

MASTERING THE ART OF FRENCH COOKING

—

JULIA CHILD
October 31st, 1960

As the author of more than a dozen bestselling cookbooks and the presenter of numerous successful cookery television programmes from the 1960s onwards, chef Julia Child was responsible for inspiring millions of Americans to be more creative in the kitchen. It was her first book, however, that made the biggest impact, published in 1961 to rave reviews and strong sales that continue to this day. In October 1961, months before its release, she wrote to her editor at Alfred A. Knopf publishers with a list of 28 potential titles for her debut. The last suggestion, *Mastering the Art of French Cuisine*, was eventually chosen.

ROLL OF MISSING MEN

—

CLARA BARTON
1865

As she worked tirelessly to care for soldiers and supply those at the frontline with medical supplies during the American Civil War, volunteer Clara Barton became known as the "Angel of the Battlefield" for her good deeds. She then continued as the war came to an end, by requesting permission from Abraham Lincoln to set up the Office of Correspondence with the Friends of the Missing Men of the United States Army, a set-up which enabled her and a small staff to reply to the thousands of frantic, unanswered letters from those awaiting word on their absent loved ones. Before long, with no such system already in place, Barton drew up a list of missing persons and had it printed in newspapers all over the country – the list seen here accompanied by a letter from Barton, reproduced to the right, was the first; many more followed.

A few years later, she founded the American Red Cross.

WASHINGTON, D. C., *June* 1, 1865.

SOLDIERS AND BROTHERS:

Please examine this Roll; and if you know what became of any man her names, or have facts of interest to surviving friends, communicate the same to me by letter, as soon as possible, with your address in full.

If any one sees his own name, or that of a comrade whom he *knows* to be living, please inform me, that it may be withheld from future rolls.

Letters of inquiry for missing soldiers may be brief—should contain the name, regiment, company, and State to which they belonged, with the full address of the writer, plainly written.

Attention will no longer be confined to those who have been prisoners, but an effort will be made to ascertain the fate of *all* missing men of the United States army during the war.

If any letter of inquiry fails to receive an answer, please write again. No apologies are necessary, and no letter will be neglected.

CLARA BARTON

Address—

Miss CLARA BARTON,

Washington, D. C.

☞ Please paste in a safe and conspicuous place. ☜

TO RETURNED SOLDIERS AND OTHERS.

WASHINGTON, D. C., *June* 1, 1865.

SOLDIERS AND BROTHERS:

Please examine this Roll; and if you know what became of any man here named, or have facts of interest to surviving friends, communicate the same to me by letter, as soon as possible, with your address in full.

If any one sees his own name, or that of a comrade whom he *knows* to be living, please inform me, that it may be withheld from future rolls.

Letters of inquiry for missing soldiers may be brief—should contain the name, regiment, company, and State to which they belonged, with the full address of the writer, plainly written.

Attention will no longer be confined to those who have been prisoners, but an effort will be made to ascertain the fate of *all* missing men of the United States army during the war.

If any letter of inquiry fails to receive an answer, please write again. No apologies are necessary, and no letter will be neglected.

CLARA BARTON.

Address—
Miss CLARA BARTON,
Washington, D. C.

OFFICERS.

Andrews, E. E., col., surg. 68th U. S. inf.
Bennett, ——, capt., co. C, 210th Pa. inf.
Bingham, Leonard P., 1st lieut., co. G, 17th Vt.
Bullard, Stephen H., maj., co. —, Mich. cav.
Butler, Frank, lieut., co. —, 51st N. Y. inf.
Caton, Milo, capt., co. D, 21st Ohio inf.
Chalmers, Hugh, 2d lt., co. E, 146th N. Y. inf.
Fish, George W., lieut., co. —, 3d Ohio inf.
Harlow, I. T., capt., co. —, 31st Me.
Harris, E. T., capt., co. —, 3d Tenn. cav.
Hunter, A. M., lt., co. —, 1st Tenn. (col.) art'y.
Hyde, Horace A., lieut., co. H, 1st Vt. cav.
Miller, Levis, capt., co. I, 6th Pa. cav.
Peirce, Gordon L., lt., co. C, 112th N. Y. inf.
Saxton, Luther W., capt., co. A, 54th Ohio inf.
Sears, D. C., lieut., co. B, 94th N. Y. inf.
West, Charles H., jr., lt., co. O, 8th N. Y. H. A.
Wilder, George O., lieut., co. —, 15th Mass. inf.

REGULARS.

Corliss, Amos, 17th inf.
Chamberlin, Oscar D., co. F, 19th inf.
Cummings, John, co. F, 12th inf.
Corbin, Monroe C., co. C, 16th inf.
Cleva, Samuel A., co. E, 11th inf.
Davis, Robert, co. A, 12th inf.
Fields, Charles F., co. A, 12th inf.
Farrar, Charles, co. A, 12th inf.
Tregaskis, Richard Alfred, co. B, 14th inf.
Heller, Daniel, co. —, 15th inf.
Lindsay, Herbert W., co. C, 12th inf.
Mitchell, John, co. G, 11th inf.
Martin, Seth, co. E, 16th inf.
McCord, George W., co. C, 14th inf.
O'Neill, John, co. A, 4th inf.
Patch, Frank T., co. C, 18th inf.
Seaton, Thomas R., co. G, 18th inf.
Tenaison, John, co. E, 14th inf.
Vantarel, Ravel, co. —, 16th inf.
Wilson, Joseph, co. G, 14th inf.
Wickham, Horace, serg., co. F, 2d inf.
Young, Silas D., co. A, 19th inf.

Conrad, Peter S., co. —, 9th vol.
Dietrich, Peter, co. I, 6th cav.
Eisele, Henry, co. H, 6th cav.
Kean, Emmett, co. E, 1st cav.
Michelbach, Henry, co. G, 5th cav.
Olinger, Charles, co. M, 1st cav.

Clarence ——, co. D, 1st art.
Devlin, Robert, bat. B, 1st art.
Gould, Charles H., bat. D, 1st a. a.
Jenks, Melville, bat. D, 7th art.
Flamer, Jeremiah, co. B, 26th col. troops.

STATE OF MAINE.

Arnold, John S., co. C, 8th vol.
Bancroft, Columbus, co. B, 16th vol.
Burnell, Henry L., corp., co. I, 8th vol.
Chadbourn, Nathan, serg't, co. F, 32d vol.
Douglass, C. R., co. A, 11th vol.
Flanders, Lewis G., co. E, 20th vol.
Gilchrist, George, co. B or E, 31st vol.
Ham, John L., serg't, co. D, 32d vol.
Hotchiss, Knox, co. E, 8th vol.
Hodges, Charles E., co. D, 11th vol.
Heald, Perham, co. A, 19th vol.
Johnson, Chas. W., serg., co. G, 32d vol.
Keech, Nelson H., co. E, 24th vol.
Williams, Luke B., co. H, 3d vol.
McCann, Alexander, co. C, 6th vol.
Norton, Joseph O., co. I, 18th vol.
Overlock, Alden, co. G, 5th vol.
Pitman, Eli, co. G, 31st vol.
Parker, Samuel D., co. E, 12th vol.
Stevens, James Orator, co. F, 19th vol.
Thomas, George W., co. C, 4th vol.
Turner, Chas. C., co. B, 6th vol.
Thayer, Albit H., co. B, 16th vol.
Taylor, John G., co. F, 32d vol.
Tuttle, Lewis, co. F, 32d vol.
Tuttle, Davis, co. F, 32d vol.
Vinal, Wooster S., co. I, 19th vol.
Wills, Isaac T., co. B, 7th vol.
Worthing, Elmar W., co. K, 19th vol.
Young, Delance, co. C, 8th vol.
Bills, Andrew J., co. M, 20th cav.
Perkins, Thomas H., co. B, 1st cav.
Whitney, Thos. C., co. A, 1st cav.
Chadbourne, Albert, bat. H, 1st heavy art.
Stover, Alvin H. P., 1st bat.
Wentworth, Caleb, co. F, 32d vol.

STATE OF NEW HAMPSHIRE.

Ames, John C., co. F, 2d vol.
Berry, James, co. K, 9th vol.
Brennan, John, co. A, 15th vol.
Clarke, Chas. C., co. I, 1st vol.
Danforth, Charles R., co. —, 7th vol.
Gilman, George W., co. H, 9th vol.
Hayes, James W., co. H, 9th vol.
Haren, Benjamin F., co. K, 9th vol.
Johnson, Albert G., co. —, 9th vol.
Kingsbury, Harlan P., co. K, 9th vol.
Lowe, Leonard, co. I, 9th vol.
Lester, William G., co. G, 5th art.
Phelps, George M., co. G, 3d vol.
Parsons, William Henry, co. B, 11th vol.
Spaulding, Fernando C., co. K, 4th vol.
Smith, Nathaniel, co. G, 5th vol.
Smith, Walter W., co. K, 6th vol.
Vincent, Rupert, co. H, 3d vol.
Willey, Edward, co. I, 6th vol.

STATE OF VERMONT.

Aiken, William A., co. A, 11th vol.
Avery, Frederick B., co. G, 3d vol.

Ball, Locl, co. D, 4th vol.
Hunt, Bradbury A., co. K, 10th vol.
Bailey, Henry U., co. A, 5th vol.
Barber, William H., co. I, 15th inf.
Bishop, Emerson, co. E, 11th vol.
Chapin, E. C., co. F, 4th vol.
Cole, Felix G., co. A, 4th vol.
Camp, Henry, co. A, 4th vol.
Crow, Henry, co. C, 5th vol.
Cheever, Moses R., co. G, 4th Bd.
Chamberlin, Convarse P., co. A, 6th vol.
Conly, Frank, co. B, 5th vol.
Davis, Leander, co. K, 10th vol.
Downer, Russel L., co. E, 5th vol.
Elkins, Moses M., co. F, 11th vol.
Forrest, Silas, co. I, 3d vol.
Fairchild, G. L., co. A, 11th vol.
Gorham, Hiram L., co. I, 4th vol.
Gelo, Aiken, co. B, 3d vol.
Himes, George C., co. F, 10th vol.
Hosmer, Francis J., co. I, 4th vol.
Ingleston, William H., co. E, 6th vol.
Kendall, Wallace, co. A, 4th vol.
Lamadon, Calvin R., co. D, 4th vol.
Melcher, William, co. F, 9th vol.
Martindale, George W. H., co. I, 11th vol.
Phillips, William H., co. —, 12th vol.
Page, Edgar W., co. I, 4th vol.
Perry, Adolphus B., co. H, 4th vol.
Robbins, George, co. F, 11th vol.
Ryerson, William, co. F, 4th vol.
Reid, Newman R., co. B, 10th vol.
Richardson, Charles E., co. E, 2d vol.
Smith, Moses G., co. A, 11th vol.
Smith, Abie R., co. D, 4th vol.
Scott, Royal G., co. F, 4th vol.
Stevens, Winthrop, co. F, 4th vol.
Slute, Henry W., co. D, 17th vol.
Sartwell, William E., co. I, 11th vol.
Stewart, Edwin W., co. A, 11th vol.
Scribner, Walter, co. G, 4th vol.
Smith, H. C., co. —, 9th vol.
Twiss, George S., co. F, 11th vol.
Tinkham, Clarence G., co. H, 11th vol.
Tucker, Milo, co. G, 9th vol.
William, Ezra G., co. G, 4th vol.
Wakefield, Joseph H., co. B, 4th vol.
Whitney, Varnum R., co. H, 1st heavy art.

Abbott, Horace M., co. D, 1st cav.
Blood, Frank J., co. K, 1st cav.
Badger, Alphonso H., co. D, 1st cav.
Butts, Harvey R., co. E, 1st cav.
Chamberlin, Wm. A., co. I, 1st cav.
Fay, Ramson Y., co. E, 1st cav.
Gilligan, Patrick C., co. D, 1st cav.
Hinds, Austin G., co. E, 1st cav.
Howard, David R., co. F, 1st cav.
Jenne, Harvey A., co. D, 1st cav.
Labanta, Henry, co. —, 1st cav.
Labonta, Lewis, co. B, 6th vol.
Morgan, Charles H., co. M, 11th cav.
Tupper, Hiram E., co. S, 1st cav.
Watson, William A., co. C, 1st cav.
Flenry, Allen B., battery K, 1st heavy art.
Hall, Charles C., battery A, 1st heavy art.
Keyes, Howard, battery K, 1st heavy art.
Kaldor, Joseph, battery F, 11th heavy art.
Macomber, Orlando, battery K, 1st heavy art.
Willey, Chester S., battery A, 1st heavy art.
Bidwell, Emory S., co. B, 5th vol.
Wardner, Col., co. E, 1st vol.

STATE OF MASSACHUSETTS.

Acker, Eldridge, co. E, 20th inf.
Adam, John, co. E, 1st inf.
Bartlett, Charles H., co. —, 15th inf.
Ball, Daniel E., co. C, 27th inf.
Bullen, Joseph W., co. A, 40th inf.
Bardwell, Orange, co. F, 37th inf.
Buffer, Elliot B., co. A, 34th inf.
Bernice, William H., co. H, 10th inf.
Bartlett, Will A., co. A, 27th inf.
Britt, Oscar G., co. C, 27th inf.
Chickering, Henry G., co. E, 34th inf.
Champney, Preston A., co. D, 25th inf.
Carroll, Robert, co. D, 24th inf.
Cooley, Milo H., co. E, 27th inf.
Carl, Robert, co. D, 34th inf.
Curtis, David R., co. G, 27th inf.
Doe, Albert W., co. K, 57th inf.
Dunn, James, co. A, 19th inf.
Dickerman, Charles C., co. D, 39th inf.
Elsbree, Frederick C., co. B, 7th inf.
Emmons, Chauncy L., co. C, 27th inf.
Emerson, George W., co. B, 21st inf.
Elsbree, Frederick O., co. C, 7th inf.
Estes, Sidney, co. H, 27th inf.
Eddy, Lafayette, co. F, 34th inf.
Frost, Charles C., co. A, 18th inf.
Fellows, Joseph E., co. B, 15th inf.
Field, Edgar, co. F, 37th inf.
Frissell, Henry J., co. G, 15th inf.
Fuller, Herbert N., co. E, 18th inf.
Fitzpatrick, Michael, co. A, 25th inf.
Gould, Oscar Emory, co. E, 23d inf.
Greenough, Archibald, co. C, 24th inf.
Howard, William F., co. I, 57th inf.
Hubbard, Calvin, co. G, 36th inf.
Hurlock, Horace P., 22d co. 2d sharp-shooters.
Hemenway, Elbert O., co. K, 39th inf.
Hurlburt, Charles H., co. C, 15th inf.
Jemisson, R. B., co. G, 36th inf.
Lalombard, Peter, co. E, 57th inf.
Lacier, Raymond, co. F, 59th inf.
Lyman, Charles Austin, co. —, 27th inf.
Little, John, co. B, 20th inf.

Lacky, John, co. —, 19th inf.
Mahr, George W., co. E, 18th inf.
Mandell, A. S., co. H, 56th inf.
Moulten, H. Harrison, co. F, 15th inf.
McWilliams, William, co. D, 17th inf.
Martin, James, co. B, 56th inf.
Newcomb, Bryant, co. E, 32d inf.
Packard, Merrick E., co. C, 27th inf.
Plimpton, Emerson F., co. F, 56th inf.
Peckham, Henry Samuel, co. E, 59th inf.
Peckham, Anson F., co. —, 15th inf.
Phipps, Mahon M., co. C, 57th inf.
Richards, John Henry, co. —, 57th inf.
Roberts, James, co. I, 18th inf.
Ripley, Brigham S., co. C, 27th inf.
Roake, John M., co. D, 34th inf.
Smith, James M., co. —, 15th inf.
Southwick, Josiah M., co. C, 18th inf.
Shaw, Charles S., co. C, 15th inf.
Stevens, Elbridge, co. A, 38th inf.
Morrison, J. T., co. C, 59th inf.
Simon, Sanford A., co. D, 40th inf.
Swift, Peres, co. D, 40th inf.
Stuart, James A., co. H, 11th inf.
Sawyer, John, co. F, 33d inf.
Thurston, John A., co. A, 40th inf.
Vilbert, George L., co. H, 15th inf.
Wood, Myron M., co. G, 140th inf.
Wodfenden, Samuel, co. C, 27th inf.
Wodfenden, John William, co. C, 27th inf.
Wilder, Charles S., co. A, 21st inf.
Willington, George F., co. H, 15th inf.
Weatherell, Andrew M., co. C, 27th inf.

STATE OF RHODE ISLAND.

Delauoh, Charles R., co. G, 1st cav.
Taylor, Herbert, co. I, 1st cav.
West, Hiram, co. A, 1st cav.
Dunlap, George, co. B, 5th art.
Edwards, George H., bat. A, 3d light art.

STATE OF CONNECTICUT.

Besancon, Pierre, co. D, 14th inf.
Burriage, G. Deming, co. G, 15th inf.
Billing, Sanford M., co. —, 21st inf.
Crossley, Benjamin, co. G, 8th inf.
Couvrese, Joel T., co. A, 11th inf.
Colburn, Jonathan S., co. I, 18th inf.
Creighton, George, co. G, 16th inf.
Hamilton, H. Nell, co. B, 11th inf.
Hints, Henry, co. E, 10th inf.
Jackman, Calvin, co. B, 7th inf.
Lyon, Olive Levi, co. E, 12th inf.
Kinne, Martin V. R., co. G, 21st inf.
Moger, Amos A., co. I, 10th inf.
McNell, Alexander, co. —, 14th inf.
Nichols, Michael, co. I, 7th inf.
Pratt, Albert C., co. G, 7th inf.
Quingley, Herbert, co. B, 11th inf.
Quingley, Edward H., co. B, 11th inf.
Richards, Charles I., co. A, 11th inf.
Sutliff, Elbert, co. K, 16th inf.
Upson, Charles A., co. B, 14th inf.
Watson, Bernard, co. —, 14th inf.
Walling, James, co. K, 14th inf.
Whitney, George F., co. I, 16th inf.
Wesley, Edward, co. E, 12th inf.
Wood, Charles H., co. B, 7th inf.

Adams, I. A., co. A, 1st cav.
Brown, Charles H., co. H, 1st cav.
Belfey, Orin T., co. —, 1st cav.
Canfield, Benjamin, co. B, 1st cav.
Greenough, Henry Walde, co. D, 1st cav.
Glena, Belna, co. B, 1st cav.
Starkweather, Eugene W., co. I, 1st cav.
Tyler, I. R., co. —, 1st cav.
Weaver, John A., co. K, 1st cav.
Downs, Amasiah, co. K, 2d heavy art.
Fitzgerald, Matthew, co. E, 2d heavy art.

STATE OF NEW YORK.

Avery, John, co. D, 146th vol.
Ambrose, Edward F., co. G, 108th inf.
Aiken, Wm., co. I, 147th inf.
Arraniggre, Edgar G., co. C, 100th inf.
Ames, Robert, co. K, 47th inf.
Burke, Timothy, co. B, 97th inf.
Bigelow, L. R., co. —, 85th inf.
Burlingame, E. A., co. —, 97th inf.
Bennett, George A., co. G, 51st inf.
Ballard, John S., co. K, 147th inf.
Barger, Lowry, co. F, 154th inf.
Bolton, Noble, co. —, 111th inf.
Besner, Moraine, co. D, 153d inf.
Boyd, Duncan W., co. C, 124th inf.
Briggs, Miles, co. K, 26th inf.
Barny, George, co. —, 85th inf.
Bishop, Samuel H., co. A, 160th inf.
Barny, John, co. —, 85th inf.
Briggs, James E., co. B, 108th inf.
Barger, L. D., co. F, 154th inf.
Boyntion, Thomas, co. G, 189th inf.
Burbanks, Jacob D., co. D, 85th inf.
Bush, J. W., co. B, 76th inf.
Bale, Joshua W., co. A, 76th inf.
Bullen, Lewis, serg., co. E, 100th inf.
Benton, D. L., co. B, 76th inf.
Brown, A. E., co. C, 152d inf.
Brown, George, co. A, 5th inf.
Beker, James A., co. H, 90th inf.
Boucher, Milen, co. H, 56th inf.
Barr, ——, co. C, 146th inf.
Baker, William, co. C, 96th inf.
Bellew, William, co. H, 140th inf.
Bulkley, Edwin A., co. E, 47th inf.
Barton, Jonathan, co. D, 119th inf.
Bannister, A. J., co. D, 64th inf.

Beals, Edward A., co. C, 85th inf.
Cushman, A. P., co. H, 100th inf.
Carter, Henry J., co. A, 179th inf.
Clinroth, Delos, co. I, 72d vol.
Carter, Henry A., co. A, 179th inf.
Canfield, Aug. W., co. D, 86th inf.
Catford, James, co. H, 13th inf.
Carson, James, 1st serg., co. D, 146th inf.
Clay, Thomas, serg., co. H, 125th inf.
Curtis, Wm. H., co. I, 146th inf.
Campbell, Jno. R., co. A, 147th inf.
Conklin, Elijah B., corp., co. —, 126th inf.
Compton, Charles W., co. —, 121st inf.
Coon, Harvey, co. A, 99th inf.
Chidester, Albert, co. H, 109th inf.
Corwin, James C., co. C, 111th inf.
Cesey, Dennis, co. A, 164th inf.
Coburn, James, co. H, 106th inf.
Conklin, A. J., co. —, 120th inf.
Church, William P., co. C, 42d inf.
Clark, Oliver P., co. B, 94th inf.
Dermont, Peter, co. H, 146th inf.
Dumount, Peter L., serg., co. A, 146th inf.
Dyke, Albert, co. F, 85th inf.
Dalton, S. R., co. K, 22d inf.
Dimmick, Samuel S., co. K, 40th inf.
Durham, R. H., co. H, 123d inf.
Duff, James F., co. C, 140th inf.
Denyes, Henry G., co. D, 150th inf.
Duel, Myron A., co. B, 142d inf.
Diamond, Frederick, co. D, 146th inf.
Denton, Jackson M., co. A, 51st inf.
Doughty, Edwin T., co. A, 48th inf.
Evans, Jeranihh, co. D, 140th inf.
Eldred, Addison M., co. E, 52d inf.
Eddy, John C., co. E, 112th inf.
Earl, William, co. —, 60th inf.
Farley, Thomas, co. K, 148th inf.
Floeger, Henry, co. C, 47th inf.
Fish, Hosea, co. A, 179th inf.
Finch, Thomas R., 1st serg., co. C, 108th inf.
Forgee, William A., co. J, 49th inf.
Fralick, William, serg., co. I, 97th inf.
Fisher, H. C., co. —, 69th inf.
Faller, Nelson P., co. E, 51st inf.
Foiger, William, jr., co. —, 49th inf.
Furrar, Charles, co. A, 12th inf.
Fairfax, Joseph, co. I, 12th inf.
Garner, Charles M., co. I, 97th inf.
Garrett, S. J., co. D, 146th inf.
Graves, S. G., co. H, 20th inf.
Graves, William T., co. H, 20th inf.
Graves, Robert T., co. C, 164th inf.
Goffe, John W., co. G, 146th inf.
Goodman, B. F., serg., co. B, 57th inf.
Gardner, Charles, co. I, 97th inf.
Hillis, Joseph, co. D, 167th inf.
Hart, William, co. B, 94th inf.
Horton, Nathan S., co. —, 49th inf.
Hecker, George, co. —, 146th inf.
Holley, Theodore W., co. —, 76th inf.
Hayes, John, co. K, 140th inf.
Hudson, William T., co. K, 85th inf.
Hudson, John, co. A, 146th inf.
Hayer, Albert, co. A, 154th inf.
Haner, Stephen, serg., co. C, 109th inf.
Holloway, Jno. H., co. D, 146th inf.
Hasball, Josiah, co. B, 146th inf.
Hunter, William, co. K, 152d inf.
Holmes, Eugene S., co. K, 117th inf.
Hodges, Charles, co. G, 121st inf.
Hughes, George, corp. serg., co. C, 99th inf.
Henry, James, serg., co. I, 76th inf.
Hecker, George, co. —, 49th inf.
Herman, F. C., co. A, 20th inf.
Hayward, S. S., co. G, 152d inf.
Haner, David, co. G, 134th inf.
Hyce, William, co. D, 146th inf.
Hudson, John, co. A, 146th inf.
Hugh, E. G., co. G, 140th inf.
Howard, John, co. H, 111th inf.
Howard, Leverett, 114th inf.
Howell, William B., corp., co. E, 124th inf.
Irish, E. W., 1st serg., co. G, 85th inf.
Johnson, James T., co. A, 104th inf.
Jones, David W., co. C, 115th inf.
Johnson, M. W., co. —, 50th eng.
Johnson, Thomas A., co. K, 179th inf.
Jones, Ezra G., co. K, 147th inf.
Johnston, William, co. —, 146th inf.
Jones, Daniel W., co. C, 115th inf.
Jones, George, co. A, 146th inf.
Jerome, James, co. F, 111th inf.
Kelley, Lutheran, co. —, 149th inf.
Kelley, Thomas, co. —, 97th inf.
Keating, Michael, co. A, 146th inf.
Keeler, Elijah R., co. C, 76th inf.
Knight, Arthur F., co. F, 117th inf.
Kessler, John A., co. B, 146th inf.
Kiddor, William, co. H, 52d inf.
Keating, Thomas, co. A, 152d inf.
Loch, William, co. E, 109th inf.
Lynch, Joseph, co. A, 117th inf.
Leroy, Ainsberg, co. —, 128th inf.
Longee, John L., co. D, 139th inf.
Lansdell, Joseph, co. A, 95th inf.
Latham, Sylvester, co. I, 96th inf.
Lutton, Thomas, co. —, 95th inf.
Lall, Gaylor, co. G, 152d inf.
Lall, G. M., co. H, 152d inf.
La Bottomy, Wm., co. D, 148th inf.
Miller, Samuel W., co. K, 121st inf.
McNeill, D. C., serg., co. E, 159th inf.
McPherson, John, co. F, 147th inf.
Madan, Wm. H., co. G, 162d inf.
Marcy, Wm. P., co. F, 152d inf.
Mailer, James R., serg., co. B, 134th inf.
Mills, Jay J., co. E, 85th inf.
Morgan, John A., co. B, 142d inf.
Maurice, Pigotto, co. K, 170th inf.
McCormick, John, serg., co. A, 152d vol.
Merrill, R. C., co. G, 118th vol.
McElroy, Wm., co. B, 121st vol.
Main, Wm. Oscar, co. A, 85th vol.
Merkle, Jos., co. A, 1st vol. Excel. brig.
Morgan, D. V. B., co. B, 93d vol.
McWalkins, Thos., co. I, 1st vol.
May, Horace, co. D, 118th vol.
McMichael, James, co. H, 66th vol.
Murphy, Peter, co. E, 152d vol.
Martin, Albert G., co. B, 24th vol.
McOmber, Otis, co. B, 76th vol.
Marsh, Edwin T., co. I, 140th vol.
Norwicke, A. Z., corp., co. B, 156th vol.
Northrop, J. R., co. —, 111th vol.
Nelson, John H., co. D, 14th vol.
Ogden, Stephen T., co. G, 111th vol.
Olmstead, J. W., co. —, 160th vol.
Prosser, E. W., co. A, 64th vol.
Peters, George, co. A, 111th vol.
Parsons, Warren H., co. H, 160th vol.
Rodney, Pacho, co. I, 51st vol.
Parsons, Henry, co. C, 40th vol.
Poor, Elijah, co. —, 92d vol.
Page, Ozias D., co. F, 146th vol.

Porter, Geo. A., co. K, 14th vol., Brooklyn.
Porter, Henry, co. E, 48th vol.
Quackenbush, George, co. —, 94th vol.
Reitley, John A., co. G, 69th vol.
Remington, Henry, co. C, 122d vol.
Reilley, Jas., co. F, 15th inf.
Ripley, Fras. A., serg., co. C, 152d vol.
Rickett, Wm., co. F, 97th vol.
Rockafeller, W. E., co. D, 85th vol.
Russell, Geo. R., co. D, 177th vol.
Radley, John, co. C, 152d vol.
Rockwell, Eldridge, co. I, 124th vol.
Stone, Alvat K., co. A, 94th vol.
Seymonr, Fred., co. D, 166th vol.
Schneider, George, co. F, 97th vol.
Snyder, K. L., co. D, 85th vol.
Smith, George, co. K, 118th vol.
Smith, Andrew, co. F, 160th vol.
Sherwood, Jones, co. G, 70th vol.
Sargent, Stanly, co. C, 152d vol.
Sherman, A. R., co. A, 117th vol.
Smith, William S., co. —, 85th vol.
Seward, A. R., co. D, 76th vol.
Scholl, Henry, co. —, 146th vol.
Smalley, George D., co. H, 140th vol.
Stockwell, Lewis, co. H, 97th vol.
Seiler, Jno. T., co. F, 140th vol.
Steger, Geo. R., co. C, 152d vol.
Schott, Henry, co. —, 146th vol.
Sampson, Thomas S., co. G, 92d inf.
Snook, James S., co. G, 152d vol.
Stevens, Wm. Thomas, co. I, 20th inf.
Smith, James A., co. K, 104th inf.
Stannard, W. W., co. D, 118th inf.
Shearman, A. R., co. F, 179th inf.
Salyer, Simeon, co. C, 120th inf.
Swanson, James, co. E, 146th inf.
Smith, George, co. K, 111th inf.
Shaylor, Henry S., co. I, 166th inf.
Tidd, Samuel V., co. K, 124th inf.
Taylor, Stephen, co. G, 97th inf.
Tilford, Benton F., co. F, 140th inf.
Taylor, James J., co. B, 93d inf.
Thomas, James L., co. A, 104th inf.
Troandell, Wm. J., co. I, 140th inf.
Taylor, Levi, co. H, 69th inf.
Taylor, Adney, co. H, 49th inf.
Tuttle, James C., co. D, 10th inf.
Taylor, Charles, co. F, 115th inf.
Taylor, Lorenzo D., co. D, 141st inf.
Terquiliger, Nelson, co. C, 120th inf.
Taylor, S. B., co. K, 147th inf.
Upham, Jared Jewel, 85th inf.
Vorhis, Jacob, co. F, 104th inf.
Vannsadall, Wesley D., co. A, 115th inf.
Van Blarcom, Isaac, co. D, 95th inf.
Van Schuyver, George, co. C, 108th inf.
Van Arman, Charles E., co. H, 69th inf.
Vantine, G. G., co. F, 106th inf.
Vale, Adrian, serg., co. D, 176th inf.
Williams, John, drummer, 226th inf.
Wellen, Augustus P., co. B, 109th inf.
Witter, Wm. Owen, co. I, 49th inf.
William, John H., co. I, 164th inf.
Webster, Elwood, co. K, 76th inf.
Weatcott, Henry C., co. F, 148th inf.
Wiley, James, co. B, 59th inf.
Weel, Wm. W., co. D, 157th inf.
Woodward, Oren B., co. I, 111th inf.
Wolf, John, co. E, 111th inf.
Waldron, Nelson, co. E, 104th inf.
Wilson, Robert, co. I, 111th inf.
Weller, John J., co. B, 66th inf.
Wisor, M. L., co. F, 90th inf.
Walston, Nelson, co. G, 164th inf.
Whitton, Joseph S., co. I, 126th inf.
Wolfe, Cristian A., co. D, 152d inf.
Warren, Nathan T., co. I, 108th inf.
Willyams, A. B., serg., co. D, 111th inf.
White, H. G., co. A, 94th inf.
Williams, Lyman W., co. F, 152d inf.
Webb, Lewis M., co. F, 147th inf.
White, Lois, co. D, 156th inf.
Yeta, Charles, co. A, 121st inf.

Alexander, Ephraim, jr., co. —, 15th cav.
Atwell, Theodore, serg., co. M, 6th cav.
Bentley, Washington, co. —, 25th cav.
Bishop, Chester, corp., co. B, 10th cav.
Boxt, Edwin, co. B, 9th cav.
Breese, Niles, co. D, 9th cav.
Barr, John, serg., co. F, 10th cav.
Bowman, Byron J., co. E, 19th cav.
Bridgee, Benjamin T., co. F, 12th cav.
Bacon, Lyman, co. B, 8th cav.
Barke, John, co. B, 9th cav.
Boyce, Ambrose A., co. I, 3d cav.
Bixby, Daniel C., co. —, 5th cav.
Brass, N. P., co. H, 3d cav.
Bayliss, Edward, co. C, 24th cav.
Bootey, John G., co. C, 9th cav.
Baker, Lamont M., serg., co. K, 10th cav.
Bronsom, Marcus D., co. H, 6th cav.
Barr, John, serg., co. F, 10th cav.
Borden, Holland, co. —, 19th cav.
Baker, Josiah, co. M, 16th cav.
Boorman, John H., co. D, 1st cav.
Bingham, Charles Elinor, co. D, 5th cav.
Coleman, James H., serg., co. C, 3d cav.
Caly, Herschell, co. I, 21st cav.
Cremor, Martin, co. F, 15th cav.
Chase, Samuel, co. I, 3d cav.
Carpenter, John, co. C, 23d cav.
Dougherty, William, co. D, 5th cav.
Dowes, Thomas, serg., co. K, 22d cav.
Davis, Henry T., co. G, 6th cav.
Evoas, Luke, co. G, 22d cav.
Estes, E. M., co. —, 3d cav.
Elmendorf, Alex. F, co. —, 24 Harris light cav.
Farnham, Charles F., co. G, 8th cav.
Farnham, Frederic, co. F, 6th cav.
Falling, Milton M., co. C, 8th cav.
Gleason, Harrison D., co. M, 22d cav.
Garrigan, Edward C., co. F, 2d cav.
Gorton, Cornelius, co. B, 16th cav.
Gifford, Edwin M., co. A, 3d cav.
Getman, David, co. I, 16th cav.
Hurdon, John M., co. G, 5th cav.
Hubbard, John, co. —, 8th cav.
Hughes, John H., serg., co. B, 24th cav.
Harvey, Burton J., co. D, 8th cav.
Hason, George R., co. —, 22d cav.
Hooks, Fred., co. —, 9th cav.
Holbrook, Archibald G., co. M, 15th cav.
Hopson, Sidney P., 6th cav.
Jackson, John W., co. F, 6th cav.
Kork, Edw., co. —, 18th cav.
Kearney, Michael, co. F, 12th cav.
Keya, Davenport, co. B, 6th cav.
Lamson, Henry, co. M, 15th cav.
LaGrange, Gaspar, co. G, 10th cav.
Lyon, Charles, co. K, 21st cav.
Munroe, George, co. F, 5th cav.
Miner, William R., co. —, 4th cav.
Mix, Albert J., co. A, 12th cav.
Morgan, Edwin L., co. F, 12th cav.
Main, Milo A., co. G, 10th cav.

Moohler, John, co. E, 2d cav.
Monroe, George, co. K, 4th cav.
Miller, Rockwell L., co. C, 5th cav.
Miner, Henry, serg., co. K, 22d cav.
Mahan, Benjamin P., co. K, 5th cav.
McMinn, Clarence L., co. B, 5d cav.
Norton, Aldred, co. B, 8th cav.
Newman, William H., serg., co. F, 5th cav.
Patterson, Orin, co. K, 24th cav.
Perine, Joseph L., co. I, 25th cav.
Pratt, George B., co. D, 10th cav.
Proad, Simeon G., co. D, 13th cav.
Raymond, William O., co. I, 5th cav.
Rustin, James W., co. D, 6th cav.
Riggs, Hiram M., co. D, 15th cav.
Rosselt, Edward, co. —, 9th cav.
Smith, Robert H., corporal, co. E, 3d cav.
Southworth, Robert, serg., co. E, 22d cav.
Smith, James, co. M, 2d cav.
Smith, James A., co. H, 22d cav.
Salisbury, Edwin, co. H, 16th cav.
Segar, Edwin, co. E, 8th cav.
Stearns, Alvin, co. D, 9th cav.
Terry, Saudder H., co. K, 16th cav.
Taylor, Alexander, co. —, 5th cav.
Trussler, J. C., serg., co. F, 16th cav.
Wunnett, Jas. A., co. —, 8th cav.
Woodhull, David E., co. E, 8th cav.
White, Martin, co. I, 18th cav.
Whipple, Marion D., co. D, 22d cav.
Watson, Thomas, co. —, 22d cav.
Warren, John M., co. A, 6th cav.
Wynkoop, Guy, co. H, 10th cav.
Younge, G. C., co. C, 22d cav.
Yeudt, Jerico F., co. D, 2d vet. cav.
Johnson, George W., co. I, 1st vet. cav.
Jones, John B., co. D, 1st vet. cav.
Roe, Henry, co. F, 1st vet. cav.
Bowen, Wm. B., co. H, 1st N. Y. drag.
Buckley, Samuel F., co. —, 2d mounted rifles.
Jones, William, co. F, 1st mounted rifles.
Allen, David H., co. A, 24th heavy art.
Baily, Robert, co. —, 8th heavy art.
Bayne, Henry C., co. A, 9th heavy art.
Bayne, George W., co. A, 4th heavy art.
Brown, Oscar, co. I, 9th heavy art.
Boss, George T., co. D, 10th heavy art.
Barbey, John, co. E, 2d heavy art.
Bodall, George D., 123d battery.
Brown, Edwin F., corp., co. A, 8th heavy art.
Brown, James Ira, co. B, 5th heavy art.
Bishop, Cassius M. C., co. M, 7th heavy art.
Blodgett, Frederick, co. D, 8th heavy art.
Clark, Ira A., co. —, 8th heavy art.
Carlson, Edwin M., serg., co. A, 144th heavy art.
Calvert, Walter L., co. I, 8th heavy art.
Cole, Edgar, co. B, 14th heavy art.
Cross, Asa, co. H, 4th heavy art.
Cook, Frank, co. F, 4th heavy art.
Church, Zenas E., co. C, 4th heavy art.
Cinoby, Horace M., co. B, 16th heavy art.
Downs, Valentine J., co. A, 2d heavy art.
Dewitt, John H., co. —, 9th heavy art.
Dunham, Russell, co. G, 9th heavy art.
Drew, Hiram, co. F, 1 heavy art.
Duvsdorf, Rudolph, co. I, 2d heavy art.
Dygert, Warner N., co. D, 2d heavy art.
Fay, John W., co. A, 3d heavy art.
Foley, Thomas, co. E, 2d heavy art.
Fish, Lester N., co. H, 7th heavy art.
Foster, Charles B., co. I, 7th heavy art.
Fanlkner, Richard, co. B, 9th heavy art.
Garfield, George, co. B, 7th heavy art.
Gerald, Frederick, co. E, 2d heavy art.
Gillett, William, co. I, 9th heavy art.
Houghtaling, Jacob H., co. B, 7th heavy art.
Holmes, Wm. S., co. K, 8th heavy art.
Hartsberg, Otto, co. E, 8th heavy art.
Jeffers, Benjamin, co. B, 7th heavy art.
Jones, David, co. —, 9th heavy art.
Johnson, George W., co. —, 9th heavy art.
Kenyon, Franklin A., co. —, 8th heavy art.
Kahle, Christian, co. D, 8th heavy art.
Lyon, James, 5th independent battery.
Leonard, Chas. H., co. A, 7th heavy art.
Longstaff, John Wm., co. B, 8th heavy art.
Loomis, John, co. M, 14th heavy art.
Lester, Wm. C., co. G, 9th heavy art.
Ladue, Ambrose, co. E, 9th heavy art.
Ledlare, John, co. A, 3d heavy art.
Lake, Romanus, co. B, 6th heavy art.
Lock, John B., serg., co. I, 7th heavy art.
McCollum, Melvin C., co. F, 8th heavy art.
Marsh, Chas., co. B, 4th heavy art.
Marcolius, Lewis, co. A, 9th heavy art.
Murray, James E., co. D, 8th heavy art.
Mosier, Edward, co. B, 9th heavy art.
McConnell, Ezr., co. E, 9th heavy art.
Mudhore, Abijah, co. B, 9th heavy art.
Martindale, Wm. J., co. 2d heavy art.
Owen, Chas. G., co. M, 14th heavy art.
Pearson, James, co. E, 8th heavy art.
Parker, Orren P., co. A, 8th heavy art.
Phelps, G. P., co. A, 14th heavy art.
Pope, Joseph, co. K, 2d heavy art.
Rumsey, George W., co. F, 8th heavy art.
Richards, Jas. M., co. B, 9th heavy art.
Rausom, John, co. A, 7th heavy art.
Rose, Adelbert, co. H, 9th heavy art.
Reily, Henry, 15th heavy art.
Ross, Elbert, co. H, 4th heavy art.
Rawson, Porter D., 24th battery.
Stiles, Geo. W., co. I, 9th heavy art.
Stapleton, Richard, co. B, 7th heavy art.
Simmons, Almon B., co. H, 8th heavy art.
Spaulding, Marimer, co. B, 14th heavy art.
Sykes, N. B., co. B, 4th heavy art.
Smith, John D., co. G, 4th heavy art.
Schreidler, George, co. D, 17th New York.
Satterlee, John, co. F, 4th heavy art.
Thornton, Judson M., co. L, 14th heavy art.
Toll, Reinhard, co. L, 9th heavy art.
Travis, Hartison, co. C, 4th heavy art.
Thomas, John B., co. H, 6th heavy art.
Tucker, James, co. C, 9th heavy art.
Waring, William B., co. A, 4th heavy art.
Wilson, Simon, 4th heavy art.
Whittemore, Marcus, co. M, 14th heavy art.
Woolsey, John, 169th bat.
Wright, John W., co. I, 2d heavy art.
Watson, James, 8th heavy art.
Watts, William, co. D, 9th heavy art.
Weldon, John, co. G, 7th heavy art.

STATE OF NEW JERSEY.

Arnold, Edwin B., co. —, 33d inf.
Bailey, William B., co. G, 15th inf.
Bloodgood, Augustus, co. —, 11th inf.
Dickerson, William J., co. D, 15th inf.
Dougherty, John W., co. H, 11th inf.
Dunn, George W., co. E, 1st inf.

Egbert, James, co. B, 15th inf.
Pinson, James, co. I, 11th inf.
Griggs, Thomas, co. —, 33d inf.
Howard, Thomas H., co. H, 19th inf.
Hyde, Wilson, co. B, 28th inf.
Lipsey, Jacob M., co. I, 10th inf.
Lovell, W. F., co. D, 1st inf.
Minion, Jacob P., co. D, 15th inf.
Muchmore, Elias D., co. C, 14th inf.
Miller, Henry, co. B, 38th inf.
Roid, JoT., co. D, 14th inf.
Shipley, Andrew J., co. C, 8th inf.
Thorne, Charles D., co. E, 10th inf.
Turner, Peter, co. K, 44th inf.
Wells, Charles J., co. C, 10th inf.
Woods, W. S., co. D, 1st inf.
Wright, W. H., co. K, 1st inf.
Wilson, Harrison, co. B, 19th inf.

Currie, W. J., co. —, 3d cav.
Eberel, Ernest, co. —, 3d cav., hussars.
Hulmes, Edward, co. M, 2d cav.
Melick, George A., co. E, 2d cav.
McPeck, Henry P., co. B, 1st cav.
Peterson, Henry, co. B, 5d cav.
Skill, Charles W., co. M, 3d cav.
Williams, Charles J., co. L, 1st cav.

PENNSYLVANIA.

Aikman, William, co. F, 116th vol.
Anthony, J. G., co. A, 59th vol.
Axtell, J. G., co. A, 148th vol.
Andrew, David W., co. D, 26th vol.
Byers, Samuel, co. B, 121 vol.
Button, Charles, co. B, 149th vol.
Black, Samuel N., co. F, 106th vol.
Bigelow, Charles A. W., co. F, 53d vol.
Bechtell, Isaac, co. J, 184th vol.
Buckley, William, co. B, 50th vol.
Bower, George W., co. K, 103d vol.
Briggs, Theron T., co. B, 145th vol.
Burdick, Chester W., co. C, 145th vol.
Boryer, S. P., co. I, 112th vol.
Bond, —, co. I, 183d vol.
Bice, James, co. —, 149th vol.
Barnes, Walter, co. G, 119th vol.
Barton, Joseph N., co. A, 6th vol.
Burnes, H. J., co. A, 57th vol.
Brock, Jacob, co. F, 103d vol.
Bennett, Byron, co. —, 141st vol.
Baran, John, co. A, 83d vol.
Bender, Flavius G., co. C, 77th vol.
Brubaker, Benjamin, co. D, 79th vol.
Coppersmith, Jno. P., co. I, 184th vol.
Criswell, Sherman M., co. B, 103d vol.
Copp, William, co. I, 142d vol.
Campbell, Amos, co. G, 11th vol.
Clark, John, co. G, 103d vol.
Conley, M. L., co. B, 138th vol.
Cowan, Espy, co. G, 191st vol.
Caworly, Thomas, co. G, 191st vol.
Campbell, Knox G., co. H, 191st vol.
Corbat, James, co. H, 99th vol.
Chamberlain, James, co. B, 191st vol.
Clemens, Wm. D., co. D, 83th vol.
Conley, Wm., co. B, 95th vol.
Culebaugh, Wm., co. K, 69th vol.
Carr, Wm., co. E, 149th vol.
Dobb, Espy, co. D, 55th vol.
Dimpsey, John H., co. A, 63d vol.
Dix, Edwin, co. C, 83d vol.
Dick, James, co. —, 79th vol.
Dunlap, S. A., co. I, 103d vol.
Derull, Eleu, co. F, 116th vol.
Dollbaugh, Jno. W., co. A, 184th vol.
Delaney, Matthew, co. B, 51st vol.
Davidson, Alex., co. G, 191st vol.
Dale, Solomon, co. D, 148th vol.
Dromm, Michael H., co. C, 85th vol.
Drawed, George C., co. C, 81st vol.
Ehrenfield, J. M., co. D, 184th vol.
Eberhart, James W., co. G, 191st vol.
Eken, Ezekiel, co. E, 105d vol.
Ellinger, John, co. I, 197th vol.
Edenddorff, George E., co. A, 157th vol.
Etters, William, co. I, 69th vol.
Etters, David, co. D, 148th vol.
Etters, Francis W., co. A, 13th vol.
Etters, Henry J., co. A, 13th vol.
Frood, George W., co. H, 148th vol.
Finley, Joseph, co. F, 48th vol.
Fay, Stephen, co. —, 106th vol.
Foster, Frank, co. H, 143d vol.
Fisher, John, co. I, 85th vol.
Gass, John T., co. B, 222 vol.
Gilbert, Henry, co. F, 53d vol.
Green, W. Henry, co. K, 141st vol.
Gee, W. H. L., co. H, 43th vol.
Geyst, J. W., co. I, 57th vol.
Green, Joseph J., co. H, 165th vol.
Grim, Henry, co. A, 48th vol.
Gibeon, David A., co. A, 55th vol.
Gordon, Robert, co. G, 69th vol.
Houston, Will., co. D, 16th vol.
Hunt, John T., co. K, 55th vol.
Hyatt, Thomas J., co. K, 118th vol.
Hyatt, James W., co. H, 118th vol.
Hershey, Abraham L., co. G, 2d vol.
Hall, John, co. B, 100th vol.
Hill, Wilson S., co. D, 141st vol.
Hill, Charles F., co. C, 72d vol.
Hern, Robert, co. I, 131th vol.
Housel, William P., co. —, 190th vol.
Hoss, Levi, co. —, 118th vol.
Heisley, F. A., co. G, 191st vol.
Haley, James B., co. —, 100th vol.
Host, Jacob, co. G, 83d vol.
Hunter, John, co. —, 155th vol.
Henderslot, David, co. E, 123d vol.
Howze, Matthew, co. E, 141st vol.
Hamilton, John R., co. H, 188th vol.
Hagan, George, co. —, 199th vol.
Hudson, Thomas K., co. K, 48th vol.
Hall, John, co. B, 100th vol.
Hawk, Michael, co. F, 103d vol.
Johnson, James E., co. L, 45th vol.
Jones, James, co. K, 9th vol.
Johnson, Harris, co. I, 45th vol.
Klinger, Ephraim, co. H, 148th vol.
Kockey, David, co. A, 184th vol.
Kelly, Henry, co. F, 138th vol.
Keyser, Jacob, co. B, 148th vol.
Kerekoonly, Julius, co. H, 56th vol.
Knox, James, co. A, 184th vol.
Kratzer, H., co. F, 76th vol.
Kinsley, Nathan P., co. H, 145th vol.
Koll, Jordan, co. F, 119th vol.
Karns, Jacob J., co. K, 149th vol.
King, John L., co. E, 118th vol.
Kave, John Oliver, co. F, 100th vol.
Kelley, George W., co. F, 101st vol.
Kephart, Samuel, co. C, 77th vol.
King, Daniel, co. B, 84th vol.
Knerp, Peter, co. —, 149th vol.
Layton, Samuel, co. A, 184th vol.
Learn, Adam, co. E, 11th vol.
Lake, Fred., co. F, 166th vol.
Laytor, Barton K., co. —, 52d vol.
Lettuer, Alfred W., co. —, 77th vol.
Livingston, George W., co. I, 190th vol.
Leo, George W., co. I, 67th vol.

Munsell, Harvey A., co. G, 99th vol.
Metcalf, Wm. H., co. —, 87th vol.
McGuire, Richard P., co. A, 55th vol.
Morse, Levi, co. F, 141st vol.
Meinhard, Ferdinand, co. H, 50th vol.
McCoy, A. J., co. I, 103d vol.
McCoy, Shannon, co. F, 138th vol.
Masters, —, co. —, 143d vol.
McDowell, John S., co. F, 77th vol.
Miller, Orlando O., co. B, 145th vol.
McKee, Charles W., co. B, 191st vol.
Margnis, Edwin, co. G, 63d vol.
Miller, Herman K., co. H, 148th vol.
McKinnon, John Y., co. H, 53d vol.
Marks, William H., co. D, 145th vol.
Morton, George H., co. I, 118th vol.
Moody, Oscar A., co. G, 150th vol.
Morris, William, co. H, 77th vol.
Matthews, F. A., co. C, 148th vol.
McCarthy, David, co. D, 68th vol.
Mosser, John, co. D, 77th vol.
Moore, Joseph H., co. H, 72d vol.
Malone, Albert M., co. E, 106th vol.
Mellon, William, co. A, 106th vol.
Meldrum, John C., co. C, 184th vol.
McConnell, Philip J., co. I, 55th vol.
Martin, Alvin A., co. D, 53d vol.
Moorhead, Howard S., co. H, 101st vol.
McNess, John H., co. H, 100th vol.
Phipps, Joseph A., co. E, 57th vol.
Parker, William H., co. D, 102d vol.
Quanee, Charles H., co. B, 145th vol.
Raush, Simon, co. B, 148th vol.
Rhinehardt, Samuel, co. I, 197th vol.
Russell, Ernest F., co. I, 141st vol.
Rhodes, William H., co. I, 145th vol.
Riddell, Royal W., co. G, 146th vol.
Reynolds, Charles M., co. H, 145th vol.
Rowland, Masters, co. F, 111th vol.
Sandt, Edward, co. A, 47th vol.
Smith, Wilbur, co. I, 52d vol.
Smith, William, co. F, 88th vol.
Surdam, Francis, co. D, 53d vol.
Scoutan, Lewis, co. F, 53d vol.
Smith, Job, co. A, 146th vol.
Starks, Charles T., co. —, 149th vol.
Stotler, Thomas, co. —, 101st vol.
Shirk, John H., co. —, 79th vol.
Scovercroft, James, co. K, 141st vol.
Shaffer, John, co. —, 57th vol.
Steel, Joseph, co. B, 191st vol.
Sayre, James, co. I, 10th vol.
Storrs, Charles, co. E, 95th vol.
Sharp, Martin L., co. F, 100th vol.
Sheriff, Charles F., co. K, 100th vol.
Stevens, George H., co. G, 77th vol.
Sorber, Andrew, co. F, 53d vol.
Trout, Jacob W., co. K, 138th vol.
Turner, James W., co. A, 211th vol.
Teeter, Christian A., co. A, 184th vol.
Tripp, George W., co. K, 143d vol.
Tillotson, Perry H., co. K, 57th vol.
Thompson, Joseph S., co. H, 183d vol.
Thompson, Cowden, co. I, 106th vol.
Truman, W. W., co. G, 191st vol.
Vancuren, Edward, co. C, 145th vol.
Vail, Gilbert B., co. G, 77th vol.
Vail, Merritt J., co. B, 143d vol.
Ward, Samuel, co. B, 135th vol.
Walker, Houston, co. B, 100th vol.
Wolford, Wm., co. B, 149th vol.
Wickerham, W. H. H., co. D, 22d vol.
Wilber, Louis W., co. D, 106th vol.
Werner, Edwin J., co. D, 65th vol.
Woodcock, Thomas, co. E, 183d vol.
Welch, Robert, co. I, 101st vol.
Wright, Edmund S., co. A, 184th vol.
Williams, John E., co. B, 22d vol.
Wilson, James, co. K, 83d vol.
Wheaton, Ambrose H., co. G, 63d vol.
Wilkinson, John, co. I, 45th vol.
Weeks, Caraden Q., co. F, 76th vol.
Wolfard, William H., co. B, 149th vol.
Whitson, Henry, co. H, 53d vol.
Whitney, Orange P., co. H, 187th vol.
Young, John, co. —, 149th vol.
Young, Philip S., co. C, 45th vol.
Young, Philip S., co. H, 101st vol.

Aikele, John J., co. H, 5th cav.
Austin, Edward, co. F, 20th cav.
Black, James A., co. D, 14th cav.
Bryan, William K., co. I, 12th cav.
Beardsley, Luther, co. L, 12th cav.
Baker, Willard, co. L, 13th cav.
Bevens, Robert, co. I, 20th cav.
Brady, Michael, co. M, 8th cav.
Brosius, Amos P., co. K, 14th cav.
Cormner, Abner P., co. B, 4th cav.
Campbell, Thomas F., co. B, 4th cav.
Coleman, A., co. K, 18th cav.
Davis, James, co. I, 5th cav.
Deming, Charles W., co. D, 16th cav.
Dyer, Joshua E., co. D, 5th cav.
Evans, Samuel P., co. F, 7th cav.
Eliis, Enos, co. I, 11th cav.
Foot, Charles, co. G, 20th cav.
Fuller, Henry, co. M, 13th cav.
Gillmore, Robert A., co. —, 12th cav.
George, Thomas, co. B, 18th cav.
Gass, John T., co. C, Ringgold battalion.
Gates, Jacob S., co. D, 13th cav.
Geary, G. S., co. D, 4th cav.
Havens, John, co. L, 19th cav.
Hottenstein, George W., co. I, 18th cav.
Humbaugh, Nathan L. H., co. A, 14th cav.
Hart, Isaac, co. B, 17th cav.
Havlin, Mathew M., co. D, 4th cav.
Ivory, Thomas, co. G, 12th cav.
Jones, Henry P., co. B, 2d cav.
Kelley, George W., co. K, 18th cav.
Lane, Amos P., co. C, 6th cav.
Levan, John, co. G, 5th cav.
Miller, Lewis, serg., co. L, 6th cav.
Margret, William, co. K, 18th cav.
McCoy, Charles E., co. B, 12th cav.
Magot, John, co. K, 18th cav.
Miller, Hamlin B., co. I, 14th cav.
McFadden, Lewis, co. I, 4th cav.
Malaby, Aaron H., co. B, 7th cav.
Mockley, Eli, co. E, 17th cav.
Miller, Lewis, co. L, 6th cav.
Myers, Joseph M., co. D, 13th cav.
McCoy, Isaac A., co. A, 9th cav.
Mastonati, Charles A., co. A, 9th cav.
Meredith, Alfred A., co. A, 22d cav.
McCoy, Alexander, co. A, 9th cav.

Meredith, Alfred A., co. A, 22d cav.
Norris, John G., co. —, 17th cav.
Nagel, George W., co. —, 18th cav.
Norris, Simon, co. G, 16th cav.
Odenheimer, John M., co. —, 6th cav.
Oliver, Adam E., co. D, 17th cav.
Penepacker, Benj. F., co. F, 12th cav.
Ramsey, Milton G., co. —, 19th cav.
Rodd, William, co. H, 20th cav.
Robbins, James S., co. K, 2d cav.
Raper, Emanuel, co. C, 14th cav.
Rees, David T., co. A, 7th cav.
Sellers, John T., co. E, 2d cav.
Smith, Samuel A., co. K, 14th cav.
Smith, James L., co. A, 13th cav.
Swearer, George S., co. H, 13th cav.
Schmidt, Charles L., co. B, 5th cav.
Shields, William, co. —, 5th cav.
Schlearbock, Conrad, co. —, 4th cav.
Snowden, John W., co. E, 2d cav.
Scott, Andrew J., co. B, 14th cav.
Smith, Dennis, co. A, 18th cav.
Sanderson, Wm. E., co. I, 3d cav.
Sargent, C. B., co. C, 14th cav.
Siebert, John, co. B, 5th cav.
Watkins, Andrew, co. —, 18th cav.
Woodburn, James S., co. F, 13th cav.
White, George, co. C, 1st cav.
Wallace, Frank, co. F, 2d cav.
Walker, James W., co. —, 5th cav.
White, Joseph, co. A, 17th cav.
Wright, Jacob, co. B, 13th cav.
Young, George H., co. F, 5th cav.
Bull, Joseph L., co. F, 2d heavy art.
Bird, George, co. F, 2d heavy art.
Boemer, Simon J., co. H, 55th heavy art.
Crawford, Sylvester, co. D, 2d heavy art.
Claybaugh, Geo. W., co. —, heavy art.
Hartwick, John, co. C, 112th heavy art.
Hassinger, Aaron, co. D, 2d heavy art.
Irvin, Charles, co. C, 2d heavy art.
Miller, Eden, co. K, 2d heavy art.
Ormsby, C. M., co. G, 2d heavy art.
Ording, George, co. C, 112th heavy art.
Rogers, Jeremiah E., co. A, 2d heavy art.
Simpson, John D., co. C, 2d heavy art.
Tovson, Jeremiah B., co. A, 2d heavy art.
Wood, James M., co. —, 2d heavy art.
Wood, George H., co. C, 2d heavy art.
Beagt, Lucian G., co. E, 2d reserves.
Belcher, Geo. W., co. B, 2d reserves.
Davison, Garrett, co. —, 9th reserves.
Huston, Wm. S., co. D, 10th reserves.
Hinkel, Jonas, co. C, 7th reserves.
Jayne, S. W., co. C, 6th reserves.
Lathrop, Halsey, co. G, 6th reserves.
Laino, John, co. D, 10th reserves.
Laughton, Robert E., co. A, 10th reserves.
McCurdy, John C., co. B, 10th reserves.
McCahon, James, co. D, 10th reserves.
McPark, Robert, co. D, 10th reserves.
Margut, Mathia, co. D, 6th reserves.
McClay, John, co. F, 11th reserves.
Otto, John, co. F, 11th reserves.
Seaton, M. A., co. G, 9th reserves.
Stansbury, Y. S., co. H, 12th reserves.
Smith, G. W., co. H, 5th reserves.
Welty, Jacob W., co. H, 7th reserves.
Woodburn, Jos. D., co. G, 11th reserves.
Williamson, Alva, co. G, 11th reserves.

Bachanan, Julius, co. I, 1st rifles.
Gillespie, James, co. K, 51st inf.
McClintock, James T., co. C, 1st rifles.
McDowell, R. C., co. I, 1st rifles.
Mattleson, John H., co. —, 1st rifles.
Roberts, Frederick T., co. —, 1st rifles.
Snyder, Jacob, co. E, 1st rifles.
Sickles, C. T., co. K, 1st rifles.

STATE OF DELAWARE.

Maxworthy, George W., co. D, 2d vol.
Rhine, Joseph, co. G, 1st vol.
Thorn, Henry T., co. D, 2d vol.

STATE OF MARYLAND.

Dake, Cornelius, co. K, 5th vol.
Gorman, Stephen, co. D, 1st vol.
Goriff, J. C., co. —, 1st vol.
Hitchins, Joseph H., co. —, 2d vol.
King, Albert, co. B, 5d vol.
King, William J., co. H, 3d vol.
Martin, Looz, co. A, 1st vol.
Mervine, John, co. H, 5d vol.
Poffinbarger, Charles, co. A, 7th vol.
Rohrer, W. H., co. —, 1st vol.
Seeger, Charles, co. F, 6th vol.
Wehn, George C., co. D, 7th vol.

DISTRICT OF COLUMBIA.

Boissonnault, M. F., co. H, 1st cav.
Cushing, James R., co. I, 1st cav.
Gidding, Henry, co. B, 1st cav.
Jones, John, co. L, Baker's cav.
Maffit, E. C., co. I, 1st cav.
Overlook, R. L., co. G, 1st cav.
Smith, William R., co. I, 1st cav.
Shafer, Frederick, co. —, 1st cav.
Tibbetts, John, co. I, 1st cav.

STATE OF OHIO.

Allen, A. E., co. G, 121st reg.
Allon, Albert R., co. G, 19th reg.
Alward, Alfred L., co. B, 125th reg.
Amour, W. Henry, co. H, 24th, after m'c'd inf.
Brown, James E., co. G, 93d reg.
Brown, Henry H., co. A, 41st reg.
Beard, Geo H., co. —, 123d reg.
Blocher, Henry D., co. B, 104th reg.
Bailey, George, co. G, 124th reg.
Cowela, George, 10th co.
Crane, John R., co. D, 100th reg.
Connally, John, co. H, 103d reg.
Cahill, Wm. P., co. A, 51st reg.
Cram, John R., co. B, 100th reg.
Cary, Asa, co. B, 21st reg.
Cayle, James P., co. G, 2d reg.
Clay, Oliver D., co. G, 123d reg.
Coit, Eureka, co. C, 123d reg.
Davis, Clinton W., co. A, 95th reg.
Dodge, David B., co. H, 100th reg.
Duffy, James, co. B, 45th reg.
Ellis, Henry M., co. G, 10th reg.
Gurney, Chas. W., co. E, 72d reg.
Hillyer, John H., co. F, 98th reg.
Harsh, Christian, co. C, 126th reg.
Henderson, David, co. B, 123d reg.
Haig, John P., co. C, 72d reg.
Kerr, Andrew, co. I, 13th reg.
Jocelyn, Alfred A., co. A, 123d reg.
Johnson, Samuel D., co. G, 177th reg.
Lee, H. B., 21st reg.
McPurdy, James, co. K, 13th reg.
McNarreR, Geo. Au. Madison, co. K, 4th reg.
McNaney, F. G., co. K, 126th reg.
Maber, Patrick, co. K, 4th reg.
Moorehead, Josiah, co. A, 102d reg.
McPurdy, James, co. K, 13th reg.
Moore, Chas., co. 14, 19th reg.
Preslman, James A., co. G, 110th reg.

Patterson, Adolphus G., co. H, 19th reg.
Parsons, George F., co. A, 124th reg.
Philips, V. B., co. H, 100th reg.
Paisley, James, co. —, 65th reg.
Rowson, Rosba, co. H, 103d reg.
Riddick, Robert G., co. —, 197th reg.
Rich, Solomon, co. H, 116th reg.
Sloan, Alexander A., co. D, 34th reg.
Sweet, Myron, co. C, 49th reg.
Stark, Gilbert J., co. —, 23d reg.
Shaw, Deloe, co. E, 103d reg.
Sheppard, Thomas J., co. E, 97th reg.
Stair, John, co. H, 100th reg.
Smith, B. P., co. A, 105th reg.
Stowe, Oscrald F., co. G, 31st reg.
Schreiner, John, co. K, 118th inf.
Tonesdale, Henry, co. H, 32d reg.
Tullis, Lindley, co. C, 24th reg.
Vail, Samuel, co. A, 49th reg.
Ward, Hiram, co. A, 103d reg.
Woodruff, William, co. —, 102d reg.
Walsh, William C., co. —, 105th reg.
Wheeler, Caleb C., co. —, 122d reg.
Withington, Thomas M., co. B, 72d reg.
Warren, Haddock, co. B, 116th reg.
Zuber, John M., co. B, 100th reg.

Barrett, George, co. G, 6th cav.
Bartges, Christian, co. F, 2d cav.
Chilson, A. W., co. —, 45th cav.
Clayton, Noel, co. D, 4th cav.
Coats, Rufus Elisha, co. —, 2d cav.
Donaldson, Richard B., co. M, 6th cav.
Fredrick, Knodel, co. —, 3d independent cav.
Krebs, Burkhard, co. —, 3d independent cav.
Johnson, W. D., co. H, 3d cav.

Lyon L., co. B, 1st art.
Stanford, Perkins, co. A, 2d art.
Volen, Henry Leopoldi, co. K, 6th art.
Wilcox, Thomas B., company M, 4th art.

STATE OF INDIANA.

Ballinger, Robert B., co. —, 46th inf.
Burris, James M., co. F, 82d inf.
Burnes, James A., co. —, 40th inf.
Evans, Charles W., co. I, 88th inf.
Farrington, Jabes, co. —, 40th inf.
Grooms, Henry G., co. D, 13th inf.
Hawkins, Martin V., co. —, 49th inf.
Hutchinson, Joseph, co. A, 2d inf.
Kurtz, Byron, co. E or I, 75th inf.
Patter, Casimer, co. —, 20th inf.
Patter, James R., co. —, 20th inf.
Reynolds, Jeremiah, co. G, 63d inf.
Rivir, John, co. F, 30th inf.
Spicer, Buell E., co. A, 5th inf.
Spicer, William E., co. G, 6th inf.
Scorlett, J. L., co. K, 12th inf.
Shoaror, Harrison, co. I, 94th inf.
West, George W., co. B, 18th inf.
Clements, Thomas A., co. B, 5th cav.
Inglish, Archibald E., co. F, 7th cav.
McCrum, James, co. —, 4th cav.
Saltz, William C., co. —, 4th cav.
Wiley, Philip, co. B, 5th cav.

STATE OF ILLINOIS.

Baker, James A., co. F, 112th inf.
Belden, William P., co. B, 72d inf.
Bull, Clark J., co. I, 93d inf.
Briggs, Wick, co. G, 95th inf.
Calvert, William, co. F, 72d inf.
Carver, Edward E., co. B, 73d inf.
Cook, Archibald, co. K, 51st inf.
Cuddington, Wm., co. I, 93d inf.
Dawson, Aaron, co. B, 30th inf.
Dann, Jerome R., co. K, 20th inf.
Devine, James D., co. K, 39th inf.
Gearheart, E. L., co. D, 8th inf.
Green, Samuel, co. H, 42d inf.
Henderson, John R., corp., co. G, 66th inf.
Kendall, Clinton A., co. —, 108th inf.
Maxham, H. C., co. H, 19th inf.
McCreery, John P., co. C, 119th inf.
McMurtry, John R., co. G, 116th inf.
Miller, James P., co. I, 31st inf.
Pomeroy, James Wm., co. C, 104th inf.
Ramsar, Chas. D., co. —, 14th and 15th batl.
Reid, Elwin, jr., co. A, 13th inf.
Reynolds, Dwight, co. D, 124 inf.
Rose, Lewis A., co. F, 42d inf.
Struble, Chas. H., co. D, 88th inf.
Sweedland, Chas. F., co. P, 30th inf.
Taylor, Jesse E., co. F, 113th inf.
Thomason, Robert H., co. C, 13th inf.
Whitney, Theo. F., co. G, 89th inf.
Williams, John A., co. G, 64th inf.
Ball, Eliphalet G., co. —, 9th cav.
Fairless, James A., co. H, 15th cav.
Fox, James D., co. —, 16th cav.
Jenks, Joseph P., co. I, 3d cav.
Roeback, Raucord, co. —, 14th cav.
Smith, Barney, co. G, 14th cav.
Watts, Francis, co. L, 14th cav.
Wildman, H. H., co. I, 16th cav.
Brown, George S., Bridge's batt., light art.
McRay, Wm. J., or Jo., Philip's Chicago bat.
Messick, Wm. T., co. E, 1st art.
Snow, Martin Van H., Chicago Board Trade bat.

STATE OF MICHIGAN.

Abernethy, Albert B., co. G, 11th inf.
Atwell, Levi, co. L, 1st engineers.
Brockway, Martin R., co. B, 4th inf.
Bressea, Dennis, co. A, 29th inf.
Boobe, John, co. A, 1st sharp-shooters.
Barry, Chester D., co. I, 20th inf.
Black, William, co. D, 16th inf.
Bishop, Joshua, co. —, 12th inf.
Cope, Martin, co. H, 17th inf.
Carr, Charles R., co. A, 25th inf.
Dark, Theodore T., co. D, 13th inf.
Duel, Charles E., co. D, 27th inf.
Decker, Jasper R., co. G, 1st engineers.
Ensign, James, co. A, 11th inf.
Hine, R. W., co. F, 24th inf.
Harmon, Henry, co. E, 19th inf.
Hoyt, John R., co. D, 21st inf.
Hill, Seymour E., co. B, 17th inf.
Hertzberg, William, co. G, 20th inf.
Johnson, James, co. I, 17th inf.
Johnson, Russell M., co. I, 17th inf.
Keeney, W. H. H., co. I, 1st inf.
Miller, W. H., 1st serg., co. C, 26th inf.
McLaughlin, Jas. M., co. —, 2d sharp-shooters.
Norton, Hiram, co. M, 1st engineers.
Nedeau, Jacob, co. E, 17th inf.
Pear, Richard, co. H, 22d inf.
Rowley, Russell, co. I, 7th inf.
Smith, Samuel, co. H, 17th inf.
Sutherland, Mason M., co. B, 1st sharp-shooters.
Schmeid, Reuben, co. F, 21st inf.
Shepherd, Solon, co. G, 1st sharp-shooters.
Sherwood, John A., co. C, 24th inf.
Sinclair, Aza, co. F, 1st engineers.
Taylor, Isaiah, co. A, 27th inf.
Van Wert, Edwin, co. E, 3d inf.
Whelen, R. M., co. G, 25th inf.
Wakeman, Clark, co. F, 21st inf.
Willits, James B., co. I, 1st sharpshooters.
Waterbury, Albert, co. H, 17th inf.
Winebrenner, John, co. A, 5th inf.

Westcot, William, co. I, 7th inf.
Budd, Schrippe, co. B, 1st cav.
Cummins, John W., co. L, 5th cav.
Clark, George M., co. L, 1st cav.
Duley, A. L., co. E, 7th cav.
Fitzgerald, co. C, 6th cav.
Frost, Allen M., co. G, 8th cav.
Groncher, Elmore R., co. B, 6th cav.
Hutton, Samuel W., co. G, 9th cav.
Hathaway, Edward P., co. M, 8th cav.
Ingledue, Eber R., co. K, 6th cav.
Marshall, George N., co. M, 4th cav.
Moore, Allen, co. M, 6th cav.
McKay, B. G., co. M, 1st cav.
Preston, Benjamin, co. K, 7th cav.
Russell, Major W., co. M, 5th cav.
Ransdell, Solomon, co. —, 6th cav.
Sherburn, Samuel, co. D, 6th cav.
Springer, Joseph, co. A, 7th cav.
Seeley, Harvey K., co. B, 6th cav.
Vincent, Albert, co. M, 1st cav.
Wilcox, Charles, co. A, 7th cav.
Willis, Henry G., co. —, 2d cav.
Wood, Charles, co. D, 11th cav.
Williams, J. D., co. I, 6th cav.

STATE OF WISCONSIN.

Brown, Edward, co. A, 13th inf.
Coburn, William J., co. A, 10th inf.
Card, Warren E., co. H, 33d inf.
Duboise, Jacob V., co. B, 10th inf.
Estey, Amos R., co. B, 21st inf.
Griggs, John A., co. —, 26th inf.
Green, L. Abner, co. I, 19th inf.
Hall, Hiram R., co. G, 13th inf.
Hitchcock, Joseph, co. K, 46th inf.
Menzies, Frederick, co. —, 5th inf.
McDonald, Isaac H., co. C, 2d inf.
Northcott, Richard, co. H, 10th inf.
Perry, Leslie, co. —, 6th inf.
Pyle, Amos M., co. K, 36th inf.
Smith, Sanford, co. E, 19th inf.
Sleeper, Hiram H., co. C, 38th inf.
Smith, Albert M., co. G, 21st inf.
Van Vickle, Walter M., co. C, 36th inf.
Webster, Alexander C., ser., co. E, 7th inf.
Wood, Walter, cor., co. A, 10th inf.
Webster, A. C., co. E, 7th inf.

MINNESOTA.

Adams, Edwin H., co. C, 4th inf.
Bond, Daniel R., co. —, 1st bat.
Harney, Joseph R., co. K, 9th reg.
Ketcham, George W., co. —, 1st reg.
Mathews, Lyman, co. E, 9th reg.

STATE OF IOWA.

Baxley, David M., co. G, 35th inf.
Buckmaster, Frederick, co. K, 15th inf.
Jacobs, Josiah R., co. H, 7th inf.
Johnson, Aaron, co. —, 19th inf.
Knight, John F., co. I, 9th inf.
Knowles, Seth, co. G, 15th inf.
Lucis, Francis M., co. C, 25th inf.
Overcroff, George, co. H, 5th inf.
Ray, William, co. —, 7th inf.
Richey, John V., co. E, 16th inf.
Treppey, William, co. K, 5th inf.
Whitten, Josiah A., co. H, 5th inf.
Whitten, John, co. B, 6th inf.
Bishard, Daniel C., co. M, 8th cav.
Dean, Henry H., co. B, 8th cav.
Frontske, Charles, co. F, 5th cav.
Littlejohn, Leverett Zenino, co. B, 4th cav.
Macy, Cyrus P., co. C, 8th cav.
Russell, W. W., co. G, 8th cav.
Wescott, Miles D., co. L, 8th cav.
Whitford, V. B., co. —, 6th cav.

STATE OF KENTUCKY.

Beatty, Wm. H., serg., co. —, 15th regiment.
Cooke, Samuel H., co. H, 4th mounted inf.
Glassman, Peter, 4th cav.
Hamilton, John D., co. D, 11th cav.
Nilest, John, co. H, 6th cav.

STATE OF MISSOURI.

Owens, Owen H., co. A, 19th cav.
Donze, J. W., co. I, 1st light artillery.

VIRGINIA.

Clutter, John L., co. I, 4th.
Broughton, William, co. F, 2d mounted inf.
Howe, Lemuel B., co. I, 5th cav.
Hobson, Norris, co. —, 1st cav.
Noble, James C., co. B, 1st cav.

STATE OF WEST VIRGINIA.

Blessing, Pius, co. C, 15th inf.
Carroll, Tunis, co. K, 1st inf.
Campbell, William R., co. I, 12th inf.
Caruthers, William R., co. A, 7th inf.
Hunt, Eugenius W., co. —, 12th inf.
Hunt, Philip, co. —, 12th inf.
Belcher, Oscar, co. A, 1st inf.
Sharp, Nicholas L., co. H, 14th inf.
Peay, William G, battery D, 1st light art.
Loring, John E., battery D, 1st light art.
Stephens, Allen, battery D, 1st light art.
Newman, Samuel G., co. —, 6th cav.

STATE OF TENNESSEE.

Barnett, John N., co. A, 2d mounted rifles.
Kirby, James M., co. K, 2d mounted rifles.
Bayles, Leroy, co. K, 2d mounted rifles.
Edwards, Troy, co. B, 5th inf.
Wilson, William S., co. —, 6th inf.
Edwards, Harry, co. B, 5th inf.
Long, J. A., co. C, 3d mounted inf.
Leep, William H. H., co. C, 3d mounted inf.
Leven, Thomas J., co. H, 2d mounted inf.
Montgomery, William T., co. —, 4th inf.
Sherman, John, construction corps.
Beverly, William S., H., co. F, 10th cav.
Godsey, Samuel, co. B, 10th cav.
Montgomery, Campbell G., co. L, 1st cav.
Tate, Frank Boyd, co. M, 6th cav.
Brown, Henry, co. M, 8th cav.

MISCELLANEOUS.

Brown, Vincent, civilian.
Bradley, John, U. S. gunboat Southfield.
Butterbold, James P., laborer.
Campbell, J. B., 18th reg., 1st bat., V. R. C.
Edwards, Leonard J., U. S. ship Granite City.
Irvine, A. M., head'q'rs 3d div'n 5th army corps.
Johnson, Geo. P., U. S. gunboat Nipsic.
Mollody, Patrick, marine battalion.
Rymer, Thos. P., signal officer, Charleston harbor.
Saule, Lewis H., co. A, 1st Berdan's Sharpsh's.
Sherwood, Henry, wagonmaster.
Nicholl, Jas L., quarterm'ster's f., 1st div. 15th A. C.
Hill, James H., civilian.
Williams, James M., U. S. gunboat Southfield.
Griffin, Thomas, alias T. Smith, steamer Clifton.
Mahoney, George, steamer Clifton.

THE SALEM WITCHES

—

AUTHOR UNKNOWN
May 28th, 1692

According to a witness, in January 1862, 11-year-old Salem resident Abigail Williams and her nine-year-old cousin Elizabeth Parris began to behave erratically and sometimes fit. Unable to find a medical reason for their behaviour, the local doctor, William Griggs, instead blamed witchcraft – a diagnosis with which the girls agreed – and before long, other girls were also claiming to be possessed. The afflicted then began to accuse various local women of being witches and soon the Salem Witch Trials were in full swing. The list seen here details just some of the accused (on the left) and their accusers. The trials lasted for more than a year, during which 20 people, most of whom were "witches", were executed.

Complaint of Severall May 28th 1692

Gooddy Carier of Andevor Tho: Carriers wife	Mary Walcott Abigail William
Gooddy fosdick of Maldin Goody pain: Mary Waren	Mary Walcott Mircy Lewes Abigail William Ann Putnam
Goody Read of marble head upon the hill by the meet'house	Mary Walcott Mircy Lewes Abigail William Ann Putnam
Gooddy Rice of Reding	Ed. Marshals wife Mary Walcott Abigall William
Goody How of Topsfield on Ipswich bounds	Mary Walcott Abigail Williams
Capt Hows brother wife vis Ja. Hows wife	Two women there abouts much affleted and suspect hir but canot sartainly say
Capt. Alldin complaind of a long time by	Mary Walcott Mircy Lewes Abigail Williams Ann Putnam Susana Sheldon
Wm. proctor	Mary Walcot Susana Shelden
Toothakors wife & daughter	Mary Walcot Abig. Williams
Capt. Flood	Mary Walcot Abigail Williams & the rest

Complaint of Severale May. 28th: 1692

gooddy Carier of Andevor	mary walcot
tho: Carerez wife ———	Abigail william
gooddy fosdick of maldin	mary walcot
Goody pain: mary waren	mircy lewes
	Abigah william
	Ann putnam
goody Read of marble head	mary walcot
apon ye hill by ye meet house	mircy lewes
	Abigah william
	Ann putnam
gooddy Rice of Reding	Ed: marshols wife
	mary walcot
	Abigah william
gooddy Stow of topsfeild	mary walcott
or Ipswich bounds	Abigail williams
Capt Stows brother wife	two women there
viz Ja: Stows wife ——	abouts much afleted
	and suspect hir but
	canot sertainly say
Capt: Alldin complaind	mary walcot
of a long time by	mircy lewes
	Abigail williams
	Ann putnam
	Susana Sheldon
Wm procter:	Mary. Walcot
	Susana. Sheldon
Toothaker wife	Mary Walcot
& daufter ——	Abig. Williams
Capt flood ———	Mary Walcot
	Abigail Williams
	& yers

Arthur Abot livis in a by place
som thing noore Meyr Appletons farme
and livis betwen Ips: Topsfeild & Wenham

Abot yt livis betwedon Ipswich
Topsfeild and Wenham

Complained of by
Mary

J'AIME, JE N'AIME PAS

—

ROLANDE BARTHES
1977

In his unconventional 1977 autobiography, *Rolande Barthes* by Rolande Barthes – a book which in itself is a list of sorts – the French sociologist, critic and theorist presents two wonderfully evocative lists: one of things he likes, and another of things he doesn't. He then muses that such things are essentially pointless.

J'aime, je n'aime pas — I like, I don't like

I like: salad, cinnamon, cheese, pimento, marzipan, the smell of new-cut hay (why doesn't someone with a "nose" make such a perfume), roses, peonies, lavender, champagne, loosely held political convictions, Glenn Gould, too-cold beer, flat pillows, toast, Havana cigars, Handel, slow walks, pears, white peaches, cherries, colors, watches, all kinds of writing pens, desserts, unrefined salt, realistic novels, the piano, coffee, Pollock, Twombly, all romantic music, Sartre, Brecht, Verne, Fourier, Eisenstein, trains, Médoc wine, having change, *Bouvard and Pécuchet*, walking in sandals on the lanes of southwest France, the bend of the Adour seen from Doctor L.'s house, the Marx Brothers, the mountains at seven in the morning leaving Salamanca, etc.

I don't like: white Pomeranians, women in slacks, geraniums, strawberries, the harpsichord, Miró, tautologies, animated cartoons, Arthur Rubinstein, villas, the afternoon, Satie, Bartók, Vivaldi, telephoning, children's choruses, Chopin's concertos, Burgundian branles and Renaissance dances, the organ, Marc-Antoine Charpentier, his trumpets and kettledrums, the politico-sexual, scenes, initiatives, fidelity, spontaneity, evenings with people I don't know, etc.

I like, I don't like: this is of no importance to anyone; this, apparently, has no meaning. And yet all this means: *my body is not the same as yours*. Hence, in this anarchic foam of tastes and distastes, a kind of listless blur, gradually appears the figure of a bodily enigma, requiring complicity or irritation. Here begins the intimidation of the body, which obliges others to endure me *liberally*, to remain silent and polite confronted by pleasures or rejections which they do not share.

(A fly bothers me, I kill it: you kill what bothers you. If I had not killed the fly, it would have been *out of pure liberalism*: I am liberal in order not to be a killer.)

WORKMEN'S ABSENCES

—

AUTHOR UNKNOWN
Circa 1250 BC

This fascinating limestone ostracon was discovered during excavations of Deir el-Medina, an ancient Egyptian village once home to families of the workmen who built the tombs in the Valley of the Kings, and features a list of reasons for the labourers' work absences in Year 40 of Ramses II. Equally as insightful are the excuses that still ring true today, such as "DRINKING WITH KHONSU", and those, like "WRAPPING THE CORPSE OF HIS MOTHER", that somehow don't.

Huynefer: month 2 of Winter, day 7 (ILL), month 2 of Winter, day 8 (ILL), month 3 of Summer, day 3 (SUFFERING WITH HIS EYE), month 3 of Summer, day 5 (SUFFERING WITH HIS EYE), day 7 (ILL), day 8 (ILL)

Amenemwia: month 1 of Winter, day 15 (EMBALMING HORMOSE), month 2 of Winter, day 7 (OFF ABSENT), month 2 of Winter, day 8 (BREWING BEER), month 2 of Winter, day 16 (STRENGTHENING THE DOOR), day 23 (ILL), day 24 (ILL), month 3 of Winter, day 6 (WRAPPING (THE CORPSE OF) HIS MOTHER)

Inhurkhawy: month 4 of Spring, day 17 (HIS WIFE WAS BLEEDING)

Neferabu: month 4 of Spring, day 15 (HIS DAUGHTER WAS BLEEDING), day 17 (BURYING THE GOD), month 2 of Summer, day 7 (EMBALMING HIS BROTHER), day 8 (LIBATING FOR HIM), month 4 of Summer, day 26 (HIS WIFE WAS BLEEDING)

Paser: month 1 of Winter, day 25 (LIBATING FOR HIS SON), month 1 of Summer, day 27 (BREWING BEER), month 2 of Summer, day 14 (ILL), day 15 (ILL)

Pakhuru: month 4 of Summer, day 4, day 5, day 6, day 7 (ILL), day 8

Seba: month 4 of Spring, day 17 (THE SCORPION BIT HIM), month 1 of Winter, day 25 (ILL), month 4 of Winter, day 8 (HIS WIFE WAS BLEEDING), month 1 of Summer, day 25, 26, 27 (ILL), month 2 of Summer, day 2, day 3 (ILL), month 2 of Summer, day 4, day 5, day 6, day 7 (ILL)

Neferemsenut: month 2 of Winter, day 7 (ILL)

Simut: month 1 of Winter, day 18 (OFF ABSENT), month 1 of Winter, day 25 (HIS WIFE WAS … AND BLEEDING), month 4 of Winter, day 23 (HIS WIFE WAS BLEEDING)

Khons: month 4 of Spring, day 7 (ILL), month 3 of Winter, day 25 (ILL), month 3 of Winter, day 26 (ILL), day 27, day 28 (ILL), month 4 of Winter, day 8 (WITH HIS GOD), month 4 of Summer, day 26 (ILL), month 1 of Spring, day 14 (HIS FEAST), day 15 (HIS FEAST)

Inuy: month 1 of Winter, day 24 (FETCHING STONE FOR QENHERKHEPSHEF), month 2 of Winter day 8 (DITTO), month 2 of Winter, day 17 (OFF ABSENT WITH THE SCRIBE), month 2 of Winter, day 24 …

Sunero: month 2 of Winter, day 8 (BREWING BEER), month 2 of Summer, day 2 (ILL), day 3, day 4, day 5, day 6, day 7, day 8 (ILL)

Nebenmaat: month 3 of Summer, day 21 (ILL), day 22 (DITTO), month 4 of Summer, day 4 (DITTO), day 5, day 6 (DITTO), day 7, day 8 (DITTO), month 4 of Summer, day 24 (ILL), day 25 (ILL), day 26 (ILL)

Merwaset: month 2 of Winter, day 17 (BREWING BEER), month 3 of Summer, day 5 (ILL), day 7, day 8 (ILL), month 3 of Summer, day 17 (ILL), day 18 (WITH HIS BOSS)

Ramose: month 2 of Winter, day 14 (ILL), day 15 (ILL), month 2 of Summer, day 2 (MOURNING HIS SON), day 3 (ILL)

Bakenmut: month 2 of Winter, day 7 (FETCHING STONE FOR THE SCRIBE)

Rahotep: month 1 of Winter, day 14 (OFFFERING TO THE GOD), month 4 of Winter, day 25 (HIS DAUGHTER WAS BLEEDING), month 2 of Summer, day 5 (WRAPPING (THE CORPSE OF) HIS SON), day 6, day 7, day 8 (DITTO), month 4 of Summer, day 7 (WITH THE SCRIBE), day 8 (WITH THE SCRIBE)

Iierniutef: month 2 of Winter, day 8 (OFF ABSENT), month 2 of Winter, day 17 (WITH THE SCRIBE), month 2 of Winter, day 23 (ILL), month 3 of Winter, day 27 (WITH THE SCRIBE), day 28 (OFF ABSENT), month 4 of Winter, day 8 (WITH THE SCRIBE), month 1 of Spring, day 14

Nakhtamun: month 1 of Winter, day 18 (BREWING BEER), month 1 of Winter, day 25 (WITH HIS BOSS), month 2 of Winter, day 13 (WITH HIS BOSS), month 2 of Winter, day 14 (WITH HIS BOSS), month 2 of Winter, day 15 (WITH HIS BOSS), month 2 of Winter, day 16 (WITH HIS BOSS), day 17, day 18 (WITH HIS BOSS), month 2 of Winter, day 24 (WITH HIS BOSS), month 3 of Winter, day 25 (WITH HIS BOSS), month 3 of Winter, day 26 (WITH HIS BOSS), month 3 of Winter, day 27 (WITH HIS BOSS), day 28 (WITH HIS BOSS), day … (WITH HIS BOSS), month 4 of Winter, day 8 (WITH THE SCRIBE), month 1 of Summer, day 16 (SUFFERING WITH HIS EYE), day 17 (SUFFERING WITH HIS EYE), month 1 of Summer, day 25 (ILL), day 26, day 27 (ILL)

Penduauu: month 1 of Spring, day 14 (DRINKING WITH KHONSU)

Hornefer: month 2 of Winter, day 13 (WITH HIS BOSS), day 14 (WITH HIS BOSS), day 15 (WITH HIS BOSS), month 2 of Winter (WITH HIS BOSS), day 16 (WITH HIS BOSS), day 17 (WITH HIS BOSS), day 23 (WITH HIS BOSS).… month … of Summer, …. (…)

Hornefer: month 2 of Summer, day 10 (ILL)

Sawadjyt: month 3 of Spring, day 23 (WITH HIS BOSS), day 24 (WITH HIS BOSS), month 4 of Spring, day 16 (HIS DAUGHTER WAS BLEEDING), month 1 of Winter, day 14 (OFFERING TO THE GOD), month 1 of Winter, day 15 (DITTO), month 1 of Winter, day 24 (LIBATING TO HIS FATHER), day 25 (DITTO), day 26(?) (DITTO), day 28(?) (WITH HIS BOSS)

Sawadjyt: month 2 of Summer, day 14 (WITH HIS BOSS)

Horemwia: month 3 of Spring, day 21 (WITH HIS BOSS), day 22 (WITH HIS BOSS), month 2 of Winter, day 8 (BREWING BEER), month 3 of Summer, day 17 (ILL), day 18 (ILL), day 21 (ILL), day 22, month 2 of Summer, day 4 (WITH HIS BOSS), month 2 of Summer, day … (WITH HIS BOSS)

Horemwia: month 4 of Summer, day 4 (ILL), day 5 (ILL), day 6 (ILL), day 7 (ILL)

Amennakht: month 4 of Spring, day 15 (WITH HIS BOSS DITTO), day 16 (DITTO), day 17 (DITTO), month 3 of Winter, day 18 (BREWING BEER), month 2 of Summer, day 4 (WITH HIS BOSS), month 3 of Summer, day 7, day 8 (WITH HIS BOSS), month 3 of Summer, day 24, day 25, day 26 (WITH HIS BOSS)

Wadjmose: month 4 of Winter, day 23 (HIS DAUGHTER WAS BLEEDING), month 4 of Summer, day 6 (BUILDING HIS HOUSE)

Nebamentet [illegible]

Hehnekhu: month 1 of Summer, day 16 (WITH HIS BOSS), day 17 (WITH HIS BOSS), month 2 of Summer, day 7 (WRAPPING (THE CORPSE OF) HIS MOTHER), day 8 (DITTO)

Nakhy: month 1 of Spring, day 14 (WITH HIS BOSS), day 15 (DITTO)

Nakhtmin: month 1 of Winter, day 25 (LIBATING), month 2 of Winter, day 7 (FETCHING STONE FOR THE SCRIBE), month 3 of Winter, day 27 (HIS WIFE WAS BLEEDING)

Pennub: month 3 of Spring, day 21 (WITH AAPEHTI), day 22 (DITTO), day 23 (DITTO), day 24 (DITTO), month 2 of Winter, day 7 (FETCHING STONE FOR THE SCRIBE), month 2 of Winter, day 8 (FETCHING STONE FOR THE SCRIBE), day 23 (WITH THE SCRIBE), day 24 (WITH THE SCRIBE), month 3 of Winter, day 28 (BREWING BEER), month 4 of Winter, day 24 (HIS MOTHER WAS ILL), day 25 (DITTO)

Aapehti: month 3 of Spring, day 21 (ILL), day 22 (ILL), day 23 (ILL), day 24 (ILL), month 4 of Spring, day 7 (ILL), day 8 (ILL), day 15 (ILL), day 16 (ILL), month 1 of Winter, day 14 (OFFERING TO THE GOD), month 1 of Winter, day 17 (ILL), month 1 of Winter, day 18 (ILL), month 1 of Summer, day 27 (ILL)

Khaemtir: month 3 of Spring, day 21 (WITH HIS BOSS), day 22 (DITTO), day 23 (DITTO), day 24 (DITTO), month 4 of Spring, day 17 (BURYING THE GOD), month 1 of Winter, day 18 (BREWING BEER), month 3 of Summer, day 8 (ILL)

Amenmose: month 2 of Winter, day 8 (BREWING BEER)

Anuy: month 1 of Winter, day 24 (FETCHING STONE FOR THE SCRIBE), month 3 of Winter, day 28 (BREWING BEER)

Wennefer: month 1 of Winter, day 14 (OFFERING TO THE GOD), month 4 of Summer, day 4 (OFFERING TO HIS GOD)

Buqentuf: month 1 of Winter, day 17 (WITH HIS BOSS), month 1 of Winter, day 18 (BREWING BEER), month 2 of Summer, day 6 (WRAPPING (THE CORPSE OF) HIS MOTHER), day 8 (DITTO)

Manninakhtef [illegible]

Huy: month 1 of Winter, day 17 (BREWING BEER), day 18 (BREWING BEER), month 2 of Winter, day 17 (BREWING BEER), month 3 of Winter, day 27 (WITH HIS BOSS), day 28 (DITTO), month 4 of Winter, day 3 (WITH HIS BOSS), month 4 of Winter, day 7 (WITH HIS BOSS), day 8 (DITTO)

Huy: month 4 of Winter, day 24 (WITH HIS BOSS), month 4 of Summer, day 25 (DITTO), day 26 (DITTO)

….: month 3 of Spring, day 21 (ILL), day 22 (ILL), day 23 (ILL), day 24 (ILL), month 4 of Spring, day 7 (ILL), day 8 (ILL), month 1 of Winter, day 24 (ILL), month 2 of Winter day 8 (BREWING BEER), month 2 of Summer, day 8 (BREWING BEER)

Paherypedjet: month 3 of Spring, day 21 (WITH AAPEHTI), day 22 (DITTO), day 23 (DITTO), day 24 (DITTO), month 4 of Spring, day 7 (DITTO), day 8 (DITTO), day 15 (DITTO), day 16 (DITTO), day 17 (DITTO), month 1 of Winter, day 14 (OFFERING TO THE GOD), month 2(?) of Winter, day 13 (…), month 3 of Winter, day 25 (WITH KHONS MAKING REMEDIES), 26 (DITTO), month 3 of Winter, day 27 (DITTO), month 1 of Summer, day 25 (MAKING REMEDIES FOR THE SCRIBE'S WIFE), day 26 (DITTO), day 27 (DITTO), month 2 of Summer, day 2 (DITTO), day 3 (DITTO), day 4, day 5, day 6, day 7, day 8 (DITTO), month 3 of Summer, day 3 (WITH KHONS MAKING REMEDIES), day 17 (WITH HOREMWIA), day 18 (WITH HOREMWIA), day 21 (DITTO), day 22, month 4 of Summer, day 4, month 4 of Summer, day 5, day 6, day 7, day 8, day 24 (ILL), day 25, day 26, month 1 of Spring, day 15 (ILL), day 16(?) (ILL)

December 19, 1956   INTEGRATED BUS SUGGESTIONS   Plurifon t L.S.

This is a historic week because segregation on buses has now been declared unconstitutional. Within a few days the Supreme Court Mandate will reach Montgomery and you will be re-boarding integrated buses. This places upon us all a tremendous responsibility of maintaining, in face of what could be some unpleasantness, a calm and loving dignity befitting good citizens and members of our Race. If there is violence in word or deed it must not be our people who commit it.

For your help and convenience the following suggestions are made. Will you read, study and memorize them so that our non-violent determination may not be endangered. First, some general suggestions:

1. Not all white people are opposed to integrated buses. Accept goodwill on the part of many.
2. The whole bus is now for the use of all people. Take a vacant se
3. Pray for guidance and commit yourself to complete non-violence in word and action as you enter the bus.
4. Demonstrate the calm dignity of our Montgomery people in your actions.
5. In all things observe ordinary rules of courtesy and good behavi
6. Remember that this is not a victory for Negroes alone, but for a Montgomery and the South. Do not boast! Do not brag!
7. Be quiet but friendly; proud, but not arrogant; joyous, but no boistrous.
8. Be loving enough to absorb evil and understanding enough to tu an enemy into a friend.

Now for some specific suggestions:

1. The bus driver is in charge of the bus and has been instructed t obey the law. Assume that he will cooperate in helping you occupy any vacant seat.
2. Do not deliberately sit by a white person, unless there is no other seat.
3. In sitting down by a person, white or colored, say "May I" or "Pardon me" as you sit. This is a common courtesy.
4. If cursed, do not curse back. If pushed, do not push back. If struck, do not strike back, but evidence love and goodwill at all times.
5. In case of an incident, talk as little as possible, and always in a quiet tone. Do not get up from your seat! Report all seriou. incidents to the bus driver.
6. For the first few days try to get on the bus with a friend in whose non-violence you have confidence. You can uphold one another by a glance or a prayer.
7. If another person is being molested, do not arise to go to his defense, but pray for the oppressor and use oral and spiritual force to carry on the struggle for justice.
8. According to your own ability and personality, do not be afraid to experiment with new and creative techniques for achieving reconciliation and social change.
9. If you feel you cannot take it, walk for another week or two. We have confidence in our people. GOD BLESS YOU ALL.

THE MONTGOMERY IMPROVEMENT ASSOCIATION
THE REV. M. L. KING, JR., PRESIDENT
THE REV. W. J. POWELL, SECRETARY

INTEGRATED BUS SUGGESTIONS
—
MARTIN LUTHER KING
December 19th, 1956

On December 1st, 1955, the course of history was changed when Rosa Parks refused to give up her bus seat for a white passenger and was subsequently arrested. For the next year, until racial segregation was deemed unconstitutional by the federal courts, a boycott of the public transport system, headed by Martin Luther King, took place. On December 19th 1956, the eve of a historic victory for those opposed to such segregation, King prepared a list of guidelines for those soon to be re-boarding the buses.

10 COMMANDMENTS FOR CON MEN

—

VICTOR LUSTIG

1936

"Count" Victor Lustig was a con man of considerable note. Born in 1890, by the 1930s he was wanted by approximately 45 law enforcement agencies worldwide for a plethora of crimes. He had 25 known aliases and spoke five languages. He cunningly gained $5,000 from Al Capone, one of the most notorious and feared criminals of the age. Better still, in 1925, Lustig posed as a government official in Paris, took five businessmen on a tour of the Eiffel Tower, and then "sold" it to one of them as 7,300 tonnes of scrap metal. The con went so well he tried it again soon after. In 1936, Lustig wrote a list of commandments for aspiring con men.

1. Be a patient listener (it is this, not fast talking, that gets a con-man his coups).

2. Never look bored.

3. Wait for the other person to reveal any political opinions, then agree with them.

4. Let the other person reveal religious views, then have the same ones.

5. Hint at sex talk, but don't follow it up unless the other fellow shows a strong interest.

6. Never discuss illness, unless some special concern is shown.

7. Never pry into a person's personal circumstances (they'll tell you all eventually).

8. Never boast. Just let your importance be quietly obvious.

9. Never be untidy.

10. Never get drunk.

GOBBLEFUNK

—

ROALD DAHL
Early 1980s

In 1982, *The BFG* was published – a magical and wildly successful children's book in which a Big Friendly Giant blows pleasant dreams through the windows of young children. As he was creating the story, renowned author Roald Dahl set about creating a new vocabulary for the enormous protagonist: a 238-word language that he ultimately named, "Gobblefunk". Words that made the cut included, "humplecrimp", "swallomp", "crumpscoddle" and, most memorably, "snozzcumber". The list you see here was written by Dahl as he brainstormed, and offers a snapshot of "Gobblefunk" in its infancy.

The Fleshlumpeating Giant

a <u>notmucher</u>, a squeakpip.

cronky	~~manhugging giant~~	troggy	~~jumpsy~~
crinky	~~fizzlecump~~	paggle	dropsy
corky	~~bottle wart~~	~~pibbling~~	~~swipsy~~
	gumplewink	~~dibbling~~	kicksey
blivver(ing)	~~swigfiddle~~	ristling	fruggler
stoching	~~squiffsquiddle~~	~~blunketing~~	~~grobswitch~~
protching	flushbuckling	pranky	crodswitch
mickering (aww)	whopsy-waddling	filking	kickswitch
	~~pongswizzler~~	pilching	~~grobby~~
~~swish~~	~~scumscrewer~~	~~scoddling~~	~~lickswitch~~
	bagblurter	slidger	dissible
	~~fizzwiggler~~	~~squiggling~~	sliggy
	spitzwargler	squibbling	
	spitzwoggler	squinkling	~~bunkledoodle~~
	~~buzzbunger~~	squeakling	grob fatch
	bizzfizz	~~squmping~~	~~grobswitch~~
	buzzfuzz	scumping	~~wimplesquiffer~~
	baghangar	~~scuddling~~	<u>snipply</u>
	bophanger	swiddling	grilky
	wash-hinger	~~squiffling~~	gronky
	spongewiggler	slunging	grouty
	~~codswallop~~	grobbled	~~cream puffnut~~
	~~muckfrumping~~	squiffly-jumpsy	
	splatchwinkling		~~snog winker~~
	~~crodscollop~~	rag-rasper	~~ring beller~~
	shardlelly	~~rotrasper~~	phizz-whizz
	~~spatchwinkle~~		chidler or tottle =
	~~swishfiggler~~	~~scrumplet~~	child
	swogglewop	squiffler	schweinwein
	gunzleswipe	sludge	squinky
	pifflemutter	pong-ping-pong	scud
			~~squeakpip~~

he skimmed land-bar,
lemon + fruit-cake.

The Fleshlumpeating Giant

a rotmucher, a squeakpip.

mandigggg giant

Cronky	~~fistecrunp~~	Troggy	~~jumpy~~
crinky	~~bottle-wart~~	faggle	dropey
Corky	fumple-wonk	~~fittling~~	~~snippy~~
	~~squifzle~~	dibbling	kicksey
	squiffsquiffle	ristling	fruggler
blivver(ing)	flushbunkling	~~blunketing~~	~~gobswifol~~
sloching	whopsy-waddling	prunking	crodswitch
protching	~~pongswoszler~~	filking	kickswitch
mickeling (away)	~~scumscrewer~~	pit-pilchey	~~frobly~~
	bagbluster	~~scuddling~~	lickswish
	~~fizzwizzler~~	slidger	dissible
Swish...	spitzwaggler	~~squiggling~~	sliggy
...	spitzwoggler	squibbling	
...	~~buzzbuzzer~~	squeakling	~~funkledoodle~~
	bizzfizz	squeackling	frobfatch
	buzzfuzz	~~squimping~~	~~frobswish~~
	baghenger	scumping	~~loppleguffler~~
	bophanger	~~scuddling~~	snipply ~~splongfler~~
	wash-hinger	swiddling	grilky
	spongewiggler	~~squiffling~~	fronky
	codswallop	slunging	frouby
	~~muckfrumping~~	grobbled	cream ~~puffrut~~
	splatchwonkling	squiffly-jumpsy	
	~~crodscollop~~		~~guog-winkler~~
	shedbelly	ragrasper	~~raghatter~~
	~~spatchwinkle~~	~~sorrasper~~	phizz-whizz
	~~swishjiggler~~		chidler or foffle = child.
	swogglewop	~~scrumplet~~	schwinwein
	funzle swipe	squiffler	squinky
	pifflemuffer	sludge	squeakpip sui

pong-pig-pong

TOPICS TO BE INVESTIGATED
—

LEONARDO DA VINCI
1489

Leonardo da Vinci's fascination with every aspect of the human body is apparent in much of his work; the famous Vitruvian Man drawing – a now iconic sketch of a man whose supposedly ideal proportions were based on those discussed in the writings of Roman architect Vitruvius – being a prime example. It was around this time, in 1489, that Leonardo wrote in one of his notebooks, from right to left as was his wont, a list of topics to be investigated in his quest to become an expert anatomist.

What nerve is the cause of movement of the eye and makes the movement of one eye draw the other

on closing the eyelids

on raising the eyelids

on lowering the eyelids

on shutting the eyes

on opening the eyes

on raising the nostrils

on opening the lips with the teeth closed

on bringing the lips to a point

on laughing

on [the expression of] wonder

describe the origin of man when he is generated in the womb

and why an infant of eight months does not live

what is sneezing

what is yawning

epilepsy

spasm

paralysis

trembling with cold

sweating

tiredness

hunger

sleep

thirst

lust

on the nerve which causes movement from the shoulder to the elbow

on movement from the elbow to the hand

from the wrist to the beginning of the fingers

from the beginning of the fingers to their middle

and from the middle to the last joint

on the nerve which causes movement of the thigh

and from the knee to the foot and from the ankle to the toes

and also to their middle

and of the rotation of the leg

NEW YER'S GUIFTES GIUEN TO THE QUENE'S MAIESTIE

—

QUEEN ELIZABETH I
1578–9

Every New Year's Day of her 44-year reign, from 1559 until 1603, Queen Elizabeth I would amass hundreds of gifts from members of the royal household in a tradition that began centuries before, but which Elizabeth actively encouraged like no other. Although a voluntary arrangement, gifts came from almost all who served her, and the urge to furnish her with something she would adore was undeniable. The Queen even offered presents to some in return albeit of low value and often boasting her image. After each gift exchange a list was drawn up of Her Highness's takings, beginning with Lords and Ladies and ending with her lowly staff.

New Yer's Guiftes giuen to the QUENE'S MAIESTIE *at her Highnes Manor of Richmond, by these Persons whose Names hereafter do ensue, the First of January, the Yere abouesaid.*

	£.	s.	d.
By the Lady *Margret* Countes of *Darby*, a trayne gowne of tawny vellat.			
Delivered to *Rauff Hope*, Yoman of her Roobes.			
By Sir *Nicholas Bacon*, Knight, Lorde Keper of the Greate Seale of Inglande, in golde and siluer	13	6	8
By the Lorde *Burley*, Lorde High Treausorour of Inglande, in golde	20	0	0
By the Lorde Marquis of *Winchester*, in golde	20	0	0
Delivered to *Henry Sackford*, Grome.			

EARLES.

	£.	s.	d.
By therle of *Leycetour*, Master of the Horses, a verey feyer juell of golde, being a clocke fully furnished with small diamonds pointed, and a pendaunte of golde, diamonds, and rubyes, very smale; and upon eche side a lozenge diamonde, and an apple of golde enamuled grene and russet.			
Delivered to the Lady *Hawarde*.			
By therle of *Arondell*, in golde	30	0	0
By therle of *Shrewesbury*, in golde	20	0	0
By therle of *Darby*, in golde	20	0	0
By therle of *Sussex*, Lorde Chamberleyn, in golde	20	0	0
By therle of *Lincoln*, Lord Admirall of Inglande, in golde	10	0	0
Delivered to the aforesaid *Henry Sackford*.			
By therle of *Warwyck*, a juell of golde, being a very great tophas set in gold, ennamuled with 8 perles pendant.			
Delivered to the Lady *Hawarde*.			
By therle of *Bedforde*, in golde	20	0	0
Delivered to the foresaid *Henry Sackford*.			
By therle of *Oxforde*, a very feyer juell of golde, wherein is a helmet of golde and small diamonds furnished, and under the same is five rubyes, one bigger then threst, and a small diamond brokenne; and all threst of the same juell furnesshed with small diamonds.			
Delivered to the Lady *Hawarde*.			
By therle of *Rutlande*, in golde	10	0	0
By therle of *Huntingdon*, in golde	10	0	0
By therle of *Penbroke*, in golde	20	0	0
By therle of *Northumberlande*, in golde	10	0	0
By therle of *Southampton*, in golde	20	0	0
Delivered to the foresaid *Henry Sackford*.			
By therle of *Hertford*, a small peyer of writing tabells enamuled with a grashopper, all of golde, ennamuled grene on the backsyde, and a pynne of golde having a small perle at thende thereof.			

Anno Regni
Regine the xxxj

Newe Yeres Guiftes geuen to the Quenes
maiestie at her highnes Manor of Richmond
by thise persons whose names hereafter do
ensue the ffirst of Januarij the yere aforesaid

Elizabeth R

By the Lady Margett Countes of Darby a Trayne Gowne of Tawny satten ... as to Iust ... her Cristi

By Sr Nicholas Baron knight Lorde keper of the great Seale of England in golde and Selute ... li vj xiij

By the Lorde Burley Lorde high Treasorer of England in golde ... xx li his highe Cristi ... sema

By the Lorde Marques of Wynchester in golde ... xx li

Earles

By therle of Lyncto M of the horse avery fyre hull of golde being a Clock garnesshed fully wt Diamond ... gh to the Lady Canard
and Rubyes with aptident of Diamond and Rubyes and an Appoll of golde Emmamuld grene and Russet

By the erle of Arondell in golde ... xx li

By therle of Shrowesbury in golde ... xx li

By Therle of Darby in golde ... xx li ... as to the pfutes in Cristi

By Therle of Sussex Lorde Chamberlyn in golde ... xx li

By Therle of Lincolne Lorde Admirall of England in golde ... xx li

By Therle of Warwyck a Iuell of golde being a greate Topas set in golde Emmamuld, wt sxx pyrles pendant ... xx li gh to the Lady Canard

By Therle of Bedford in golde ... xx li

By therle of Oxforde a fyne Iuell of golde wherein is a billett of golde and small Diamond sixnesse &c ... Dx to his futhered Cristi
and sendes the same to Rubyth one bigger then thother and all thrust of the same Iuell sxxesshed wt small Diamond

By Therle of Rutland in golde ... x li ... gh to the Lady Canard

By Therle of Huntingdon in golde ... x li

By Therle of Penbroke in golde ... xx li

By Therle of Northumberlande in golde ... xx li ... Dx to his pfutes in Cristi

By Therle of Southampton in golde ... x li

By Therle of Hertford a small ... xx li

By therle of *Ormonde*, a very fayre juell of golde, whearin are three large emeraldes sett in roses white and redd, one bigger than the other twoo; all the rest of the same juell garnished with roses and flowers enamuled, furnished with very smale dyamonds and rubyes; aboute the edge very smale perles; and in the bottome is parte of a flower-de-luce garnished with smale diamondes, rubyes, and one sapher, with three meane pearles pendaunte, two of them smale; the backsyde a flower-de-luce enamuled greene.

By therle of *Surr'*, a gyrdill of tawny vellat embrawdred with sede perle, the buckyll and pendant of golde.

Delivered to the Lady *Hawarde*.

VICOUNT.

By the Vicounte *Mountague*, in golde	10	0	0

Delivered to the foresaid *Henry Sackford*.

DUCHESSES, MARQUISSES, AND COUNTESS.

By the Duches of *Suffolke*, a lylly pot of agathe, a lylly flower going owte of it garnsshed with roses of rubyes and diamonds hanging at two small cheynes of golde.

Delivered to the Lady *Hawarde*.

By the Duches of *Somerset*, in golde and silver	18	6	8
By the Lady Marques of *Winchester*, in golde	10	0	0

Delivered to the foresaid *Henry Sackford*.

By the Lady Marques of *Northampton*, a gyrdill of golde with buckells and pendants of golde, garneshed with sparks of rubyes and diamonds, and also 10 perles set in colletts of golde.

Delivered to the Lady *Hawarde*.

By the Countes of *Shrewesbury*, a mantyll of tawny satten enbrawdred with a border of Venice golde and silver, lyned with white taphata, and faced with white satten.

By the Countes of *Warwyk*, a cap of black vellat with 13 buttons of golde, in every of them eyther a ruby or diamonde; and a knot of small perle, with a garter and a byrde upon the same; and a perle pendant.

Delivered to the foresaid *Rauf Hoope*.

By the Countes of *Sussex*, in golde	10	0	0

Delivered to the foresaid *Henry Sackford*.

By the Countess of *Bedford*, a foreparte of white satten, enbrawdred with black sylke and golde, with two feyer borders of Venice golde and sede perle enbrawdred.

Delivered to the foresaid *Rauf Hoope*.

By the Countes of *Lincoln*, a jug of marbill garnesshed with golde, per oz. 18 oz. di. qr.

Remaynyng with *John Astley*, Master of the Juells.

By the Countes of *Huntingdon*, in golde	8	0	0

Delivered to the foresaid *Henry Sackford*.

By the Countes of *Oxford*, a foreparte of a kyrtyll of white satten enbrawdred with flowers of silver, and two borders of golde and sede perle enbrawdred upon black vellat.

Delivered to the foresaid *Rauf Hoope*.

By the Countes of *Penbroke*, doager, in golde	12	0	0
By the Countes *Penbroke*, junior, in golde	10	0	0
By the Countes of *Northumberlande*, in golde	10	0	0
By the Countes of *Southampton*, in golde	10	0	0

Delivered to the foresaid *Henry Sackford*.

By the Countes of *Essex*, a greate cheyne of amber slightly garneshed with golde and small perle.

Delivered to the *Lady Hawarde*.

By the Countes of *Rutlande*, in golde	10	0	0

Delivered to the foresaid *Henry Sackford*.

By the Countes of *Kent*, doager, a mufler of purple vellat, enbrawdred with Venice and damaske golde and perle.

Delivered to Mrs. *Elizabeth Knowlls*.

By the Countes of *Kent*, junior, a foreparte of a kyrtyll network, floureshed with golde and tufts of sundry coloured sylke.

Delivered to the foresaid *Rauf Hoope*.

By the Vicecountes of *Mountague*, in golde	10	0	0

BUSSHOPS.

By the Archebusshop of *Yorke*, in golde	30	0	0
By the Busshop of *Ely*, in golde	30	0	0
By the Busshop of *Dureham*, in golde	30	0	0
By the Busshop of *London*, in golde	20	0	0
By the Busshop of *Winchester*, in golde	20	0	0
By the Busshop of *Salisbury*, in golde	20	0	0
By the Busshop of *Lincoln*, in golde	20	0	0
By the Busshop of *Norwiche*, in golde	20	0	0
By the Busshop of *Worcetour*, in golde	20	0	0
By the Busshop of *Lichfelde*, in golde and silver	8	6	8
By the Busshop of *Hereford*, in golde	10	0	0
By the Busshop of *Seint David*, in golde	10	0	0
By the Busshop of *Karlyle*, in golde	10	0	0
By the Busshop of *Bathe*, in golde	10	0	0
By the Busshop of *Peterborough*, in golde	10	0	0
By the Busshop of *Glocestour*, in golde	10	0	0
By the Busshop of *Chicester*, in golde	10	0	0
By the Busshop of *Rochester*, in golde	10	0	0

LORDES.

By the Lorde of *Burgavenny*, in golde	30	0	0

Delivered to the foresaid *Henry Sackford*.

By the Lorde *Howarde*, a lock of golde, black ennamuled, garneshed with 16 small diamonds.

Delivered to the Lady *Hawarde*.

By the Lorde *Russell*, a cawle of here, garneshed with buttons of golde, within ennamuled, and set with ragged perle.

Delivered to the Mrs. *Elizabeth Knowlls*.

By the Lorde *Riche*, in golde	10	0	0
By the Lorde *Darcy of Chyche*, in golde	10	0	0
By the Lorde *Shandowes*, in golde and silver	6	13	4
By the Lorde *North*, in golde	10	0	0
By the Lorde *Paget*, in golde	10	0	0
By the Lorde *Stafford*, in golde	10	0	0
By the Lorde *Compton*, in golde	10	0	0
By the Lorde *Norrys of Rycote*, in golde	10	0	0
By the Lorde *Lumley*, in golde	10	0	0
By the Lorde *Wharton*, in golde	10	0	0
By the Lorde *Morley*, in golde	10	0	0

Delivered to the foresaid *Henry Sackford*.

By the Lorde *Cobham*, a dublet of white satten lyned with murry, white sarcenet leyed with a pasmane of golde and sylke.

Delivered to the foresaid *Rauf Hope*.

By the Lorde *Henry Haward*, a juell of golde, being a ded tre with mysaltow, set at the rote with sparks of diamonds and rubys.

BARONESSES.

By the Lady Baronesse *Burleigh*, 36 buttons of golde, one broken.

Delivered to the Lady *Haward*.

By the Lady Barones *Howarde*, Dowager, in golde	10	0	0

Delivered to the forsaid *Henry Sackford*.

By the Lady Barones *Howard*, jun. a juell of golde, garnesshed with rubys and diamonds, and thre smale perles pendant.

Delivered to the same Lady *Hawarde*.

By the Lady Barones *Cobham*, a petticote of crymsen rewed with silver.

By the Lady Barones *Dacres*, a gowne of wrought vellat.

Delivered to the forsaid *Rauf Hope*.

By the Lady Barones *Tayleboyes*, in golde 10 0 0

Delivered to the forsaid *Henry Sackford*.

By the Lady Barones *Shandowes*, douger, a feyer skarf of grene sersenet enbrawdred with byrds and flowers of sylke and golde of sundry collours, frenged with Venice golde, and lyned with murry sarceonet.

By the Lady Barones *Shandowes*, jun. a vale of black networke flurreshed with flowers of silver and a small bone lace.

Delivered to Mrs. *Elizabeth Knowlls*.

By the Lady Barones *Seint John Bletzelow*, in golde 10 0 0

Delivered to the forsaid *Henry Sackford*.

By the Lady Barones *Paget*, the Lord's wyf, a pettycote of cloth of golde, stayned black and white, with a bone lace of golde and and spangells leyed lyke waves of the see.

Delivered to the foresaid *Rauf Hope*.

By the Barones *Paget Darce*, a small cheyne of golde, with a luer of golde hanging at it, on thone syde a white dove, and on thother syde a hawke with a button white ennamuled.

By the Lady Barones *Cheyny*, a carcanet of golde, cont' 8 peces, with byrds and frute ennamuled.

Delivered to the foresaid Lady *Hawarde*.

By the Lady Barones *Awdeley*, a foreparte of a kyrtill of orenge collored satten.

Delivered to the foresaid *Rauf Hope*.

By the Lady Barones *Barkeley*, in golde 10 0 0
By the Lady Barones *Bookehurst*, in golde 5 0 0
By the Lady Barones *Norris*, in golde 10 0 0

Delivered to the forsaid *Henry Sackford*.

By the Lady Barones *Sheffelde*, a kyrtyll of purple satten, with roses of white lawne enbrawdred with golde unlyned.

Delivered to the foresaid *Rauf Hope*.

By the Lady *Vere*, Mr. *Bartewe's* wyf, a vale oof open worke with golde and spangills.

Delivered to Mrs. *Elizabeth Knowlls*.

By the Lady Barones *Morley*, a pettycote of white satten all over enbrawdred with roses of golde; and 3 gards, likewyse enbrawdred, lyned with white satten, and frenged with sylke and golde.

Delivered to the forsaid *Rauf Hope*.

By Therle of Northumberland in gote [col] vi li [right note]

By Therle of Southampton in gote [col] vi li

By Therle of Hertford a small pryer of worktng Tablett w a grene hopper all of gote enamnled grene on the backside and a small prynt of gote having a small perle at the vnder therof

By Therle of Osmonde a fayrr Juell of gote w an ex that large Entralde set in Roff white w one out higgte then Roff d two all theff greneyffin a Roff and fflowers enamled all theff flowerds w very small diamonds verdr [right] d to the Lady Haward

By Therle of Essex a gredull of Tawny scrllat enbrawdrd w the perle the birkyll and pendant of gote

By the viscount Mountague in gote [col] vi li [right note]

By the Duches of Suffolke a belly pot of Agathe belly fflowert gomy gost ex A garnefficd w Roffs of Rubyes and diamonds havtng at two small Chyrues of gote [right] d to the Lady Haward

By the Duches of Somerset in gote and Silvr [col] viij li ... [right] ... [right] ...

By the Lady Marques of Northampton a Gredull of gote w Rubyell and pendant of gote garnefficd w Roffs of Rubyes and diamonds and also p perles set in Collette of gote [right] d to the Lady Haward

By the Comtes of Shroffbury a Mantyll of Tawny Sattyn enbrawdrd w a bordr of goote gote and Silvr lyned w Roff white Taphata and faced w Roff Sattyn

By the Countes of Warwyck a Cap of black scllat w xij zim buttons of gote in evy of them a zuby or a diamond and a knot of small perle w agatres g abyzde vpon the same w apparll pendant [right] d to the forsaid Ront Hope

By the Comtes of Suffex in gote [col] vi li [right note]

By the Countes of Bedford a forente of wlight Sattin enbrawdrd w black silke and gote w two fayrr bordrs of verment gote and set perle enbrawdrd [right] d to the forsaid Rauf Hope

By the Comtes of Lincoln a Juct of Markill garnefficd w gote perl [right] d to the forsaid ...

By the Comtes of Huntingdon in gote [col] viij li [right] ...

By the Countes of Bedford a forgote of a kyrtyll of wight Sattey enbrawdrd w fflowers of Silu and two bordrs of gote and set perle enbrawdrd vpon black scllat [right] d forsaid Henry Sackfort

By the Comtes of Pembroke Margrt in gote

By the Comtes of Pembroke Jnul in gote [col] vij li

By the Comtes of Northumberland in gote [col] vi li [right note]

By the Comtes of Southampton in gote [col] vi li

By the Comtes of Essex a petratt wchyne of Amber slghgtly garnefficd w gote and small perle [right] d to the Lady Haward

By the Countes of Rutlande in gote [col] vi li [right] ...

By the Comtes of Kent Margt a muffler of purple scllat enbrawdrd w veluet g Damaske gote g perle d w Mr Elizath Hawards

By the Comtes of Kent Jnul a fayrr of abyzhall network ffloureffin w gote dud tufft of sundry colord silke [right] d to the forsaid Anne Hope

By the vicecomitte Mountague in gote [col] vi li

By therchebusshop of yorke in gote [col] xxx li

By the Busshop of Ely in gote [col] xxx li

By the Busshop of Durhm in gote [col] xxx li

By the Busshop of London in gote [col] xxx li

By the Busshop of worcester in gote [col] xx li

By the Busshop of Salisbury in gote [col] xx li

By the Busshop of Lincoln in gote [col] xx li

By the Busshop of Norwich in gote [col] xviij li

By the Busshop of worcett in gote [col] xvij li

By the Busshop of Lichfelde in gote and Silvr [col] xviij li ... [right] ... [right] d to the forsaid ... Sackfort

By the Busshop of Hereford in gote [col] v li

By the Busshop of Sent David in gote [col] v li

By the Busshop of Karliell in gote [col] v li

By the Busshop of Bathe in gote [col] v li

By the Busshop of Peterburgh in gote [col] v li

By the Busshop of Glocett in gote [col] v li

By the Busshop of Chichester in gote [col] v li

By the Busshop of Rochester in gote [col] v li

By the Lorde of Burgheuny in gote [col] v li

By the Lorde Hayward alias of gote black enameiled garnefficd w zi zym small diamonds [right] d Lady Haward

By the Lorde Russell annell of that garnefficd w buttons of gote wm enamelled and set w Ragged perle [right] d to the Lady Lennett

By the Lorde Dacre in gote [col] v li [right] ...

By the Lorde Darcy of Chiche in gote [col] v li [right] ...

By the Lorde Chandoes in gote and Silvr [col] vi li viij ... [right] ...

By the Lorde of Wokehurst in gote [col] v li

By the Lorde Worthy in gote [col] v li [right] ...

By the Lorde Dacret in gote [col] v li

By the Lorde Stafford in gote [col] v li

By the Lorde Compton in gote [col] v li

By the Lorde Norrys of Rycote in gote [col] v li

By the Lorde Lumley in gote [col] v li

By the Lady Barrones *Wharton*, a juell of golde, wherein is a parret hanging, garnesshed with small diamonds, and a cluster of perle pendaunt lacking a ffysshe on thone syde.

Delivered to the forsaid Lady *Haward*

LADIES.

By the Lady *Mary Sydney*, a smock and two pillowbyers of cameryk, feyer wrought with black worke, and edged with a brode bone lace of black sylke.

Delivered to Mrs. *Skydmore*.

By the Lady *Mary Sem'*, wif to Mr. *Rogers*, a touthe-pike of golde made gonne fation.

Delivered to the foresaid Lady *Haward*.

By the Lady *Elizabeth Sem'*, alias *Knightlye*, a kyrtell of oring tawnye satten, edged with a passamayne of silver.

Delivered to the forsaid *Rauf Hope*.

By the Lady *Stafforde*, a juell of golde, being an agate garnished with golde, sett about with sparks of rubyes and diamonds, with a smale perle pendaunt.

Delivered to the forsaid Lady *Haward*.

By the Lady *Carowe*, a cusshen clothe camereke, blake worke, and frenged with Venice golde.

Delivered to Mrs. *Skydmore*.

By the Lady *Cheeke*, a foreparte of golde and silver networke.

Delivered to the forsaid *Rauf Hope*.

By the Lady *Butler*, in golde		6	0	0

Delivered to the foresaid *Henry Sackford*.

By the Lady *Heniaige*, a pomaunder gar' with golde and 12 sparks of rubies and perles pendaunt, per oz.

Delivered to the foresaid Lady *Haward*.

By the Lady *Waulsingham*, 4 paire of gloves set with buttons of golde.

Delivered to Mrs. *Elizabeth Knowlls*.

By the Lady *Drury*, a foreparte of clothe of silver, all over enbraudred with clothe of golde.

Delivered to the foresaid *Rauf Hope*.

By the Lady *Pawlet*, in golde		5	0	0

Delivered to the foresaid *Henry Sackford*.

By the Lady *Willoby*, Sir *Francis'* wif, tow pillowberes of camerike wrought allover withe carnatyon silke.

Delivered to Mrs. *Skydmore*.

By the Lady *Gresham*, in golde		10	0	0
By the Lady *Cromwell*, Sir *Henrye's* wif, in golde		5	0	0

Delivered to the forsaid *Henry Sackford*.

By the Lady *Ratclyf*, a vale of white worke with spangles, and a smale bone lace of silver, a swete bag, beinge of changeable silke, with a smale bone lace of golde.

The vale delivered to Mrs. *Elizabeth Knowlls*; and the bag to Mrs. *Skydmore*.

By the Lady *Frogmorton*, a large bag to put a pillow in of morre satten, allover enbrauderid with golde, silver, and silke of sondry collours, with 4 tassels of grene silke and golde; and a cusshen-cloth of networke, florisshed over with flowers of golde, silver, and silke of sondry collours, lyned with white satten.

Delivered to Mrs. *Skydmore*.

By the Lady *Cromwell*, Lorde *Cromwell's* wif, 3 sutes of ruffes of white cute worke, edged with a passamayne of white.

Delivered to Mrs. *Jane Bresett*.

By the Lorde Darcy of Chyche in golde
By the Lorde Chandoses in golde and silver
By the Lorde of Bohchurst in golde
By the Lorde Northe in golde
By the Lorde Pagett in golde
By the Lorde Stafforde in golde
By the Lorde Compton in golde
By the Lorde Norrys of Ryott in golde
By the Lorde Lumley in golde
By the Lorde Wharton in golde
By the Lorde Mosley in golde
By the Lorde Cobham a dublet of whitt satten lynid wt murry wrett shewt thrid wt a garnement of golde & silke
By the Lorde Henry Haward a juell of golde being a dead tre wt myslitoro set at the rote wt spks of diamond & rubyes

Baroness

By the Lady Barouesse Burleigh xxxxiiij buttons of golde one broken
By the Lady Barones Howarde Dowager in golde
By the Lady Barones Howard Jun a juell of golde garnesshed wt rubyes and diamonds and xvij perles pendaunt
By the Lady Barones Cobham a petticote of crymson velvett wrought wth silver
By the Lady Barones Darcey a gowne of wrought satt
By the Lady Barones Tayleboyes in golde
By the Lady Barones Chandowes Dowager a forepart of grene velvett enbraudered wt byrdes and flowers of silke and golde of sundry coller set wth spotts in golde and lynid wt murry tawronet
By the Lady Barones Chandowes Jun a vale of black networke flowryd & wt flowers of silke a small bone lace
By the Lady Barones Seint John Bletchley in golde
By the Lady Barones Pagett the Lorde wyfe a pettycote of scott of golde strayned blak and white wth about lace of golde and spangill lynid lyke wawes of the see
By the Barones Payne gwre a small cheyne & gurdle wt a tablet hanging at it on thon syde wt argus eye and on thother syde a hawke wth a button whitt ennameled
By the Lady Barones Cheyny a carcanett of golde cont xxvj pcs wt byrdes and fruit ennameled
By the Lady Barones Dudley a petticote of a kyrtell of Orenge colored satten
By the Lady Barones Darlelley in golde
By the Lady Barones Scottshurst in golde
By the Lady Barones Norrys in golde
By the Lady Barones Chffelld a kyrtell of purple satten wt roses of white lawne enbraudered wt golde rubyes &c
By the Lady Dere Mr Baskeweis wyfe a vale of open worke wth golde and spangill
By the Lady Barones Morley a pettycote of whitt satten alen enbraudered with roses of golde and nj gards likewise enbraudered lynid wth whitt satten and fatryned wth silke and golde a juell of golde
By the Lady Barones Wharton neggpem wt apparrett hanging garnesshed wt small diamond and a fusses of pearll pendaunt lacking a fusses on thoneside

Ladies

By the Lady Mary Sydney a smok and two pillowbyers of camerek seye wrought wth clark worke and edged wth a brode bone lace of blak silke
By the Lady Mary Som wyfe to Mr Roger a tomb robe of golde made yonne salucy
By the Lady Lizabeth Som alio Lughlley a kyrtell of Oring tawnye satten edged wt a passamayne of silver
By the Lady Stafforde a juell of golde being an agate set about wth sparks of rubyes & diamonds with a small perle pendaunt
By the Lady Carowe & Crofton clothe camerek blak work and fatryned wt prime golde
By the Lady Cheek a fore parte of golde and silv networke
By the Lady Dudle in golde
By the Lady De maye a pomander garr wt golde and vj sparks of rubies & perles pendaunt rn
By the Lady Mawlinghton my paint of glooes set wth buttons of golde
By the Lady Drury a fore parte of cloth of silv alon enbraudered wth a lace of golde
By the Lady Pawlet in golde
By the Lady Willoby & ffrauuc wth two pillowberes of camerik wrought allen wth carnatyon silk
By the Lady Griffin in golde
By the Lady Cromwell & he myed wyfe in golde
By the Lady Catlyn a vale of whitt worke wth spanglt and a small bone lace of silv a forte being of carnyscall silk wth a small bone lace of golde
By the Lady ffyngmerton a large bag to put a pillowe in of merie satten allen enbraudered wth golde shute silke of sundry coller wt nj tassells of grene silke and golde and a cusshon cloth of networke florisshed on wth flowers of golde silk and silke of sundry coller lynid with white satten
By the Lady Cromwell Lorde Cromwell wyfe nj sutes of ruffes of whitt cutworke edged wth a passamayne of white
By the Lady Wilsforde thre pece of lawne wrought wt white and florisshed wt golde
By the Lady Markey a case of sleabes of Oringe colo satten
By the Lady Crofte a pettcote of carnation satten enbraudered wt flewers of silk of sundry collors
By the Lady Bowche thre peces cutwork florisshed wt golde

By the Lady *Wilforde*, thre peces of lawne, wroughte with white and florisshed with golde.

Delivered to Mrs. *Skydmore*.

By the Lady *Marvey*, a paire of sleaves of oringe-colour satten.

Delivered to the forsaid *Rauf Hope*.

By the Lady *Crofts*, a peticote of carnation satten, enbrawderid with flowers of silke of sondry collours.

Delivered to the same *Rauf Hope*.

By the Lady *Souche*, thre peces of superior cut-worke, florisshd with golde.

Delivered to Mrs. *Skydmore*.

KNIGHTS.

By Sir *Frauncis Knowles*, Treasorour of our Householde, 3 angells	10	0	0
By Sir *James Crofts*, Comptrolor of the same, in di. sovereignes	10	0	0

Delivered to the forsaid *Henry Sackford*.

By Sir *Chrystopher Hatton*, Vice-chamberlen, a carkanet and a border of golde; the same carkanet contayning seven redd roses of golde, in every of them very smale diamondes, and in the topp a garnet and eight troches of meane pearles, four in every troche, and fourteen perles pendante, being lose; and the said border containing twenty-four redd roses of golde garnished with a very smale diamonde, in every of them a garnet and perle pendaunte, garnished with very small seed perle, and seven open pendants of golde; every one of them garnished with very small dyamondes, three meane perles, and thedges garnished with a very small seed perle.

Delivered to the Lady *Haward*.

By Sir *Frauncis Waulsingham*, Pryncipall Secretary, a night-gowne of tawney satten, allover enbraderid, faced with satten like heare collour.

Delivered to the forsaid *Rauf Hope*.

By Mr. *Thomas Wilson*, Esquire, also Secretary, a cup of agath, with a cover and garnisshment of golde enamuled, the same agath crased in dyvers places, per oz. 17 oz. qrt.

Delivered to Mr. *Asteley*, Mr. Threausorour of the Juells.

By Sir *Rauf Sadler*, Chauncellor of the Duchey	15	0	0
By Sir *Waulter Mildmay*, Chauncellor of the Exchequer, in angells	10	0	0
By Sir *William Cordell*, Master of the Rolles, in golde	10	0	0

Delivered to the forsaid *Henry Sackford*.

By Sir *Henry Sydney*, Lorde Deputie of Irelande, a feyer juell of golde, with a Dyana, fully garnisshed wythe dyamonds, one biggar than the rest, three rubyes, two pearles, and a pearle pendante; the backsyde a ship.

Delivered to the Lady *Hawarde*.

By Sir *William Damsell*, Recevor of the Courte of Wardes	10	0	0
By Sir *Owine Hopton*, Livetenant of the Tower	10	0	0

Delivered to the forsaid *Henry Sackford*.

By Sir *Thomas Hennaige*, Treasoror of the Chamber, a proper ringe of golde ennamulled in the top thereof, an white rubye without a foyle, with a grahounde in it.

By Sir *Edwarde Horsey*, Captayne of thile of Wight, a touthe picke of golde, the top beinge garnesshed with a faire emeraude, a dyamond, and ruby, and other smale dyamonds and rubies, with two perles pendaunt.

Delivered to the Lady *Hawarde*.

By Sir *Guilbarte Dethicke*, alias *Garter*, Principall Kinge at Armes, a booke at armes.

By Sir *Christopher Haydon*, in golde	10	0	0
By Sir *Henry Cromwell*, in golde	10	0	0

Delivered to the foresaid *Henry Sackford*.

...was samayne of white ◊

By the Lady Wilforde that perce of lawne wroughte w'th white and florisshed w'th golde ◊ &c to m'r Shdmore

By the Lady Markby a yarde of Sleaves of Crimes rolle Satten ◊ &c to the p'sons Ramp' Hope

By the Lady Crofte a petticte of Carnation' Satten enbrawdered w'th flowers of silk of sondry cellors ◊ &c to the same Ramp' Hope

By the Lady Sondes that perce cut worke florisshed w'th golde ◊ &c to m'r Shdmore

Knight

By S'r ffraunces Knowles Treasoror of the houssholde in Angells ◊ &c to the p'sons h' Sussex

By S'r James Croft Comptroler of the same in d' sove'raignes ◊ &c to the p'sons h' Sussex

By S'r Christopher Hatton v'ce chamberleyn a Carkett and a border for the hed of golde cont' xiij roses Resses of golde in euy of them very smale Dyamonde & in the top a garnet and vij Troches of mene perle iij in euy Troche & euy pearled pendaunte beinge lose &c &c to the Lady Hawarde

By S'r ffrance Wauls'm principall Secretary a night Cowne of Tawney Satten allow' enbradred fared w'th Satten like heare colle ◊ &c to the p'sons Ramp' Hope

By m'r Thom's Wilson Esquire also Secretary a Cup of Agath w'th a cou' and garnisshment of golde enamlled the same Agath raised in dyu'rs plac's vyz ◊ &c to m'r Asker W'ch Customer ...

By S'r Rauf Sadler chancello' of the Duchy ◊ &c

By S'r Wauter Mildmay Chaunceller of the Checquer in Angells ◊ &c to the p'sons h' Sussex

By S'r Will'm Cordell M'r of the Rolles in golde ◊ &c

By S'r Henry Sydney lorde de'putie of Ireland a feyre Juell of golde w't a Dyana is fully garnisshed wythe Dyamond &c ◊ &c to the Lady Hawarde

By S'r Will'm Damsell Rec'ver of the courte of wardes ◊ &c to the p'sons h' Sussex

By S'r Owine Hopton lieutenant of the Tower ◊ &c

By S'r Thomas Henneage Treasoror of the Chamber a proper Cupp of golde enamulled in the Top therof an white Antyke vont a feyle w'ch a grahornde in it ◊ &c to the Lady Hawarde

By S'r Edwarde Horsly Captayne of Thisle of wight a Tothe pike of golde the top beinge garnisshed w't a faier enbrawde a Dyamond & Ruby & other smale Dyamond and Rubis w'th ij pestes pendaunt ◊

By S'r Gillbarte Dethyk alias Garter princhpall kinge at Armes a booke at Armes ◊ &c

By S'r Christopher Haydon in golde ◊ &c to the p'sons h' Sussex

By S'r Henry Cromwell in golde ◊ &c to m'r Shdmore

By S'r Gawine Carowe a smok of camery w' wroughte w'th blake worke & edged w'th bone lace of golde ◊ &c

By S'r Thom's Gresshm in golde ◊ &c

By S'r John Thymne in golde ◊ &c to the p'sons h' Sussex

By S'r Henry Lee a Juell of golde beinge a faier Emrande cut & enamyld hartwyse ◊ &c to the La'y Hawarde

By S'r Willi Drury a yarde of mytteyn of blake vellet enbrawdered w'th Damaske golde and lyned w'th vnsheorne vellat carnation ◊ &c to m'r Elizabeth Knowll

By S'r Amyas Pawlet a peyre of Tisshue of Carnation golde & silu' cut & dam' perle .xxij. ◊ &c to the p'sons Ramp' Hope

By S'r Edwarde Clere in golde ◊ &c to the p'sons h' Sussex

Gentlewomen

By m'rs Blaunche Parry apeir of Braslett of Cornelion' golde two small perles betwyxt euy hed vout x' xxxti ◊ &c to the Lady Hawarde

By m'rs ffraunces Howarde two Iuells of Enghis clothe florisshed at the sides therof w'th golde thother w'th silu' w'th spangles ◊ &c to m'r Jane Dorssell

By m'rs Elizabethe Knowles a feyre Cup of blake vellat ga'd w' longe a Gelt of enamelled ◊ &c to the p'sons Ramp' Hope

By m'rs Edmund iij peces of net worke w'th frayges and thredy of golde ◊ &c to m'r Shdmore

By m'rs Shdmer aforesaide w' bodyes and Sleakes of Satten ytmyr' role w't lyned w'th murre Taphata w't'e ij Iares of golde and silu' and henged w'th like golde and silu' ◊ &c to the p'sons Ramp' Hope

By m'rs Snowe Syx hand kercheers faier wroughte and edged w'th nde yassemayne of golden ◊ &c to m'r Shdmore

By m'rs Barth'o a Iare of Russet silke and sede perle ◊ &c to m'rs Elizabeth Knowll

By m'rs Chaworth six hand kerchiues of Holland wroughte w'th blake worke and enyed w'th a smale bone Iare of golde and silu' and an Asse of golde enamlled ◊ &c one hand kercher to m'r m'rs Shdmore and the asse of like La' Sandes

By m'rs Weste a faire Scarse of grene Net worke florisshed w'th yold and silu' and edged at bothe end w'th a brode bone Iare and at the side w'th a narrow yassemane of gold and silu' and lyned w'th murre sortene to ◊ &c to m'rs Elizabeth Knowll

By m'rs Kathryn Newton a forpte of a kirtill of Tawney Satten enbrad'rd w'th yardes of golde and silu' lyned with white sercenet ◊ &c to the p'sons Ramp' Hope

By m'rs Markby Syx hand kerchers of camery'ke faier wroughte w'th blake silk edged w'a smale bone Iare of golde and silu' ◊ &c to m'r Shdmore

By m'rs D... iiij faire hand kerchers of camerike of blake frayge work edged w'a brode bone Iare of gold ◊

By m'rs Jane D... iij a partelet and Ruffe of lawne wrought w'th white worke w'a blake speris vey wt y'vij nethe benydes ◊ &c to m'r Jane Dorssell

By m'rs Townesend a chayne of Amber beade and monts of pearll ◊ &c to the La' Hawarde

By m'rs Cave two pillowberes of Holland wroughte w'th blake silk & edged w't a yassemane of blake silk ◊

By m'r Litchfelde a faire lokinge glasse set in a frame of purple Taphata allo' faire enbrawdered w'th sede perle and Damaske golde ◊ &c to m'r Shdmore

By m'rs Clark foure ayons of Sleaves of lawne wroughte w'th knitworke stryped w'th yolde and silu' and edged w'th a bone Iare of golde and silu' ◊

By m'rs Elizabeth Howarde a vale of networke florisshed w'th gold and frayngeth of gold & smale bone Iare of golde ◊ &c to m'rs Elizabeth Knowll

... w'th perles vey smale ◊ &c to the Lady Hawarde

By Sir *Gawine Carowe*, a smoke of cameryke, wrought with blake worke, and edged with bone lace of golde.

Delivered to Mrs. *Skydmore*.

By Sir *Thomas Gresham*, in golde	10	0	0
By Sir *John Thynne*, in golde	5	0	0

Delivered to the foresaid *Henry Sackford*.

By Sir *Henry Lee*, a juell of golde, being a faire emeraude, cut lozanged hartwise.

Delivered to the Lady *Hawarde*.

By Sir *William Drury*, a paire of myttows of blake vellet enbraudered with damaske golde, and lyned with unshorne vellat carnation.

Delivered to Mrs. *Elizabeth Knowlls*.

By Sir *Amyas Pawlet*, a pece of tyssue of carnation golde and siluer, cont' 18 yedrs qr.

Delivered to the foresaid *Rauf Hope*.

By Sir *Edwarde Clere*, in golde.

Delivered to the foresaid *Henry Sackford*.

GENTILWOMEN.

By Mrs. *Blanche Parry*, a peir of brasletts of Cornelion hedds two small perles betwixt every hed, gar' with golde.

Delivered to the Lady *Haward*.

By Mrs. *Fraunces Howarde*, two sute of ruffes of stitched clothe florisshed at the sides, thone withe golde, thother with siluer with spangles.

Delivered to Mrs. *Jane Bressills*.

By Mrs. *Elizabethe Knowles*, a fayre cap of black vellat, gar' ith longe agetts golde enamuled.

Delivered to the foresaid *Rauf Hope*.

By Mrs. *Edmonds*, three peces of networke with spangles and threds of golde.

Delivered to Mrs. *Skydmore*.

By Mrs. *Skydmore*, a foreparte with bodyes and sleaves of satten, ginger colour, cut, lyned with murre taphata, with two laces of golde and siluer, and frenged with like golde and siluer.

Delivered to the foresaid *Rauf Hope*.

By Mrs. *Snowe*, six handkercheues, faire wroughte and edged, with a passamayne of golde.

Delivered to Mrs. *Skydmore*.

By Mrs. *Bapteste*, a lace of russet silke and sede perle.

Delivered to Mrs. *Elizabeth Knowlls*.

By Mrs. *Chaworthe*, two handkerchives of Hollande, wroughte with blacke worke, and edged with a smale bone lace of golde and siluer; and an asse of golde enamuled.

The handekerchers with Mrs. *Skydmore*; and the asse with the Lady *Haward*.

By Mrs. *Weste*, a faire scarfe of grene networke florisshed with golde and siluer, and edged at bothe ends with a brode bone lace, and at the side with a narrowe passamane of golde and siluer, and lyned with murre serceonete.

Delivered to Mrs. *Elizabeth Knowlls*.

By Mrs. *Katherin Newton*, a forepart of a kirtill of tawny satten, enbroderid with gardes of golde and siluer, lyned with white sercenet.

Delivered to the foresaid *Rauf Hope*.

By Mrs. *Marbery*, six handekerchers of cameryke faire wrought with blacke silke, edged with a smale bone lace of golde and siluer.

By Mrs. *Digby*, six faire handkerchers of camerike of blake Spanish worke, edged with a brode bone lace of golde and siluer.

By Mrs Clark fownde a payre of Sleaves of lawne wrought wt blackworke striped wt golde and
silv and edged wt a bone lace of golde and silv

By Mrs Elizabeth Howarde a rale of Networke florysshed wt gold and fraynged of golde & smale bone   *By to Mrs Charleys knowll*
lace of golde

By Mrs Wingefeld nightegowne and a border of Bewgolde and fob: perles very smale   *By to the Lady Howard*

By Mrs Hermon a fayre Smok the Sleaves wrought wt blak silke and edged wt gold   *By to the Lady Chedmore*

By Mrs Tayler a Coife and a fforehed clothe of blak edged wt a smal bone lace of gold & fob of gold wt silke

By Mrs Twiste sixe Corkhandcheffes wrought wt blak silke and edged wt golde and a conte of   *By to Mr Chedmore and the clark By to Mr Saul Vaughan*

Three of lawne wrought wt spanisshe worke

By Mrs Nele sixe handcherchers of Camerike edged wt bone lace of gold and silv   *By to Mr Chedmore*

By Mrs Barley sixe handcherchers likewyse edged wt browne golde   *By to Mr Gant master*

By Mrs Mountayne a postell of fyne Camerike wrought wt flowers of blak silke   *By to Mr Blanne perry*

By Mrs Dane three yerds of Lawne

By Mrs Crokson a kyrchtrosse of white Sipers florysshed wt wt silv   *By to Mrs Chedmore*

By Mrs Huggynes my handcherchers fayre wrought wt spanisshe worke

By Mrs Anne Shelton sixe handcherchers edged wt black worke wt a passamayne of gold & silv

By Mrs Julio a dublet of Crymsen Satten cut & lacde wt a passamayne of silv   *By to the besaid knyght gent*

By Mrs Dale in Dublate and a forepte of clothe of gold garnysshed wt passamayne of golde

By Mrs Alley a fayre Carle of Damaske golde wrthe pippes and flowers garnysshed   *By to Mr Chedmore*
wt smale seade perle

Chaplyns   By derfeldeacon Carlisle in golde   *ii li*   *By to the forsaid knyght gent*

By Absolon Clerk of the closet abole ronked in a Prtose of Tysshu garnysshed wt Silver and guilte   *By ma by Mr Tonckford*

Gentilmen   By Mr Phillip Sydney a wast coate of white Sarstonet enybred and enbrawdered wt golde Silv and   *By to Mr Chedmore*
Silke of divs collors wt a passmane lace of golde and Silver rownde abought it

By Mr Lawnse Bowes a hat of Tawny Taphata enbrandered wt fcorpions of venne golde and a border   *By to the forsaid knyght gent*
garnysshed wt seden worke

By Mr John Harrynton a bole of Chrystall wt out arm yerd wt golde enamled about the mouth sployed   *ma of xii oz dj*   wt wt... *By lyghtly wt hys han...*

By Mr Edwarde Basse in golde   *x li*   *By of Sir Sir Pter*

By Mr Dyer a forepte of white Satten wt a brode garde of purple Satten enbrawdered wt   *By to the besaid knyght gent*
venne golde silv and fob perle unlyned

By Mr Stanhope a Dublate of Orynge tawnie Satten wt a brode passamayne of silv and
buttons of the same

By Mr ffowke Grevill a smale Juell wherme is a mother of perle garnysshed wt three smale dyamondes   *By to the La Hunnesden*
twe smale Enbits and my perles pendaunte

By Mr Smythe Constorll twe boxtle of Camerike   *By to Mr Blanne perry*

By Mr Benedicke Spenolle a forepte of white & tawnie Satten alenforte enbrandered wt golde   *the fopte p the fope the flanne...*
and silv and twe fannes of Strawe wrought wt silke of sondry colls   *wt wt Eliz knowll*

By Mr Welly a forke of agathe garnysshed wt golde   *By to the Lady Howarde*

By Mr Winefeld a play fayre Ante the lynke side and worke of mother of perle the cafe of crymsen   *mr ger mr the Esquill Smyth*
veluet enbrandered wt flowers the inside grene Veluet

By Mr Newby a raine of Salt wt a fountem ginger rolle enbrandered wt borders of gold & silv lyned wt white Sarstonet   *By to the forsaid La hope*

By Mrs Dort: Howwike twe rolls of Orynge flowers and donde Jenyfer

By Dort: wt twe lyke rolls

By Dort: Julie twe lyke rolls   *By to Mr Chedmore*

By John He minger way & pothian Gitternes presentid

By John Lyrke a nyothian & twoe of bores & a glasse of peare plomes

By Jo: Smyth fend also Taile Mr dote a fayre marshe pane wt a Castell in myddes

By John Dudley Saryeaunte of the pastry a fayre xxx wt Amyers   *By to Mr Chedmore*

By Willm Huggyns a forke yerbs paste bed of Stitonet enbrandered by smale Smite berryes   *By to Mrs Eliz Howarth*

By Mr Edwarde Stafforde twe bares of golde and silv   *By to the forsaid La hope*

By Mr Thomas Lawley Captayne of ye gamesen a forest of blak veluet wt bodyes of feathers wt
rened wt white Sarstonet felt wt longe aglytts of golde white enamelde

By Mark Anthony Vaisdell my tempse glasses   *By to Mrs Baptist*

By Ambrose Lupo a boy of lute stronge

By Petrucho a bote of Italien wt pyrtures of the lyfe & mrtem rhosses of God

By Charles Smyth a smale Juell benng a Sallamaunder a smale Enbte wt smale Dyamondes   *By to the La Howard*
and wt smale perles pendaunte   *By ma by Mr Lucost*

By Peter Wolfe a songe boke   *By to Mrs Baptist*

By Anthonias Dhenotro a smale boke in Italien meter

By Mr Henry Brenkr a peece of stitched clothe wrought in yelb worke   *ph yerk & By to La hope*

By Mr Willm Unssell a payre of gleaves garnysshed wt gold and silk worke   *By to Mr Eliz Howarth*

By Smythin Slete a Drail Kyrtomalla & cut of copper and gyulte   *By ma by Mr Lucost*

By Morys Watkins my larkes in a Cay   *By to Mrs Blanne perry*

Delivered to Mrs. *Skydmore*.

By Mrs. *Bissels*, a partelet and ruffs of lawne wrought with white worke, with a blake sipers upon yt, gar' wythe bewgles.

Delivered to Mrs. *Jane Brissetts*.

By Mrs. *Townesend*, a cheyne of ambey, jeate, and mouther of pearll.

Delivered to the Lady *Hawarde*.

By Mrs. *Cave*, two pillowberes of Hollande, wroughte with blacke silke, and edged with a passamane of blacke silke.

By Mrs. *Lichefelde*, a fare lokinge glasse set in a case of purple taphata, allou' fare enbrawdered with seade perle and damaske golde.

By Mrs. *Sackefourde*, a paire of sleaves of lawne wrought with knit worke, striped with golde and siluer, and edged wtih a bone lace of golde and siluer.

Delivered to Mrs. *Skydmore*.

By Mrs. *Elizabeth Howarde*, a vale of networke florisshed with gold and spangles of gold, and smale bone lace of golde.

Delivered to Mrs. *Elizabeth Knowlls*.

By Mrs. *Wingefeld*, a chaine and a border of bewegels and seed perles very smale.

Delivered to the Lady *Haward*.

By Mrs. *Hermon*, a faire smoke, the sleves wroughte with blake silke, and edged with gold.

By Mrs. *Taylor*, a coif and forehed clothe of blake, edged with a smale bone lace of gold, and roses of gold and silke.

Delivered to Mrs. *Skydmore*.

By Mrs. *Twiste*, six towthclothes wroughte with blake silke, and edged with golde; and a sute of ruffes of lawne, wroughte with Spanisshe worke.

The toth clothes delivered to Mrs. *Skydmore*; and the ruffes delivered to Mrs. *Jane Brissetts*.

By Mrs. *Note*, six handkerchers of camerike, edged with bone lace of gold and siluer.

By Mrs. *Barley*, six handekerchers, lykewyse edged with Venice golde.

Delivered to Mrs. *Skydmore*.

By Mrs. *Mountague*, a pertelet of fyne cameryke, wroughte with flowers of blake silke.

Delivered by Mrs. *Jane Bressett*.

By Mrs. *Dane*, thre peces of lawne.

Delivered to Mrs. *Blanche Parry*.

By Mrs. *Crokson*, a night coyf of white Cipers florisshed ouer with siluer.

By Mrs. *Huggaynes*, four handekerchers faire wroughte with Spanyshe worke.

By Mrs. *Amye Shelton*, sixe handkercheves edged with black worke with a passamaine of golde and siluer.

Delivered to Mrs. *Skydmore*.

By Mrs. *Julio*, a dublet of crymsen satten, cut and laide with a passamayne of siluer.

By Mrs. *Dale*, a dublate and foreparte of clothe of gold, garnisshed with a passamayne of golde.

Delivered to the forsaid *Rauf Hope*.

By Mrs. *Allen*, a fayre cawle of damaske golde, with pypes and flowers garnished with a smale seade perle.

Delivered to Mrs. *Skydmore*.

CHAPLYNS.

By Archedeacon *Carewe*, in golde £10.

Delivered to the forsaid *Henry Sackford*.

By Enych ap Elice a spall Norfomalls & cut off corper and ymilts ———————— to Iyena by Mr Surton

By Morys Walton vbay sarkes in a Cage ———————— to Mrs Blane[...] pany

Suma totalis of all the money given to hee Maiestie and delivered in man and forme above declared

iiij ml viiij xviij viij s

Elizabeth R

[marginalia annotations at right]

[faint annotations at bottom]

By *Absolyn*, Clerc of the Closet, a boke couered with cloth of tyssue, garnesshed with siluer and guilte. With her Majestie, by Mr. *Sackford*.

GENTILMEN.

By Mr. *Philip Sydney*, a wastcoate of white sarceonet, quylted and enbrawdred with golde, siluer, and silke of diuers collors, with a pasmane lace of golde and siluer rownde aboughte it.
Delivered to Mrs. *Skydmore*.

By Mr. *Rauffe Bowes*, a hat of tawny taphata, enbrauderid with scorpions of Venice golde, and a border garnisshed with sede perle.
Delivered to the forsaid *Rauf Hope*.

By Mr. *John Harington*, a bole of christall without a couer, grasd, garnisshed with gold enamuled about the mouth and fote, per oz. 4 oz. 3 qr. di.
With Mr. *Asteley*, Master of the Juells.

By Mr. *Edward Basshe*, in golde £10.
Delivered to *Henry Sackford*.

By Mr. *Dyer*, a foreparte of white satten, with a brode garde of purple satten, enbraudered withe Venice golde, silluer, and sede perle, unlyned.

By Mr. *Stanhope*, a dublate of oringe tawnie satten with a brode passamayne of siluer and buttons of the same.
Delivered to the foresaid *Rauf Hope*.

By Mr. *Foulke Grevill*, a smale juell, being a lambe of mother-of-perle, garnished with two smale dyamonds, two smale rubies, and three perles pendante.
Delivered to the Lady *Hawarde*.

By Mr. *Smythe Coustom'*, two boults of camerycke.
Delivered to Mrs. *Blanch Pary*.

By Mr. *Beinedicke Spenolle*, a foreparte of white and tawnie satten, al ouer faire, enbrauderid with golde and siluer; and two fannes of strawe, wrought with silke of sondry collours.
The foreparte with *Rauf Hope*; the fannes with Mrs. *Elizabeth Knowll*.

By Mr. *Wolly*, a forke of agathe garnisshed with golde.
Delivered to the Lady *Hawarde*.

By Mr. *Lychfeld*, a very fayre lute, the backeside and necke of mother-of-perle, the case of crymsen vellat, enbrawedered with flowers, and the inside grene vellate.
With her Majestie, by *Charles Smyth*.

By Mr. *Newton*, a paire of sleves of satten, ginger collour, enbrauderid with borders of gold and siluer, lined with white sarceonet.
Delivered to the foresaid *Rauf Hope*.

By Mr. Doctor *Hewicke*, two potts of oringe flowers, and cande jenger.

By Doctor *Mr.* two lyke potts.

By Doctor *Julio*, two lyke potts.

By *John Hemnigeway*, Apotticary, sittornes preservid.

By *John Ryche*, Apotticary, abrycos two boxes, and two glasses of peare pomes.
Delivered to Mrs. *Skydmore*.

By *John Smythesone*, alias *Taylor*, Master Cooke, a fayre march pane with a cattell in myddes.

By *John Dudley*, Sargeaunte of the Pastry, a fayre pye of quynces.

By *William Huggans*, a fere grete bad of sarceonet, enbraudered, sixteen smale swete bagges.
Delivered to Mrs. *Skydmore*.

By Mr. *Edwarde Stafforde*, two laces of golde and siluer.
Delivered to Mrs. *Elizabeth Knowlls*.

By Mr. *Thomas Layton*, Captayne of Garnesey, a gowne of blacke vellat, with bodyes and sleaves cut, lyned with white sarceonet, and sett with longe agletts of golde white enamuled.

Delivered to the forsaid *Rauf Hope*.

By *Marke Anthony Gaiardell*, four Venyse glasses.

By *Ambrose Lupo*, a box of lute-strynge.

By *Petricho*, a boke of Italian, with pictures of the lyfe and metomerpheses of Oved.

Delivered to Mr. *Baptest*.

By *Charles Smythe*, a small juell, being a salamaunder, a smale ruby, two smale dyamonds, and three smale perles pendaunte.

Delivered to the Lady *Haward*.

By *Peter Wolfe*, five songe books.

With her Majestie, by Mr. *Knevet*.

By *Anthonias Phenotus*, a smale booke in Italian meter.

Delivered to Mr. *Baptest*.

By Mr. *Henry Bronker*, a pese of stitched clothe wrought with gold cont' fifteen yerds di.

Delivered to *Rauf Hope*.

By Mr. *William Russell*, a paire of gloves, garnished with gold and sede perle.

Delivered to Mrs. *Elizabeth Knowlls*.

By *Guylham Sketh*, a dyall noctornalla, di. onc' of copper, and guylte.

With her Majestie, by Mrs. *Knevet*.

By *Morrys Watkins*, eighteen larkes in a cage.

Delivered to Mrs. *Blanch Parry*.

Summa totalis of all the money giuen to her Maiestie, and deliuered in man' and fourme aboue declared   497   13   4

FATHER'S OBJECTIONS

—

CHARLES DARWIN
1831

In August 1831, having recently graduated from Cambridge and soon to become a clergyman, 22-year-old Charles Darwin was invited on a two-year expedition to South America aboard the HMS *Beagle*, in the role of Captain's Companion. That voyage became the most important of his life, for it was there, while studying fossils and wildlife along the coastline, that he truly became a scientist; and it was on his return that his ground-breaking book on evolution, *On the Origin of Species*, was born. Before he could even set foot on the boat, however, his father supplied him with a list of objections to the trip. Seen here are those objections written in Darwin's hand in a letter to his Uncle Josiah, who went on to talk his brother around.

(1) Disreputable to my character as a Clergyman hereafter

(2) A wild scheme

(3) That they must have offered to many others before me, the place of Naturalist

(4) And from its not being accepted there must be some serious objection to the vessel or expedition

(5) That I should never settle down to a steady life hereafter

(6) That my accommodations would be most uncomfortable

(7) That you should consider it as again changing my profession

(8) That it would be a useless undertaking

(1) Dis reputable to my character as a Clergyman hereafter

(2) A wild scheme

(3) That they must have offered to many others before me, the place of Naturalist

(4) And from its not being accepted there must be some serious objection to the vessel or expedition

(5) That I should never settle down to a steady life hereafter

(6) That my accomodations would be most uncomfortable

(7) That you should consider it as again changing my profession

(8) That it would be a useless undertaking

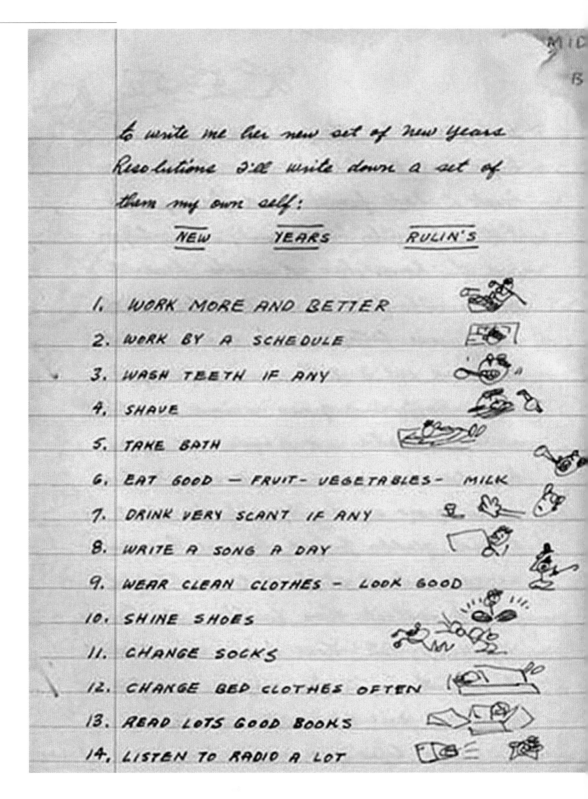

to write me her new set of new years
Resolutions I'll write down a set of
them my own self:

NEW   YEARS   RULIN'S

1. WORK MORE AND BETTER
2. WORK BY A SCHEDULE
3. WASH TEETH IF ANY
4. SHAVE
5. TAKE BATH
6. EAT GOOD — FRUIT- VEGETABLES- MILK
7. DRINK VERY SCANT IF ANY
8. WRITE A SONG A DAY
9. WEAR CLEAN CLOTHES — LOOK GOOD
10. SHINE SHOES
11. CHANGE SOCKS
12. CHANGE BED CLOTHES OFTEN
13. READ LOTS GOOD BOOKS
14. LISTEN TO RADIO A LOT

NEW YEAR'S RULIN'S
—
WOODY GUTHRIE
1941

Woody Guthrie was an iconic American folk singer responsible for recording more than 400 songs during his all too brief career, the most notable being the hugely famous "This Land Is Your Land" in 1944. A couple of years before unveiling that one to the public, with 1943 soon to begin, Guthrie wrote and illustrated this impossibly charming list of New Year's "Rulin's" in his journal.

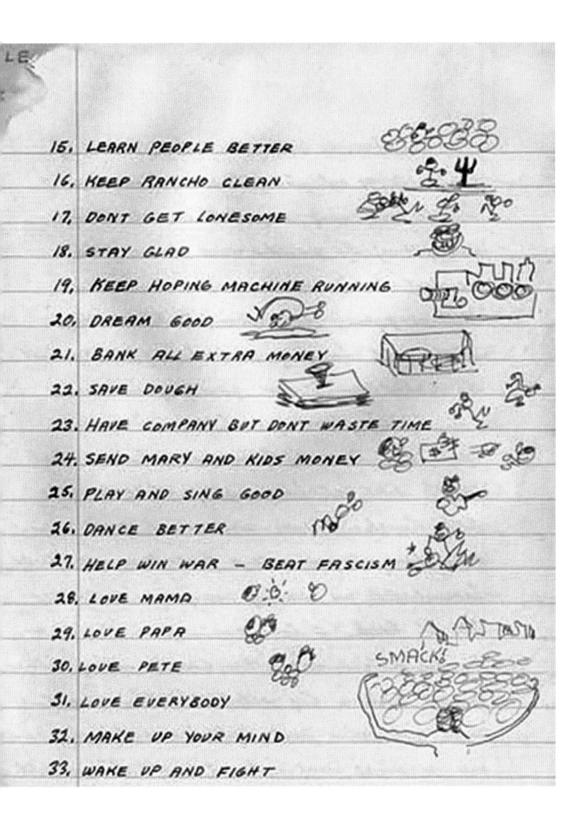

15. LEARN PEOPLE BETTER

16. KEEP RANCHO CLEAN

17. DON'T GET LONESOME

18. STAY GLAD

19. KEEP HOPING MACHINE RUNNING

20. DREAM GOOD

21. BANK ALL EXTRA MONEY

22. SAVE DOUGH

23. HAVE COMPANY BUT DON'T WASTE TIME

24. SEND MARY AND KIDS MONEY

25. PLAY AND SING GOOD

26. DANCE BETTER

27. HELP WIN WAR — BEAT FASCISM

28. LOVE MAMA

29. LOVE PAPA

30. LOVE PETE

31. LOVE EVERYBODY

32. MAKE UP YOUR MIND

33. WAKE UP AND FIGHT

SMACK!

MUST MAKE EFFORT TO DO

—

MARILYN MONROE
Late 1955

As 1955 came to a close, Marilyn Monroe wrote this motivational set of New Year's Resolutions in one of her address books – a list that, if followed, would hopefully lead to another 12 months as successful as the last. Monroe was 29 years old at the time and had already filmed an impressive number of movies, including *The Seven Year Itch*, released that year, and just recently had been accepted as a student at Lee Strasberg's renowned Actors Studio. Judging by the list, she was determined to make the most of her opportunities.

Must make effort to do

Must have the discipline to do the following–

z – go to class–my own <u>always</u>–without fail

x – go as often as possible to observe Strasberg's other private classes

g – <u>never</u> miss my actors studio sessions

v – <u>work</u> whenever possible–on class assignments–and <u>always keep working on the acting exercises</u>.

u – start attending Clurman lectures–also Lee Strasberg's directors' lectures at theater wing–enquire about both

l – keep looking around me–only much more so–<u>observing</u>–but not only myself but others and everything–take things (it) for what they (it's) are worth.

y – must make strong effort to work on current problems and phobias that out of my past has arisen–making much much much more more more more more effort in my analysis. And be there <u>always</u> on time–no excuses for being <u>ever</u> late.

w – if possible take at least one class at university–in literature–

o – follow RCA thing through.

p – try to find someone to take dancing from–body work (creative)

t – take care of my instrument–personally & bodily (exercise)

try to enjoy myself when I can–I'll be miserable enough as it is.

RULES OF PALSHIP

—

NOËL COWARD
August 1915

In August 1915, at just 16 years of age and in an effort to minimise arguments in what was an incredibly close and sometimes turbulent friendship, future playwright Noël Coward and his best friend, the actress Esmé Wynne, drew up an endearing list of 16 "Rules of Palship", to be signed and followed by both parties. The list proved successful; the pair remained friends for some years.

RULES OF PALSHIP BETWEEN ESMÉ WYNNE AND NOËL COWARD

(1). We must not tease each other and if we begin we must stop directly we are asked.

(2). We must take it in turns to go and see one another and if one goes twice running to the other's house, the other must do the same afterwards.

(3). We must *never* split on one another even if the PALSHIP is dissolved and we must hold all confidences sacred.

(4). We must share all profits in any transaction made together, however slight the help of the other may be. Profits are excluded from any expenses incurred during the said transaction.

(5). In case of serious quarrel a week or a fortnight may be taken to think things over before abolishing the PALSHIP.

(6). If one hits the other either in anger or fun, he must allow the other to hit back. Any other offence must be paid for.

(7). We must stick up for each other against anyone or anything, and stand by each other in all danger.

(8). We must tell each other all secrets concerned with ourselves, others confidences may be held sacred even from one another.

(9). We must not talk RELIGION unless it is enevitable.

(10). When writing to mutual friends we must tell each other, we must also tell each other what we have said in the letter.

(11). We must swear by "HONOUR AS A PAL" and hold it THE most sacred of bonds in the world.

(12). We must tell each other what we think about the other's appearance or behaviour.

(13). We must go straight to one another in case of mischief being made and believe NOTHING unless it comes from the other's own lips.

(14). NO ONE not even our Parents may keep us from one another.

(15). If any other rules are formed or thought of they must be added (with the consent of both) at the end of this document.

(16). NO OTHER PERSON may be admitted into our PALSHIP or SECRETS.

SIGNATURE OF BOTH

(Signed)

Dated August the 11th 1915.

A LITTLE BILL OF FARE

—

MARK TWAIN
1870s

As he journeyed around Europe in the late 1870s writing his travelogue, *A Tramp Abroad*, American author Mark Twain grew increasingly tired of an abundance of what he described as "fair-to-middling" food. He explained:

"The number of dishes is sufficient; but then it is such a monotonous variety of unstriking dishes [...] Three or four months of this weary sameness will kill the robustest appetite."

As the end of his trip neared, Twain began to prepare for his return to the US by compiling the following – an enormous list of the foods he had longed for the most, all of which were to be prepared and consumed when he arrived home.

It has now been many months, at the present writing, since I have had a nourishing meal, but I shall soon have one—a modest, private affair, all to myself. I have selected a few dishes, and made out a little bill of fare, which will go home in the steamer that precedes me, and be hot when I arrive—as follows:

Radishes. Baked apples, with cream

Fried oysters; stewed oysters. Frogs.

American coffee, with real cream.

American butter.

Fried chicken, Southern style.

Porter-house steak.

Saratoga potatoes.

Broiled chicken, American style.

Hot biscuits, Southern style.

Hot wheat-bread, Southern style.

Hot buckwheat cakes.

American toast. Clear maple syrup.

Virginia bacon, broiled.

Blue points, on the half shell.

Cherry-stone clams.

San Francisco mussels, steamed.

Oyster soup. Clam Soup.

Philadelphia Terapin soup.

Oysters roasted in shell, Northern style.

Soft-shell crabs. Connecticut shad.

Baltimore perch.

Brook trout, from Sierra Nevadas.

Lake trout, from Tahoe.

Sheep-head and croakers, from New Orleans.

Black bass from the Mississippi.

American roast beef.

Roast turkey, Thanksgiving style.

Cranberry sauce. Celery.

✓ Radishes.
Baked apples, ~~iced~~, with cream.
Fried oysters; stewed oysters. Frogs.

American coffee, with real cream.

American butter, ~~fresh & sweet~~.
Fried chicken, southern style.
Porter-house steak, ~~with mushrooms~~.

Saratoga potatoes.
Broiled chicken, American style.
Hot biscuits Southern style. ✶
Hot wheat-bread, Southern style. Hot light rolls.
Hot buckwheat cakes.
American ~~breakfast~~ toast.
Clear maple syrup.
Virginia bacon, broiled.

~~Oysters~~

Blue-points, on the half shell.

Cherry-stone clams.
San Francisco Mussels, ~~~~ steamed.
Oyster soup. Clam soup.
~~Shelled~~ Oysters roasted in the shell — northern style. ✶
Philadelphia Terrapin soup.
Soft-shell ~~crabs~~.
(Connecticut shad.

Baltimore perch.

Brook trout, from Sierra Meadows.

Lake trout, from Tahoe.

Sheep-head & croakers, from
New Orleans.

Black bass from the Mississippi.

Roast wild turkey. Woodcock.

Canvas-back-duck, from Baltimore.

Prairie liens, from Illinois.

Missouri partridges, broiled.

'Possum. Coon.

Boston bacon and beans.

Bacon and greens, Southern style.

Hominy. Boiled onions. Turnips.

Pumpkin. Squash. Asparagus.

Butter beans. Sweet potatoes.

Lettuce. Succotash. String beans.

Mashed potatoes. Catsup.

Boiled potatoes, in their skins.

New potatoes, minus the skins.

Early rose potatoes, roasted in the ashes, Southern style, served hot.

Sliced tomatoes, with sugar or vinegar. Stewed tomatoes.

Green corn, cut from the ear and served with butter and pepper.

Green corn, on the ear.

Hot corn-pone, with chitlings, Southern style.

Hot hoe-cake, Southern style.

Hot egg-bread, Southern style.

Hot light-bread, Southern style.

Buttermilk. Iced sweet milk.

Apple dumplings, with real cream.

Apple pie. Apple fritters.

Apple puffs, Southern style.

Peach cobbler, Southern style

Peach pie. American mince pie.

Pumpkin pie. Squash pie.

All sorts of American pastry.

Fresh American fruits of all sorts, including strawberries which are not to be doled out as if they were jewelry, but in a more liberal way.
Ice-water—not prepared in the ineffectual goblet, but in the sincere and capable refrigerator.

NEWTON'S SINS

—

SIR ISAAC NEWTON
1662

Sir Isaac Newton is undoubtedly one of the most influential scientists in human history. In 1668, he built the world's first successful reflecting telescope; then, in 1687, he published *Philosophiæ Naturalis Principia Mathematica*, a hugely important book in which he laid out the laws of motion and universal gravitation. In 1964, 300 years after he made his mark on the world, a page in one of his notebooks, penned cryptically in 1662, was finally decoded; on it, addressed to God, was a list of sins 19-year-old Newton had committed.

Before Whitsunday 1662.

1. Using the word (God) openly
2. Eating an apple at Thy house
3. Making a feather while on Thy day
4. Denying that I made it.
5. Making a mousetrap on Thy day
6. Contriving of the chimes on Thy day
7. Squirting water on Thy day
8. Making pies on Sunday night
9. Swimming in a kimnel on Thy day
10. Putting a pin in Iohn Keys hat on Thy day to pick him.
11. Carelessly hearing and committing many sermons
12. Refusing to go to the close at my mothers command.
13. Threatning my father and mother Smith to burne them and the house over them
14. Wishing death and hoping it to some
15. Striking many
16. Having uncleane thoughts words and actions and dreamese.
17. Stealing cherry cobs from Eduard Storer
18. Denying that I did so
19. Denying a crossbow to my mother and grandmother though I knew of it
20. Setting my heart on money learning pleasure more than Thee
21. A relapse
22. A relapse
23. A breaking again of my covenant renued in the Lords Supper.
24. Punching my sister
25. Robbing my mothers box of plums and sugar
26. Calling Derothy Rose a jade
27. Glutiny in my sickness.
28. Peevishness with my mother.
29. With my sister.
30. Falling out with the servants
31. Divers commissions of alle my duties
32. Idle discourse on Thy day and at other times
33. Not turning nearer to Thee for my affections
34. Not living according to my belief
35. Not loving Thee for Thy self.
36. Not loving Thee for Thy goodness to us
37. Not desiring Thy ordinances
38. Not long for Thee in [illegible]
39. Fearing man above Thee
40. Using unlawful means to bring us out of distresses
41. Caring for worldly things more than God
42. Not craving a blessing from God on our honest endeavors.
43. Missing chapel.
44. Beating Arthur Storer.

45. Peevishness at Master Clarks for a piece of bread and butter.
46. Striving to cheat with a brass halfe crowne.
47. Twisting a cord on Sunday morning
48. Reading the history of the Cn champions on Sunday

Since Whitsunday 1662

1. Glutony
2. Glutony
3. Using Wilfords towel to spare my own
4. Negligence at the chapel.
5. Sermons at Saint Marys (4)
6. Lying about a louse
7. Denying my chamberfellow of the knowledge of him that took him for a [illegible] sot.
8. Neglecting [illegible] to pray 3
9. Helping Pettit to make his water watch at 12 of the clock on Saturday night

THE PILLOW BOOK

—

SEI SHŌNAGON
Circa 996

Born circa 966, Sei Shōnagon was a Japanese court lady responsible for writing *The Pillow Book*, a truly wonderful collection of hundreds of observational notes that paint a vivid, amusing and often touching picture of life in 11th-century Japan. Much of the book is written in list form, with headings such as "Pleasing things", "Infuriating things", "Things it's frustrating and embarrassing to witness", and those seen here.

Rare Things

A son-in-law who's praised by his wife's father. Likewise, a wife who's loved by her mother-in-law.

A pair of silver tweezers that can actually pull out hairs properly.

A retainer who doesn't speak ill of his master.

A person who is without a single quirk. Someone who's superior in both appearance and character, and who's remained utterly blameless throughout his long dealings with the world.

You never find an instance of two people living together who continue to be overawed by each other's excellence and always treat each other with scrupulous care and respect, so such a relationship is obviously a great rarity.

Copying out a tale or a volume of poems without smearing any ink on the book you're copying from. If you're copying it from some beautiful bound book, you try to take immense care, but somehow you always manage to get ink on it.

Two women, let alone a man and a woman, who vow themselves to each other forever, and actually manage to remain on good terms to the end.

Things that should be small

Thread for sewing something in a hurry. The hair of women in the lower classes. The voice of someone's daughter. Lampstands.

Things now useless that recall a glorious past

A fine embroidery-edged mat that's become threadbare.

A screen painted in the Chinese style, that's now turned dark and discoloured and developed a scarred surface.

A painter with poor eyesight.

A switch of false hair seven or eight feet long, that's now fading and taking on a reddish tinge.

Grape-coloured fabric when the ash dye has turned.

A man who was a great lover in his day but is now old and decrepit.

A tasteful house whose garden trees have been destroyed by fire. The pond is still there, but it's now uncared for and thick with pond weed.

Repulsive things

The back of a piece of sewing. Hairless baby mice tumbled out of their nest. The seams of a leather robe before the lining's been added. The inside of a cat's ear. A rather dirty place in darkness.

夏は夜。

月のころはさらなり。

やみもなほ、蛍の多く飛びちがひたる。

また、ただ一つ二つなど、ほのかにうち光りて行くもをかし。

雨など降るもをかし。

ELOQUENT SILENCE

—

WALT WHITMAN
1865

In 1865, as the world reeled following the assassination of Abraham Lincoln, *Leaves of Grass* poet Walt Whitman began work on an elegy to mark the death of the US President, a man for whom Whitman held great admiration. As he prepared to write the mourning poem that would eventually be known as *When Lilacs Last in the Dooryard Bloom'd*, Whitman brainstormed by drawing up a list of words related to such loss.

sorrow (saxon)
grieve
sad
mourn (sax)
    "   ing
    "   ful
melancholy
dismal
heavy-hearted
tears
black
sobs -ing
sighing
funeral rites
wailing
lamenting
mute grief
eloquent silence
bewail
bemoan
deplore
regret deeply
loud lament
pitiful
loud weeping
violent lamentation

anguish
wept sore
depression
pain of mind
passionate regret
afflicted with grief
cast down
downcast
gloomy
serious
sympathy
moving compassion
tenderness
tender-hearted
full of pity
obscurity
partial or total darkness
(as the gloom of a forest – gloom of midnight)
cloudy
cloudiness
    "   of mind
mind sunk in gloom
soul   "   "   "

dejection
dejected

sorrow (excess)
grieve
sad
mourn (2 usc)
    " ing
    " ful
melancholy
dismal
heavy-hearted
tears
black
sobs - ing
sighs
funeral rites
wailing
lamenting
mute grief
eloquent silence
bewail
bemoan
deplore
regret deeply
loud lament
pitiful
loud weeping
violent lamentation

anguish
wept sore
depression
pain of mind
passionate regret
afflicted with grief
cast down
downcast
gloomy
serious
sympathy
more compassion
tenderness
tender hearted
full of pity
obscurity
partial } darkness
or total }
(as the gloom of a
    forest — gloom
    of midnight)
cloudy
cloudiness
    "   of mind
mind sunk in gloom
soul   "   "   "
Dejection
dejected

[shades?] of night
heavy
dull – sombre
sombre shades
    "   ness
affliction
oppress – oppressiove
    "   ion
prostration
humble – humility
suffering – silent suffering
burdensome
Distress – distressing
Calamity
Extreme anguish (either of mind or
body)
Misery
torture
harrassed
weighed down
trouble
deep affliction
plaintive
Calamity
disaster
something that strikes down – ~~as by~~
~~Almighty~~

shades of night
heavy
dull — sombre
sombre shades
" ness
affliction
oppress — oppressive
          "   ion
prostration
humble — humility
suffering — silent suffering
burdensome
Distress — distressing
Calamity
Extreme anguish, (either of
                    mind or body)
Misery
torture   Calamity
harrassed   Disaster
weighed down   somethy that strikes
trouble.   down — as by
deep affliction   Almighty
plaintive

ADVICE TO YOUNG LADIES

—

THE LADIES' POCKET MAGAZINE
1830

Established in 1824 *The Ladies' Pocket Magazine* was one of few publications to cater for women of the Georgian era and was filled with stories, readers' letters, etiquette guides and fashion. In the first issue of 1830, sandwiched between a piece called "Effects of Beauty" and another titled "The Ladies' Toilet", was printed this list of "Advice to young ladies".

ADVICE TO YOUNG LADIES.

If you have blue eyes, you need not languish.

If black eyes, you need not leer.

If you have pretty feet, there is no occasion to wear short petticoats.

If you are doubtful as to that point, there can be no harm in letting them be long.

If you have good teeth, do not laugh for the purpose of shewing them.

If you have bad ones, do not laugh less than the occasion may justify.

If you have pretty hands and arms, there can be no objection to your playing on the harp, if you play well.

If they are disposed to be clumsy, work tapestry.

If you have a bad voice, rather speak in a low tone.

If you dance well, dance but seldom.

If you dance ill, never dance at all.

If you sing well, make no previous excuses.

If you sing indifferently, hesitate not a moment when you are asked, for few people are judges of singing, but every one is sensible of a desire to please.

If you would preserve beauty, rise early.

If you would preserve esteem, be gentle.

If you would obtain power, be condescending.

If you would live happily, endeavour to promote the happiness of others.

THE LADIES' POCKET MAGAZINE
1824

TEN FAVORITE AMERICAN NOVELS

—

NORMAN MAILER
1988

In January 1988, Pulitzer Prize-winning American author Norman Mailer was asked by editors of the *Reader's Catalogue* – a curated directory of 75,000 novels that you might find in a local bookshop, all of which could be delivered to one's door – to choose ten of his favourite novels for inclusion in the next edition. He responded with this list, saying,

"With the exception of Huckleberry Finn, *which I reread recently, the other nine books were devoured in my freshman year at Harvard, and gave me the desire, which has never gone completely away, to be a writer, an American writer."*

Ten Favorite American Novels

U.S.A. John Dos Passos

Huckleberry Finn Mark Twain

Studs Lonigan James T. Farrell

Look Homeward, Angel Thomas Wolfe

The Grapes of Wrath John Steinbeck

The Great Gatsby F. Scott Fitzgerald

The Sun Also Rises Ernest Hemingway

Appointment in Samarra John O'Hara

The Postman Always Rings Twice James M. Cain

Moby-Dick Herman Melville

LIST

Of the sporting LADIES who is arrived from all the principal Towns in Great Britain and Ireland, to take their Pleasure at Leith Races, on Monday the 3d of June 1776.

COme sporting Ladies now approach,
Those cannot walk must hire a coach
On Monday to Leith sands repair,
Where you may breath the wholesome air,
Let there be seen your pretty faces,
And chuse your riders at the races.
So many has from all airths come
This year, I wish you all get room;
A hundred is already booked,
This year the sands are overstocked.
You'll own Ladies 'tis but right,
To tell of all that clean and tight,
For sure you ill deserve your hire,
When you your riders set on fire.
we will describe as far's we're able,
and tell their names who keep clean stables
At back of Bess wynd we'll begin,
And tell their names that stay within,
There's first the Flowers of forrest fair
There's few with her that can compare,
For handsome shape and temper free,
And honest to the last degree.
Her maiden name is Miss Clerk,
who deals with her is at no loss.
There's pretty miss Maxwell & miss Jean,
Two handsome ladies neat and clean,
miss Stevenson, miss Peggy Bruce,
Are all too good for common use,
there's witty Sally Buchan too,
Each one of those above will do,

Next lucky G——e in Miln's square,
For your own sake beware of her,
For such a dirty set she keeps,
Few clean within her house she keeps.
The commonest that walks the street,
She'll make them serve for little meat,
And when they cold and hunger feel,
what can the poor things do but steal.

But we'll proceed to tell more names,
Of several ladies of the game,
A squad last night arriv'd in town,
Some of them black some of them brown,
It was in the evening pretty late,
And lodging being ill to get,
Unto a lady they apply'd,
Immediately she them supply'd.

The one was Kate from Inverness,
with rosy cheeks and neat plain dress.
So black her eyes and white her skin,
She wou'd almost tempt a priest to sin
In Anchor close please call upon her,
I hope the girl will act with honour.

There's Sally, Mary, Bet, and Jean,
Are all arriv'd from Berdeen,
Expects their Chance among the rest,
But yet I dont admire their taste,
Their lodging mean few will incline,
to call at foot of Niddery's wynd. viz.

Next Jenny Simpson from Montrose,
as fresh as buxome as a rose,
Her een like stars or diamonds bright,
wou'd light to your bed at night.
as sweet a nymph as treads the ground,
Into Gray's Close she may be found.

Next pretty Betty from Dundee,
Jean Sim, Peg Peery all the three,
Begg'd to be listed 'mong the core,
Declares they never rode before,
who please to see them on them call,
opposite the Lawn-market well.

Joan, and Rachel, both from Perth,
From whom I dread you may get skaith,
therefore from them you'd best keep back
Least afterwards you little crack,
that you with them had ought to do,
they are not fit at all for you.
and cause I fear of your after grudging,
I will not tell you of their lodging.

there's Katie Broun a chatering Parrat,
whose tap's as red as any carrot,
Is latety from Dunfermline come,
and with Bess Jackson ta'n a room,
they both this spring's been at the grazing
their dress and looks are both amazing,
that pleaded they might be reported,
their room as yet was not reforted,
In Castle wynd they're to be found,
and will be seen on the race grounp.

N. B. As there will be published a new List every day during the Races, Ladies who incline to be booked, will loose no time in giving in their Names.

LIST OF THE SPORTING LADIES

—

AUTHOR UNKNOWN
1776

Prostitution was rampant in 18th-century Great Britain and an accepted activity by most – so much so, in fact, that local guides were often printed in an effort to promote (and sometimes warn against, as you will soon see) various ladies working in each area. This particular example was written in 1776 in Scotland and lists, in verse, those women who were available on the day of an incredibly popular horse racing event in Leith on the 3rd June. As noted at the foot of this anonymously authored list, new editions were circulated every day.

Rodney

Roddy

Roderick

(Rudolph)

Rudy

→ Rollo

Roland

Reggy

(Reginald) ✓

Romeo

1.65
.10
1.05

1.75   3.30
5
2.30   1.65

2.30
1.65
3.95

Thirty-five-year-old Robert May was working as an advertising copywriter for a department store when, in early 1939, his boss tasked him with writing a "cheery" book to give to the store's customers that year. The one he came up with months later was *Rudolph the Red-Nosed Reindeer*. It was subsequently handed out, for free, to 2.5 million shoppers in the alone. Luckily for May, his boss tran rights to him in 1946. The list seen a snapshot of what could have been list of names being considered for th penned in May's hand. Early favou Rollo, Reginald and the eventual winn

LEONDARDO'S TO-DO LIST

—

LEONARDO DA VINCI
1510

Leonardo da Vinci remains one of history's most recognisable polymaths – a genius who excelled as a sculptor, painter, engineer, inventor, musician, mathematician, cartographer, writer, architect, scientist and geologist. He was also an expert anatomist, and in approximately 1510 he travelled to the University of Pavia's medical school to dissect and then draw some corpses. Sometime before he left, on a page of his notebook thick with notes and sketches of the brain, nerves and veins, Leonardo wrote a list, both of things to do and take.

Have Avicenna translated. 'On the Utilities'.

Spectacles with case, firestick, fork, bistoury, charcoal, boards, sheets of paper, chalk, white, wax, forceps, pane of glass, fine-tooth bone saw, scalpel, inkhorn, pen-knife. Zerbi, and Angnolo Benedetti. Get hold of a skull. Nutmeg.

Observe the holes in the substance of the brain, where there are more or less of them.

Describe the tongue of the woodpecker and the jaw of a crocodile.

Give the measurement of the dead using his finger.

The book 'On Mechanical Science' precedes that 'On the Utilities'. Get your books on anatomy bound. Boots, stockings, comb, towel, shirts, shoe-laces, shoes, pen-knife, pens, a skin for the chest, gloves, wrapping paper, charcoal.

Mental matters that have not passed through the *senso comune* are vain and they beget nothing but the prejudiced truth. And because such discourses arise from poverty of wit, such reasoners are always poor, and if they are born rich they will die poor in old age because it seems that Nature revenges herself on those who want to work miracles, so that they have less than quieter men. And those who want to grow rich in a day live for a long time in great poverty, as happens, and will happen to eternity – the alchemists, searchers after the creation of gold and silver, and those engineers who want dead water to give itself moving life with perpetual motion, and the supreme fool, the necromancer and enchanter.

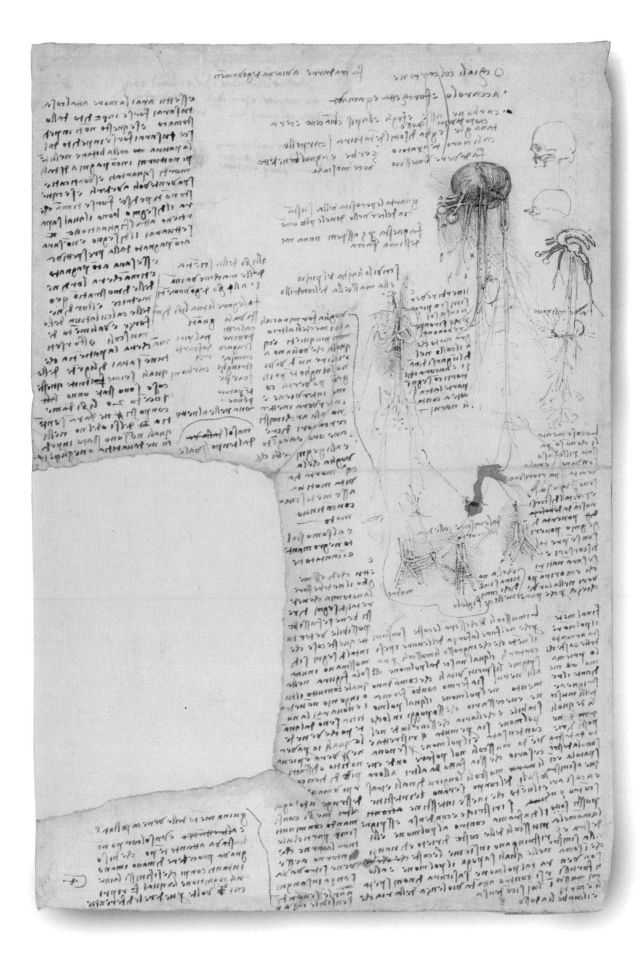

How My Life Has Changed
Hilary North

I can no longer flirt with Lou.
I can no longer dance with Mayra.
I can no longer eat brownies with Suzanne Y.
I can no longer meet the deadline with Mark.
I can no longer talk to George about his daughter.
I can no longer drink coffee with Rich.
I can no longer make a good impression on Chris.
I can no longer smile at Paul.
I can no longer hold the door open for Tony.
I can no longer confide in Lisa.
I can no longer complain about Gary.
I can no longer work on a project with Donna R.
I can no longer get to know Yolanda.
I can no longer call the client with Nick.
I can no longer contribute to the book drive organized by Karen.
I can no longer hang out with Millie.
I can no longer give career advice to Suzanne P.
I can no longer laugh with Donna G.
I can no longer watch Mary Ellen cut through the bull shit.
I can no longer drink beer with Paul.
I can no longer have a meeting with Dave W.
I can no longer leave a message with Andrea.
I can no longer gossip with Anna.
I can no longer run into Dave P. at the vending machine.
I can no longer call Steve about my computer.
I can no longer compliment Lorenzo.
I can no longer hear Herman's voice.
I can no longer trade voice mails with Norman.
I can no longer ride the elevator with Barbara.
I can no longer be happy about Jennifer's pregnancy.
I can no longer walk with Adam.
I can no longer say hello to Steven every morning.
I can no longer see the incredible view from the 103rd Floor of the South Tower.
I can no longer take my life for granted.

HOW MY LIFE HAS CHANGED

—

HILARY NORTH
2001

On the morning of September 11th, 2001, having decided to stop en route in order to vote, Hilary North was late for work. Had she turned up on time, it's almost certain that she would have perished along with 176 of her co-workers, for her office was situated on the 103rd floor of the World Trade Center's South Tower, approximately 20 floors above the entry point of the hijacked jet airliner. Hilary wrote this list shortly after the tragedy; a recording of it being read aloud was featured in the Sonic Memorial Project, an audio archive of reactions to the event from all over the world.

OUTFIT FOR AN EXCURSION

—

HENRY DAVID THOREAU
1857

In 1854 Henry David Thoreau published *Walden*, his first-hand account of a two-year stay in a cabin he built in the woodland of Massachusetts in the mid-1840s – an experiment in simple living, independence and survival. After that he made three trips to Maine, the last of which was a 12-day jaunt that occurred in 1857 with a canoe, a companion and an Indian guide. He later described his packing list – which, as it happens, is anything but simple – for such a trip.

The following will be a good outfit for one who wishes to make an excursion of *twelve* days into the Maine woods in July, with a companion, and one Indian for the same purposes that I did.

Wear, — a check shirt, stout old shoes, thick socks, a neck ribbon, thick waistcoat, thick pants, old Kossuth hat, a linen sack.

Carry, — in an India-rubber knapsack, with a large flap, two shirts (check), one pair thick socks, one pair drawers, one flannel shirt, two pocket-handkerchiefs, a light India-rubber coat or a thick woollen one, two bosoms and collars to go and come with, one napkin, pins, needles, thread, one blanket, best gray, seven feet long.

Tent, — six by seven feet, and four feet high in middle, will do; veil and gloves and insect-wash, or, better, mosquito-bars to cover all at night; best pocket-map, and perhaps description of the route; compass; plant-book and red blotting-paper; paper and stamps, botany, small pocket spy-glass for birds, pocket microscope, tape-measure, insect-boxes.

Axe, full size if possible, jackknife, fish-lines, two only apiece, with a few hooks and corks ready, and with pork for bait in a packet, rigged; matches (some also in a small vial in the waist-coat pocket); soap, two pieces; large knife and iron spoon (for all); three or four old newspapers, much twine, and several rags for dishcloths; twenty feet of strong cord, four-quart tin pail for kettle, two tin dippers, three tin plates, a fry-pan.

Provisions. — Soft hardbread, twenty-eight pounds; pork, sixteen pounds; sugar, twelve pounds; one pound black tea or three pounds coffee, one box or a pint of salt, one quart Indian meal, to fry fish in; six lemons, good to correct the pork and warm water; perhaps two or three pounds of rice, for variety. You will probably get some berries, fish, &c., beside.

A gun is not worth the carriage, unless you go as hunters. The pork should be in an open keg, sawed to fit; the sugar, tea or coffee, meal, salt, &c., should be put in separate water-tight India-rubber bags, tied with a leather string; and all the provisions, and part of the rest of the baggage, put into two large India-rubber bags, which have been proved to be water-tight and durable. Expense of preceding outfit is twenty-four dollars.

An Indian may be hired for about one dollar and fifty cents per day, and perhaps fifty cents a week for his canoe (this depends on the demand). The canoe should be a strong and tight one. This expense will be nineteen dollars.

Such an excursion need not cost more than twenty-five dollars apiece, starting at the foot of Moosehead, if you already possess or can borrow a reasonable part of the outfit. If you take an Indian and canoe at Oldtown, it will cost seven or eight dollars more to transport them to the lake.

BELIEF & TECHNIQUE FOR MODERN PROSE

—

JACK KEROUAC
1958

In 1958, a year after the publication of his magnum opus – the sprawling, rambling *On the Road* – American beat poet and novelist Jack Kerouac sent a letter to friend and publisher Donald Allen that included this, a "list of essentials" for writers of modern prose, written in his own inimitable style. The next year, with Kerouac's blessing, it was printed in *Evergreen Review*, the literary magazine then edited by Allen.

*****BELIEF & TECHNIQUE FOR MODERN PROSE*****

List of Essentials

****

1. Scribbled secret notebooks, and wild typewritten pages, for yr own joy
2. Submissive to everything, open, listening
3. Try never get drunk outside yr own house
4. Be in love with yr life
5. Something that you feel will find its own form
6. Be crazy dumbsaint of the mind
7. Blow as deep as you want to blow
8. Write what you want bottomless from bottom of the mind
9. The unspeakable visions of the individual
10. No time for poetry but exactly what is
11. Visionary tics shivering in the chest
12. In tranced fixation dreaming upon object before you
13. Remove literary, grammatical and syntactical inhibition
14. Like Proust be an old teahead of time
15. Telling the true story of the world in interior monolog
16. The jewel center of interest is the eye within the eye
17. Write in recollection and amazement for yourself
18. Work from pithy middle eye out, swimming in language sea
19. Accept loss forever
20. Believe in the holy contour of life
21. Struggle to sketch the flow that already exists intact in mind
22. Dont think of words when you stop but to see picture better
23. Keep track of every day the date emblazoned in yr morning
24. No fear or shame in the dignity of yr experience, language & knowledge
25. Write for the world to read and see yr exact pictures of it
26. Bookmovie is the movie in words, the visual American form
27. In praise of Character in the Bleak inhuman Loneliness
28. Composing wild, undisciplined, pure, coming in from under, crazier the better
29. You're a Genius all the time
30. Writer-Director of Earthly movies Sponsored & Angeled in Heaven

BACK TO SCHOOL
COMMANDMENTS

—

SYLVIA PLATH
January 1953

In December 1952, at 20 years of age, future Pulitzer Prize-winning poet and author Sylvia Plath broke her leg while skiing in New York – an accident which resulted in a brief stay in hospital and, most frustratingly, a cast on her leg for two months. As she prepared to return to Smith College, downbeat yet eager to get back to classes and see her new love interest, Myron Lotz, she wrote two lists: first, a three-point reminder to appear calm in front of Myron, and second, a set of "Back to School Commandments" to keep her focused.

1   I will not overwhelm him by breathless over-enthusiasm.
2   I will not throw myself at him physically.
3   I <u>will</u> be moderate, yet intense, and interested.

————————

Back to School Commandments

1   Keep a CHEERFUL FRONT continuously.
2   <u>Science</u> – don't get upset. You have to get an A so you have to learn this. You <u>can</u>: You proved it by getting 2 good test marks.
3   <u>Unit</u> – Don't panic. Ask for an extension if you need it. Write allegory paper this weekend. You were in infirmary a week if he needs excuses.
4   <u>Davis</u>[n] – ask for extension if you need it. You've done enough words theoretically anyway. Do paper for him in exam period.
5   See Schnieders. Be calm, even if it is a matter of life & death.
6   Get <u>Mlle</u> written.
7   DO EXERCISES
8   Get a lot of sleep: afternoon naps if necessary
9   Remember: 5 months is not eternity. 2 months is not eternity. Even if it looks that way now.
10 Attitude is everything: so KEEP CHEERFUL, even if you fail your science, your unit, get a hateful <u>silence</u> <u>from</u> <u>Myron</u>, no dates, no praise, no love, nothing. There is a certain clinical satisfaction in seeing just how bad things can get.

P.S. Remember – you're a hell of a lot better off than 9/10 of the world anyway!

Love,

Syl

WHEN I COME TO BE OLD

—

JONATHAN SWIFT
1699

Irish author and cleric Jonathan Swift is best known for *Gulliver's Travels*, a biting satirical novel first published in 1726 that went on to sell millions of copies. It was only after Swift's death, in 1745, that a list of resolutions was found amongst his personal papers, written in 1699 when he was 32 and comprising of advice directed at his future self.

When I come to be old. 1699.

Not to marry a young Woman.

Not to keep young Company unless they reely desire it.

Not to be peevish or morose, or suspicious.

Not to scorn present Ways, or Wits, or Fashions, or Men, or War, &c.

Not to be fond of Children, or let them come near me hardly.

Not to tell the same Story over and over to the same People.

Not to be covetous.

Not to neglect decency, or cleenlyness, for fear of falling into Nastyness.

Not to be over severe with young People, but give Allowances for their youthfull follyes, and Weeknesses.

Not to be influenced by, or give ear to knavish tatling Servants, or others.

Not to be too free of advise nor trouble any but those that desire it.

To desire some good Friends to inform me wch of these Resolutions I break, or neglect, & wherein; and reform accordingly.

Not to talk much, nor of my self.

Not to boast of my former beauty, or strength, or favor with Ladyes, &c.

Not to hearken to Flatteryes, nor conceive I can be beloved by a young woman, et eos qui hereditatem captant, odisse ac vitare.

Not to be positive or opinionative.

Not to sett up for observing all these Rules; for fear I should observe none.

When I come to be old   1699

Not to marry a young Woman.

Not to keep young Company unless they realy desire it.

Not to be peevish or morose, or suspicious

Not to scorn present Ways, or Witt, or Fashions, or Men, or War, &c.

Not to be fond of Children, ~~but let them~~ ~~~~

Not to tell the same Story over & over to the same People.

Not to be covetous.

Not to neglect decency, or cleanlyness, for fear of falling into Nastyness.

Not to be severe with young People, but give allowances for their youthfull
    follyes, and Weaknesses

Not to be influenced by, or give ear to knavish tatling Servants, or others.

Not to be too free of advise, nor trouble any but those that desire it.

To ~~keep~~ desire some good Friend to inform me wch of these Resolutions I
    break, or neglect, & wherein; and reform accordingly.

Not to talk much, nor of my self.

Not to boast of my former beauty, or strength, or favor with Ladyes, &c

Not to hearken to Flatteryes, nor conceive I can be beloved by a young
    woman. et eos qui hereditatem captant ~~~~ odisse ac vitare.

Not to be positive or opiniatre.

Not to sett up for observing all these Rules; for fear I should observe none.

Houdini's

SCENE AND PROP. LIST

Open and close in full stage. (Palace.)

Time of act—About 25 minutes.

As I leave stage soaking wet in bathing suit, require two dressing rooms nearest stage (6 in company). Couch in dressing room.

Require a small trap in center of stage, not less than 8 inches square (8x8 inches) two feet in rear of front cloth.

Must have use of Fire Hose to reach from side of stage, about 3 feet past center of stage. Hose is used in view of audience.

Please see to it that the water in Hose is run off. It must be clear, so that audience can see through same.

100 gallons of Boiling water (must be boiling).

We carry four brass tubs to hold this water, which must be filled ready on stage **before** each performance.

Prepare a chute, or get-away, for 250 gallons of water, from the small 8x8-inch trap to most convenient spot underneath stage. The outlet in our Water Cloth is 6 inches in Diameter.

Our Water Carpet must be flied after each show back of stage, for which we require a strong batten.

Two small occasional tables (gold if possible, and 4 gold chairs) and 18 Bent-wood Chairs.

A run or stair case, so that committee from audience can come over footlights onto stage.

A small, clean looking (mahogany colored if possible) step ladder about 3 feet 6 inches high.

Two 20 feet and two 16 feet lengths of Lumber 4 inches by 2 inches (4x2 inches), or battens would do, which must be 4 inches wide.

PLEASE DO NOT PURCHASE ANYTHING AT MY EXPENSE

HOUDINI'S SCENE AND PROP. LIST

—

HARRY HOUDINI
Circa 1900

The great Harry Houdini was a master escapologist who wowed audiences by somehow escaping from a wide range of breathtaking predicaments. In 1912 he unveiled to the public what would be his most famous act, Houdini Upside Down!, in which he would hang, head first and underwater, in a device named the Chinese Water Torture Cell and then break free against all odds. Houdini performed the trick for 14 years, until his death in 1926. Before each and every show, this list was supplied to the venue.

REASONS FOR ADMISSION

—

WEST VIRGINIA HOSPITAL FOR THE
INSANE
1864–1889

In 1858, building work began on what would eventually become the West Virginia Hospital for the Insane, a 250-capacity psychiatric hospital located on 269 acres of land in the city of Weston, West Virginia. Progress was slow due to a pause in construction brought on by the American Civil War, but six years later its doors finally opened and the first set of patients were admitted for care. The list seen here, published in 1993, details the official "reasons for admission" of the hospital's patients between 1864 and 1889, as recorded in its logbook.

REASONS FOR ADMISSION
WEST VIRGINIA HOSPITAL FOR THE INSANE (WESTON)
OCTOBER 22, 1864 to DECEMBER 12, 1889

Amenorrhea
Asthma
Bad company
Bad habits & political Excitement
Bad whiskey
Bite of rattle snake
Bloody flux
Brain fever
Business nerves
Carbonic acid gas
Carbuncle
Cerebral softening
Cold
Congestion of brain
Constitutional
Death of sons in war
Decoyed into the army
Deranged masturbation
Desertion by husband
Diphtheria
Disappointed affection
Disappointed love
Disappointment
Dissipation of nerves
Dissolute habits
Dog bite
Domestic affliction
Domestic Trouble
Doubt about his mothers Ancestors
Dropsy
Effusion on the brain
Egotism
Epileptic fits
Excessive sexual abuse

Excitement as officer
Explosion of a shell nearby
Exposure and hereditary
Exposure and quackery
Exposure in Army
Fall from horse
False confinement
Feebleness of intellect
Fell from horse in war
Female disease
Fever and loss of law suit
Fever and Nerved
Fever and Jealousy
Fighting fire
Fits and desertion of husband
Gastritis
Gathering in the head
Greediness
Grief
Gunshot wound
Hard study
Hereditary predisposition
Hysteria
Ill treatment by husband
Imaginary female trouble
Immoral life
Imprisonment
Indigestion
Intemperance
Intemperance & business Trouble
Interference
Jealousy and religion
Kick of horse
Kicked in the head by a horse

Laziness

Liver and social disease

Loss of arm

Marriage of son

Masturbation & syphilis

Masturbation for 30 years

Medicine to prevent conception

Menstrual deranged

Mental excitement

Milk fever

Moral sanity

Novel reading

Nymphomania

Opium habit

Over action of the mind

Over heat

Over study of religion

Over taxing mental powers

Parents were cousins

Pecuniary losses

Periodical fits, tobacco & Masturbation

Political excitement

Politics

Puerperal

Religious enthusiasm

Religious Excitement

Remorse

Rumor of husband murder

Salvation Army

Scarlatina

HOSPITAL F

Seduction

Seduction & disappointment

Self Abuse

Severe labor

Sexual abuse and stimulants

Sexual derangement

Shooting of daughter

Small pox

Snuff eating for 2 years

Softening of the brain

Spinal irritation

Sun stroke

Superstition

Suppressed masturbation

Suppression of menses

The War

Time of life

Trouble

Uterine derangement

Venereal Excesses

Vicious vices in early life

Women

Women trouble

GAS

BOILER HOUSE
& KITCHEN

THE INSANE

LAWN

AIN

LAWN

THE EIGHT KINDES OF DRUNKENNES

—

THOMAS NASHE

1592

Born in 1567, Thomas Nashe was a popular Elizabethan satirist who made his name writing plays, poetry, novels and pamphlets – small, cheaply produced books that were largely seen as dispensable, and which were all the rage in London in the late 1600s amongst the reading public. One of Nashe's most popular pamphlets was *Pierce Penniless, His Supplication to the Divell*, a quite cutting look at modern society from which this entertaining list – The Eight Kindes of Drunkennes – is taken.

THE EIGHT KINDES OF DRUNKENNES

The first is ape drunke; and he leapes, and singes, and hollowes, and daunceth for the heauens: the second is lion drunke; and he flings the pots about the house, calls his hostesse whore, breakes the glasse windowes with his dagger, and is apt to quarrell with anie man that speaks to him: the third is swine drunke; heauie, lumpish, and sleepie, and cries for a little more drinke, and a fewe more cloathes: the fourth is sheepe drunke; wise in his conceipt, when he cannot bring foorth a right word: the fifth is mawdlen drunke; when a fellowe will weepe for kindnes in the midst of ale, and kisse you, saying, "By God, captaine, I loue thee. Goe thy wayes; thou dost not thinke so often of me as I doo of thee; I would (if it pleased God) I could not loue thee as well as I doo;" and then he puts his finger in his eye, and cryes: the sixt is Martin drunke; when a man is drunke, and drinkes himselfe sober ere he stirre: the seuenth is goate drunke; when, in his drunkennes, he hath no minde but on lecherie: the eighth is fox drunke—when he is craftie drunke, as manie of the Dutchmen bee, that will neuer bargaine but when they are drunke.

Ape Drunke

HANDKERCHIEF FLIRTATIONS.

Drawing across the lips—Desirous of an acquaintance.
Drawing across the eyes—I am sorry.
Taking it by the center—You are too willing.
Dropping—We will be friends.
Twirling in both hands—Indifference.
Drawing across the cheek—I love you.
Drawing through the hands—I hate you.
Letting it rest on the right cheek—Yes.
Letting it rest on the left cheek—No.
Twisting in the left hand—I wish to be rid of you.
Twisting in the right hand—I love an-other.
Folding it—I wish to speak with you.
Over the shoulder—Follow me.
Opposite corners in both hands—Wait for me.
Drawing across the forehead—We are watched.
Placing on right ear—You have chang-ed.
Letting it remain on the eyes—You are cruel.
Winding around the fore-finger—I am engaged.
Winding around the third finger—I am married.
Putting in the pocket—No more at pres-ent.

The Loving Heart.

"Let me whisper in your ear,
Noiseless as the falling dew,
Words I'd have you only hear,
'Darling one, I love but you!'"

I LOVE YOU!   DO YOU LOVE ME?

Look these words within your heart,
That they never may be free;
Keep them wheresoe'er thou art,
And let me, dearest, hold the Key.

To One I Love

"I HAVE loved thee long and well,
Yet never dared my love to tell;—
Hear it now in language plain,
Let me cease to sigh in vain,
            I love thee !

Oh ! when next we meet, my heart,
In joy or woe, will take its part;
I'll seek thine eyes, and I'll see there,
If I may hope, or in despair
            Must love thee !"

Your Lover,

....

THE STANDARD

BEAU CATCHER.

—CONTAINS—

The Loving Heart; To one I Love;
Flirtation of the Handkerchief, Fan
Parasol, Glove; and Language
of Flowers.

THE STANDARD BEAU CATCHER

—

AUTHOR UNKNOWN

Late 1800s

In 1890, a pamphlet by the name of *The Standard Beau Catcher* was published that acted as a flirtation guide for the discerning Victorian lady. In it could be found a number of lists, the majority of which revealed the hidden meanings behind various movements made by those holding gloves, fans, parasols and handkerchiefs – a secret code that seemingly failed to catch on. Also included was a brief guide to the 'Language of Flowers'.

GLOVE FLIRTATIONS.

Biting the tips—I wish to be rid of you.
Clenching them, rolled in right hand—No.
Drawing half way on left hand—Indifference.
Dropping both of them—I love you.
Dropping one of them—Yes.
Folding up carefully—Get rid of your company.
Holding with tips downward—I wish to be acquainted.
Holding loose in right hand—Be contented.
Holding loose in left hand—I am satisfied.
Left hand, naked thumb exposed—Do you love me?
Putting them away—I am vexed.
Right hand, naked thumb exposed—Kiss me.
Smoothing out gently—I wish I were with you.
Striking over the hand—I am displeased.
Striking over the shoulder—Follow me.
Tapping the chin—I love another.
Tossing them up gently—I am engaged.
Turning them inside out—I hate you.
Twirling around the fingers—Be careful, we are watched.
Using them as a fan—Introduce me your company.

FAN FLIRTATIONS.

Carrying in right hand—You are too willing.
Carrying in right hand, in front of face—Follow me.
Carrying in left hand—Desirous of acquaintance.
Closing it—I wish to speak with you.
Drawing across the forehead—We are watched.
Drawing across the cheek—I love you.
Drawing across the eyes—I am sorry.
Drawing through the hand—I hate you.
Dropping—We will be friends.
Fanning fast—I am engaged.
Fanning slow—I am married.
Letting it rest on the right cheek—Yes.
Letting it rest on the left cheek—No.
Open and shut—You are cruel.
Open wide—Wait for me.
Shut—I have changed.
Placing on right ear—You have changed.
Twirling in left hand—I wish to get rid of you.
Twirling in right hand—I love another.
With handle to lips—Kiss me.

PARASOL FLIRTATIONS.

Carrying it elevated in left hand, — Desiring acquaintance.
Carrying it elevated in right hand, — You are too willing.
Carrying it closed in left hand, — Meet on the first crossing.
Carrying it closed in right hand by side, — Follow me.
Carrying it in front of you, — No more at present.
Carrying it over the right shoulder, — You can speak to me.
Carrying it over the left shoulder, — You are too cruel.
Closing it,—I wish to speak to you.
Dropping it.—I love you.
End of tip to lips,—Do you love me?
Folding it up,—Get rid of your company.
Letting it rest on right cheek.—Yes.
Letting it rest on left cheek.—No.
Striking it on the hand, — I am very much displeased.
Swinging by handle on left side, — I am engaged.
Swinging by handle on right side, — I am married.
Tapping the chin gently, — I am in love with another.
Twirling it around, — Be careful, we are watched.
Using it as a fan. — Introduce me to your company.
With handle to lips,—Kiss me.

LANGUAGE OF FLOWERS.

Arbor Vitæ,—Unchanging Friendship.
Apple Blossom,—My Preference.
Alyssum,—Worth above Beauty.
Aspen Tree,—Sorrow.
Blue Canterberry Bell,—Fidelity.
China Pink,—Hate.
Coreopsis,—Love at first sight.
Dead Leaves,—Heavy Heart.
Forget-me-not,—True Love.
Geranium,—Lost Hope.
Hazel,—Let us bury the Hatchet.
Hawthorne,—Hope.
Heliotrope,—You are Loved.
Ivy,—Friendship.
Lily of the Valley,—Happy again.
Linden Tree,—Marriage.
Marigold,—I'm Jealous.
Myrtle,—Unalloyed Affection.
Pansy,—Think of Me.
Pea,—Meet me by Moonlight.
Peach Blossom,—My heart is thine.
Phlox,—Our Souls are United.
Pink, red,—Woman's Love.
Rose,—Perfect Beauty.
Rose Bud,—My Heart knows no Love.
Rose Geranium,—You are preferred.
Sweet William,—Let this be our last.
Tulip,—Declare your Love.
Wall Flower,—You will find me true.
Yellow Lily,—You are a Coquette.

YOU'VE GOT TO DIG IT TO DIG IT, YOU DIG?

—

THELONIOUS MONK
1960

It's no exaggeration to say that in the 1940s, legendary jazz pianist and composer Thelonious Monk was a pioneer in the world of bebop – a musical genius, some would say, whose influence is still felt. In 1960, a couple of years before the release of his most successful album, *Monk's Dream*, he relayed a typically colourful selection of suggestions to his friend, saxophonist Steve Lacy, who transcribed his words into the list of advice seen here.

T.MONK'S ADVICE (1960)

JUST BECAUSE YOU'RE NOT A DRUMMER, DOESN'T MEAN THAT YOU DON'T HAVE TO KEEP TIME.

PAT YOUR FOOT + SING THE MELODY IN YOUR HEAD, WHEN YOU PLAY.

STOP PLAYING ALL (THAT BULLSHIT) THOSE WEIRD NOTES, PLAY THE MELODY!

MAKE THE DRUMMER SOUND GOOD.

DISCRIMINATION IS IMPORTANT.

YOU'VE GOT TO DIG IT TO DIG IT, YOU DIG?

ALL REET!

ALWAYS KNOW… (MONK)

IT MUST BE ALWAYS NIGHT, OTHERWISE THEY WOULDN'T NEED THE LIGHTS.

LET'S LIFT THE BAND STAND!!

I WANT TO AVOID THE HECKLERS.

DON'T PLAY THE PIANO PART, I'M PLAYING THAT. DON'T LISTEN TO ME. I'M SUPPOSED TO BE ACCOMPANYING YOU!

THE INSIDE OF THE TUNE (THE BRIDGE) IS THE PART THAT MAKES THE OUTSIDE SOUND GOOD.

DON'T PLAY EVERYTHING (OR EVERY TIME); LET SOME THINGS GO BY. SOME MUSIC JUST IMAGINED. WHAT YOU DON'T PLAY CAN BE MORE IMPORTANT THAN WHAT YOU DO.

ALWAYS LEAVE THEM WANTING MORE.

A NOTE CAN BE SMALL AS A PIN OR AS BIG AS THE WORLD, IT DEPENDS ON YOUR IMAGINATION.

STAY IN SHAPE! SOMETIMES A MUSICIAN WAITS FOR A GIG, + WHEN IT COMES, HE'S OUT OF SHAPE + CAN'T MAKE IT.

WHEN YOU'RE SWINGING, SWING SOME MORE! (WHAT SHOULD WE WEAR TONIGHT? SHARP AS POSSIBLE!)

DON'T SOUND ANYBODY FOR A GIG, JUST BE ON THE SCENE. THOSE PIECES WERE WRITTEN SO AS TO HAVE SOMETHING TO PLAY, + TO GET CATS INTERESTED ENOUGH TO COME TO REHEARSAL.

YOU'VE GOT IT! IF YOU DON'T WANT TO PLAY, TELL A JOKE OR DANCE, BUT IN ANY CASE, YOU GOT IT! (TO A DRUMMER WHO DIDN'T WANT TO SOLO).

WHATEVER YOU THINK CAN'T BE DONE, SOMEBODY WILL COME ALONG + DO IT. A GENIUS IS THE ONE MOST LIKE HIMSELF.

THEY TRIED TO GET ME TO HATE WHITE PEOPLE, BUT SOMEONE WOULD ALWAYS COME ALONG + SPOIL IT.

JUST BECAUSE YOU'RE NOT A DRUMMER, DOESN'T MEAN THAT YOU DON'T HAVE TO KEEP TIME.

PAT YOUR FOOT & SING THE MELODY IN YOUR HEAD, WHEN YOU PLAY.

STOP PLAYING ALL (THAT BULLSHIT) THOSE WIERD NOTES, PLAY THE MELODY!

MAKE THE DRUMMER SOUND GOOD.

DISCRIMINATION IS IMPORTANT.

YOU'VE GOT TO DIG IT TO DIG IT, YOU DIG?

ALL REET!

ALWAYS KNOW... (MONK)

IT MUST BE ALWAYS NIGHT, OTHERWISE THEY WOULDN'T NEED THE LIGHTS.

LET'S LIFT THE BANDSTAND!! (I WANT)

AVOID THE HECKLERS.

DON'T PLAY THE PIANO PART, I'M PLAYING THAT. DON'T LISTEN TO ME, I'M SUPPOSED TO BE ACCOMPANING YOU!

THE INSIDE OF THE TUNE (THE BRIDGE) IS THE PART THAT MAKES THE OUTSIDE SOUND GOOD.

DON'T PLAY EVERYTHING (OR EVERYTIME); LET SOME THINGS GO BY. SOME MUSIC JUST IMAGINED. WHAT YOU DON'T PLAY CAN BE MORE IMPORTANT THAN WHAT YOU DO PLAY.

A NOTE CAN BE SMALL AS A PIN OR AS BIG AS THE WORLD, IT DEPENDS ON YOUR IMAGINATION.

STAY IN SHAPE! SOMETIMES A MUSICIAN WAITS FOR A GIG, & WHEN IT COMES, HE'S OUT OF SHAPE & CAN'T MAKE IT.

WHEN YOU'RE SWINGING, SWING SOME MORE! (WHAT SHOULD WE WEAR TONIGHT! SHARP AS POSSIBLE!)

ALWAYS LEAVE THEM WANTING MORE.

DON'T SOUND ANYBODY FOR A GIG, JUST BE ON THE SCENE. THOSE PIECES WERE WRITTEN SO AS TO HAVE SOMETHING TO PLAY, & TO GET CATS INTERESTED ENOUGH TO COME TO REHEARSAL.

YOU'VE GOT IT! IF YOU DON'T WANT TO PLAY, TELL A JOKE OR DANCE, BUT IN ANY CASE. YOU GOT IT! (TO A DRUMMER WHO DIDN'T WANT TO SOLO).

WHATEVER YOU THINK CAN'T BE DONE, SOMEBODY WILL COME ALONG & DO IT. A GENIUS IS THE ONE MOST LIKE HIMSELF.

THEY TRIED TO GET ME TO HATE WHITE PEOPLE, BUT SOMEONE WOULD ALWAYS COME ALONG & SPOIL IT.

GALILEO'S SHOPPING LIST

—

GALILEO GALILEI
1609

In August 1609, Galileo Galilei presented his latest telescope to the public – an instrument built using pre-made spectacle lenses that boasted an approximate magnification of 8x. Although it was effective, Galileo was determined to improve on the design; however, the only way to do so would be to take full control and make his own lenses. The shopping list seen here, written by Galileo on the back of a letter dated November 23rd, 1609, shows, amongst other items, the equipment needed for such an endeavour. In January 1610, he wrote a letter in which he announced the discovery of Jupiter's moons, spotted thanks to improvements to his telescope.

Scarfarotti e cappelletto per Vinc.o.
La cassa delle robe di Mar[in]a.
Lente, ceci bianchi, risi, uva passa, farro.
Zucchero, pepe, garofani, cannella, spezie, confetture.
Sapone, aranci.
Pettine d'avorio n.° 2.
Malvagia da i S.i Sagredi.
Palle d'artiglieria n.° 2.
Canna d'organo di stagno.
Vetri todeschi spianati.
Spianar cristallo di monte.
Pezzi di specchio.
Tripolo, ~~spantia~~
Lo specchiaro all'insegna del Re.
In calle delle aqque si fanno sgubie.
Trattare in materia di scodelle di ferro, o di gettarle in pietre, o vero come le palle d'artiglieria.
Privilegio per il vocabolario.
Ferro da spianare.
Pece greca.
Feltro, specchio per fregare.
Follo.
Pareggiarsi col S. Mannucci, et rendergli l'Edilio.

[TRANSLATION]

Shoes and hat for Vincenzo.
The case of wares for Marina.
Lentils, white chickpeas, rice, raisins, spelt.
Sugar, pepper, cloves, cinnamon, spices, jams.
Soaps, oranges.
Two ivory combs.
Malvasia by Lords Sagredo.
Two artillery balls.
Organ pipe of tin.
German lenses, polished.
Have rock crystal polished.
Pieces of mirror.
Tripolitan, ~~'spantia'~~
The mirror-maker under the insignia of the Kmg.
Small iron tuning chisels made in the *Calle delle Acque*.
To haggle about iron bowls, or to make them out of stone, or like the artillery balls.
Privilege for the vocabulary.
Iron plane.
Greek pitch.
Felt, mirror to rub.
Wool.
Pay debts to Lord Mannucci and give him back the Edilio.

Sacc[...]etti a affettate p[er] [...]

La Cassa delle robe di Mar[t]a

Lente. Ceci bianchi, Risi. Uva
passa. Farro.

Zucchero. pepe. garofani, Cannella
Spezie, confetture.

Sapori, aranci.

Pettine d'auorio n° 2.

Maluagia da i S[igno]ri Sagredi.

Palle d'Artiglieria n° 2

Canna d'Organo di Stagno

Vetri Todeschi spianati.

Spianar Cristallo di M[on]te

Pezzi di specchio

Tripolo, ~~Hearth~~

Co Specchiaro all'insegna
del Rè.

I' Calle delle agque di [...] fano
Sgubio

Prottore ò materia di s[...]delle di ferro, ò di Gettarle
in pietre, ò uero come le
Palle d'Artiglieria.

Priuilegio p[er] il Vocabolario

Ferro da spianare.

Pece greca

Soltro - specchio p[er] tregare

Sotto

pareggiare col S[...] Manucci; et
rendergli l'Edilio

IMMACULATE HEART COLLEGE ART DEPARTMENT RULES

—

CORITA KENT
Circa 1967

For 30 years until 1968, Sister Mary Corita headed the art department at Immaculate Heart College, a Catholic college in Los Angeles which quickly became known for its forward-thinking art classes. Indeed, Sister Mary herself was a leading light in the Pop Art movement thanks to her unique and bold screen printing; she was also good friends with such people as Alfred Hitchcock, Saul Bass and John Cage. During her time teaching at the college, she wrote a list of rules for the department.

IMMACULATE HEART COLLEGE ART DEPARTMENT RULES

RULE ONE: Find a place you trust and then try trusting it for a while.

RULE TWO: General duties of a student: pull everything out of your teacher. Pull everything out of your fellow students.

RULE THREE: General duties of a teacher: pull everything out of your students.

RULE FOUR: Consider everything an experiment.

RULE FIVE: Be self disciplined. This means finding someone wise or smart and choosing to follow them. To be disciplined is to follow in a good way. To be self disciplined is to follow in a better way.

RULE SIX: Nothing is a mistake. There's no win and no fail. There's only make.

RULE SEVEN: The only rule is work. If you work it will lead to something. It's the people who do all of the work all the time who eventually catch on to things.

RULE EIGHT: Don't try to create and analyse at the same time. They're different processes.

RULE NINE: Be happy whenever you can manage it. Enjoy yourself. It's lighter than you think.

RULE TEN: "We're breaking all the rules. Even our own rules. And how do we do that? By leaving plenty of room for x quantities." John Cage

HELPFUL HINTS: Always be around. Come or go to everything. Always go to classes. Read anything you can get your hands on. Look at movies carefully, often. Save everything – it might come in handy later.

HARRY S. TRUMAN'S LOVE LIST

—

HARRY S. TRUMAN
June 28th, 1957

The 33rd US President, Harry Truman, was married to his wife, Bess, for 53 years after having met her in high school. On each of their anniversaries – June 28th – he would write her a letter; however, on their 38th wedding anniversary he did something a little different and instead gave her this, a list of each of their preceding anniversaries and a brief summary of that year.

June 28, 1920	One happy year.
June 28, 1921	Going very well.
June 28, 1922	Broke and in a bad way.
June 28, 1923	Eastern Judge. Eating.
June 28, 1924	Daughter 4 mo. old.
June 28, 1925	Out of a job.
June 28, 1926	Still out of a job.
June 28, 1927	Presiding Judge – eating again.
June 28, 1928	All going well. Piano. Al Smith.
June 28, 1929	Panic, in October.
June 28, 1930	Depression. Still going.
June 28, 1931	Six year old daughter.
June 28, 1932	Roads finished.
June 28, 1933	Employment Director.
June 28, 1934	Buildings finished. Ran for the Senate.
June 28, 1935	U.S. Senator Gunston.
June 28, 1936	Resolutions Philadelphia. Roosevelt reelected.
June 28, 1937	Great time in Washington.
June 28, 1938	Very happy time. Margie 14.
June 28, 1939	Named legislation.
June 28, 1940	Senate fight coming.
June 28, 1941	Special Senate Committee. Margie wants to sing.
June 28, 1942	Also a happy time.
June 28, 1943	Lots of work.
June 28, 1944	Talk of V.P. Bad business.
June 28, 1945	V.P. & President. War end.
June 28, 1946	Margie graduate & singer. 80th Congress.
June 28, 1947	Marshall Plan & Greece & Turkey. A grand time 28th Anniversary.
June 28, 1948	A terrible campaign. Happy day.
June 28, 1949	President again. Another happy day.
June 28, 1950	Korea – a terrible time.
June 28, 1951	Key West – a very happy day.
June 28, 1952	All happy. Finish, Jan. 20, 1953.
June 28, 1953	Back home. Lots of *Roses*.
June 28, 1954	A happy 35th.
June 28, 1955	All cut up but still happy.
June 28, 1956	A great day – more elation.
June 28, 1957	Well here we are again, as Harry Jobes would say.

Only 37 to go for the diamond jubilee!

June 28, 1920   One happy year.

June 28, 1921   Going very well.

June 28, 1922   Broke and in a bad way.

June 28, 1923   Eastern Judge. Eating

June 28, 1924   Daughter 4 mo. old.

June 28, 1925   Out of a job.

June 28, 1926   Still out of a job.

June 28, 1927   Presiding Judge - eating again

June 28, 1928   All going well. Piano.

June 28, 1929   Al Smith   Panic in October.

June 38, 1930   Depression. Still going.

June 28, 1931   Six year old daughter

June 28, 1932   Roads finished

June 28, 1933   Employment Director.

June 28, 1934   Buildings finished.
               Ran for the Senate

June 28, 1935   U.S. Senator. Gunston.

June 28, 1936   Resolutions Philadelphia.
               Roosevelt reelected.

June 28, 1937 Grand time in Washington.

June 28, 1938 Very happy time. Margie 14.

June 28, 1939 Named legislation.

June 28, 1940 Senate fight comming.

June 28, 1941 Special Senate Committee
Margie wants to sing.

June 28, 1942 Also a happy time

June 28, 1943 Lots of work.

June 28, 1944 Talk of V.P. Bad business

June 28, 1945 V.P. & President. War End

June 28, 1946 Margie graduate & singer
80th Congress.

June 28, 1947 Marshall Plan + Greece + Turkey
A grand time 28th Anna

June 28, 1948 A terrible campaign. Happy day.

June 28, 1949 President again. Another happy day.

June 28, 1950 Korea — a terrible time.

June 28, 1951 Key West — a very happy day.

June 28, 1952 All happy. Finish Jan 20, 1953

June 28, 1953 Back home Lots of Roses.

June 28, 1954 A happy 35th

June 28, 1955 All cut up but still happy.

June 28, 1956 A great day – more election.

June 28, 1957 Well here we are again
as ~~Harry~~ Jones would say.

Only 37 to go for the
diamond jubilee!

H.S.T.

HOW TO WRITE

—

DAVID OGILVY
September 7th, 1982

British-born David Ogilvy was one of the original "ad men". In 1948, he started what would eventually be known as Ogilvy & Mather, the Manhattan-based advertising agency that has since been responsible for some of the world's most iconic ad campaigns, and in 1963 he wrote *Confessions of an Advertising Man*, a bestselling book that is still to this day considered essential reading for all who enter the industry. *Time* magazine called him "the most sought-after wizard in today's advertising industry" in the early 1960s. His name, and that of his agency, have been mentioned more than once in *Mad Men* for good reason.

On September 7th, 1982, Ogilvy sent an internal memo to all employees of his advertising agency, Ogilvy & Mather. It was titled "How to Write", and consisted of this list of advice.

The better you write, the higher you go in Ogilvy & Mather. People who *think* well, *write* well.

Woolly minded people write woolly memos, woolly letters and woolly speeches.

Good writing is not a natural gift. You have to *learn* to write well. Here are 10 hints:

(1) Read the Roman-Raphaelson book on writing. Read it three times.

(2) Write the way you talk. Naturally.

(3) Use short words, short sentences and short paragraphs.

(4) Never use jargon words like *reconceptualize*, *demassification*, *attitudinally*, *judgmentally*. They are hallmarks of a pretentious ass.

(5) Never write more than two pages on any subject.

(6) Check your quotations.

(7) Never send a letter or a memo on the day you write it. Read it aloud the next morning – and then edit it.

(8) If it is something important, get a colleague to improve it.

(9) Before you send your letter or your memo, make sure it is crystal clear what you want the recipient to do.

(10) If you want ACTION, *don't write*. Go and *tell* the guy what you want.

REJECTING *WITTGENSTEIN'S MISTRESS*
—

DAVID MARKSON
Date Unknown

Wittgenstein's Mistress by David Markson is not your average novel. Written largely in single sentence paragraphs, it tells the story of a lady who is convinced that she is alone is this world – that no other human beings exist. When published in 1988, it received strong reviews and is now considered to be his masterpiece; in 1999, fellow novelist David Foster Wallace called it "pretty much the high point of experimental fiction in this country". Despite the praise garnered after publication, it wasn't all plain sailing. The list you see here, handwritten by the book's exasperated author, details each of the rejections he received before *Wittgenstein's Mistress* eventually found a home at Dalkey Archive Press. They total 54.

1 – Asher – Harper & Row – No

2 – Cannon – Dutton? – No

3 – Talese – HM Co – No –

4 – Silberman – Summit – <u>Brilliant</u> / Classy – No

5 – Strachan – FSG – <u>Too</u> <u>Brilliant</u> / not know who – No

6 – Sifton – Viking – Admin, not love – rhythm – No

7 – Knopf – Lish want – cannot get through – No (Lee Goerner said no)

8 – Entrekin – S&S – nice letter – No

9 – Phillips – Little Brown – not "love" enough – No

10 – Sale – Putnam – not sort of voice can get into – No

11 – Landis – Morrow – No –

12 – Ann Patty – Poseidon – No

13 – Tom Engelhart – Pantheon – No

14 – Freedgood – Random – Admire writing – not love – No

15 – Stewart – Atheneum – Doesn't thicken – No

16 – Peter Davison – Atlantic Monthly Press – <u>Brilliant</u> – Hummed – No

17 – Tom Wallace – Norton – No

18 – Barbara Grossman – Crown – <u>Brilliant</u> – 25yrs ahead of its time – No

19 – Godine – No

20 – Catherine Court – Penguin – <u>Didn't understand</u> – No

21 – Lish – Knopf – asked for it back – No

22 – Fred Jordan – Grove – No

23 – Irene Skolnick – HBJ – she <u>love</u> – cldn't get 2nd reader – No

24 – Karen Brazillar – Persea – <u>Brilliant</u> – <u>Can't do</u> – No

25 – Bob Wyatt – Ballantine – No

26   Shoemaker – North Point – Brilliant creative No

27 – Roger Angell – NY'er – No concessions – Hard to stay with – No

28 – Pantheon – 2nd Ed (via Lish) – <u>Brilliant</u> – No

29 – Fran McCullough – Dial – No

30 – St. Martins – <u>Brilliant</u> – <u>Beattie 100% Right</u> – No

31 – Delacorte – No

32 – Braziller – No

33 – Sam Vaughan – Doubleday – No

34 – Vanguard – No

35 – Donald I. Fine – No

36 – Congdon – Congdon & Weed – No

37 – Cork Smith – Ticknor & Fields – No

38 – Fisketjon – Random House – No

39 – Raebuth – Horizon 5/7/84 – spoke 3/85 – personal problems – can't do but wld – maybe later

40 – Carrol – Carroll & Geoff – No

41 – Lish – Knopf – Had asked – No

42 – Scribner's – No

43 – Pushcart Press – No

44 – McPherson & Co – No

45 – Putnam – 2nd Ed. Stacy Kramer – No

46 – New Directions – Abish & Laughlin – rejection slip – No – told Walter never read it

47 – Juri Jurevis – SoHo Press – No

48 – Overlook – No

49 – Weidenfield & Nicholson – No

50   Sun & moon – No

51   Algonquin – No

52   Delphinium Press – Joe Papaleo – <u>Brilliant</u> – <u>spectacular</u> – No

53   William Abraham – No

54   Thunder's Mouth – No

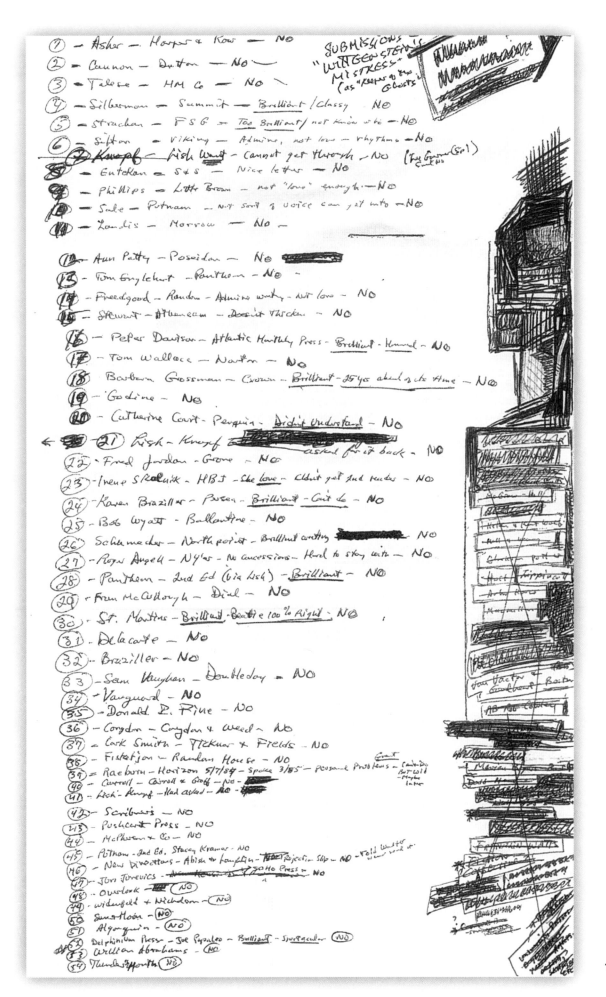

① — Asher — Harper & Row — NO

② — Cannon — Dutton — NO

③ — Talese — HM Co — NO

④ — Silberman — Summit — Brilliant / Classy — NO

⑤ — Strachan — FSG — Too Brilliant / not know who — NO

⑥ — Sifton — Viking — Admire, not love — rhythms — NO

⑦ — Knopf — Lish Want — Cannot get through — NO (Fog Guerne (Sol))

⑧ — Entreken — S&S — Nice letter — NO

⑨ — Phillips — Little Brown — not "long" enough — NO

⑩ — Sale — Putnam — Not sort of voice can get into — NO

⑪ — Landis — Morrow — NO

⑫ — Ann Patty — Poseidon — NO

⑬ — Tom Englehart — Pantheon — NO

⑭ — Freedgood — Random — Admire work — not love — NO

⑮ — Stewart — Atheneum — Doesn't thicken — NO

⑯ — Peter Davison — Atlantic Monthly Press — Brilliant — Kennel — NO

⑰ — Tom Wallace — Norton — NO

⑱ — Barbara Grossman — Crown — Brilliant — 25 yrs ahead of its time — NO

⑲ — Godine — NO

⑳ — Catherine Court — Penguin — Didn't Understand — NO

← ㉑ Lish — Knopf — asked for it back — NO

㉒ — Fred Jordan — Grove — NO

㉓ — Irene Skolnick — HBJ — She love — didn't get 2nd reader — NO

㉔ — Karen Braziller — Persea — Brilliant — Can't do — NO

㉕ — Bob Wyatt — Ballantine — NO

㉖ — Schumacher — North point — Brilliant writing — NO

㉗ — Roger Angell — NY'er — No concessions — Hard to stay with — NO

㉘ — Pantheon — 2nd Ed (via Lish) — Brilliant — NO

㉙ — Fran McCullough — Dial — NO

㉚ — St. Martins — Brilliant — Beattie 100% Right — NO

㉛ — Delacorte — NO

㉜ — Braziller — NO

㉝ — Sam Vaughan — Doubleday — NO

㉞ — Vanguard — NO

㉟ — Donald D. Rine — NO

㊱ — Corydon — Corydon & Weed — NO

㊲ — Cork Smith — Ticknor & Fields — NO

㊳ — Fistarjon — Random House — NO

㊴ — Raeburn — Horizon 5/7/84 — Spoke 3/85 — personal Problems — Grant — can't do But told — maybe later

㊵ — Carroll — Carroll & Graff — NO

㊶ — Lish — Knopf — Had asked — NO

㊷ — Scribner's — NO

㊸ — Pushcart Press — NO

㊹ — McPherson & Co — NO

㊺ — Pitman — 2nd Ed. Stacey Kramer — NO

㊻ — New Directions — Abish + Laughlin — Projection Slip — NO — Told Waite

㊼ — Jon Jurevics — SOHO Press — NO

㊽ — Overlook — NO

㊾ — Widenfeld + Nicholson — NO

㊿ — Sun + Moon — NO

— Algonquin — NO

— Delphinium Press — Joe Papaleo — Brilliant — Spectacular — NO

— William Abrahams — NO

— Thunders Mouth — NO

LOVECRAFT'S WEIRD IDEAS

—

H.P. LOVECRAFT
Circa 1930

In a letter dated January 1920, much revered horror author H.P. Lovecraft revealed to Reinhardt Kleiner that he had recently begun compiling a list of "ideas and images for subsequent use in fiction". He went on, "For the first time in my life, I am keeping a 'commonplace book'—if that term can be applied to a repository of gruesome and fantastick thoughts." Fourteen years later he handed the now sprawling list to a curious friend with an explanatory note that read:

"This book consists of ideas, images, & quotations hastily jotted down for possible future use in weird fiction. Very few are actually developed plots—for the most part they are merely suggestions or random impressions designed to set the memory or imagination working. Their sources are various—dreams, things read, casual incidents, idle conceptions, & so on."

1 *Demophon* shivered when the sun shone upon him. (Lover of darkness = ignorance.)

2 Inhabitants of *Zinge*, over whom the star Canopus rises every night, are always gay and without sorrow.

3 The shores of Attica respond in song to the waves of the Aegean.

4 Horror Story—Man dreams of falling—found on floor mangled as tho' from falling from a vast height.

5 Narrator walks along unfamiliar country road,—comes to strange region of the unreal.

6 In Ld Dunsany's "Idle Days on the Yann": The inhabitants of the antient Astahahn, on the Yann, do all things according to antient ceremony. Nothing new is found. "Here we have fetter'd and manacled Time, who wou'd otherwise slay the Gods."

7 *Horror Story:* The sculptured hand—or other artificial hand—which strangles its creator.

8 Hor. Sto.: Man makes appt. with old enemy. Dies—body keeps appt.

9 Dr. Eben Spencer plot.

10 Dream of flying over city. [Celephaïs]

11 Odd nocturnal ritual. Beasts dance and march to musick.

12 Happenings in interval between preliminary sound and striking of clock—ending: "It was the tones of the clock striking three".

13 House and garden—old—associations. Scene takes on strange aspect.

14 Hideous sound in the dark.

15 Bridge and slimy black waters. [Fungi—The Canal.]

16 The walking dead—seemingly alive, but—

17 Doors found mysteriously open and shut &c.—excite terror.

18 Calamander-wood—a very valuable cabinet wood of Ceylon and S. India, resembling rosewood.

19 Revise 1907 tale—painting of ultimate horror.

20 Man journeys into the past—or imaginative realm—leaving bodily shell behind.

21 A very ancient colossus in a very ancient desert. Face gone—no man hath seen it.

22 Mermaid Legend—*Encyc. Britt.* XVI—40.

23 The man who would not sleep—dares not sleep—takes drugs to keep himself awake. Finally falls asleep—and *something* happens— Motto from Baudelaire p. 214. [Hypnos]

24 Dunsany—"Go-By Street": Man stumbles on dream world—returns to earth—seeks to go back—succeeds, but finds dream world ancient and decayed as though by thousands of years.

1919

25 Man visits museum of antiquities—asks that it accept a bas-relief *he has* just made—*old* and learned curator laughs and says he cannot accept anything so modern. Man says that 'dreams are older than brooding Egypt or the contemplative Sphinx or garden-girdled Babylonia' and that he had fashioned the sculpture in his dreams. Curator bids him shew his product, and when he does so curator shews horror, asks who the man may be. He tells modern name. "No—*before that*" says curator. Man does not remember except in dreams. Then curator offers high price, but man fears he means to destroy sculpture. Asks fabulous price—curator will consult directors.

Add good development and describe nature of bas-relief. [Cthulhu]

26 Dream of ancient castle stairs—sleeping guards—narrow window—battle on plain between men of England and men of yellow tabards with red dragons. Leader of English challenges leader of foe to single combat. They fight. Foe unhelmeted, *but there is no head revealed*. Whole army of foe

fades into mist, and watcher finds himself to be the English knight on the plain, mounted. Looks at castle, and sees a peculiar concentration of fantastic clouds over the highest battlements.

27 *Life and Death:* Death—its desolation and horror—bleak spaces—sea-bottom—dead cities. But Life—the greater horror! Vast unheard-of reptiles and leviathans—hideous beasts of prehistoric jungle—rank slimy vegetation—evil instincts of primal man—Life is more horrible than death.

28 *The Cats of Ulthar:* The cat is the soul of antique AEgyptus and bearer of tales from forgotten cities of Meroë and Ophir. He is the kin of the jungle's lords, and heir to the secrets of hoary and sinister Africa. The Sphinx is his cousin, and he speaks her language; but he is more ancient than the Sphinx, and remembers that which she hath forgotten. [used]

29 Dream of Seekonk—ebbing tide—bolt from sky—exodus from Providence—fall of Congregational dome.

30 Strange visit to a place at night—moonlight—castle of great magnificence &c. Daylight shews either abandonment or unrecognisable ruins—perhaps of vast antiquity.

31 Prehistoric man preserved in Siberian ice. (See Winchell—*Walks and Talks in the Geological Field*—p. 156 et seq.)

32 As dinosaurs were once surpassed by mammals, so will man-mammal be surpassed by insect or bird—fall of man before the new race.

33 Determinism and prophecy.

34 Moving away from earth more swiftly than light—past gradually unfolded—horrible revelation.

35 Special beings with special senses from remote universes. Advent of an external universe to view.

36 Disintegration of all matter to electrons and finally empty space assured, just as devolution of energy to radiant heat is known. Case of *acceleration*—man passes into space.

37 Peculiar odour of a book of childhood induces repetition of childhood fancy.

38 Drowning sensations—undersea—cities—ships—souls of the dead. Drowning is a horrible death.

39 *Sounds*—possibly musical—heard in the night from other worlds or realms of being.

40 Warning that certain ground is sacred or accursed; that a house or city must not be built upon it—or must be abandoned or destroyed if built, under penalty of catastrophe.

41 The Italians call *Fear* La figlia della Morte—the daughter of Death.

42 Fear of *mirrors*—memory of dream in which scene is altered and climax is hideous surprise at seeing oneself in the water or a mirror. (Identity?) [Outsider?]

43 Monsters born living—burrow underground and multiply, forming race of unsuspected daemons.

44 Castle by pool or river—reflection fixed thro' centuries—castle destroyed, reflection lives to avenge destroyers weirdly.

45 Race of immortal Pharaohs dwelling beneath pyramids in vast subterranean halls down black staircases.

46 Hawthorne—unwritten plot: Visitor from tomb—stranger at some publick concourse followed at midnight to graveyard where he descends into the earth.

47 From "Arabia" *Encyc. Britan.* II—255: Prehistoric fabulous tribes of Ad in the south, Thamood in the north, and Tasm and Jadis in the centre of the peninsula. "Very gorgeous are the descriptions given of Irem, the City of Pillars (as the Koran styles it) supposed to have been erected by Shedad, the latest despot of Ad, in the regions of Hadramaut, and which yet, after the annihilation of its tenants, remains entire, so Arabs say, invisible to ordinary eyes, but occasionally, and at rare intervals, revealed to some heaven-favoured traveller." Rock excavations in N. W. Hejaz ascribed to Thamood tribe.

48 Cities wiped out by supernatural wrath.

49 AZATHOTH—hideous name.

50 *Phleg*'e-thon—a river of liquid fire in Hades.

51 Enchanted garden where moon casts shadow of object or ghost invisible to the human eye.

52 Calling on the dead—voice or familiar sound in adjacent room.

53 Hand of dead man writes.

54 Transposition of identity.

55 Man followed by invisible *thing*.

56 Book or MS. too horrible to read—warned against reading it—someone reads and is found dead. Haverhill incident.

57 Sailing or rowing on lake in moonlight—sailing into invisibility.

58 A queer village—in a valley, reached by a long road and visible from the crest of the hill from which that road descends—or close to a dense and antique forest.

59 Man in strange subterranean chamber—seeks to force door of bronze—overwhelmed by influx of waters.

60 Fisherman casts his net into the sea by moonlight—what he finds.

61 A terrible pilgrimage to seek the nighted throne of the far daemon-sultan *Azathoth*.

62 Live man buried in bridge masonry according to superstition—or black cat.

63 Sinister names—Nasht—Kaman-Thah.

64 Identity—reconstruction of personality—man makes duplicate of himself.

65 Riley's fear of undertakers—door locked on inside after death.

66 Catacombs discovered beneath a city (in America?).

67 An impression—city in peril—dead city—equestrian statue—men in closed room—clattering of hooves heard from outside—marvel disclosed on looking out—*doubtful* ending.

68 Murder discovered—body located—by psychological detective who pretends he has made walls of room transparent. Works on fear of murderer.

69 Man with unnatural face—oddity of speaking—found to be a *mask*—Revelation.

70 *Tone of extreme phantasy:* Man transformed to island or mountain.

71 Man has sold his soul to devil—returns to family from trip—life afterward—fear—culminating horror—novel length.

72 Hallowe'en incident—mirror in cellar—face seen therein—death (claw-mark?).

73 Rats multiply and exterminate first a single city and then all mankind. Increased size and intelligence.

74 Italian revenge—killing self in cell with enemy—under castle. [used by FBL, Jr.]

75 Black Mass under antique church.

76 Ancient cathedral—hideous gargoyle—man seeks to rob—found dead—gargoyle's jaw bloody.

77 Unspeakable dance of the gargoyles—in morning several gargoyles on old cathedral found transposed.

78 Wandering thro' labyrinth of narrow slum streets—come on distant light—unheard-of rites of swarming beggars—like Court of Miracles in *Notre Dame de Paris*.

79 Horrible secret in crypt of ancient castle—discovered by dweller.

80 Shapeless living *thing* forming nucleus of ancient building.

81 Marblehead—dream—burying hill—evening—unreality. [Festival?]

82 Power of wizard to influence dreams of others.

1920

83 Quotation: "…a defunct nightmare, which had perished in the midst of its wickedness, and left its flabby corpse on the breast of the tormented one, to be gotten rid of as it might."—Hawthorne

84 Hideous cracked discords of bass musick from (ruin'd) organ in (abandon'd) abbey or cathedral. [Red Hook]

85 "For has not Nature, too, her grotesques—the rent rock, the distorting lights of evening on lonely roads, the unveiled structure of man in the embryo, or the skeleton?" Pater—*Renaissance* (da Vinci).

86 To find something horrible in a (perhaps familiar) book, and not to be able to find it again.

87 *Borellus* says, "that the Essential Salts of animals may be so prepared and preserved, that an ingenious man may have the whole ark of Noah in his own Study, and raise the fine shape of an animal out of its ashes at his pleasure; and that by the like method from the Essential Salts of humane dust, a Philosopher may, without any criminal necromancy, call up the shape of any dead ancestor from the dust whereinto his body has been incinerated." [Charles Dexter Ward]

88 Lonely philosopher fond of cat. Hypnotises it—as it were—by repeatedly talking to it and looking at it. After his death the cat evinces signs of possessing his personality. N. B. He has trained cat, and leaves it to a friend, with instructions as to fitting a pen to its right fore paw by means of a harness. Later writes with deceased's own handwriting.

89 Lone lagoons and swamps of Louisiana—death daemon—ancient house and gardens—moss-grown trees—festoons of Spanish moss.

1922?

90 *Anencephalous* or brainless monster who survives and attains prodigious size.

91 Lost winter day—slept over—20 yrs. later. Sleep in chair on summer night—false dawn—old scenery and sensations—cold—old persons now dead—horror—frozen?

92 Man's body dies—but corpse retains life. Stalks about—tries to conceal odour of decay—detained somewhere—hideous climax. [Cool Air]

93 A place one has been—a beautiful view of a village or farm-dotted valley in the sunset—which one cannot find again or locate in memory.

94 Change comes over the sun—shews objects in strange form, perhaps restoring landscape of the past.

95 Horrible Colonial farmhouse and overgrown garden on city hillside—overtaken by growth. Verse "The House" as basis of story. [Shunned House]

96 Unknown fires seen across the hills at night.

97 Blind fear of a certain woodland hollow where streams writhe among crooked roots, and where on a buried altar terrible sacrifices have occur'd—Phosphorescence of dead trees. Ground bubbles.

98 Hideous old house on steep city hillside—Bowen St.—beckons in the night—black windows—horror unnam'd—cold touch and voice—the welcome of the dead.

1923

99 Salem story—the cottage of an aged witch—wherein after her death are found sundry terrible things.

100 Subterranean region beneath placid New England village, inhabited by (living or extinct) creatures of prehistoric antiquity and strangeness.

101 Hideous secret society—widespread—horrible rites in caverns under familiar scenes—one's own neighbour may belong.

102 Corpse in room performs some act—prompted by discussion in its presence. Tears up or hides will, etc.

103 Sealed room—or at least no lamp allowed there. Shadow on wall.

104 Old sea-tavern now far inland from made land. Strange occurrences—sound of lapping of waves—

105 Vampire visits man in ancestral abode—is his own father.

106 A *thing* that sat on a sleeper's chest. Gone in morning, but something left behind.

1923

107 Wall paper cracks off in sinister shape—man dies of fright. [Rats in Walls]

108 Educated mulatto seeks to displace personality of white man and occupy his body.

109 Ancient negro voodoo wizard in cabin in swamp—possesses white man.

110 Antediluvian—Cyclopean ruins on lonely Pacific island. Centre of earthwide subterranean witch cult.

111 Ancient ruin in Alabama swamp—voodoo.

112 Man lives near graveyard—how does he live? Eats no food.

113 Biological-hereditary memories of other worlds and universes. Butler—*God Known and Unk*. p. 59. [Belknap]

114 Death lights dancing over a salt marsh.

115 Ancient castle within sound of weird waterfall—sound ceases for a time under strange conditions.

116 Prowling at night around an unlighted castle amidst strange scenery.

117 A secret living thing kept and fed in an old house.

1924

118 Something seen at oriel window of forbidden room in ancient manor house.

119 Art note—fantastick daemons of Salvator Rosa or Fuseli (trunk-proboscis).

120 Talking bird of great longevity—tells secret long afterward.

121 Photius tells of a (lost) writer named Damascius, who wrote *Incredible Fictions, Tales of Daemons, Marvellous Stories of Appearances from the Dead*.

122 Horrible things whispered in the lines of Gauthier de Metz (13th cen.) *Image du Monde*.

123 Dried-up man living for centuries in cataleptic state in ancient tomb.

124 Hideous secret assemblage at night in antique alley—disperse furtively one by one—one seen to drop something—a human hand—

125 Man abandon'd by ship—swimming in sea—pickt up hours later with strange story of undersea region he has visited—mad??

126 Castaways on island eat unknown vegetation and become strangely transformed.

127 Ancient and unknown ruins—strange and immortal bird who *speaks* in a language horrifying and revelatory to the explorers.

128 Individual, by some strange process, retraces the path of evolution and becomes amphibious. ∴ Dr. insists that the particular amphibian from which *man* descends is not like any known to palaeontology. To prove it, indulges in (or relates) strange experiment.

1925

129 *Marble Faun* p. 346—strange and prehistorick Italian city of stone.

130 N. E. region call'd "Witches' Hollow"—along course of a river. Rumours of witches' sabbaths and Indian powwows on a broad mound rising out of the level where some old hemlocks and beeches formed a dark grove or daemon-temple. Legends hard to account for. Holmes—*Guardian Angel*.

131 Phosphorescence of decaying wood—call'd in New England "fox-fire".

132 Mad artist in ancient sinister house draws *things*. What were his models? Glimpse. [Pickman's Model]

133 Man has miniature shapeless Siamese twin—exhib. in circus—twin surgically detached—disappears—does hideous things with malign life of his own. [HSW—Cassius]

134 Witches' Hollow novel? Man hired as teacher in private school misses road on first trip—encounters dark hollow with unnaturally swollen trees and small cottage (light in window?). Reaches school and hears that boys are forbidden to visit hollow. One boy is strange—teacher sees him visit hollow—odd doings—mysterious disappearance or hideous fate.

135 Hideous world superimposed on visible world—gate through—power guides narrator to ancient and forbidden book with directions for access.

136 A secret language spoken by a very few old men in a wild country leads to hidden marvels and terrors still surviving.

137 Strange man seen in lonely mountain place talking with great winged thing which flies away as others approach.

138 Someone or something cries in fright at sight of the rising moon, as if it were something strange.

139 DELRIO asks "An sint unquam daemones incubi et succubae, et an ex tali congressu proles nasci queat?" [Red Hook]

140 Explorer enters strange land where some atmospheric quality darkens the sky to virtual blackness—marvels therein.

1926

141 Footnote by Haggard or Lang in *The World's Desire:* "Probably the mysterious and indecipherable ancient books, which were occasionally excavated in old Egypt, were written in this dead language of a more ancient and now forgotten people. Such was the book discovered at Coptos, in the ancient sanctuary there, by a priest of the Goddess. 'The whole earth was dark, but the moon shone all about the Book.' A scribe of the period of the Ramessids mentions another in indecipherable ancient writing. 'Thou tellest me thou understandest no word of it, good or bad. There is, as it were, a wall about it that none may climb. Thou art instructed, yet thou knowest it not; this makes me afraid.' Birch *Zeitschrift*, 1871 pp. 61–64. *Papyrus Anastasi* I, pl. X, l. 8, pl. X l. 4. Maspero, *Hist. Anc.*, pp. 66–67."

142 Members of witch-cult were buried face downward. Man investigates ancestor in family tomb and finds disquieting condition.

143 Strange well in Arkham country—water gives out (or was never struck —hole kept tightly covered by a stone ever since dug)—no bottom—shunned and feared—what lay beneath (either unholy temple or other very ancient thing, or great cave-world). [Fungi—The Well]

144 Hideous book glimpsed in ancient shop—never seen again.

145 Horrible boarding house—closed door never opened.

146 Ancient lamp found in tomb—when filled and used, its light reveals strange world. [Fungi]

147 Any very ancient, unknown, or prehistoric object—its power of suggestion—forbidden memories.

148 Vampire *dog*.

149 Evil alley or enclosed court in ancient city—Union or Milligan Pl. [Fungi]

150 Visit to someone in wild and remote house—ride from station through the night—into the haunted hills—house by forest or water—terrible things live there.

151 Man forced to take shelter in strange house. Host has thick beard and dark glasses. Retires. In night guest rises and sees host's clothes about—also *mask* which was the apparent face of *whatever* the host was. Flight.

152 Autonomic nervous system and subconscious mind *do not reside in the head*. Have mad physician decapitate a man but keep him alive and subconsciously controlled. Avoid copying tale by W. C. Morrow.

1928

153 Black cat on hill near dark gulf of ancient inn yard. Mew hoarsely—invites artist to nighted mysteries beyond. Finally dies at advanced age. Haunts dreams of artist—lures him to follow—strange outcome (never wakes up? or makes bizarre discovery of an elder world outside 3-dimensioned space?). [used by Dwyer]

154 Trophonius—cave of. Vide Class. Dict. and *Atlantic* article.

155 Steepled town seen from afar at sunset—*does not light up at night*. Sail has been seen putting out to sea. [Fungi]

156 Adventures of a disembodied spirit—thro' dim, half-familiar cities and over strange moors—thro' space and time—other planets and universes in the end.

157 Vague lights, geometrical figures, &c., seen on retina when eyes are closed. Caus'd by rays from *other dimensions* acting on optick nerve? From *other planets?* Connected with a life or phase of being in which person could live if he only knew how to get there? *Man afraid to shut eyes*—he has been somewhere on a terrible pilgrimage and this fearsome seeing faculty remains.

158 Man has terrible wizard friend who gains influence over him. Kills him in defence of his soul—walls body up in ancient cellar—BUT—the dead wizard (who has said strange things about soul lingering in body) *changes bodies with him …* leaving him a conscious corpse in cellar. [Thing on Doorstep]

159 Certain kind of deep-toned stately music of the style of the 1870's or 1880's recalls certain visions of that period—gas-litten parlours of the dead, moonlight on old floors, decaying business streets with gas lamps, &c.—under terrible circumstances.

160 Book which induces sleep on reading—cannot be read—determined man reads it—goes mad—precautions taken by aged initiate who knows—protection (as of author and translator) by incantation.

161 Time and space—past event—150 years ago—unexplained. Modern period—person intensely homesick for past says or does something which is psychically transmitted back and *actually causes* the past event.

162 Ultimate horror—grandfather returns from strange trip—mystery in house—wind and darkness—grandf. and mother engulfed—questions forbidden—somnolence—investigation—cataclysm—screams overheard—

163 Man whose money was *obscurely* made loses it. Tells his family he must go *again* to THE PLACE (horrible and sinister and extra-dimensional) where he got his gold. Hints of possible pursuers—or of his possible non-return. He goes—record of what happens to him—or what happens at his home when he returns. Perhaps connect with preceding topic. Give fantastic, quasi-Dunsanian treatment.

164 Man observed in a publick place with features (or ring or jewel) identified with those of man long (perhaps generations) buried.

165 Terrible trip to an ancient and forgotten tomb.

166 Hideous family living in shadow in ancient castle by edge of wood near black cliffs and monstrous waterfall.

167 Boy rear'd in atmosphere of considerable mystery. Believes father dead. Suddenly is told that father is about to return. Strange preparations—consequences.

168 Lonely bleak islands off N. E. coast. Horrors they harbour—outpost of cosmic influences.

169 What hatches from primordial egg.

170 Strange man in shadowy quarter of ancient city possesses something of immemorial archaic horror.

171 Hideous old book discovered—directions for shocking evocation.

1930

172 Pre-human idol found in desert.

173 Idol in museum *moves* in a certain way.

174 Migration of Lemmings—Atlantis.

175 Little green Celtic figures dug up in an ancient Irish bog.

176 Man blindfolded and taken in closed cab or car to some very ancient and secret place.

177 The *dreams* of one man actually *create* a strange half-mad world of quasi-material substance in *another dimension*. *Another man*, also a dreamer, blunders into this world in a dream. What he finds. Intelligence of denizens. Their dependence on the first dreamer. What happens at his death.

178 A very ancient tomb in the deep woods near where a 17th

century Virginia manor-house used to be. The undecayed, bloated thing found within.

179 Appearance of an ancient god in a lonely and archaic place—prob. temple ruin. Atmosphere of beauty rather than horror. Subtle handling—presence revealed by faint sound or shadow. Landscape changes? Seen by child? Impossible to reach or identify locale again?

180 A general house of horror—nameless crime—sounds—later tenants—(Flammarion) (novel length?).

181 Inhabitant of another world—face masked, perhaps with human skin or surgically alter'd to human shape, but body alien beneath robes. Having reached earth, tries to mix with mankind. Hideous revelation. [Suggested by CAS]

182 In ancient buried city a man finds a mouldering prehistoric document *in English and in his own handwriting*, telling an incredible tale. Voyage from present into past implied. Possible actualisation of this.

183 Reference in Egyptian papyrus to a secret of secrets under tomb of high-priest Ka-Nefer. Tomb finally found and identified—trap door in stone floor—staircase, and the illimitable black abyss.

184 Expedition lost in Antarctic or other weird place. Skeletons and effects found years later. Camera films used but undeveloped. Finders develop—and find strange horror.

185 Scene of an urban horror—Sous le Cap or Champlain Sts.—Quebec—rugged cliff-face—moss, mildew, dampness—houses half-burrowing into cliff.

186 Thing from sea—in dark house, man finds doorknobs &c. *wet* as from touch of *something*. He has been a sea-captain, and once found a strange temple on a volcanically risen island.

1931

187 Dream of awaking in vast hall of strange architecture, with sheet-covered forms on slabs—in positions similar to one's own. Suggestions of disturbingly non-human outlines under sheets. One of the objects moves and throws off sheet—non-terrestrial being revealed. Sugg. that *oneself* is also such a being—mind has become transferred to body on other planet.

188 Desert of rock—prehistoric door in cliff, in the valley around which lie the bones of uncounted billions of animals both modern and prehistoric—some of them puzzlingly gnawed.

189 Ancient necropolis—bronze door in hillside which opens as the moonlight strikes it—focussed by ancient lens in pylon opposite?

1932

190 Primal mummy in museum—awakes and changes place with visitor.

191 An odd wound appears on a man's hand suddenly and without apparent cause. Spreads. Consequences.

1933

192 Thibetan ROLANG—Sorcerer (or NGAGSPA) reanimates a corpse by holding it in a dark room—lying on it mouth to mouth and repeating a magic formula with all else banished from his mind. Corpse slowly comes to life and stands up. Tries to escape—leaps, bounds, and struggles—but sorcerer holds it. Continues with magic formula. Corpse sticks out tongue and sorcerer bites it off. Corpse then collapses. Tongue become a valuable magic talisman. If corpse escapes—hideous results and death to sorcerer.

193 Strange book of horror discovered in ancient library. Paragraphs of terrible significance copies. Later unable to find and verify text. Perhaps discover body or image or charm under floor, in secret cupboard, or elsewhere. Idea that book was merely hypnotic delusion induced by dead brain or ancient magic.

194 Man enters (supposedly) own house in pitch dark. Feels way to room and shuts door behind him. Strange horrors—or turns on lights and finds alien place or presence. Or finds past restored or future indicated.

195 Pane of peculiar-looking glass from a ruined monastery reputed to have harboured devil-worship set up in modern house at edge of wild country. Landscape looks vaguely and unplaceably *wrong* through it. It has some unknown time-distorting quality, and comes from a primal, lost civilisation. Finally, hideous things in other world seen through it.

196 Daemons, when desiring an human form for evil purposes, take to themselves the bodies of hanged men.

197 Loss of memory and entry into a cloudy world of strange sights and experiences after shock, accident, reading of strange book, participation in strange rite, draught of strange brew, &c. Things seen have vague and disquieting familiarity. Emergence. Inability to retrace course.

1934

198 Distant tower visible from hillside window. Bats cluster thickly around it at night. Observer fascinated. One night wakes to find self on unknown black circular staircase. In tower? Hideous goal.

199 Black winged thing flies into one's house at night. Cannot be found or identified—but subtle developments ensue.

200 Invisible Thing felt—or seen to make prints—on mountain top or other height, inaccessible place.

201 Planets form'd of invisible matter.

202 A monstrous derelict—found and boarded by a castaway or shipwreck survivor.

203 A return to a place under dreamlike, horrible, and only dimly comprehended circumstances. Death and decay reigning—town fails to light up at night—Revelation.

204 Disturbing conviction that all life is only a deceptive dream with some dismal or sinister horror lurking behind.

205 Person gazes out window and finds city and world dark and dead (or oddly changed) outside.

206 Trying to identify and visit the distant scenes dimly seen from one's window—bizarre consequences.

207 Something snatched away from one in the dark—in a lonely, ancient, and generally shunned place.

208 (Dream of) some vehicle—railway train, coach, &c.—which is boarded in a stupor or fever, and which is a fragment of some past or ultra-dimensional world—taking the passenger out of reality—into vague, age-crumbled regions or unbelievable gulfs of marvel.

209 Special Correspondence of *N. Y. Times*—March 3, 1935: "Halifax, N. S.—Etched deeply into the face of an island which rises from the Atlantic surges off the S. coast of Nova Scotia 20 m. from Halifax is the strangest rock phenomenon which Canada boasts. Storm, sea, and frost have graven into the solid cliff of what has come to be known as Virgin's Island an almost perfect outline of the Madonna with the Christ Child in her arms.

"The island has sheer and wave-bound sides, is a danger to ships, and is absolutely uninhabited. *So far as is known, no human being has ever set foot on its shores.*"

210 An ancient house with blackened pictures on the walls—so obscured that their subjects cannot be deciphered. Cleaning—and revelation. Cf. Hawthorne—"Edw. Rand. Port.

211 Begin story with presence of narrator—inexplicable to himself—in utterly alien and terrifying scenes (dream?).

212 Strange human being (or beings) living in some ancient house or ruins far from populous district (either old N. E. or far exotic land). Suspicion (based on shape and habits) that it is not *all* human.

213 Ancient winter woods—moss—great boles—twisted branches—dark—ribbed roots—always dripping. …

214 Talking rock of Africa—immemorially ancient oracle in desolate jungle ruins that *speaks* with a voice out of the aeons.

215 Man with lost memory in strange, imperfectly comprehended environment. Fears to regain memory—a *glimpse*. …

216 Man idly shapes a queer image—some power impels him to make it queerer than he understands. Throws it away in disgust—but something is abroad in the night.

217 Ancient (Roman? prehistoric?) stone bridge washed away by a (sudden and curious?) storm. *Something* liberated which had been sealed up in the masonry of years ago. Things happen.

218 Mirage in *time*—image of long-vanish'd pre-human city.

219 Fog or smoke—assumes shaped under incantations.

220 Bell of some ancient church or castle rung by some unknown hand—a thing … or an invisible Presence.

221 Insects or other entities from space attack and penetrate a man's head and cause him to *remember* alien and exotic things—possible displacement of personality.

222 Quoted as motto by John Buchan: "The effect of night, of any flowing water, of lighted cities, of the peep of day, of ships, of the open ocean, calls up in the mind an army of anonymous desires and pleasures. Something, we feel, should happen; we know not what, yet we proceed in quest of it."—*R. L. Stevenson.*

FUMBLERULES OF GRAMMAR

—

WILLIAM SAFIRE
Late 1979

Late 1979, *New York Times* political columnist and presidential speechwriter William Safire compiled a list of 36 "Fumblerules of Grammar" – rules of writing, all of which are humorously self-contradictory – and published them in his popular *New York Times Magazine* column, "On Language". Ten years later, he devoted a book to the same subject. Those 36 fumblerules can be seen below, along with another 18 that later featured in Safire's book *Fumblerules: A Lighthearted Guide to Grammar and Good Usage*.

1. Remember to never split an infinitive.
2. A preposition is something never to end a sentence with.
3. The passive voice should never be used.
4. Avoid run-on sentences they are hard to read.
5. Don't use no double negatives.
6. Use the semicolon properly, always use it where it is appropriate; and never where it isn't.
7. Reserve the apostrophe for it's proper use and omit it when its not needed.
8. Do not put statements in the negative form.
9. Verbs has to agree with their subjects.
10. No sentence fragments.
11. Proofread carefully to see if you any words out.
12. Avoid commas, that are not necessary.
13. If you reread your work, you will find on rereading that a great deal of repetition can be avoided by rereading and editing.
14. A writer must not shift your point of view.
15. Eschew dialect, irregardless.
16. And don't start a sentence with a conjunction.
17. Don't overuse exclamation marks!!!
18. Place pronouns as close as possible, especially in long sentences, as of 10 or more words, to their antecedents.
19. Hyphenate between sy-llables and avoid un-necessary hyphens.
20. Write all adverbial forms correct.
21. Don't use contractions in formal writing.
22. Writing carefully, dangling participles must be avoided.
23. It is incumbent on us to avoid archaisms.
24. If any word is improper at the end of a sentence, a linking verb is.
25. Steer clear of incorrect forms of verbs that have snuck in the language.
26. Take the bull by the hand and avoid mixing metaphors.
27. Avoid trendy locutions that sound flaky.
28. Never, ever use repetitive redundancies.
29. Everyone should be careful to use a singular pronoun with singular nouns in their writing.
30. If I've told you once, I've told you a thousand times, resist hyperbole.
31. Also, avoid awkward or affected alliteration.
32. Don't string too many prepositional phrases together unless you are walking through the valley of the shadow of death.
33. Always pick on the correct idiom.

34. "Avoid overuse of 'quotation "marks."'"

35. The adverb always follows the verb.

36. Last but not least, avoid clichés like the plague; seek viable alternatives.

37. Never use a long word when a diminutive one will do.

38. Employ the vernacular.

39. Eschew ampersands & abbreviations, etc.

40. Parenthetical remarks (however relevant) are unnecessary.

41. Contractions aren't necessary.

42. Foreign words and phrases are not apropos.

43. One should never generalize.

44. Eliminate quotations. As Ralph Waldo Emerson said, "I hate quotations. Tell me what you know."

45. Comparisons are as bad as clichés.

46. Don't be redundant; don't use more words than necessary; it's highly superfluous.

47. Be more or less specific.

48. Understatement is always best.

49. One-word sentences? Eliminate.

50. Analogies in writing are like feathers on a snake.

51. Go around the barn at high noon to avoid colloquialisms.

52. Who needs rhetorical questions?

53. Exaggeration is a billion times worse than understatement.

54. capitalize every sentence and remember always end it with a point

CHRISTOPHER HITCHENS'
COMMANDMENTS

—

CHRISTOPHER HITCHENS
2010

Christopher Hitchens was a divisive journalist, author and critic who was never anything but outspoken when discussing religion, a subject that was particularly close to his heart and which he debated regularly and with passion. In 2010, in a piece written for *Vanity Fair* on the subject of the Ten Commandments, titled "The New Commandments", he argued, with some tongue-in-cheek, that they should be revised, updated for our times. His piece ended with these suggested replacements.

Do not condemn people on the basis of their ethnicity or *color*.

Do not ever use people as private property.

Despise those who use violence or the threat of it in sexual relations.

Hide your face and weep if you dare to harm a child.

Do not condemn people for their inborn *nature*—why would God create so many homosexuals only in order to torture and destroy them?

Be aware that you too are an animal and dependent on the web of nature, and think and act accordingly.

Do not imagine that you can escape judgment if you rob people with a false prospectus rather than with a knife.

Turn off that fucking cell phone—you can have no idea how *un*important your call is to us.

Denounce all jihadists and crusaders for what they are: psychopathic criminals with ugly delusions.

Be willing to renounce any god or any religion if any holy commandments should contradict any of the above.

OLYMPIC VICTOR LIST

—

AUTHOR UNKNOWN
3rd Century AD

In 1897, in the Egyptian city of Oxyrhynchus, this fragment of papyrus bearing Greek script was found by archaeologists who later concluded that it dates back to the middle of the 3rd century AD. Due to its condition, a complete transcript is impossible; however, what we do know is this: written on it is a list of winners – known as a "victor list" – at various Ancient Olympic Games, beginning, top-left, with the 75th Games in 480 BC and ending, bottom-right, with the 83rd in 448 BC; winners include Damagetos of Rhodes (boxing), Astylos of Croton (stadion run) and Leontiscus of Messana (wrestling); and for each year, 13 events are listed in the following order.

στάδιον	*stadion run (192.27 metre sprint)*
δίαυλος	*2 stadia run*
δόλιχος	*dolichos (2000 metre run)*
πένταθλον	*pentathlon*
πάλη	*wrestling*
πύξ	*boxing*
παγκράτιον	*pancration (combined wrestling and boxing)*
παίδων στάδιον	*boys' stadio*
παίδων πάλη	*boys' wrestling*
παίδων πύξ	*boys' boxing*
ὁπλίτης	*hoplite (running in armour)*
τέθριππον	*four horse chariot race*
κέλης	*horse riding*

179

HOW TO ATTAIN SMARTNESS

—

EDNA WOOLMAN CHASE
1954

In 1914, having steadily worked her way up from the mail room, Edna Woolman Chase became editor-in-chief of *Vogue* magazine, a role she held until her retirement 38 years later. Two years after stepping down, Chase wrote her autobiography, *Always in Vogue*, in which she presented a list of advice for ladies on "how to attain smartness".

Perhaps this is as good a place as any to set down, as concisely as I can, [the] code on how to attain smartness that, over a long life and through years of dealing with a capricious art, I have found to be the most serviceable. Much of it is obvious, but every season new, young eyes become style-conscious and I believe it bears repetition.

Point #1: Study yourself with the unblinking eye of your meanest enemy. Could that throat, so like a swan to your lover, perhaps be considered a long, skinny neck, thrust forward at a cranelike angle, by one who cares for you less? Or could that short neck and submissive little chin, which make you so cuddlesome, could they, with the years, develop into a thick, indeterminate oneness, with that middle-aged hump at the back? Are your legs or upper arms too thin or too fat? Do you have pretty hands and nails, so that you can permit yourself eye-attracting gestures and jewelry, or are they large and capable, profiting from a decent anonymity? And your hair? Is it sexy or serviceable? This questionnaire could go on indeterminately, but its point, I think, is clear. Your person is the material you have to work with.

Study yourself with dispassionate eyes *and* in a three-ply mirror. It is a grueling ordeal, but it pays off. Remember your enemy, the rival who sees you always in 3-D. Make sure you are at least as well informed as she.

Point #2: This does not have to do with clothes; it does have to do with good grooming, a vital part of fashion, and I think it is valid. Set your dressing table in front of a window, so that the uncompromising light of day will fall evenly upon your face when you are making up. If, because of architectural reasons, this is impossible, place it so the light, day or artificial, comes equally from both sides. This will help you to achieve a well-blended make-up and to do your hair becomingly. Also always have your hand mirror within reach, that you may see yourself from the side and back as well as from the front.

Point #3: Choose for yourself clothes that play up your good points and subdue your bad. Have you pretty legs, but a thick middle? Perhaps your hips depress you, but from the waist up you are a Tanagra figurine? Or have you the lean, lithe flanks of a Diana yet are overly emphasized above? For this silhouette the French have an apt expression: "*Beaucoup de monde au balçon*" — a lot of people in the balcony. These are the assets and defects you must be aware of.

Know thyself and dress accordingly is the great fashion edict. Certain cliche warnings on the whole are probably sound; if you are partridge-plump a print of cabbage roses may not be for you. On the other hand, if you are small and slim the dictum that you should wear only "dainty" jewelry is groundless. If you yearn for chunks, go ahead. A massive bracelet makes a slender wrist more fragile. There are times when the truly chic woman achieves style and individuality through breaking with tradition, but remember! Revolution takes experience. It can take money as well, which brings us to…

Point #4: In fashion do *not* have the courage of your mistakes. Since you are human you will make them, yet if you want a reputation for elegance hide them. They are expensive, yes, which is one reason you should read *Vogue*, so that you will make fewer of them, but you must be brave. If you've pulled a fearful boner, if the dress or hat so beguiling in the shop is a dud in the home, pitch it out. Give it to some dear relation or send it to the thrift shop: don't wear it. To be considered well dressed, you must be it continuously. Not in fits and starts.

Point #5: Select clothes appropriate to the life you lead. The wildly inappropriate

garment is usually the mistake of youth, before the discipline of taste and budget has had the time to sink in. Although the temptation may be strong, even in maturity, to purchase the dress that would be knockout for a unique occasion and completely out of key the rest of the time, unless you're rich, don't succumb. Compromise. Obviously, if you sense that a certain ravishing garment will cause him to pop the question don't be a fool. Buy it.

Point #6: The allotment of budget. There are certain articles in one's wardrobe on which one not only may, but should, splurge. Within reason, of course. Remember this is a Quaker speaking. A good cashmere sweater will last for years. Your winter coat should be the very best you can afford. It is meant to survive several seasons, keep you warm, and be worn every day. The same is true of your tailored suit. It should be of good fabric and well cut. Also your street shoes should be the best. Smart, comfortable, and with a medium heel. For walking the city streets they should not have open toes and heels. This misbegotten fashion I have already dwelt on at length. Keep your shoes in good repair; you prolong their life indefinitely.

Economize on evening slippers. They are fragile and unless you are a debutante the wear you exact from them will probably be limited. If you are a debutante you will want several pairs, but they need not be expensive.

Point #7: Don't buy too much. There is nothing to sap the morale and dull the appearance like a closet full of half-worn, no-longer-at-their-peak clothes. With the exception of the aforementioned staples — coats, sits, and street shoes, which should last several seasons — buy only what you need at the time, make it serve you well, and get rid of it.

Point #8: In your wardrobe consider color carefully. If you use restraint you will find it makes both for elegance and economy. This does not mean you have to be drab and monotonous; if your clothes are interchangeable, shoes and accessories doing duty with several dresses and suits instead of only one, you will achieve greater variety at less cost. Don't get a blue hat and a red bag and a brown coat and black shoes, each good in itself but as incompatible as whisky and wine. Plan your wardrobe as a whole. Don't just buy it, compose it.

Point #9: Consider color; don't get set in concrete as to what colors you can and cannot wear. To be adamant on the subject of black or brown, shrimp pink or almond green is nonsense. Quite possibly with the right shades of rouges, lipstick, and powder we can wear them. Another thing to remember is that as we grow older we can frequently change our color spectrum with flattering results.

Point #10:

A: Dress your age. A hat that really belongs above a mature, thoughtful face is far more flattering, and incidentally in better taste, than a cute pixie cap. Clothes that are too young paradoxically make their wearer look older. Remember that the interesting men of the world *like women who appear youthful but who are not pathetic carbon copies of the girls they were.* On the other hand, clothes that are too sophisticated do not imbue the youthful wearer with the femme fatale look she longs to achieve, but tend, on the contrary, to give her a comically childlike appearance.

B: As you grow older, cover up. Aging flesh is not appealing. Whether a Bikini bathing suit on a charming young body is modest or immodest is a matter of the current mode or local morals or good taste; it has nothing to do with aestheticism, but too much revelation of a figure that is too thin, too fat, or too old can be lamentable.

For the older woman, misty tulle scarves in the evening or little jackets or stoles are pleasant bits of decorative fancy.

Point #11

A: Stand up when you buy a hat. This may sound daft, but it is rooted in wisdom. Few ladies, we trust, are so foolish as to buy a hat without viewing it from the profile and three-quarter angles as well as from the front, but many a lady fails to realize that her hat must be integrated with the rest of her, that it must be in proportion to her entire body. If you see what you secretly feel to be an enchanting reflection in the milliner's mirror, restrain yourself yet a moment. Stand up, move a few feet away, and view yourself in the altogether. Are you small, so that under a wide brim you look strangely like a gnome under a toadstool? Are you tall, so that too small a hat is reminiscent of a thimble on a broomstick? What looks enchanting in one dimension, sitting down, may be a different story in the round and long.

B: Just as you should stand up when you buy a hat so should you sit down when you buy a dress. It may be all good when you are erect, but how does it sit? Is it so full that it lies in puddles on the floor? Does the wrap-around skirt fall open? Is it so tight that it rides above your knees? Sit down in it in front of the mirror, and then walk, enough to make sure it doesn't bind. There is nothing more aggravating than a too narrow skirt on one who likes to stride freely.

Point #12: Pare down the nonessentials. This does not mean eschew jewels and flowers, scarves and bows and hair ornaments; it does mean to use them with discretion, to integrate them into your costume so that they are a deliberate accent, the perfect finishing touch. The observer, and you, should feel that with whatever you have chosen you are complete. Without it there would be something lacking. This system is infinitely more satisfactory than tossing gewgaws on yourself because they happen to be kicking around the bureau drawer.

Point #13: Let us now suppose your wardrobe is admirably chosen from every point of view and that even if you are wealthy you have adopted as your own a slogan I coined for *Vogue* long ago: "More Taste than Money." It is still so much our philosophy of good dressing that annually we bring out a "More Taste than Money" issue, proving our premise in page after page of fashions that are admirable rather than costly.

The same point of view has resulted in our more recent and very popular "Young Nillionaire" feature. Taste is better than money at any age, but if one has youth, a good figure, and is well informed on fashion, thanks to the ready-to-wear industry and *Vogue*'s guidance, one can be well dressed on surprisingly little outlay.

Yet even when every article is chosen with foresight and taste there is still one great fashion law to bear in mind. As in cooking or bartending, so in good dressing: the mixture is the secret. Never be guilty of wearing fancy shoes with a sports costume, an elaborate hat with a simple tailored suit. Do not wear long earrings for traveling or carry a businesslike leather bag with a filmy summer frock. Ask yourself always, Am I harmoniously put together, am I appropriately clad for the deed at hand, and I free of nonessentials? If you can truthfully answer yes, you are a well-dressed woman.

CONTEMPT FOR:

—

WALKER EVANS AND JAMES AGEE
December 26th, 1937

In 1936, famed photographer Walker Evans collaborated with writer and close friend James Agee to produce what would eventually become, five years later, *Let Us Now Praise Famous Men* – a powerful, well-received book that documented the lives of three farming families in Depression-era America. Their original intention, however, had been to write and shoot an article for *Fortune* magazine. *Fortune* had other ideas and rejected their hard work in 1937. With nothing to show for the past year's work but an unwanted article, Evans and Agee were left feeling tired and angry. On December 26th they both sat down and wrote lists of the things they hated the most.

James Agee's list

Contempt or hatred for:
The Anglo Saxon tristesse
the Anglo Saxon optimism
Anglo Saxon men in relation to their women
Anglo Saxon women
English girls
female athletes
intellectual women
most women who say fuck, shit, fart, etc
most women who do not
all women who like dirty jokes
most women who do not
the liking for dirty jokes
limited editions, especially when signed
literary pornography
handsome volumes
slim volumes
zest
gusto
Rabelaisianism
book reviewers
sex education
literature
moving picture versions of Shakespeare, famous novels, and the lives of famous people
famous people
fame
English slang
the Americanisms of Englishmen
the Anglicisms of Americans
the Anglicisms of Englishmen
the professional American
"smart" women
"smart" people
those who live in the Barbizon Plaza
doctors
plays about doctors
The Group Theatre
Orson Welles's lighting
Archibald MacLeish's courage
whatever was responsible for my maternal grandmother, for Mrs. Saunders, for my mother, for my stepfather, for my sister's trouble, for sexual pain, for the pain of sexual love.
every conception of motherhoods functions
those who bring forth, and up, children
those who despise them
those who say that things are slowly working themselves out towards the best
everything about William Shakespeare expect William Shakespeare and his own writing
      "   "   Christ except himself as I presume him, Dostoevsky, Blake, Kafka.
those who say, 'if only everyone would love one another'
the Van Gogh show at the Museum of Modern Art

the Surrealist show at same
those who saw these shows
everything about Salvador Dali except a few of his paintings
Tchelitchev
Julien Levy
Film Groups, Guilds, Sociétés, etc.,
theatres which show the best foreign films
the word film
the word shot
the words cinema, swing, stuff, reactionary, swell, modest, contact, sexual intercourse, coitus, classical historical objective, act
     of kind, conventional, unconventional, poet, art, cultivated, mind, integrity, love, God, cozy, cunning, sweet, etc etc; such
     as, angle.
Walter Winchell
Bohemians
Lucius Beebe
pedantic wit
those who use no effort not to have their lives and thinking governed by their feelings
those who are not sceptical of their own premises
all self-confessed mystics and mahatmas who permit even one disciple
sensitive young men
unconsciousness of the self-betrayal of spoken language
peasant art in other than peasant contexts
old furniture
period interiors
the distortions which every falsehood imposes on every truth
most whose feelings get hurt
those who carry off unpleasant incidents with laughter
pipes and pipe smokers
the libraries of clergy men
Alice in Wonderland
dog-lovers
the words pooch and mutt
the words prostie, bordello, etc.
the elaborate oaths of prep school boys
dictionaries of slang
the New Republic
Josef Stalin
Leon Trotsky
Karl Marx
Jane Austen
Paul Rotha
all books on movies
women through whose crotch you can see daylight when their knees are together
any creased droop under the breast
social crediters
American children who speak French
Every confusion of friendship and business
the face of Max Eastman
Walt Disney's human beings
most of the public of Disney and of Clair
publishers
journalists who like their jobs
     "   who say they don't but do

12 26 37 NYC

contempt for:

men who try to fascinate women with their minds;

gourmets, liberals, cultivated women;

writers;

successful artists who use the left to buttress their standing;

the sex life of America;

limited editions, "atmosphere", Bennington College, politics;

men of my generation who became photographers during the
    depression;

journalism, new dealers, readers of the New Yorker;

the corner of Madison Avenue and 56th Street;

the public;

Richard Wagner, radio announcers;

hobbies and hobbyists;

the soul of Josef von Sternberg;

the gay seventies', eighties, nineties, or hundreds;

art in America, the artist of America, the art lovers of
    America, the art patrons of America, the art museums of
    America, the art directors of America, the wivwes and
    mistresses and paramours of the artists of America; the
    etchings and the christmas cards and the woodcuts and the
    paintings and the letters and the memoirs and the talk
    and the beards or the cleanshaven faces of the artists
    of America;

for college bred intellectual communists with private incomes;

for safe experimentation in living or in expression;

for merrie England;

for critics;

for passing away, passing on, going on, leaving us; instead of
    dying;

for school spirit, Christmas spirit, gallant spirit, and
    whatever is meant by The American Spirit;

```
                    The Bohemian Dinner.
                    ────────────────────

The ride down town.
The Washington Square district.
The "bohemian" restaurant.
The descending steps.
The narrow hall-way.
The semi darkness.
The checking the hat.
The head waiter.
The effusive greeting.
The corner table.
The candle light.
The brick walls.
The "artistic atmosphere".
The man who plays the piano.
The wailing sounds.
The boy fiddler.
The doleful discords.
The other diners.
The curious types.
The long hair.
The low collar.
The flowing tie.
The loose clothes.
The appearance of food.
The groan.
The messy waiter.
The thumb in the soup.
The grated cheese.
The twisted bread.
The veal paté.
The minced macaroni.
The cayenne pepper.
The coughing fit.
The chemical wine.
The garlic salad.
The rum omelette.
The black coffee.
The bénédictine.
The Russian cigarette.
The "boatman's song".
The mock applause.
The 'tempermental' selection.
The drowsy feeling.
The snooze.
The sudden awakening.
The appearance of the check.
The dropped jaw.
The emptied pockets
The last penny.
The bolt for the door.
The hat.
The street.
The lack of car fares
The long walk up town.
The limping home.
The Bed.
```

THE BOHEMIAN DINNER

—

CHARLES GREEN SHAW
Circa 1930

Born in New York in 1892, Charles Green Shaw was an abstract painter whose artworks are still celebrated to this day in a number of prestigious art museums. He was also, at various points in his life, a writer, poet, illustrator and journalist. Most interestingly, however, for the purposes of this book at least, Shaw was an avid list maker. The delightful example seen here, in which he describes a recent visit to a "bohemian" restaurant in Manhattan in list form, is typically entertaining.

10 COMPOSERS I LIKE BEST

—

LUCAS ARMORY
January 2011

In January 2011, chief music critic at the *The New York Times*, Anthony Tommasini, concluded a two-week project in which he discussed the world's finest composers by unveiling a list he had personally compiled: The Top 10 Composers. As can be expected, much discussion was generated by his list, but it was a written response from eight-year-old Lucas Amory, son of noted violists Misha Amory and Hsin-Yun Huang, that really stood out.

The Top 10 Composers, by Anthony Tommasini

1. Bach
2. Beethoven
3. Mozart
4. Schubert
5. Debussy
6. Stravinsky
7. Brahms
8. Verdi
9. Wagner
10. Bartok

Hi Mr Tommasini,

I read about you in the newspaper. Like you, I adore music. So I've written two lists: The 10 Greatist Composers and: The Ones I Like Best. Lets start with 10 Greatist:

1, 2, 3: You're right about those: Bach, Beethoven, and Mozart.
4:       I disagree about that; I'd go with Haydn. Haydn is as good as Mozart, but goes with 4.
4A: If I hurt your feelings I'm sorry.
5:       This one my dad chose for me: Schubert. I gotta say, I'll have to agree. I don't know why, but I'll do it.
6:       This is hard. I'll go with Brahms. He was supposed to be lower but when I learned he burned his music...
7:       Tchaikovsky. Most definaly. He was an awesome composer.
8, 9:   Chopin is 8. Schumanns nine.
10:      Lizst?

TURN OVER FOR THE TEN COMPOSERS I LIKE BEST

Zwei Seiten: Letzte Aufzeichnungen zur „Kunst der Fuge".

Ist in der Ausgabe von **B. W.** 25¹ in vorliegender Notirung nicht mitgetheilt.

Canon al roverscio
et per augmentationem.

1. Even though my favorite piece is Tchaikovskys Violin Concerto, someone else is beside him: Schumann. Schumann wins.

[drawing]

1A: Uh-huh you get the picture
2:      Tchaikovsky.
3:      Rachmaninoff.
4:      Lizst
5:      Chopin
6:      Schubert
7:      You won't believe it: Paganini
8:      Rossini
9:      Prokoviev
10:    Grieg

Well, thats about it.

Sincerly,

Lucas Amory

P.S. I go to Lucy Moses School. I'm 8 years old.

THURBER'S RULES

—

JAMES THURBER

1949

As a successfully published and much-loved author, cartoonist and satirist whose work regularly found a home on the pages of *The New Yorker*, James Thurber was often the recipient of unsolicited manuscripts from aspiring writers. So much so, in fact, that in his 1949 book, *Thurber Country*, he printed the following list with an introduction that read, "I have established a few standing rules of my own about humor, after receiving dozens of humorous essays and stories from strangers over a period of twenty years."

1. The reader should be able to find out what the story is about.

2. Some inkling of the general idea should be apparent in the first five hundred words.

3. If the writer has decided to change the name of his protagonist from Ketcham to McTavish, Ketcham should not keep bobbing up in the last five pages. A good way to eliminate this confusion is to read the piece over before sending it out, and remove Ketcham completely. He is a nuisance.

4. The word "I'll" should not be divided so that the "I" is on one line and "'ll" on the next. The reader's attention, after the breaking up of "I'll," can never be successfully recaptured.

5. It also never recovers from such names as Ann S. Thetic, Maud Lynn, Sally Forth, Bertha Twins, and the like.

6. Avoid comic stories about plumbers who are mistaken for surgeons, sheriffs who are terrified by gunfire, psychiatrists who are driven crazy by women patients, doctors who faint at the sight of blood, adolescent girls who know more about sex than their fathers do, and midgets who turn out to be the parents of a two-hundred-pound wrestler.

I have a special wariness of people who write opening sentences with nothing in mind, and then try to create a story around them. These sentences, usually easy to detect, go like this: "Mrs. Ponsonby had never put the dog in the oven before," "'I have a wine tree, if you would care to see it,' said Mr. Dillingworth," and "Jackson decided suddenly, for no reason, really, to buy his wife a tricycle." I have never traced the fortunes of such characters in the stories I receive beyond the opening sentence, but, like you, I have a fair notion of what happens, or doesn't happen, in "The Barking Oven," "The Burgundy Tree," and "A Tricycle for Mama."

THE GODFATHER

—

FRANCIS FORD COPPOLA
Circa 1970

Few movies in the history of cinema have garnered as much praise as *The Godfather*, Francis Ford Coppola's sublimely directed crime saga set in 1940s New York. Each and every aspect of the film is close to perfect, including an impressive roster of acting talent that included Marlon Brando, Al Pacino, James Caan and Robert Duvall. However, it could have been so different. Here, from one of Coppola's notepads, is a list of potential cast members, written before production began.

CAST

Don Corleone:	Marlon Brando
John Marley	Laurence Olivier
Carlo Ponti*	*Frank Dekova
Michael Corleone:	*Al Pacino
	*Scott Marlowe
Robert di Niro	Mike Margota
Art Genovese	(Richard Romanos)
Dustin Hoffman	Jimmy Caan
Mike Parks	~~Martin Sheen~~
SONNY CORLEONE:	
	*Jimmy Caan
Tony Lo Bianco	Carmine Caridi
~~Peter Falk~~	*Scott Marlowe
Al Letteiri	*Don Gordon
	*(Tony Zerbe)
	*Lou Antonio
	(Paul Banteo)
	Robert Viharo
	(Rudy Solari)
	John Saxon
	John Brascia
	Johnny Sette (7)
	Adam Roake
Harry Guardino	Ben Gazzara
TOM HAGEN:	Ben Piazza
	*Robert Duvall
	Tony Zerbe
	*Peter Donat

MYSTERIES OF OPIUM REVEAL'D

—

DR. JOHN JONES
1700

In 1700, English physician Dr. John Jones wrote *Mysteries of Opium Reveal'd*, possibly the first treatise to tackle the subject of opium at a time when, despite its numerous dangerous side effects, it was freely available and used by many to cure and treat all manner of ailments. Much of Jones' book takes the form of lists, two of which are seen here: "The Effects of Opium taken in an Excessive Quantity" and "The seeming Contradictions in the Effects of Opium".

The Effects of Opium taken in an Excessive Quantity.

1. A Heat at Stomach.
2. A sense of Weight at Stomach (sometimes.)
3. Gaity of Humour at first.
4. Sardonick Laughter afterward.
5. Laxity, and Debility of all Parts.
6. Alienation of the Mind.
7. Loss of Memory.
8. Darkness of the Eyes.
9. Laxity of the Cornea.
10. Appearance of divers Colours.
11. Deadness of the Eyes to the View.
12. Faltring of the Tongue.
13. A Sopor.
14. A flow, and wide Pulse.
15. A high Colour.
16. Looseness of the Jaw, and Lips.
17. Intumescence of the Lips.
18. Difficulty of Breathing.
19. Fury, and Madness.
20. Venereal Fury.
21. Priapisms.
22. Violent Itchings.
23. Nausea's.
24. Swimmings in the Head.
25. Vertigo's.
26. Vomitings.
27. Hiccoughs.
28. A turbulent Pulse.
29. Convulsions, and Cold Sweats.
30. Faintings and Leipothymies.
31. Cold Breath.
32. Death.

Such as escape it generally have,

33. Plentiful Purging.
34. Sweats that smell of the Opium.
35. Violent Itchings in the Skin.

The seeming Contradictions in the Effects of Opium.

1. It causes Sleeping, and Watching.
2. It causes, and prevents Sweat.
3. It relaxes, and stops Loosenesses.
4. It stops Fluxes, and causes that of Sweat, &c.
5. It stupifies the Sense of Feeling, yet irritates by that Sense to Venery.
6. It causes Stupidity, and Promptitude in Business; Cloudiness, and Serenity of Mind.
7. It excites the Spirits, and quiets them.
8. It is very hot, yet cools in Fevers.
9. It is hot, and bitter; yet lessens Appetite, even in Cold Stomachs.
10. It stops, and promotes Urine.
11. It relaxes, and weakens; yet enables us to undergo Labours, Journeys, &c.
12. It causes, and prevents Abortions.
13. It stops Vomiting above all things; yet causes most violent, tedious, and dangerous Vomitings.
14. It stops Purging in a most eminent manner; yet sometimes causes it.
15. It is very acrimonious, yet (as all say) obtunds Acrimony; however, it allays Pain proceeding from Acrimony.
16. It causes a furious Madness; yet composes the Spirits above all things.
17. It causes Dropsies; yet sometimes cures them (as Willis says.)
18. It causes Palsies; yet have I known it to cure a Palsie.
19. It causes Driness in the Mouth; yet takes off Thirst in Fevers.
20. It cures, and causes a Hiccough.
21. It stanches Blood; yet causes the Blood to come outward, (as appears by the Efflorescence, or Redness of the Skin that it causes) yet moves the Menses and Lochia.
22. We have many Instances of it promoting, and hindering Critical Motions.
23. It raises very weak People, (when nothing besides will do it) yet it kills other weak People.
24. It causes, and cures Convulsions.
25. It causes Relaxation, and Contraction of the same Parts.
26. It Relaxes; yet causes Rigidity, Tension, and Erection of the Penis, Priapisms, &c.

AVAILABLE NAMES

—

CHARLES DICKENS

1855–65

Over the course of his illustrious career, Charles Dickens created hundreds of characters to inhabit his many novels, short stories and plays. Understandably, thinking of names for these characters, and indeed titles for the works, was quite a task, and so Dickens kept lists of such things to be considered for future use. Those seen here were kept in a single notebook that he called *Memoranda* and used from 1855 until 1865; it also contained story ideas, snippets of dialogue and general brainstorming.

AVAILABLE NAMES

Titles for books

THE LUMBER ROOM.
SOMEBODY'S LUGGAGE.
TO BE LEFT TILL CALLED FOR.
SOMETHING WANTED.
EXTREMES MEET.
NOBODY'S FAULT.
THE GRINDSTONE.
ROKESMITH'S FORGE.
OUR MUTUAL FRIEND.
THE CINDER HEAP.

TWO GENERATIONS.
BROKEN CROCKERY.
DUST.
THE HOME DEPARTMENT.
THE YOUNG PERSON.
NOW OR NEVER.
MY NEIGHBOURS.
THE CHILDREN OF THE FATHERS.
NO THOROUGHFARE.

Girls from Privy Council Education lists.

LELIA.
MENELLA.
RUBINA.
IRIS.
REBECCA.

ETTY.
REBINAH.
SEBA.
PERSIA.
ARAMANDA.

DORIS.
BALZINA.
PLEASANT.
GENTILLA.

Boys from Privy Council Education lists.

DOCTOR.
HOMER.
ODEN.
BRADLEY.

ZERUBBABEL.
MAXIMILIAN.
URBIN.
SAMILIAS.

PICKLES.
ORANGE.
FEATHER.

Girls and Boys from Ditto.

AMANDA, ETHLYNIDA; BOETIUS, BOLTIUS.

More Boys.

ROBERT LADLE.
JOLY STICK.
BILL MARIGOLD.
STEPHEN MARQUICK.
JONATHAN KNOTWELL.
PHILIP BROWNDRESS.
HENRY GHOST.

GEORGE MUZZLE.
WALTER ASHES.
ZEPHANIAH FERRY (or FURY).
WILLIAM WHY.
ROBERT GOSPEL.
THOMAS FATHERLY.
ROBIN SCRUBBAN.

More Girls.

SARAH GOLDSACKS.
ROSETTA DUST.
SUSAN GOLORING.
CATHERINE TWO.
MATILDA RAINBIRD.
MIRIAM DENIAL.
SOPHIA DOOMSDAY.

ALICE THORNEYWORE.
SALLY GIMBLET.
VERITY MAWKYARD.
BIRDIE NASH.
AMBROSINA EVENTS.
APAULINA VERNON.
NELTIE ASHFORD.

[Untitled list]

TOWNDLING.
MOOD.
GUFF.
TREBLE.
CHILBY.
SPESSIFER.
WODDER.
WHELPFORD.
FENNERCK.
GANNERSON.
CHINKERBLE.
BINTREY.
FLEDSON.
HIRLL.
BRAYLE.
MULLENDER.
TRESLINGHAM.
BRANKLE.
SITTERN.
DOSTONE.
CAY-LON.
SNOWELL.
LOTTRUM.
LAMMLE.
FROSER.
HOLBLACK.
MULLEY.
REDWORTH.
REDFOOT.
TARBOX (B).
TINKLING.
DUDDLE.
JEBUS.
POWDERHILL.
GRIMMER.
SKUSE.
TITCOOMBE.
CRABBLE.
SWANNOCK.
TUZZEN.
TWEMLOW.
SQUAB.
JACKMAN.
SUGG.

BREMMIDGE.
SILAS BLODGET.
MELVIN BEAL.
BUTTRICK.
EDSON.
SANLORN.
LIGHTWORD.
TITBULL.
BANGHAM.
KYLE—NYLE.
PEMBLE.
MAXEY.
ROKESMITH.
CHIVERY.
SLYANT.
QUEEDY.
BESSELTHUR.
MUSTY.
GROUT.
TERTIUS JOBBER.
AMON HEADSTON.
STRAYSHOTT.
HIGDEN.
MORFIT.
GOLDSTRAW.
BARREL.
INGE.
JUMP.
JIGGINS.
BONES.
COY.
DAWN.
TATKIN.
DROWVEY.
PUDSEY.
WABBLER.
PEEX—SPEEX.
GANNAWAY.
MRS. FLINKS.
FLINX.
JEE.
HARDEN.
MERDLE.
MURDEN.

TOPWASH.
PORDAGE.
DORRET—DORRIT.
CARTON.
MINIFIE.
SLINGO.
JOAD.
KINCH.
MAG.
CHELLYSON.
BLENNAM—CL.
BARDOCK.
SNIGSWORTH.
SWENTON.
CASBY—BEACH.
LOWLEIGH—LOWELY.
PIGRIN.
YERBURY.
PLORNISH.
MAROON.
BANDY-NANDY.
STONEBURY.
MAGWITCH.
MEAGLES.
PANCKS.
HAGGAGE.
PROVIS.
STILTINGTON.
PEDSEY.
DUNCALF.
TRICKLEBANK.
SAPSEA.
READYHUFF.
DUFTY.
FOGGY.
TWINN.
BROWNSWORD.
PEARTREE.
SUDDS.
SILVERMAN.
KIMBER.
LAUGHLEY.
LESSOCK.
TIPPINS.

MINNITT.
RADLOWE.
PRATCHET.
MAWDETT.
WOZENHAM.
STILTWALK.
STILTINGSTALK.
STILTSTALKING.
RAVENDER.
PODSNAP.
CLARRIKER.
COMPERY.
STRIVER—STRYVER.
PUMBLECHOOK.
WANGLER.
BOFFIN.
BANTINCK.
DIBTON.
WILFER.
GLIBBERY.
MULVEY.
HORLICK.
DOOLGE.
GANNERY.
GARGERY.
WILLSHARD.
RIDERHOOD.
PRATTERSTONE.
CHINKIBLE.
WOPSELL.
WOPSLE.
WHELPINGTON.
WHELPFORD.
GAYVERY.
WEGG.
HUBBLE.
URRY.
KIBBLE.
SKIFFINS.
WODDER.
ETSER.
AKERSHEM.

LIVE AS WELL AS YOU DARE

—

SYDNEY SMITH
February 16th, 1820

In February 1820, on learning that his good friend Lady Georgiana Morpeth was suffering from a bout of depression, noted English essayist and clergyman Sydney Smith sent her a precious letter filled with sound advice, to be followed in an effort to overcome "low spirits". Smith presented his wise words in the form of a list.

Foston, Feb. 16th, 1820

Dear Georgiana,

Nobody has suffered more from low spirits than I have—so I feel for you. Here are my prescriptions.

1st Live as well as you dare.

2nd Go into the shower-bath with a small quantity of water at a temperature low enough to give you a slight sensation of cold.

3rd Amusing books.

4th Short views of human life—not further than dinner or tea.

5th Be as busy as you can.

6th See as much as you can of those friends who respect and like you.

7th And of those acquaintances who amuse you.

8th Make no secret of low spirits to your friends, but talk of them freely—they are always worse for dignified concealment.

9th Attend to the effects tea and coffee produce upon you.

10th Compare your lot with that of other people.

11th Don't expect too much from human life—a sorry business at the best.

12th Avoid poetry, dramatic representations (except comedy), music, serious novels, melancholy sentimental people, and every thing likely to excite feeling or emotion not ending in active benevolence.

13th Do good, and endeavour to please everybody of every degree.

14th Be as much as you can in the open air without fatigue.

15th Make the room where you commonly sit, gay and pleasant.

16th Struggle by little and little against idleness.

17th Don't be too severe upon yourself, or underrate yourself, but do yourself justice.

18th Keep good blazing fires.

19th Be firm and constant in the exercise of rational religion.

20th Believe me, dear Georgiana, your devoted servant, Sydney Smith

S. SMITH
"PRESCRIPTION SPECIALIST"

56 GREEN STREET   LONDON, WI

FOR. Lady G. Morpeth

R

Live as well as you dare
— daily
Amusing books
— chapter, twice daily
Do good
— twice weekly

REG. NO. _____   S. Smith
                                           M.D.
DATE 16th February 1820

ADDRESS

A LOVE LIST

—

EERO SAARINEN
1954

Finnish-American architect Eero Saarinen was a man most notably responsible for designing, amongst other stunning buildings and structures, the Gateway Arch in St. Louis, Missouri – a seemingly gravity-defying steel archway which is the largest of its kind on earth. In 1954, Saarinen married art critic Aline Bernstein Louchheim; soon after the wedding, he wrote her a list.

I — FIRST I RECOGNIZED THAT YOU WERE VERY CLEVER

II — THAT YOU WERE VERY HANSOME

III — THAT YOU WERE PERCEPTIVE

IV — THAT YOU WERE ENTHUSIASIC.

V — THAT YOU WERE GENEROUS.

VI — THAT YOU WERE BEAUTIFUL

VII — THAT YOU WERE TERRIBLY WELL ORGANIZED

VIII — THAT YOU WERE FANTASTICALLY EFFICIENT

IX — THAT YOU DRESS VERY VERY WELL

IIIA — THAT YOU HAVE A MARVELOUS SENSE OF HUMOR

X — THAT YOU HAVE A VERY VERY BEATIFUL BODY.

XI — THAT YOU ARE UNBELIEVABLY GENEROUS TO ME.

XII — THAT THE MORE ONE DIGS THE FOUNDATIONS THE MORE AND MORE ONE FINDS THE SOLIDEST OF GRANIT FOR YOU AND I TO BUILD A LIFE TOGETHER UPON (I KNOW THIS IS NOT A GOOD SENTENCE)

I — FIRST I RECOGNIZED THAT YOU WERE
VERY CLEVER

II — THAT YOU WERE VERY HANSOME

III — THAT YOU WERE PERCEPTIVE

IV — THAT YOU WERE ENTHUSIASIC.

V — THAT YOU WERE GENEROUS.

VI — THAT YOU WERE BEAUTIFUL

VII — THAT YOU WERE TERRIBLY WELL ORGANIZED

VIII — THAT YOU WERE FANTASTICALLY EFFICIENT

IX — THAT YOU ~~WILL~~ DRESS VERY VERY WELL

IIIa — THAT YOU HAVE A MARVELOUS SENCE
OF HUMOR

X THAT YOU HAVE A VERY VERY BEUTIFUL
BODY.

XI THAT YOU ARE UNBELIEVABLY GENEROUS
TO ME.

XII THAT THE MORE ONE DIGS THE
FOUNDATIONS THE MORE AND MORE
ONE FINDS THE SOLIDEST OF
GRANIT FOR YOU AND I TO BUILD
A LIFE TOGETHER UPON
↳ I KNOW THIS IS NOT
A GOOD SENTENCE

COCKTAIL!

—

F. SCOTT FITZGERALD
January 1926

F. Scott Fitzgerald was one of the most famous novelists of the 20th century, having been responsible for writing such classics as *The Great Gatsby* and *Tender is the Night*. He was also notorious for his excessive drinking during the Roaring Twenties and spent much of the decade topped up with alcohol, ultimately to the detriment of his health. It seems quite apt, then, to find, in a letter written to Blanche W. Knopf, a list in which he conjugates the verb "to cocktail".

Present	I cocktail	We cocktail
	Thou cocktail	You cocktail
	It cocktails	They cocktail
Imperfect	I was cocktailing	
Perfect (pastdefinate)	I cocktailed	
Past perfect	I have cocktailed	
Conditional	I might have cocktailed	
Pluperfect	I had cocktailed	
Subjunctive	I would have cocktailed	
Voluntary Sub.	I should have cocktailed	
Preterite	I did cocktail	
Imperative	Cocktail!	
Interrogative	Cocktailest thou? (Dos't Cocktail?) (or Wilt Cocktail?)	
Subjunctive Conditional	I would have had to have cocktailed	
Conditional Subjunctive	I might have had to have cocktailed	
Participle	Cocktailing	

℅ Guaranty Trust
1, Rue des Italiennes

Dear Blanche:

    I hate like hell to have to decline all those invitations but as this is three days too late I've no choice. As "cocktail", so I gather, has become a verb, it ought to be be conjugated at least once, so 'ere goes

Present   I cocktail   We cocktail
           Thou ~~You~~ cocktail   You cocktail
           It cocktails   They cocktail

Imperfect   I was cocktailing

Perfect   I cocktailed
(past definate)

Past perfect   I have cocktailed

Conditional   I might have cocktailed

Pluperfect   I had cocktailed

Subjunctive   I would have cocktailed

Voluntary Sub.   I should have cocktailed

Preterite   I did Cocktail

Imperative   Cocktail!

Interrogative   Cocktailest thou? (Dost Cocktail)
                       (or Wilt cocktail?)

Subjunctive Conditional   I would have had to have cocktailed

Conditional Subjunctive   I might have had to have
                                      cocktailed

Participle   Cocktailing

I find this getting dull, and would much

HENRY MILLER'S 11 COMMANDMENTS

—

HENRY MILLER
Circa 1932

Henry Miller was an innovative author who broke the rules, quite literally, and saw his now classic novels banned in the US until a 1964 ruling by the Supreme Court decided they weren't obscene. He did, however, have his own boundaries. In the early 1930s, as he wrote what would become his first published novel – the hugely influential *Tropic of Cancer* – he wrote a list of 11 commandments, to be followed by himself.

COMMANDMENTS

1. Work on one thing at a time until finished.

2. Start no more new books, add no more new material to "Black Spring."

3. Don't be nervous. Work calmly, joyously, recklessly on whatever is in hand.

4. Work according to Program and not according to mood. Stop at the appointed time!

5. When you can't *create* you can *work*.

6. Cement a little every day, rather than add new fertilizers.

7. Keep human! See people, go places, drink if you feel like it.

8. Don't be a draught-horse! Work with pleasure only.

9. Discard the Program when you feel like it—but go back to it next day. *Concentrate. Narrow down. Exclude.*

10. Forget the books you want to write. Think only of the book you *are* writing.

11. Write first and always. Painting, music, friends, cinema, all these come afterwards.

BRAINES.

—

A.T. (PRACTITIONER IN PHISICKE AND CHIRURGERIE.)

1596

From the concisely titled self-help medical book, *A Rich Store-house or Treasury for the Diseased. Wherein, are many approved Medicines for diuers and sundry Diseases, which haue been long hidden, and not come to light before this time. Now set foorth for the great benefit and comfort of the poorer sort of people that are not of abillitie to go to the Physitions*, comes two lists: the first, of things that were then, in 1596, considered "good" for the brain; the second, of things thought to be "ill" for the brain.

Braines.

A Rule to knowe what thinges are good and holosome for the Braine.

To smell to Camamill or Muske, + To eate Sage, but not ouermuch, + To drinke Wine measurablie, + To keepe the Head warme, + To washe your Hands often, + To walke measurablie, + To sleepe measurablie, + To heare litle noise or Musicke or singers, + To eate Mustarde & Pepper, + To smell the sauoue of Red-roses, & to washe the Temples of your Head often with Rose-Water.

These Thinges are ill for the Braine.

All maner of Braines, + Gluttony, + Drunkennes, + Late Suppers, + To sleepe much after meate, + Anger, + Heauines of minde, + To stand much bare-headed, + Corrupt Aires, + To eate ouermuch or hastely, + Ouermuch heate in Trauaylinge or Labouringe, + Ouermuch Watching, + Ouermuch Colde, + Ouermuch Bathing, + Milke, + Cheese, + Garlicke, + Oynions + Ouermuch Knocking or Noise, & to smell a white Rose.

Cap. 144.

¶ A Rule to knowe what thinges are good and holosome for the Braine.

To smell to Camamill or Muske, + To eate Sage, but not ouermuch, + To drinke Wine measurablie, + To keepe the Head warme, + To washe your Hands often, + To walke measurablie, + To sleepe measurablie,— + To heare litle noise of Musicke or singers, + To eate Mustarde & Pepper, + To smell the sauour of Red-roses, & to washe the Temples of your Heade often with Rose-Water. +

Cap. 145.

¶ These Thinges are ill for the Braine.

+ All maner of Braines, + Gluttony, + Drunkennes, + Late Suppers, + To sleepe much after meate, + Anger, + Heauines of minde, + To stande much bare-headed, + Corrupt Aires, + To eate ouermuch or hastely, + Ouermuch heate in Trauaylinge or Labouringe, + Ouermuch Watching, + Ouermuch Colde, + Ouermuch Bathing, + Milke, + Cheese, + Garlicke, + Oynions + Ouermuch Knocking or Noise, & to smell to a white + Rose. +

SIMPLE RULES FOR LIFE IN LONDON

—

RUDYARD KIPLING
June 9th, 1908

Rudyard Kipling is one of the most famous writers in modern history, having written, in 1894, a story collection by the name of *The Jungle Book* that has since been enjoyed in various forms by many millions of people, but which was just one of countless poems, stories and essays he penned. On June 9th, 1908 he wrote a particularly important piece: a letter to his youngest daughter, 12-year-old Elsie, who was soon to be travelling to London many miles away, in which this list of "rules for Life in London" was included.

Dear Bird,

[…]

I send you a few simple rules for Life in London.

1. Wash early and often with soap and hot water.

2. Do not roll on the grass of the parks. It will come off black on your dress.

3. Never eat penny buns, oysters, periwinkles or peppermints on the top of a bus. It annoys the passengers.

4. Be kind to policemen. You never know when you may be taken up.

5. Never stop a motor bus with your foot. It is not a croquet ball.

6. Do not attempt to take pictures off the wall of the National Gallery, or to remove cases of butterflies from the National History Museum. You will be noticed if you do.

7. Avoid late hours, pickled salmon, public meetings, crowded crossings, gutters, water-carts and over-eating.

Ever your

Daddo

213

THE FAKE BOOKS OF CHARLES DICKENS

—

CHARLES DICKENS
October 1851

In 1851, Charles Dickens and his family moved to Tavistock House, the London home in which he would go on to write *A Tale of Two Cities*, *Bleak House* and *Little Dorrit*. All was close to perfect, but there was one small dilemma: he didn't have in his possession enough books to fill the many bookshelves offered by his new abode. Rather than purchase more reading material, Dickens' creative solution was to instead fill the gaps with fake books, the witty titles of which he had invented and then supplied, by letter, to a local bookbinder named Thomas Robert Eeles. The list read as follows.

History of a Short Chancery Suit
Catalogue of Statues of the Duke of Wellington
Five Minutes in China. 3 vols.
Forty Winks at the Pyramids. 2 vols.
Abernethy on the Constitution. 2 vols.
Mr. Green's Overland Mail. 2 vols.
Captain Cook's Life of Savage. 2 vols.
A Carpenter's Bench of Bishops. 2 vols.
Toots' Universal Letter-Writer. 2 vols.
Orson's Art of Etiquette.
Downeaster's Complete Calculator.
History of the Middling Ages. 6 vols.
Jonah's Account of the Whale.
Captain Parry's Virtues of Cold Tar.
Kant's Ancient Humbugs. 10 vols.
Bowwowdom. A Poem.
The Quarrelly Review. 4 vols.
The Gunpowder Magazine. 4 vols.
Steele. By the Author of "Ion."
The Art of Cutting the Teeth.
Matthew's Nursery Songs. 2 vols.
Paxton's Bloomers. 5 vols.
On the Use of Mercury by the Ancient Poets.
Drowsy's Recollections of Nothing. 3 vols.
Heavyside's Conversations with Nobody. 3 vols.
Commonplace Book of the Oldest Inhabitant. 2 vols.
Growler's Gruffiology, with Appendix. 4 vols.
The Books of Moses and Sons. 2 vols.
Burke (of Edinburgh) on the Sublime and Beautiful. 2 vols.
Teazer's Commentaries.
King Henry the Eighth's Evidences of Christianity. 5 vols.
Miss Biffin on Deportment.
Morrison's Pills Progress. 2 vols.
Lady Godiva on the Horse.
Munchausen's Modern Miracles. 4 vols.
Richardson's Show of Dramatic Literature. 12 vols.
Hansard's Guide to Refreshing Sleep. As many volumes as possible.

DICKENS' BOOKS

FORTY WINKS
AT THE
PYRAMIDS

CRIME

CHARLES DICKENS

DICKENS' BOOKS

LADY GODIVA
ON THE
HORSE

FICTION

CHARLES DICKENS

DICKENS' BOOKS

ORSON'S
ART OF
ETIQUETTE

ESSAYS/LETTERS

CHARLES DICKENS

DICKENS' BOOKS

THE
QUARRELLY
REVIEW

FICTION

VOL I.

DICKENS' BOOKS

PAXTON'S
BLOOMERS

FICTION

VOL 3.

DICKENS' BOOKS

JONAH'S
ACCOUNT OF
THE WHALE

NON-FICTION

CHARLES DICKENS

DICKENS' BOOKS

KANT'S
ANCIENT
HUMBUGS

BIOGRAPHY

VOL 8.

DICKENS' BOOKS

THE ART OF
CUTTING
TEETH

CRIME

CHARLES DICKENS

DICKENS' BOOKS

FIVE
MINUTES
IN CHINA

FICTION

VOL 2.

THE DON'TS AND BE CAREFULS

—

MOTION PICTURE PRODUCERS AND
DISTRIBUTORS OF AMERICA
1927

In 1927, the Motion Picture Producers and
Distributors of America produced and published
a list, titled *The Don'ts and Be Carefuls*, in an effort
to clean up Hollywood's increasingly controversial
output and help the studios avoid further clashes
with the country's regional censorship boards.
The list consisted of 11 things to be completely
avoided in future movies (the "Don'ts"), and 25
things that required careful consideration before
inclusion (the "Be Carefuls"). Much to their
annoyance, the list was unenforceable, and so
to some extent ignored. In 1930 it was ditched
in favour of the Motion Picture Production Code,
which in turn gave way to the MPAA film rating
system we now know.

"The Don'ts and Be Carefuls"

Motion Picture Producers and Distributors of America, 1927

Resolved, That those things which are included in the following list shall not
appear in pictures produced by the members of this Association, irrespective of the
manner in which they are treated.

1. Pointed profanity — by either title or lip — this includes the words "God,"
   "Lord," "Jesus," "Christ" (unless they be used reverently in connection
   with proper religious ceremonies), "hell," "damn," "Gawd," and every other
   profane and vulgar expression however it may be spelled;
2. Any licentious or suggestive nudity — in fact or in silhouette; and any
   lecherous or licentious notice thereof by other characters in the picture;
3. The illegal traffic in drugs;
4. Any inference of sex perversion;
5. White slavery;
6. Miscegenation (sex relationships between the white and black races);
7. Sex hygiene and venereal diseases;
8. Scenes of actual childbirth — in fact or in silhouette;
9. Children's sex organs;
10. Ridicule of the clergy;
11. Willful offense to any nation, race or creed;

And be it further resolved, That special care be exercised in the manner in which
the following subjects are treated, to the end that vulgarity and suggestiveness be
eliminated and that good taste may be emphasized:

1. The use of the flag;
2. International relations (avoiding picturizing in an unfavorable light another
   country's religion, history, institutions, prominent people, and citizenry);
3. Arson;
4. The use of firearms;
5. Theft, robbery, safe-cracking, and dynamiting of trains, mines, building, etc.
   (having in mind the effect which a too-detailed description of these may have
   upon the moron);
6. Brutality and possible gruesomeness;
7. Techniques of committing murder by whatever method;
8. Methods of smuggling;
9. Third-degree methods;
10. Actual hangings or electrocutions as legal punishment for crime;
11. Sympathy for criminals;
12. Attitude toward public characters and institutions;
13. Sedition;
14. Apparent cruelty to children and animals;
15. Branding of people or animals;

16. The sale of women, or of a woman selling her virtue;
17. Rape or attempted rape;
18. First-night scenes;
19. Man and woman in bed together;
20. Deliberate seduction of girls;
21. The institution of marriage;
22. Surgical operations;
23. The use of drugs;
24. Titles or scenes having to do with law enforcement or law-enforcing officers;
25. Excessive or lustful kissing, particularly when one character or the other is a "heavy."

MARRY/NOT MARRY

—

CHARLES DARWIN
July 1838

In July 1838, 21 years before his ground-breaking book, *On the Origin of Species*, was published, 29-year-old naturalist Charles Darwin found himself facing a difficult decision: whether or not to propose to the love of his life, Emma Wedgwood. This was his handwritten solution – a list of pros and cons of marriage that includes such gems as "better than a dog anyhow" and "not forced to visit relatives". Indeed, the pros were too numerous to ignore, and six months later they were wed. The couple remained married until Darwin's death in 1882. They had ten children.

This is the Question

Marry

Children — (if it Please God) — Constant companion, (& friend in old age) who will feel interested in one, — object to be beloved & played with. — better than a dog anyhow. — Home, & someone to take care of house — Charms of music & female chit-chat. — These things good for one's health. — Forced to visit & receive relations but terrible loss of time. —

W My God, it is intolerable to think of spending ones whole life, like a neuter bee, working, working, & nothing after all. — No, no won't do. — Imagine living all one's day solitarily in smoky dirty London House. — Only picture to yourself a nice soft wife on a sofa with good fire, & books & music perhaps — Compare this vision with the dingy reality of Grt. Marlbro' St.

Not Marry

No children, (no second life), no one to care for one in old age.— What is the use of working 'in' without sympathy from near & dear friends — who are near & dear friends to the old, except relatives

Freedom to go where one liked — choice of Society & little of it. — Conversation of clever men at clubs — Not forced to visit relatives, & to bend in every trifle. — to have the expense & anxiety of children — perhaps quarelling — Loss of time. — cannot read in the Evenings — fatness & idleness — Anxiety & responsibility — less money for books &c — if many children forced to gain one's bread. — (But then it is very bad for ones health to work too much)

Perhaps my wife wont like London; then the sentence is banishment & degradation into indolent, idle fool —

Marry, Marry, Marry Q.E.D.

Marry

This is the

Children — (if it Please God) — Constant companion,
(& friend in old age) who will feel interested in one, — object to be
— better than a dog anyhow. —
beloved & played with. — Home, & someone
to take care of house — Charms of music &
female chit-chat. — These things good for
one's health. — but terrible loss of time. —

My God, it is intolerable to think of
spending one's whole life, like a neuter
bee, working, working, & nothing after
all. — No, no won't do. — Imagine living
all one's day solitarily in smoky dirty London
House. — Only picture to yourself a nice
soft wife on a sofa with good fire,
& books & music perhaps — Compare this
vision with the dingy reality of Gt. Marlbro'
Marry — Marry — Marry Q.E.D.

Not Marry

No children, (no second life) no one to care for one in old age. — What is the use of working without sympathy from near & dear friends — who are near & dear friends to the old. except relatives

Freedom to go where one liked — choice of Society & little of it. — Conversation of clever men at clubs — Not forced to visit relatives, & to bend in every trifle. — to have the expense & anxiety of children — perhaps quarrelling — Loss of time. — cannot read in the Evenings — fatness & idleness — Anxiety & responsibility — less money for books &c — if many children forced to gain one's bread. — (But then it is very bad for one's health to work too much)

Perhaps my wife wont like London; then the sentence is banishment & degradation into indolent, idle fool —

VONNEGUT'S COMMITMENTS

—

KURT VONNEGUT
January 26th, 1947

By January 1947, less than two years after escaping captivity during World War II and a few years before his writing career took off, Kurt Vonnegut had been married to his first wife, Jane, for 16 months. She was also pregnant with their first child, a situation which prompted Vonnegut to produce a contract in which was listed a number of commitments for him to adhere to – essentially an amusingly worded promise to take care of certain household chores. Kurt and Jane went on to have three children; they also adopted all three of his sister's children following her tragic death in 1957.

I, Kurt Vonnegut, Jr., that is, do hereby swear that I will be faithful to the commitments hereunder listed:

I. With the agreement that my wife will not nag, heckle, and otherwise disturb me, on the subject, I promise to scrub the bathroom and kitchen floors once a week, on a day and hour of my own choosing. Not only that, but I will do a good and thorough job, and by that she means that I will get *under* the bathtub, *behind* the toilet, *under* the sink, *under* the icebox, *into* the corners; and I will pick up and put in some other location whatever movable objects happen to be on said floors at the time so as to get under them too, and not just around them. Furthermore, while I am undertaking these tasks I will refrain from indulging in such remarks as "Shit," "Goddamn sonofabitch," and similar vulgarities, as such language is nervewracking to have around the house when nothing more drastic is taking place than the facing of Necessity. *If I do not live up to this agreement*, my wife is to feel free to nag, heckle and otherwise disturb me until I am driven to scrub the floors anyway—*no matter how busy I am.*

II. I furthermore swear that I will observe the following minor amenities:

> a. I will hang up my clothes and put my shoes in the closet when I am not wearing them;

> b. I will not track dirt into the house needlessly, by such means as not wiping my feet on the mat outside, and by wearing my bedroom slippers to take out the garbage, and other things;

> c. I will throw such things as used up match folders, empty cigarette packages, the piece of cardboard that comes in shirt collars, etc, into a wastebasket instead of leaving them around on chairs or the floor;

> d. After shaving I will put my shaving equipment back in the medicine closet;

> e. In case I should be the direct cause of a ring around the bathtub after taking a bath, I will, with the aid of Swift's Cleanser and a brush, *not* my washcloth, remove said ring;

> f. With the agreement that my wife collects the laundry, places it in a laundry bag, and leaves the laundry bag in plain sight in the hall, I will take said laundry to the Laundry not more than three days after said laundry has made its appearance in the hall; I will furthermore bring the *clean* laundry back from the Laundry within two weeks after I have taken it, dirty that is;

> g. When smoking I will make every effort to keep the ashtray which I am using at the time upon a surface that does not slant, sag, slope, dip, wrinkle, or give way upon the slightest provocation; such surfaces may be understood to include stacks of books precariously mounted on the edge of a chair, the arms of the chair that has arms, and my own knees;

h. I will not put out cigarettes upon the sides of, or throw ashes into either the red leather waste-basket, or the stamp waste-basket which my loving wife made me for Christmas, 1945, as such practise noticeably impairs the beauty, and ultimate practicability of said waste-baskets;

i. In the event that my wife makes a request of me, and that request cannot be regarded as other than reasonable and wholly within the province of a man's work (when his wife is pregnant, that is), I will comply with said request within three days after my wife has presented it: It is understood that my wife will make no reference to the subject, other than saying thank you, of course, *within these three days*; if, however, I fail to comply with said request after a more substantial length of time has elapsed, my wife shall be completely justified in nagging heckling and otherwise disturbing me, until I am driven to do that which I should have done;

j. An exception to the above three-day time limit is the taking out of the garbage, which, as any fool knows, had better not wait that long; I will take out the garbage within three *hours* after the need for disposal has been pointed out to me by my wife. It would be nice, however, if, upon observing the need for disposal with my own two eyes, I should perform this particular task upon my own initiative, and thus not make it necessary for my wife to bring up a subject that is moderately distasteful to her;

k. It is understood that, should I find these commitments in any way unreasonable or too binding upon my freedom, I will take steps to amend them by counter-proposals, constitutionally presented and politely discussed, instead of unlawfully terminating my obligations with a simple burst of obscenity, or something like that, and the subsequent persistent neglect of said obligations;

l. The terms of this contract are understood to be binding up until that time after the arrival of our child, (to be specified by the doctor,) when my wife will once again be in full possession of all her faculties, and able to undertake more arduous pursuits than are now advisable.

SIGNATURE

KURT VONNEGUT

A DECALOGUE OF CANONS FOR OBSERVATION IN PRACTICAL LIFE

—

THOMAS JEFFERSON
1825

In 1825, the year before his death, Thomas Jefferson – the third US President and a Founding Father of the United States of America – was asked by a father to supply some words of wisdom to his young son, Thomas Jefferson Smith, who had recently been named after the President. Jefferson graciously responded with a handwritten letter, at the end of which was a ten-point list of advice for the youngster, titled, "A Decalogue of Canons for observation in practical life".

A Decalogue of Canons for observation in practical life.

1.   Never put off till tomorrow what you can do to-day.
2.   Never trouble another for what you can do yourself.
3.   Never spend your money before you have it.
4.   Never buy a what you do not want, because it is cheap; it will be dear to you.
5.   Pride costs us more than hunger, thirst and cold.
6.   We never repent of having eaten too little.
7.   Nothing is troublesome that we do willingly.
8.   How much pain have cost us the evils which have never happened!
9.   Take things always by their smooth handle.
10. When angry, count ten, before you speak; if very angry, an hundred.

a Decalogue of Canons for observation in practical life.

1. Never put off till tomorrow what you can do to-day.
2. Never trouble another for what you can do yourself.
3. Never spend your money before you have it.
4. Never buy a what you do not want, because it is cheap; it will be dear to you.
5. Pride costs us more than hunger, thirst and cold.
6. We never repent of having eaten too little.
7. Nothing is troublesome that we do willingly.
8. How much pain have cost us the evils which have never happened!
9. Take things always by their smooth handle.
10. When angry, count ten, before you speak; if very angry, an hundred.

TEN COMMANDMENTS OF GUITAR PLAYING
—
CAPTAIN BEEFHEART
Late 1970s

Captain Beefheart was a musician and singer who, despite little commercial success, captured the hearts of many and influenced a whole raft of performers who followed. His 1969 album, *Trout Mask Replica*, is regarded a masterpiece by many and sits firmly in numerous "Greatest Album" lists. In 1976, Moris Tepper joined Beefheart's Magic Band to play guitar – a position he held until Beefheart's retirement in 1982. It was during this period that Tepper was handed the "Ten Commandments of Guitar Playing", as written by Beefheart himself.

1. Listen to the birds.
   That's where all the music comes from. Birds know everything about how it should sound and where that sound should come from. And watch hummingbirds. They fly really fast, but a lot of times they aren't going anywhere.

2. Your guitar is not really a guitar.
   Your guitar is a divining rod. Use it to find spirits in the other world and bring them over. A guitar is also a fishing rod. If you're good, you'll land a big one.

3. Practice in front of a bush.
   Wait until the moon is out, then go outside, eat a multi-grained bread and play your guitar to a bush. If the bush doesn't shake, eat another piece of bread.

4. Walk with the devil.
   Old Delta blues players referred to guitar amplifiers as the "devil box." And they were right. You have to be an equal opportunity employer in terms of who you're bringing over from the other side. Electricity attracts devils and demons. Other instruments attract other spirits. An acoustic guitar attracts Casper. A mandolin attracts Wendy. But an electric guitar attracts Beelzebub.

5. If you're guilty of thinking, you're out.
   If your brain is part of the process, you're missing it. You should play like a drowning man, struggling to reach shore. If you can trap that feeling, then you have something that is fur bearing.

6. Never point your guitar at anyone.
   Your instrument has more clout than lightning. Just hit a big chord then run outside to hear it. But make sure you are not standing in an open field.

7. Always carry a church key.
   That's your key-man clause. Like One String Sam. He's one. He was a Detroit street musician who played in the fifties on a homemade instrument. His song "I Need a Hundred Dollars" is warm pie. Another key to the church is Hubert Sumlin, Howlin' Wolf's guitar player. He just stands there like the Statue of Liberty — making you want to look up her dress the whole time to see how he's doing it.

8. Don't wipe the sweat off your instrument.
   You need that stink on there. Then you have to get that stink onto your music.

9. Keep your guitar in a dark place.
   When you're not playing your guitar, cover it and keep it in a dark place. If you don't play your guitar for more than a day, be sure you put a saucer of water in with it.

10. You gotta have a hood for your engine.
    Keep that hat on. A hat is a pressure cooker. If you have a roof on your house, the hot air can't escape. Even a lima bean has to have a piece of wet paper around it to make it grow.

THINGS DOING AND TO BE DONE

—

THOMAS EDISON
January 3rd, 1888

Born in 1847, Thomas Edison remains to this day one of the most prolific inventors in history with an impressive 1093 patents to his name in the United States alone. Some of his biggest breakthroughs included the invention of the phonograph, the development of the first practical incandescent light bulb, and the design of the Kinetograph, an early motion picture camera. It is therefore no surprise to learn that Edison relied on to-do lists that could make the busiest of us feel comparatively slothful. This five-page example was written in January 1888 – notable entries include "Electrical Piano", "Artificial Ivory" and "Ink for Blind",

Things doing and to be done;

Cotton Picker
New Standard Phonograph
Hand turning phonograph.
New Slow Speed cheap Dynamo.
New Expansion Pyromagnetic Dynamo.
Deaf Apparatus
Electrical Piano
Long distance standard Telephone transmitter
which employs devices of recording phonogh
Telephone Coil of Fe by H in Parafine or other insulator
Platina Point Trans using new phono Recorder devices;
Grd Battery for Telephone;
"   "   "   "   Long distance
"   "   "   "   Phonoplex
"   "   "   "   Jump telegraph
"   "   "   "   Volt motor,

Improved Magnetic Bridge for practical work
Motograph Mirror
"   Relay
"   Telophone practical.

Artificial Cable.
Phono motor to work on 100 volt ckts
Duplicating Phono Cylinders
Deposit in Vacuo on Lace gold & silver
also on Cotton Molten Chemical compound of lustrous
surface to imitate silk — also reg plating system
Vacuous Ore milling Large Machine;
Magnetite Seperator Large   "
Locking Material for Iron sand.

THINGS DOING AND TO BE DONE

Artificial Silk

Artificial filiments

NEW 17's —

Uninflammable Insulating Material

Good wax for phonograms

Phonographic Clock

Large Phonograph for Novels etc

Pig Iron Exprmts with Electricity & Magnetism

Malleablezing Cast iron in Vacuo

Drawing fine wire.

Toy phonograph for Dolls

Cable Motograph

Very Loud Matograph Telephone with
1/3 sez phonogh motor.

Magneto Telephone nearly actual contact and magnet
compression of an adjustable rubber piece as in new phono

Snow Compressor

Glass plate water On- Reperator

Tinned faced iron for Stove Castings

Refining Copper Electrically

Quad neutral relay

Cheap low induct Cap insulating material
for Lead Cable people —

Constant mould for non foundry

THINGS DOING AND TO BE DONE

200 Volt 20 cp lamp

Cheap pressure Indicator

Recording Volt Indicator

Box balancing System

Alternating Machine & Transformer

Silver Surface Switches

Vulcanizing the 7¢ African Rubber adulterant.

Platinum wire Ice cutting Machine,

Silver wire wood Cutting system

Silvering or Coppering bolting Cloth in Vac for durability

S Motor altered own with new devices for C speed

Expansion Mirror Plat-Irid- wire in Vacuo

Photoghy through Opaque Screens;

Photoghy by causing heat at the Critical points -

Boron fil.

Hg out of Lamp

Phonoplex Repeater

Squirting glass sheet tube &c Etc Nickel moulds

Artificial Mother Pearl.

Red Lead pencils equal to Graphite

India Ink

Tracing Cloth

Ink for Blind

THINGS DOING AND TO BE DONE

Fluffy Incandescent Burner for gas

Regenerative Kerosene burner

Centralized arc in Arc Lamp

Carmen Tesla Arc Lamp test

Straightening alternating Cts by street Dynamo

ERR Continuous reducers

Electroplating Machine for Schenectady

Condenser Transformer

Sqr ft diffraction gratings on silver by 5000 inch dia tool
Special precision lathe for ornamental purposes —

Photo Scintillations.

Cheap plan produce Mimeograph surfaces

Miners battery & Lamp

Sorting Coal from Slate Machine

Butter direct from Milk

Burning asphalt Candles by high chimney

Magnets RR signals

Soften ink of books transfer to Cop plate & plate
to obtain matrix

Telephone Repeater

Substitute for Hard rubber

Artificial Ivory

Soften Vegetable Ivory to press in sheets

Various battery on Lolande Type

Revolving Thermo

THINGS DOING AND TO BE DONE

Call or Indicator for Jump teligh

Marine telegraphy

Long distance speaking tube filled H_2O 2 dia pressure.

Lead plate battery for modifying alternating Current.

Two revolving bands in battery lead forced pass in liquid close together & out into seperate Chambers to peroxidize one & reduce by gas the other —

Siren phonogh —

Perm mag like an Electromag of discs hard steel high polish seperately magnetized & forced together powerfully .005" thick ——

Telephone working molecularly

Ear tubes formed ~~more~~ crescent drawn wire

Long strip 50 cp carbon under stress & index for Cheap Voltmeter.

Chalk Battery.

Dynamo or motor long tube in long magnetic field top & bottom contacts forcing water through generates current by its passage.

Naphthalene in Benzol in oil cups for Lubricant.

Diamagnetimeter. Capillary tube liquid rising repelled by powerful magnet, also iron solution to pump ——

(Thermo battery Slide Copper oxidized then plated over surface oxide a nickel to make good Contact. Iron if possible ——

Disk phonogh

237

11 RULES FOR BOX-OFFICE
APPEAL

—

PRESTON STURGES
1941

In 1940, American film-maker and "father of the screwball comedy" Preston Sturges made his directorial debut with *The Great McGinty*, a political satire that was warmly received by critics. The film was also enjoyed by the Academy of Motion Picture Arts and Sciences, and particularly its screenplay, written by Sturges, which was later awarded an Oscar. For the next few years, he continued to produce his best work. In 1941, just as his star was rising, Sturges drew up a list: "eleven rules for box-office appeal".

1. A pretty girl is better than an ugly one.
2. A leg is better than an arm.
3. A bedroom is better than a living room.
4. An arrival is better than a departure.
5. A birth is better than a death.
6. A chase is better than a chat.
7. A dog is better than a landscape.
8. A kitten is better than a dog.
9. A baby is better than a kitten.
10. A kiss is better than a baby.
11. A pratfall is better than anything.

DEGREES OF VAGABOND

—

THOMAS HARMAN

1566

In 1566, Thomas Harman published *A Caveat or Warning for Common Cursitors, Vulgarly called Vagabonds*, a book that aimed to shine a light on what he believed to be the devious rogues of society. As well as retelling stories of thievery, detailing the techniques of such criminals and providing a dictionary of rogues' secret language ("Thieves' Cant"), each of the book's first 23 chapters were named after a different class of vagabond, as identified by Harman. Those chapter titles soon became the following popular list, as described in William Harrison's *Description of England* 11 years later.

The several disorders and degrees amongst our idle vagabonds:

1. Rufflers [thieving beggars, apprentice uprightmen]
2. Uprightmen [leaders of robber bands]
3. Hookers or anglers [thieves who steal through open windows with hooks]
4. Rogues [rank-and-file vagabonds]
5. Wild rogues [those born of rogues]
6. Priggers of prancers [horse thieves]
7. Palliards [male and female beggars, traveling in pairs]
8. Fraters [sham proctors, pretending to beg for hospitals, etc.]
9. Abrams [feined lunatics]
10. Fresh-water mariners or whipjacks [beggars pretending shipwreck]
11. Dummerers [sham deaf-mutes]
12. Drunken tinkers [thieves using the trade as a cover]
13. Swadders or peddlers [thieves pretending to be peddlers]
14. Jarkmen [forgers of licenses] or patricoes [hedge priests].

Of womenkind

1. Demanders for glimmer or fire [female beggars pretending loss of fire]
2. Bawdy baskets [female peddlars]
3. Morts [prostitutes and thieves]
4. Autem [married] morts
5. Walking [unmarried] morts
6. Doxies [prostitutes who begin with uprightmen]
7. Dells [young girls, incipient doxies]
8. Kinchin morts [female beggar children]
9. Kinchin coes [male beggar children].

WILD ROGUES

DRUMMERERS

DRUNKEN TINKERS

SWADDERS

KINCHIN MORTS

ABRAMS

RUFFLERS

JARKMEN

UPRIGHTMEN

WHIPJACKS.

VERTIGO

—

PARAMOUNT
October 24th, 1957

As production on the movie adaptation of the novel *D'entre les morts* began in 1957, behind the scenes a tug of war developed between its director, Alfred Hitchcock, and studio, Paramount – all because of its title. Hitchcock wanted *Vertigo*, and nothing less. The studio repeatedly shot it down and offered a selection of alternatives that included *Tonight is Ours* and *The Mad Carlotta*. Still, Hitchcock refused to budge. Weeks later, on October 24th, 1957, Paramount executive Sam Frey tried one last time to change Hitchcock's mind and sent him this list of suggestions.

Yet again, Hitchcock stood firm. Paramount threw in the towel.

Afraid to Love
Alone in the Dark
The Apparition
Behind the Mask
Carlotta
Checkmate
Conscience
Cry from the Rooftop
The Dark Tower
Deceit
Deceitful
Deception
Don't Leave Me
Dream Without Ending
The Face
Variations
Footsteps
For the Last Time
The Hidden life
In the Shadows
The Investigator
A Life Is Forever
The Lure
Malice
The Mask and the Face
The Mask Illusion
My Madeleine
~~A Matter of Fact~~
Never Leave Me
Night Shade
Nothing Is Forever
Now and Forever
Past, Present and Future
The Phantom
The Second Chance
The Shadow
Shadow and Substance
Shadow on the Stairs Shock
Steps on the Stairs Terror
To Live Again
Tonight Is Ours
Too Late My Love
Two Kinds of Women
The Unknown
Wanted
Without A Trace
The Witness

PARAMOUNT PRESENTS

JAMES STEWART
KIM NOVAK
IN ALFRED HITCHCOCK'S
MASTERPIECE

'VERTIGO'

CO STARRING
BARBARA BEL GEDDES WITH TOM HELMORE HENRY JONES DIRECTED BY ALFRED HITCHCOCK SCREENPLAY BY ALEC COPPEL & SAMUEL TAYLOR TECHNICOLOR®
BASED UPON THE NOVEL 'D'ENTRE 'LES MORTS' BY PIERRE BOILEAU AND THOMAS NARCEJAC MUSIC BY BERNARD HERRMANN

SEVEN SOCIAL SINS

—

MOHANDAS GANDHI
October 1947

In October 1947, Mohandas Gandhi handed a piece of paper to his visiting grandson, Arun Gandhi, upon which was written the following: a list that he said contained "the seven blunders that human society commits, and that cause all the violence". The next day, Arun returned home to South Africa with the list, never to see his grandfather again. Gandhi was assassinated three months later. The very same list was originally published by Gandhi in his journal, *Young India*, in 1925, where it was titled, "Seven Social Sins".

Wealth without work.

Pleasure without conscience.

Knowledge without character.

Commerce without morality.

Science without humanity.

Worship without sacrifice.

Politics without principles.

BODY PARTS FOR WHICH I AM GRATEFUL

—

TINA FEY

2011

American comedian Tina Fey first made a name for herself as a writer and performer on *Saturday Night Live*, a stint that began in the mid-1990s. However, it was for her television show *30 Rock*, which she created in 2006, that she won the affections of many millions and countless awards. These two lists – one of women's supposed deficiencies, the other of the body parts for which she is grateful – were written by Fey and printed in her 2011 memoir, *Bossypants*.

At any given moment on planet Earth, a woman is buying a product to correct one of the following "deficiencies":

- big pores
- oily T-zone
- cankles
- fivehead
- lunch lady arms
- nipples too big
- nipples too small
- breasts too big
- breasts too small
- one breast bigger than the other
- one breast smaller than the other (How are those two different things? I don't know.)
- nasal labial folds
- "no arch in my eyebrows!"
- FUPA (a delightfully crude acronym for a protruding lower belly)
- muffin top
- spider veins
- saddlebags
- crotch biscuits (that's what I call the wobbly triangles on one's inner thighs)
- thin lashes
- bony knees
- low hairline
- calves too big
- "no calves!"
- "green undertones in my skin"
- and my personal favorite, "bad nail beds"

[...]

If you don't have a good body, you'd better starve the body you have down to a neutral shape, then bolt on some breast implants, replace your teeth, dye your skin orange, inject your lips, sew on some hair, and call yourself the Playmate of the Year.

How do we survive this? How do we teach our daughters and our gay sons that they are good enough the way they are?

We have to lead by example. Instead of trying to fit an impossible ideal, I took a personal inventory of all my healthy body parts for which I am grateful:

- Straight Greek eyebrows. They start at the hairline at my temple and, left unchecked, will grow straight across my face and onto yours.

- A heart-shaped ass. Unfortunately, it's a right-side-up heart; the point is at the bottom.

- Droopy brown eyes designed to confuse predators into thinking I'm just on the verge of sleep and they should come back tomorrow to eat me.

- Permanently rounded shoulders from years of working at a computer.

- A rounded belly that is pushed out by my rounded posture no matter how many sit-ups I do. Which is mostly none.

- A small high waist.

- A wad of lower-back fat that never went away after I lost my "baby weight." One day in the next ten years, this back roll will meet up with my front pouch, forever obscuring my small high waist, and I will officially be my mother.

- Wide-set knockers that aren't so big but can be hoisted up once or twice a year for parades.

- Good strong legs with big gym teacher calves that I got from walking pigeon-toed my whole life.

- Wide German hips that look like somebody wrapped Pillsbury dough around a case of soda.

- My father's feet. Flat. Bony. Pale. I don't know how he even gets around, because his feet are in my shoes.

I would not trade any of these features for anybody else's. I wouldn't trade the small thin-lipped mouth that makes me resemble my nephew. I wouldn't even trade the acne scar on my right cheek, because that recurring zit spent more time with me in college than any boy ever did.

BODY PARTS FOR WHICH I AM GRATEFUL

MICHELANGELO'S SHOPPING LIST

—

MICHELANGELO
1518

Having been commissioned by Pope Leo X to design and craft the San Lorenzo facade, the Italian artist known to most as Michelangelo spent his time travelling to and from Pietrasanta to quarry marble for the ultimately unrealised project. It was during this frustrating period that he wrote a list of foods on the back of a letter dated March 18th, 1518 – it is believed by some to be a three-meal shopping list, charmingly illustrated for the benefit of his illiterate servant; others imagine it to simply be a recollection of meals gone by; on the other hand, it could of course just be a doodle from the mind of a hungry artist. We will never know for certain.

pani dua
un bochal di vino
una aringa
tortegli

—————

una insalata
quatro pani
un bochal di tondo
un quartuccio di bruscho
un piatello di spinaci
quatro alice
tortelli

—————

sei pani
dua minestre di finochio
una aringa
un bochal di tondo

[TRANSLATION]

two bread rolls
a jug of wine
a herring
tortelli

—————

a salad
four bread rolls
a jug of full-bodied wine
a quarter of dry wine
a dish of spinach
four anchovies
tortelli

—————

six bread rolls
two dishes of fennel
a herring
a jug of full-bodied wine

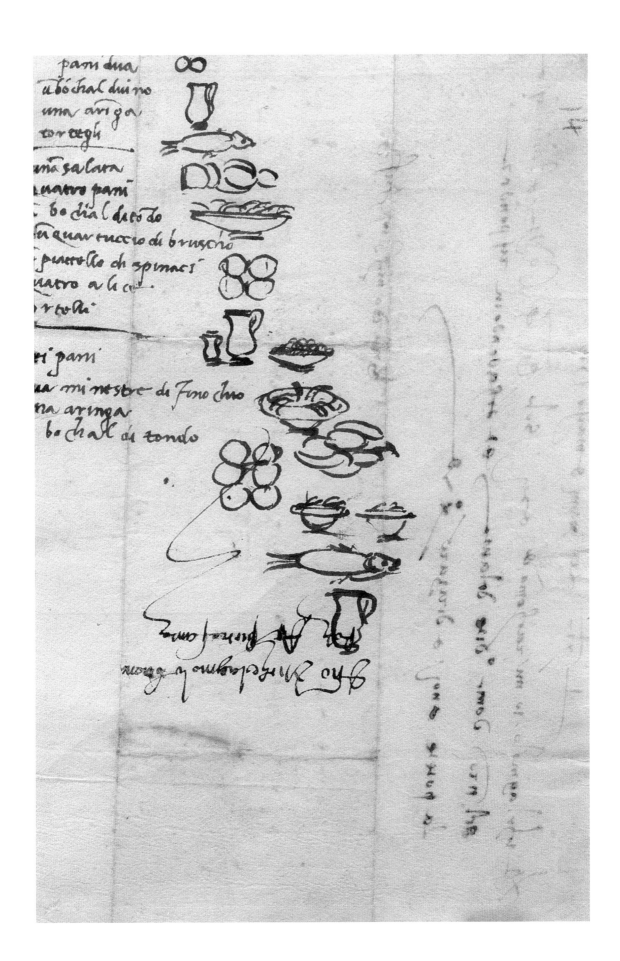

pani dua
u bochal dui vino
una ariga
tortegli

uña salata
quatro pani
bo dial dato do
un quartuccio di bruscio
i puncelло di spinaci
quatro a le ce.
tortelli

i pani
una minestre di finochio
una aringa
bochal di tondo

SIMILES AND COMPARISONS

—

RAYMOND CHANDLER
Date Unknown

Raymond Chandler, much-loved author of such books as *The Big Sleep* and *Farewell, My Lovely*, was an American detective fiction novelist known for lacing his stories with memorable turns of phrase, snappy one-liners and lyrical similes with apparent ease. When it came to the latter, Chandler prepared by keeping lists of similes in his notebooks, ready to be plucked out for future use. This is just one example.

As noiseless as a finger in a glove

Lower than a badger's balls (!!) (Vulgar—belly)

As systematic as a madam counting the take

About as French as a doughnut (i.e. not French at all)

His face was long enough to wrap twice around his neck

As much sex appeal as a turtle

A nose like a straphanger's elbow

As clean as an angel's neck

Smart as a hole through nothing

A face like a collapsed lung

So tight his head squeaks when he takes his hat off

As cold as a nun's breeches

High enough to have snow on him

As shiny as a clubwoman's nose

He sipped like a hummingbird drinking dew from a curled leaf

As gaudy as a chiropractor's chart

A mouth like wilted lettuce

His smile was wide, about three quarters of an inch

A thready smile

As cold as Finnegan's feet

As rare as a fat postman (Cissy)

The triangular eye of a squirrel

Longer than a round trip to Siam

As cute as a washtub

Lonely as a caboose of a fifty car freight

A great long gallows of a man with a ravaged face and a haggard eye

A sea sick albatross

SCOTT'S TURKEY RECIPES

—

F. SCOTT FITZGERALD
Date Unknown

When he wasn't writing such classics as *The Great Gatsby* and *Tender is the Night*, American novelist F. Scott Fitzgerald could often be found filling his many notebooks with anecdotes, jokes, lyrics, observations on life and ideas for future books. Indeed, judging from those which were published posthumously, from 1932 until his death eight years later it seems he was keen to document as much of his thought process as possible. As can be seen here, he also wrote a number of lists, this particular example being a tongue-in-cheek rundown of 13 ways to use leftover turkey.

TURKEY REMAINS AND HOW TO INTER THEM WITH NUMEROUS SCARCE RECIPES

At this post holiday season, the refrigerators of the nation are overstuffed with large masses of turkey, the sight of which is calculated to give an adult an attack of dizziness. It seems, therefore, an appropriate time to give the owners the benefit of my experience as an old gourmet, in using this surplus material. Some of the recipes have been in the family for generations. (This usually occurs when rigor mortis sets in.) They were collected over years, from old cook books, yellowed diaries of the Pilgrim Fathers, mail order catalogues, golf-bats and trash cans. Not one but has been tried and proven—there are headstones all over America to testify to the fact.

Very well then: here goes:

1. *Turkey Cocktail:* To one large turkey add one gallon of vermouth and a demijohn of angostura bitters. Shake.

2. *Turkey à la Français:* Take a large ripe turkey, prepare as for basting and stuff with old watches and chains and monkey meat. Proceed as with cottage pudding.

3. *Turkey and Water:* Take one turkey and one pan of water. Heat the latter to the boiling point and then put in the refrigerator. When it has jelled, drown the turkey in it. Eat. In preparing this recipe it is best to have a few ham sandwiches around in case things go wrong.

4. *Turkey Mongole:* Take three butts of salami and a large turkey skeleton, from which the feathers and natural stuffing have been removed. Lay them out on the table and call up some Mongole in the neighborhood to tell you how to proceed from there.

5. *Turkey Mousse:* Seed a large prone turkey, being careful to remove the bones, flesh, fins, gravy, etc. Blow up with a bicycle pump. Mount in becoming style and hang in the front hall.

6. *Stolen Turkey:* Walk quickly from the market, and, if accosted, remark with a laugh that it had just flown into your arms and you hadn't noticed it. Then drop the turkey with the white of one egg—well, anyhow, beat it.

7. *Turkey à la Crême:* Prepare the crême a day in advance. Deluge the turkey with it and cook for six days over a blast furnace. Wrap in fly paper and serve.

8. *Turkey Hash:* This is the delight of all connoisseurs of the holiday beast, but few understand how really to prepare it. Like a lobster, it must be plunged alive into boiling water, until it becomes bright red or purple or something, and then before the color fades, placed quickly in a washing machine and allowed to stew in its own gore as it is whirled around. Only then is it ready for hash. To hash, take a large sharp tool like a nail-file or, if none is handy, a bayonet will serve the purpose—and then get at it! Hash it well! Bind the remains with dental floss and serve.

9. *Feathered Turkey:* To prepare this, a turkey is necessary and a one pounder cannon to compel anyone to eat it. Broil the feathers and stuff with sage-brush, old clothes, almost anything you can dig up. Then sit down and simmer. The feathers are to be eaten like artichokes (and this is not to be confused with the old Roman custom of tickling the throat.)

10. *Turkey à la Maryland:* Take a plump turkey to a barber's and have him shaved, or if a female bird, given a facial and a water wave. Then, before killing him, stuff with old newspapers and put him to roost. He can then be served hot or raw, usually with a thick gravy of mineral oil and rubbing alcohol. (Note: This recipe was given me by an old black mammy.)

11. *Turkey Remnant:* This is one of the most useful recipes for, though not, "chic," it tells us what to do with the turkey after the holiday, and how to extract the most value from it. Take the remnants, or, if they have been consumed, take the various plates on which the turkey or its parts have rested and stew them for two hours in milk of magnesia. Stuff with moth-balls.

12. *Turkey with Whiskey Sauce:* This recipe is for a party of four. Obtain a gallon of whiskey, and allow it to age for several hours. Then serve, allowing one quart for each guest. The next day the turkey should be added, little by little, constantly stirring and basting.

13. *For Weddings or Funerals:* Obtain a gross of small white boxes such as are used for bride's cake. Cut the turkey into small squares, roast, stuff, kill, boil, bake and allow to skewer. Now we are ready to begin. Fill each box with a quantity of soup stock and pile in a handy place. As the liquid elapses, the prepared turkey is added until the guests arrive. The boxes delicately tied with white ribbons are then placed in the handbags of the ladies, or in the men's side pockets.

There I guess that's enough turkey talk. I hope I'll never see or hear of another until—well, until next year.

9. Today, how do you associate to the following, described in one word?

New York: *great*

Elvis: ~~fat~~ *fat* ~~boring~~

Ringo: *friend*

Yoko: *love*

Howard Cosell: *hum*

George: *lost*

Bootlegs: *good*

Elton: *nice*

Paul: *extraordinary*

Bowie: *thin*

M.B.E: *shit*

JOHN: *great*

10. Is there any advise that you can give to the teenagers of today?

grow up!

— read Sugar Blues by ~~~~

it was a pleasure, hope ya dig it. ~John Lennon~

Thank you very much for your time and consideration.

ELVIS: FAT

—

JOHN LENNON
1976

In 1976, a young man named Stuart took a chance and sent six pages of interview questions to one of the most famous people on the planet, John Lennon. Much to his surprise, a reply soon arrived. Here we have Question 9, in which he offered a list of ten things and asked Lennon to describe each with a single word. Interestingly, four years later, Howard "Ham" Cosell would announce the death of Lennon to millions in the US during a televised game of American football.

BOOKS YOU OUGHT TO READ

—

ERNEST HEMINGWAY
1935

In the spring of 1934, a 22-year-old aspiring novelist named Arnold Samuelson hitch-hiked from Minnesota to Key West, Florida to meet his idol, Ernest Hemingway. Hoping at best to spend ten minutes in the company of the "greatest writer alive", Samuelson was quickly stunned to instead be taken under the author's wing and spent the best part of the next year as Hemingway's deckhand aboard his boat, *Pilar*. It was on that first day that Hemingway offered his first piece of advice to his young visitor: upon learning that he was yet to read *War and Peace*, Hemingway said, "That's a damned good book. You ought to read it. We'll go up to my workshop and I'll make out a list you ought to read."

Stephen Crane –
      The Blue Hotel
      The Open Boat.
Madame Bovary – Gustave Flaubert
Dubliners – James Joyce –
The Red and The Black – By Stendhal –
(OF Human Bondage – Somerset Maugham) –
Anna Karenina – Tolstoy –
War and Peace – Tolstoy –
Buddenbrooks – Thomas Mann –
Hail and Farewell – George Moore –
Brothers Karamazov – Doestoevsky –
Oxford Book of English Verse –
The Enormous Room – EE Cummings.
Wuthering Heights – Emily Bronte
Far Away and Long Ago – W.H. Hudson –
The American – Henry James.

Basket. Ball.

The ball to be an ordinary Association foot ball.

1. The ball may be thrown in any direction with one or both hands.

2. The ball may be batted in any direction with one or both hands (never with the fist).

3. A player cannot run with the ball, the player must throw it from the spot on which he catches it, allowance to be made for a man who catches the ball when running at a good speed.

4. The ball must be held in or between the hands, the arms or body must not be used for holding it.

5. No shouldering, holding, pushing, tripping or striking in any way the person of an opponent shall be allowed. The first infringement of this rule by any person shall count as a foul, the second shall disqualify him until the next goal is made, or if there was evident intent to injure the person, for the whole of the game, no substitute allowed.

6. A foul is striking at the ball with the fist, violation of rules 3 and 4, and such as described in rule 5.

7. If either side makes three consecutive fouls it shall count a goal for the opponents (consecutive means without the opponents in the meantime making a foul).

8. A goal shall be made when the ball is thrown or batted from the grounds into the basket and stays there, providing those defending the goal do not touch or disturb the goal. If the ball rests on the edge and the opponent moves the basket it shall count as a

BASKET. BALL.

—

JAMES NAISMITH
December 6th, 1891

In December 1891, having been asked to invent a new indoor game for his students during the winter months, a Canadian teacher named James Naismith wrote this 13-point list of rules and attached it to the wall of a gym at the YMCA Training School in Springfield, Massachusetts. In fact, the game he had just invented was basketball. Over the years the list evolved to include rules for such things as dribbling and dunking. Today, the official rules of basketball, as approved by the FIBA, are 80 pages long. The original draft of this list was sold by Sotheby's auction house in 2012 for $4.3 million.

goal.

9. When the ball goes out of bounds it shall be thrown into the field, and played by the person first touching it. In case of a dispute the umpire shall throw it straight into the field. The thrower in is allowed five seconds, if he holds it longer it shall go to the opponent. If any side presists in delaying the game, the umpire shall call a foul on them.

10. The umpire shall be judge of the men, and shall note the fouls, and notify the referee when three consecutive fouls have been made. He shall have power to disqualify men according to Rule 5.

11. The referee shall be judge of the ball and shall decide when the ball is in play, in bounds, and to which side it belongs, and shall keep the time. He shall decide when a goal has been made, and keep account of the goals with any other duties that are usually performed by a referee.

12. The time shall be two fifteen minutes halves, with five minutes rest between.

13. The side making the most goals in that time shall be declared the winners. In case of a draw the game may, by agreement of the captains, be continued until another goal is made.

First draft of Basket Ball rules.
Hung in the gym that the boys might
learn the rules - Dec. 1891 James Naismith
6-28-31.

DON'TS FOR WOMEN RIDERS

—

UNIQUE CYCLING CLUB OF CHICAGO
June 21st, 1895

On June 21, 1895, the *Newark Sunday Advocate* ran an alarming story, syndicated from *New York World*, about a recent gathering of the Unique Cycling Club of Chicago – an event that saw two lady riders publicly shamed for having the audacity to turn up wearing short skirts over their bloomers. The story can be seen here, as can a list that followed the piece, printed in an effort to better educate female cyclists in light of the bloomer fiasco and titled, "Don'ts for Women Riders".

DON'TS FOR WOMEN RIDERS

Don't be a fright.
Don't faint on the road.
Don't wear a man's cap.
Don't wear tight garters.
Don't forget your toolbag
Don't attempt a "century."
Don't coast. It is dangerous.
Don't criticise people's "legs."
Don't boast of your long rides
Don't wear loud hued leggings
Don't cultivate a "bicycle face."
Don't refuse assistance up a hill.
Don't wear clothes that don't fit.
Don't "talk bicycle" at the table.
Don't neglect a "light's out" cry.
Don't wear jewelry while on a tour.
Don't race. Leave that to the scorchers.
Don't imagine everybody is looking at you.
Don't go to church in your bicycle costume.
Don't wear laced boots. They are tiresome.
Don't keep your mouth open on dirty roads.
Don't converse while in a scorching position.
Don't go out after dark without a male escort.
Don't contest the right of way with cable cars.
Don't wear a garden party hat with bloomers.
Don't wear white kid gloves. Silk is the thing.
Don't chew gum. Exercise your jaws in private.
Don't tempt fate by riding too near the curbstone.
Don't ask, "What do you think of my bloomers?"
Don't use bicycle slang. Leave that to the boys.
Don't discuss bloomers with every man you know.
Don't think you look as pretty as every fashion plate.
Don't go out without a needle, thread and thimble.
Don't allow your dear little Fido to accompany you.
Don't scratch a match on the seat of your bloomers.
Don't try to have every article of your attire "match."
Don't let your golden hair be hanging down your back.
Don't appear in public until you have learned to ride well.
Don't try to ride in your brother's clothes "to see how it feels."
Don't overdo things. Let cycling be a recreation, not a labor.
Don't ignore the laws of the road because you are a woman.
Don't throw your legs over the handle bar and coast down hill.
Don't scream if you meet a cow. If she sees you first, she will run.
Don't cultivate everything that is up to date because you ride a wheel.
Don't emulate your brother's attitude if he rides parallel with the ground.
Don't undertake a long ride if you are not confident of performing it easily.
Don't appear to be up on "records" and "record smashing." That is sporty.

FRANKLIN'S 13 VIRTUES

—

BENJAMIN FRANKLIN
1726

Benjamin Franklin was a high achiever, to say the least: at various stages of his life he was a scientist, musician, printer, author, businessman and politician – a diverse range of roles, somehow all mastered by one man. As if that wasn't enough, he even had a hand in the formation of the United States of America. All of which is to say, his attitude to life and work is certainly worth studying for anyone attempting to better themselves, the list seen here being a perfect start: a set of 13 virtues to live by, written by 20-year-old Franklin in 1726 in an attempt to "live without committing any fault at any time". And follow them he did, until his death at 84, all the while keeping notes on his progress.

1.   TEMPERANCE. Eat not to dullness; drink not to elevation.

2.   SILENCE. Speak not but what may benefit others or yourself; avoid trifling conversation.

3.   ORDER. Let all your things have their places; let each part of your business have its time.

4.   RESOLUTION. Resolve to perform what you ought; perform without fail what you resolve.

5.   FRUGALITY. Make no expense but to do good to others or yourself; i.e., waste nothing.

6.   INDUSTRY. Lose no time; be always employ'd in something useful; cut off all unnecessary actions.

7.   SINCERITY. Use no hurtful deceit; think innocently and justly, and, if you speak, speak accordingly.

8.   JUSTICE. Wrong none by doing injuries, or omitting the benefits that are your duty.

9.   MODERATION. Avoid extreams; forbear resenting injuries so much as you think they deserve.

10.   CLEANLINESS. Tolerate no uncleanliness in body, cloaths, or habitation.

11.   TRANQUILLITY. Be not disturbed at trifles, or at accidents common or unavoidable.

12.   CHASTITY. Rarely use venery but for health or offspring, never to dulness, weakness, or the injury of your own or another's peace or reputation.

13.   HUMILITY. Imitate Jesus and Socrates.

TEMPERANCE.

Eat not to dulness: drink not to elevation.

	Sun.	M.	T.	W.	Th.	F.	S.
Temp.							
Sil.							
Ord.	*	*		*		*	
Res.	*	*	*		*	*	*
Fru.		*				*	
Ind.		*				*	
Sinc.			*				
Jus.							
Mod.							
Clea.							
Tran.							
Chas.							
Hum.							

RESCUE ETIQUETTE

—

MARK TWAIN
1962

In 1962, 52 years after the death of humourist Mark Twain, a collection of his previously unseen writing was published in the form of a book titled *Letters from the Earth*. Included in that book, along with numerous pieces on such subjects as religion and morality, is an extract from an "unfinished burlesque of books on etiquette" of Twain's which sees him list, in order of importance, 27 types of people and furniture to be rescued from boarding house fires.

In assisting at a fire in a boarding house, the true gentleman will always save the young ladies first—making no distinction in favor of personal attractions, or social eminence, or pecuniary predominance—but taking them as they come, and firing them out with as much celerity as shall be consistent with decorum. There are exceptions, of course, to all rules; the exceptions to this one are:

Partiality, in the matter of rescue, to be shown to:

1. Fiancées.
2. Persons toward whom the operator feels a tender sentiment, but has not yet declared himself.
3. Sisters.
4. Stepsisters.
5. Nieces.
6. First cousins.
7. Cripples.
8. Second cousins.
9. Invalids.
10. Young-lady relations by marriage.
11. Third cousins, and young-lady friends of the family.
12. The Unclassified.

Other material in boarding house is to be rescued in the following order:

13. Babies.
14. Children under 10 years of age.
15. Young widows.
16. Young married females.
17. Elderly married ditto.
18. Elderly widows.
19. Clergymen.
20. Boarders in general.
21. Female domestics.
22. Male ditto.
23. Landlady.
24. Landlord.
25. Firemen.
26. Furniture.
27. Mothers-in-law.

MY FAVORITE BOOKS

—

EDITH WHARTON
1909

Novelist Edith Wharton was born in 1862 in New York and stayed there until the turn of the century, plying her trade as a writer. It wasn't until 1920, at which point she had settled in France, that she wrote *The Age of Innocence*, her 12th novel and the one that would see her awarded a Pulitzer Prize for Fiction – the first ever to be awarded to a woman. She was also nominated for a Nobel Prize in Literature on three occasions. In 1909, she wrote a list of her favourite books.

My Favorite Books, 1909

Faust; Goethe
Shakespeare
Divina Commedia; Dante Alighieri
Seneca the Younger
Giacomo Leopardi, John Keats
Blaise Pascal: *Pensées & Provinciales*
Schopenhauer
Origin of Species; Charles Darwin
Walt Whitman; *The Leaves of Grass*
Nietzsche: *Jenseits v. gut u Böse* (Beyond Good and Evil); *Genealogie der Moral* (On the Genealogy of Morality); *Wille zur Macht* (The Will to Power)
Lettres de Flaubert
Goethe's Conversations with Eckermann
Le Rouge et la noir; Stendhal
La Chartreuse de Parme; Stendhal
Mme Bovary; Gustave Flaubert
The Egoist; George Meredith
Anna Karenina; Leo Tolstoy
Harry Richmond; George Meredith
The Portrait of a Lady; Henry James
Adolphe; Benjamin Constant
Manon Lescaut; Abbé Prévost
Tyndall's Essays

CELESTIAL EMPORIUM OF BENEVOLENT KNOWLEDGE

—

JORGE LUIS BORGES
1942

In 1942, Argentine writer Jorge Luis Borges penned *El idioma analítico de John Wilkins* ("The Analytical Language of John Wilkins"), an essay in which he discussed the difficulties associated with man's repeated attempts to classify all that existed. He did this, primarily, by focusing on a universal language proposed by 17th-century philosopher John Wilkins which divided the contents of the universe into 40 *genera*, each of which gave an object its first two letters; those categories were then split into 241 *differences* which offered another letter, and those differences were then divided into 2,030 *species* to add the final fourth letter – for example, Salmon becomes Zana: Za would identify "fish" (the genus), Zan would identify "squamous river fish" (the difference), and Zana would identify "largest red-fleshed kind" (the species). Borges was unimpressed and ridiculed the idea, comparing the system's "ambiguities, redundancies and deficiencies" to this delightful and now infamous taxonomy of the animal kingdom found in *Celestial Emporium of Benevolent Knowledge*, an ancient Chinese encyclopaedia which, unbeknownst to the countless people who went on to be influenced by it, didn't actually exist outside of Borge's imagination.

Those that belong to the emperor

Embalmed ones

Those that are trained

Suckling pigs

Mermaids (or Sirens)

Fabulous ones

Stray dogs

Those that are included in this classification

Those that tremble as if they were mad

Innumerable ones

Those drawn with a very fine camel hair brush

Et cetera

Those that have just broken the flower vase

Those that, at a distance, resemble flies

A LIBERAL DECALOGUE

—

BERTRAND RUSSELL
December 16th, 1951

Bertrand Russell was a distinguished philosopher and the person responsible for writing *On Denoting*, a seminal essay described as "that paradigm of philosophy". He was also, at various points in his lifetime, a mathematician, social critic and teacher. In 1951 he wrote a piece on liberalism in *The New York Times Magazine*, at the end of which was this set of commandments to be passed on by teachers. It was later reprinted in his autobiography, titled, "A Liberal Decalogue".

Perhaps the essence of the Liberal outlook could be summed up in a new decalogue, not intended to replace the old one but only to supplement it. The Ten Commandments that, as a teacher, I should wish to promulgate, might be set forth as follows:

1. Do not feel absolutely certain of anything.

2. Do not think it worth while to proceed by concealing evidence, for the evidence is sure to come to light.

3. Never try to discourage thinking for you are sure to succeed.

4. When you meet with opposition, even if it should be from your husband or your children, endeavour to overcome it by argument and not by authority, for a victory dependent upon authority is unreal and illusory.

5. Have no respect for the authority of others, for there are always contrary authorities to be found.

6. Do not use power to suppress opinions you think pernicious, for if you do the opinions will suppress you.

7. Do not fear to be eccentric in opinion, for every opinion now accepted was once eccentric.

8. Find more pleasure in intelligent dissent than in passive agreement, for, if you value intelligence as you should, the former implies a deeper agreement than the latter.

9. Be scrupulously truthful, even if the truth is inconvenient, for it is more inconvenient when you try to conceal it.

10. Do not feel envious of the happiness of those who live in a fool's paradise, for only a fool will think that it is happiness.

HENSLOWE'S INVENTORY

—

PHILIP HENSLOWE
March 10th, 1598

Born in the 1550s, Philip Henslowe was a famous theatre owner whose establishments, particularly The Rose, were in direct competition with William Shakespeare's Globe Theatre. Between 1592 and 1603 he kept a record of his financial dealings, box office takings, etc., in what is now known as *Henslowe's Diary* – a historically invaluable document that throws light on the industry of that period like no other. Featured in that diary is this wonderful Elizabethan inventory of props relating to the Admiral's Men, Henslowe's resident performing company for many years.

The inventory taken of all the properties for my Lord Admiral's Men on the 10th of March 1598

Item: 1 rock, 1 cage, 1 tomb, 1 Hell mouth.

Item: 1 tomb of Guido, 1 tomb of Dido, 1 bedstead.

Item: 8 lances, 1 pair of stairs for *Phaeton*.

Item: 2 steeples, and 1 chime of bells, and 1 beacon.

Item: 1 hecfor for the play of Phaeton, the limbs dead.

Item: 1 globe, and 1 golden scepter; 3 clubs.

Item: 2 marchpanes, and the city of Rome.

Item: 1 golden fleece; 2 rackets; 1 bay tree.

Item: 1 wooden hatchet; 1 leather hatchet.

Item: 1 wooden canopy; old Mahomet's head.

Item: 1 lion skin; 1 bear's skin; and Phaeton's limbs, and Phaeton chariot; and Argus' head.

Item: Neptune's fork and garland.

Item: 1 crozier's staff; Kent's wooden leg.

Item: Iris's head, and rainbow; 1 little altar.

Item: 8 vizards; Tamburlaine's bridle; 1 wooden mattock.

Item: Cupid's bow, and quiver; the cloth of the sun and moon.

Item: 1 boar's head and Cerberus's 3 heads.

Item: 1 caduceus; 2 moss banks, and 1 snake.

Item: 2 fans of feathers; Belin Dun's stable; 1 tree of golden apples; Tantalus's tree; 9 iron targets.

Item: 1 copper target, and 17 foils.

Item: 4 wooden targets; 1 greave armour.

Item: 1 sign for Mother Redcap; 1 buckler.

Item: Mercury's wings; Tasso's picture; 1 helmet with a dragon; 1 shield with 3 lions; 1 elm bowl.

Item: 1 chain of dragons; 1 gilt spear.

Item: 2 coffins; 1 bull's head; and 1 vulture.

Item: 3 tumbrils, 1 dragon in *Faustus*.

Item: 1 lion; 2 lion heads; 1 great horse with his legs; 1 sack-butt.

Item: 1 wheel and frame in the *Siege of London*.

Item: 1 pair of wrought gloves.

Item: 1 pope's mitre.

Item: 3 Imperial crowns; 1 plain crown.

Item: 1 ghost's crown; 1 crown with a sun.

Item: 1 frame for the heading in *Black John*.

Item: 1 black dog.

Item: 1 cauldron for the Jew.

ROSE vs GLOBE

MIDWESTERNISMS

—

DAVID FOSTER WALLACE
1997

In April 2011, almost three years after his suicide, David Foster Wallace's unfinished novel, *The Pale King* – a sprawling, brilliant and often difficult work largely set in offices of the Internal Revenue Service in the Midwestern United States – was published. Research for the novel had begun long before, in 1997, the year after publication of his magnum opus, *Infinite Jest*, at which point it had a working title of *Sir John Feelgood* ("SJF"). One of Wallace's first tasks had been to write, in his spiral notebook, this list of "Midwesternisms".

- Pronouncing 'theater' like it had a y in it – theayter theyater
- Pronouncing 'vehicle' with a h – pronouncing the h in 'vehicle'
- Solicism: 'Itty-tiny.' 'An itty-tiny little man
- 'Because you know why?'
- Preceding a question with 'Question': 'Question. Why aren't office supplies a revenue expenditure instead of an operating expense.'
  Malaprops
- 'The office encouraged them that whoever had a problem should…'
- 'This stuff's all been mulling around in my head.'
- 'The more I keep [?], I realise how little I know.'
- 'That irks my feelings.'
- 'He would have made short work of me in a hurry.'
- 'The thing is that I'm serious.'
- 'It just got all scrabbled up in my head.'
- 'Involved' for 'evolved.' 'And it involved into a bad situation.'
- 'I had a circumstance happen.'
- 'Whatnot.' 'and whatnot.'
- 'Set' for 'sit.' 'Set down. Go on and set yourself down here.'
- Academic stutter (not a true stutter; the stutter of compression and density, the plosive a bottleneck – 'The the the the radical discontent of business under the New Deal.'
- 'Just let them get it under their belt and chew on it a while.'

`97

"He'd like for you
to call him"

Midwesternisms ②

theayter

- Prouncing `theater` like it had a y in it — theayter
- Pronouncing `vehicle` with an h — pronouncing the h in `vehicle`
- Solecism: `Itty-tiny.` `An itty-tiny little man`
- `Because you know why?`
- Preceding a question with `Question.` : `Question. Why isn't
office supplies a revenue expenditure instead of an operating expense.`

    Malaprops
- `The office encouraged them that whoever had a
problem should...`
- `This stuff's all been mulling around in my head.`
- `The more I keep cunning, I realize how little I know`
- `That irks my feelings.`
- `He would have made short work of me in a hurry.`
- `The thing is that I'm serious.`
- `It just got all scrabbled up in my head.`
- `Involved` for `evolved.` `And it involved into a bad situation.`
- `I had a circumstance happen.`
- `whatnot.` `and whatnot.`
- `Set` for `sit` `Sit down. Go on and set yourself down here.`
- Academic stutter (not a true stutter; the stutter of
- the compression and density, the plosive a bottleneck —
`The the the the the radical discontent of ~~taxpayers~~ business
under the New Deal.`
- `Just let them get it under their belt and chew on it
a while.`

NAMING THE PHONOGRAPH

—

THOMAS EDISON
November 1877

In November 1877, prolific American inventor Thomas Edison debuted his latest project, the "phonograph", a ground-breaking device that was capable of not just recording sound, but also replaying it, and which directly inspired the development of the gramophone some years later. Prior to naming his new invention, Edison and his colleagues came up with dozens of potential monikers for the device – most bearing prefixes of Greek or Latin origin – and collated them in this list.

T. A. Edison.

Auto-Electrograph = Electric Pen
Tel-autograph
Tel-autophone
Polyphone = Manifold Sounder
Autophone = Self sounder
Kosmophone = Universal Sounder
Acoustophone = Sound hearer = Audible speaker
Octophone = Ear-sounder = speaker
Anitphone = Back-talker
Liguphone = Clear speaker
Minuttophone = Minute-sounder
Meistophone = Smallest sounder
Anchiphone = Near sounder or speaker
Palmatophone = <u>Vibration sounder</u>
Chronophone = Time-announcer = Speaking clock
Didaskophone = Teaching speaker = Portable teacher
Glottophone = Language sounder or speaker
Climatophone = Weather announcer
Atmophone = Fog sounder or Vapor-speaker
Palmophone = Pendulum sounder or Sounding pendulum
Pinakophone = Speaking Register
Hemerologophone = Speaking almanac
Kalendophone = Speaking Calendar
Sphygmophone = Pulse speaker
Halmophone = Heart-beat-sounder
Seismophone = Earthquake sounder
Electrophone = Electric speaker
Brontophone = Thunder sounder
Klangophone = Bird-cry sounder
Surigmophone = Whistling sounder
Bremophone = Wind sounder
Bittako-phone = Parrot speaker
Krogmophone = Croaking or Cawing sounder
Hulagmophone = Barking sounder
Trematophone = Sound borer
Telephemist telephemy telepheme
Electrophemist electrophemy electropheme
Phemegraph = speech writer
Omphegraph-gram = voice writer or recorder
Melodograph Melograph Melpograph-gram = song writer
Epograph = speech writer, lecture or sermon
Rhetograph = speech writer
Kinemograph = motion writer
Atmophone = vapor or steam sound
Aerophone = air-sound
Symphraxometer = pressure measurer
Synothemeter = pressure measurer
Orcheograph = vibration record
Orcheometer

Menlo Park, N. J., '87

Auto - Electrograph : Electric Pen
Tel - autograph
Tel - autophone -
Polyphone = Manifold Sounder
Autophone = Self sounder
Kosmophone = Universal Sounder
Acoustophone = Sound hearer - = Audible speaker
Otophone = Ear - sounder = speaker.
Antiphone = Back - talker
Liquphone = Clear speaker
Minuthophone = minute - sounder
Meistophone = smallest sounder
Anchiphone = Near Sounder or speaker
Palmatophone = Vibration sounder
Chronophone = Time - announcer = Speaking Clock
Didaskophone = Teaching speaker = Portable teacher
Glottophone = Language sounder or speaker
Climatophone = Weather announcer.
Atmophone = Fog sounder. or Vapor - speaker.

Palmophone = Pendulum sounder or Sounding Pendulum
Pinakophone = Speaking Register.
Hemerologophone = Speaking almanac
Kalendophone = Speaking Calendar
Sphygmophone = Pulse speaker
Halmophone = Heart-beat-sounder
~~Tertrophone =~~
Seismophone = Earthquake sounder
Electrophone = Electric Speaker.
Brontophone = Thunder sounder
Klangophone = Bird-coy sounder
Surigmophone = Whistling sounder
Bremophone = Wind sounder
Bittako-phone = Parrot speaker
Krogmophone = Croaking or Cawing sounder
Hulagmophone = Barking sounder
Trematophone = Sound borer.

Telephemist. telephemy. telepheme.
Electrophemist. electrophemy. electropheme.

Phemegraph. - speech writer.
Omphegraph. gram. - voice writer or recorder.

Melodograph. Melograph. Melpograph. - grem. song writer.

Epograph - speech writer lecture or sermon
Rhetograph =   "   " .

Kinemograph = motion writer.

Atmophone ~~atmophone~~ = vapor or steam sound.
aerophone = air - sound.

Symphroxometer = pressure measurer.
Synothemeter - = pressure measurer.
Orcheograph = vibration record
Orcheometer

279

THINGS TO WORRY ABOUT

—

F. SCOTT FITZGERALD
1933

Scottie was just 11 years old and at camp many miles away from her family when, in August 1933, she received a heartening letter of advice from home. It was written by her father, F. Scott Fitzgerald, a man responsible for penning some of the most acclaimed novels of recent times and someone for whom the art of writing letters was clearly a breeze. This particular missive contained a charming and timeless list of things for his daughter to worry/not worry about.

Things to worry about:

Worry about courage
Worry about cleanliness
Worry about efficiency
Worry about horsemanship
Worry about …

Things not to worry about:

Don't worry about popular opinion
Don't worry about dolls
Don't worry about the past
Don't worry about the future
Don't worry about growing up
Don't worry about anybody getting ahead of you
Don't worry about triumph
Don't worry about failure unless it comes through your own fault
Don't worry about mosquitoes
Don't worry about flies
Don't worry about insects in general
Don't worry about parents
Don't worry about boys
Don't worry about disappointments
Don't worry about pleasures
Don't worry about satisfactions

Things to think about:

What am I really aiming at?
How good am I really in comparison to my contemporaries in regard to:
(A) Scholarship
(B) Do I really understand about people and am I able to get along with them?
(C) Am I trying to make my body a useful instrument or am I neglecting it?

With dearest love,

MARILYN MONROE'S DREAM LOVERS

—

MARILYN MONROE
1951

In 1951, as they flicked through a copy of the *Academy Players Directory* and discussed the actors of the day, 25-year-old rising starlet Marilyn Monroe turned to roommate and fellow actress, Shelley Winters, and said, "Wouldn't it be nice to be like men and just get notches in your belt and sleep with the most attractive men and not get emotionally involved?" Before long, they were sitting with pen in hand writing lists of the actors they would like to bed in such circumstances. Monroe's wish list can be seen here.

Zero Mostel

Eli Wallach

Charles Boyer

Jean Renoir

Lee Strasberg

Nick Ray

John Huston

Elia Kazan

Harry Belafonte

Yves Montand

Charles Bickford

Ernest Hemingway

Charles Laughton

Clifford Odets

Dean Jagger

Arthur Miller

Albert Einstein

List No. 114

QUALITIES OF CIVILISED PEOPLE
—

ANTON CHEKHOV
March 1886

In March 1886, at the age of 26, acclaimed Russian author and physician Anton Chekhov wrote an honest letter of advice to his troubled older brother, Nikolai, a talented painter and writer who, despite being just 28 himself, had for many years been plagued by alcoholism to the point where he often slept on the streets, his days a blur; his notable skills as an artist largely untapped. The letter contained a list, seen here – eight qualities exhibited by "civilized" people – and was essentially Anton's attempt at knocking some sense into the brother he was slowly losing.

Sadly, his efforts were ultimately futile. Nikolai passed away three years later.

To my mind, well-bred people ought to satisfy the following conditions:

1. They respect the individual and are therefore always indulgent, gentle, polite and compliant. They do not throw a tantrum over a hammer or a lost eraser. When they move in with somebody, they do not act as if they were doing him a favor, and when they move out, they do not say, "How can anyone live with you!" They excuse noise and cold and overdone meat and witticisms and the presence of others in their homes.

2. Their compassion extends beyond beggars and cats. They are hurt even by things the naked eye can't see. If for instance, Pyotr knows that his father and mother are turning gray and losing sleep over seeing their Pyotr so rarely (and seeing him drunk when he does turn up), then he rushes home to them and sends his vodka to the devil. They do not sleep nights the better to help the Polevayevs, help pay their brothers' tuition, and keep their mother decently dressed.

3. They respect the property of others and therefore pay their debts.

4. They are candid and fear lies like the plague. They do not lie even about the most trivial matters. A lie insults the listener and debases him in the liar's eyes. They don't put on airs, they behave in the street as they do at home, and they do not try to dazzle their inferiors. They know how to keep their mouths shut and they do not force uninvited confidences on people. Out of respect for the ears of others they are more often silent than not.

5. They do not belittle themselves merely to arouse sympathy. They do not play on people's heartstrings to get them to sigh and fuss over them. They do not say, "No one understands me!" or "I've squandered my talent on trifles! I am […]" because this smacks of a cheap effect and is vulgar, false and out-of-date.

6. They are not preoccupied with vain things. They are not taken in by such false jewels as friendships with celebrities, handshakes with drunken Plevako, ecstasy over the first person they happen to meet at the Salon de Variétés, popularity among the tavern crowd. They laugh when they hear, "I represent the press," a phrase befitting only Rodzeviches and Levenbergs. When they have done a penny's worth of work, they don't try to make a hundred rubles out of it, and they don't boast over being admitted to places closed to others. True talents always seek obscurity. They try to merge with the crowd and shun all ostentation. Krylov himself said that an empty barrel has more chance of being heard than a full one.

7. If they have talent, they respect it. They sacrifice comfort, women, wine and vanity to it. They are proud of their talent, and so they do not go out carousing with trade-school employees or Skvortsov's guests, realizing that their calling lies in exerting an uplifting influence on them, not in living with them. What is more, they are fastidious.

8. They cultivate their aesthetic sensibilities. They cannot stand to fall asleep fully dressed, see a slit in the wall teeming with bedbugs, breathe rotten air, walk on a spittle-laden floor or eat off a kerosene stove. They try their best to tame and ennoble their sexual instinct … […] to endure her logic and never stray from her. What's the point of it all? People with good breeding are not as coarse as that. What they look for in a woman is not a bed partner or horse sweat, […] not the kind of intelligence that expresses itself in the ability to stage a fake pregnancy and tirelessly reel off lies. They—and especially the artists among them—require spontaneity, elegance, compassion, a woman who will be a mother, not a […] They don't guzzle vodka on any old occasion, nor do they go around sniffing cupboards, for they know they are not swine. They drink only when they are free, if the opportunity happens to present itself. For they require a *mens sana in corpore sano*.

And so on. That's how well-bred people act. If you want to be well-bred and not fall below the level of the milieu you belong to, it is not enough to read *The Pickwick Papers* and memorize a soliloquy from *Faust*. It is not enough to hail a cab and drive off to Yakimanka Street if all you're going to do is bolt out again a week later.

You must work at it constantly, day and night. You must never stop reading, studying in depth, exercising your will. Every hour is precious.

PRESIDENT ROOSEVELT'S LIST OF BIRDS

—

THEODORE ROOSEVELT
1908

In 1908, as she worked on a new edition of her book, *Birds of Washington and Vicinity*, American historian Lucy Maynard asked then US President Theodore Roosevelt whether she could include mention of some of the birds he had seen near the White House. Roosevelt, an avid birdwatcher, replied, "I'll do better for you than that, I'll make you a list of all the birds I can remember having seen since I have been here." And here is that list: 93 birds seen in Washington by Roosevelt during his seven and a half years in power.

NIGHT HERON. Five spent winter of 1907 in swampy country about one-half mile west of Washington Monument.

MOURNING DOVE.

QUAIL.

RUFFED GROUSE. One seen on Rock Creek.

SHARP-SHINNED HAWK.

RED-SHOULDERED HAWK.

*SPARROW HAWK. A pair spent the last two winters on and around the White House grounds, feeding on the Sparrows—largely, thank Heaven, on the English Sparrows.

*SCREECH OWL. Steady resident on White House grounds.

*SAW-WHET OWL. A pair spent several weeks by the south portico of the White House, 1905.

KINGFISHER.

*YELLOW-BILLED CUCKOO.

HAIRY WOODPECKER.

*DOWNY WOODPECKER.

*SAPSUCKER.

*RED-HEADED WOODPECKER. Nests (one pair) on White House grounds.

*FLICKER. Nests (several pairs) on White House grounds.

WHIP-POOR-WILL.

NIGHTHAWK.

*CHIMNEY SWIFT.

*HUMMINGBIRD.

KINGBIRD.

GREAT CRESTED FLYCATCHER.

PHŒBE.

WOOD PEWEE.

HORNED LARK.

*CROW.

*FISH CROW.

*ORCHARD ORIOLE. One pair nested in White House grounds.

BOBOLINK.

RED-WINGED BLACKBIRD.

*BALTIMORE ORIOLE.

MEADOWLARK.

*PURPLE GRACKLE. Nests on White House grounds. Very abundant in early spring.

*PURPLE FINCH.

*THISTLE BIRD (Goldfinch).

VESPER SPARROW.

*WHITE-THROATED SPARROW. Sings; this year sang now and then all through the winter.

*TREE SPARROW.

*CHIPPIE (Chipping Sparrow). Nests.

BUSH SPARROW (Field Sparrow).

*SNOW BIRD (Junco).

*SONG SPARROW. Nests.

*FOX SPARROW.

*CARDINAL.

TOWHEE.

*INDIGO-BIRD. Nests.

TANAGER.

PURPLE MARTIN.

*BARN SWALLOW.

TREE SWALLOW.

BANK SWALLOW.

*CEDAR BIRD.

LOGGER-HEAD SHRIKE.

*RED-EYED VIREO. Nests.

*WARBLING VIREO. Nests.

*BLACK AND WHITE WARBLER. Nests.

*BLUE YELLOW-BACKED WARBLER (Parula Warbler).

*CAPE MAY WARBLER.

*SUMMER YELLOWBIRD. Nests.

*BLACK-THROATED BLUE WARBLER.

*BLACK-THROATED GREEN WARBLER.

*MYRTLE WARBLER.

*MAGNOLIA WARBLER.

*CHESTNUT-SIDED WARBLER.

*BAY-BREASTED WARBLER.

*BLACKPOLL WARBLER.

*BLACKBURNIAN WARBLER.

PRAIRIE WARBLER.

OVEN-BIRD.

WATER THRUSH.

KENTUCKY WARBLER.

*YELLOWTHROAT.

CHAT.

*BLUE-WINGED WARBLER.

*CANADIAN WARBLER.

*REDSTART. Nests on White House grounds.

PIPIT.

MOCKINGBIRD.

*CATBIRD. Nests on White House grounds.

THRASHER.

HOUSE WREN.

*CAROLINA WREN.

MARSH WREN.

*BROWN CREEPER.

*WHITE-BREASTED NUTHATCH.

*TUFTED TIT. Nest on White House grounds.

*CHICKADEE.

*GOLDEN-CROWNED KINGLET.

*RUBY-CROWNED KINGLET.

GNATCATCHER.

*WOOD THRUSH. Nests on White House grounds.

*BLUEBIRD.

*ROBIN. Nests on White House grounds.

PRESIDENT ROOSEVELT'S
LIST OF BIRDS

———

SEEN IN THE WHITE HOUSE GROUNDS AND
ABOUT WASHINGTON DURING
HIS ADMINISTRATION

———

(*Denotes a species seen on White House grounds)

NIGHT HERON. Five spent winter of 1907 in swampy country about one-half mile west of Washington Monument.

MOURNING DOVE.

QUAIL.

RUFFED GROUSE. One seen on Rock Creek.

SHARP-SHINNED HAWK.

RED-SHOULDERED HAWK.

*SPARROW HAWK. A pair spent the last two winters on and around the White House grounds, feeding on the sparrows—largely, thank Heaven, on English sparrows.

*SCREECH OWL. Steady resident on White House grounds.

*SAW-WHET OWL. A pair spent several weeks by the south portico of the White House in June, 1905.

KINGFISHER.

*YELLOW-BILLED CUCKOO.

HAIRY WOODPECKER.

*DOWNY WOODPECKER.

*SAPSUCKER.

*RED-HEADED WOODPECKER. Nests (one pair) on White House grounds.

*FLICKER. Nests (several pair) on White House grounds.

WHIP-POOR-WILL.

NIGHTHAWK.

*CHIMNEY SWIFT.

*HUMMINGBIRD.

KINGBIRD.

FELLOWSHIP ASSETS

—

FRANK LLOYD WRIGHT
1943

In 1932, Frank Lloyd Wright, arguably the most accomplished architect of all time, opened the Frank Lloyd Wright School of Architecture ("Taliesin") and welcomed 23 apprentices into his world. For the next 27 years until his death, Wright taught and lived with numerous sets of students, some of whom went on to work for his firm after graduating. To this day, Taliesin continues to take on apprentices. In his 1943 memoir, *Frank Lloyd Wright: An Autobiography*, Wright listed a Taliesin fellow's ideal qualities.

FELLOWSHIP ASSETS

I. AN HONEST EGO IN A HEALTHY BODY—GOOD CORRELATION

II. LOVE OF TRUTH AND NATURE

III. SINCERITY AND COURAGE

IV. ABILITY FOR ACTION

V. THE ESTHETIC SENSE

VI. APPRECIATION OF WORK AS IDEA AND IDEA AS WORK

VII. FERTILITY OF IMAGINATION

VIII. CAPACITY FOR FAITH AND REBELLION

IX. DISREGARD FOR COMMONPLACE (INORGANIC) ELEGANCE

X. INSTINCTIVE COOPERATION

THE BOOKSHOP

—

ITALO CALVINO
1979

Italo Calvino's 1979 book, *If on a Winter's Night a Traveler*, is an enchanting novel that sees you, the reader, attempting to buy and read Italo Calvino's novel, *If on a Winter's Night a Traveler*. In one particular passage of the story's first chapter, the following types of reading material are listed as you navigate a crowded bookshop, eager to locate Calvino's.

Books You Haven't Read;

the Books You Needn't Read;

the Books Made For Purposes Other Than Reading;

Books Read Even Before You Open Them Since They Belong To The Category Of Books Read Before Being Written;

the Books That If You Had More Than One Life You Would Certainly Also Read But Unfortunately Your Days Are Numbered;

the Books You Mean To Read But There Are Others You Must Read First;

the Books Too Expensive Now And You'll Wait Till They're Remaindered;

the Books ditto When They Come Out In Paperback;

Books You Can Borrow From Somebody;

Books That Everybody's Read So It's As If You Had Read Them, Too;

the Books You've Been Planning to Read for Ages;

the Books You've Been Hunting for Years Without Success;

the Books Dealing With Something You're Working On At The Moment;

the Books You Want to Own So They'll Be Handy Just in Case;

the Books You Could Put Aside Maybe To Read This Summer;

the Books You Need To Go With Other Books On Your Shelves;

the Books That Fill You With Sudden, Inexplicable Curiosity, Not Easily Justified;

the Books Read Long Ago Which It's Now Time To Reread;

the Books You've Always Pretended To Have Read And Now It's Time To Sit Down And Really Read Them;

the New Books Whose Author Or Subject Appeals To You;

the New Books By Authors Or On Subjects Not New (for you or in general);

New Books By Authors Or On Subjects Completely Unknown (at least to you)

VERB LIST COMPILATION:
ACTIONS TO RELATE TO ONESELF
—

RICHARD SERRA
1967–68

In the late 1960s, American sculptor Richard Serra wrote *Verb List Compilation: Actions to Relate to Oneself* – four columns mainly composed of verbs in their infinitive form, all of which describe actions that can be carried out on materials during the artistic process. He then used the list as a blueprint for his later work.

to roll	to curve
to crease	to lift
to fold	to inlay
to store	to impress
to bend	to fire
to shorten	to flood
to twist	to smear
to dapple	to rotate
to crumple	to swirl
to shave	to support
to tear	to hook
to chip	to suspend
to split	to spread
to cut	to hang
to sever	to collect
to drop	of tension
to remove	of gravity
to simplify	of entropy
to differ	of nature
to disarrange	of grouping
to open	of layering
to mix	of felting
to splash	to grasp
to knot	to tighten
to spill	to bundle
to droop	to heap
to flow	to gather

to roll	to curve
to crease	to sift
to fold	to inlay
to store	to impress
to bend	to fire
to shorten	to flood
to twist	to smear
to dapple	to rotate
to crumple	to swirl
to shave	to support
to tear	to hook
to chip	to suspend
to split	to spread
to cut	to hang
to sever	to collect
to drop	of tension
to remove	of gravity
to simplify	of entropy
to differ	of nature
to disarrange	of grouping
to open	of layering
to mix	of felting
to splash	to grasp
to knot	to tighten
to spill	to bundle
to droop	to heap
to flow	to gather

to scatter   to modulate
to arrange   to distill
to repair   of waves
to discard   of electromagnetic
to pair   of inertia
to distribute   of ionization
to surfeit   of polarization
to compliment   of refraction
to enclose   of simultaneity
to surround   of tides
to encircle   of reflection
to hide   of equilibrium
to cover   of symmetry
to wrap   of friction
to dig   to stretch
to tie   to bounce
to bind   to erase
to weave   to spray
to join   to systematize
to match   to refer
to laminate   to force
to bond   of mapping
to hinge   of location
to mark   of context
to expand   of time
to dilute   of carbonization
to light   to continue

to scatter
to arrange
to repair
to discard
to pair
to distribute
to surfeit
to complement
to enclose
to surround
to encircle
to hide
to cover
to wrap
to dig
to tie
to bind
to weave
to join
to match
to laminate
to bond
to hinge
to mark
to expand
to dilute
to light

to modulate
to distill
of waves
of electromagnetic
of inertia
of ionization
of polarization
of refraction
of simultaneity
of tides
of reflection
of equilibrium
of symmetry
of friction
to stretch
to bounce
to erase
to spray
to systematize
to refer
to force
of mapping
of location
of context
of time
of carbonization
to continue

UTOPIAN TURTLE-TOP

—

MARIANNE MOORE
1955

In 1955, while attempting to find a name for their hugely anticipated new car, Ford decided to approach the most unlikely of people to assist in the matter: Pulitzer Prize-winning poet, Marianne Moore. Moore, who was known by the wife of one Robert Young, an employee in the car manufacturer's marketing research department, was soon contacted by letter; she agreed to help and proceeded to supply them with numerous lists of delightful names, all of which are compiled here, ordered chronologically. Her final suggestion, sent to Young on December 8th, was the amazing, "Utopian Turtle-top".

Incredibly, Ford ignored all of Moore's ideas and instead named their new car, "Edsel". It flopped.

The Ford Silver Sword
Hirundo
Aerundo
Hurricane Hirundo (swallow)
Hurricane Aquila (eagle)
Hurricane Accipter (hawk)
The Impeccable
Symmechromatic
Thunderblender
The Resilient Bullet
Intelligent Bullet
Bullet Cloisonné
Bullet Lavolta
The Intelligent Whale
The Ford Fabergé
The Arc-en-Ciel (the rainbow)
Arcenciel
Mongoose Civique
Anticipator
Regna Racer (couronne à couronne) sovereign to sovereign
Aeroterre
Fée Rapide (Aérofee, Aéro Faire, Fée Aiglette, Magi-faire) Comme Il Faire
Tonnere Alifère (winged thunder)
Aliforme Alifère (wing-slender, a-wing)
Turbotorc (used as an adjective by Plymouth)
Thunderbird Allié (Cousin Thunderbird)
Thunder Crester
Dearborn Diamante
Magigravure
Pastelogram
Regina-Rex
Taper Racer
Taper Acer
Varsity Stroke
Angelastro
Astranaut
Chaparral
Tir à l'arc (bull's eye)
Cresta Lark
Triskelion (three legs running)
Pluma Piluma (hairfine, feather-foot)
Adante con Moto (description of a good motor?)
Turcotinga (turqoise cotinga—the cotinga being a South-American finch or sparrow) solid indigo
Utopian Turtle-top

BILLY WILDER'S TIPS FOR SCREENWRITERS
—

BILLY WILDER
Late 1990s

Legendary film-maker Billy Wilder was responsible for writing and/or directing some of Hollywood's most iconic movies – he worked his magic on such classics as *The Apartment*, *Some Like It Hot* and *Double Indemnity*, to name just three – and as a result remains one of the most nominated directors in the history of the Academy Awards. He was a genuine force of nature in Hollywood for much of his prolific 50-year career, and a voice worth listening to. In the late 1990s, he imparted his wisdom on the subject of film-making in the form of this list of tips for screenwriters.

1. The audience is fickle.
2. Grab 'em by the throat and never let 'em go.
3. Develop a clean line of action for your leading character.
4. Know where you're going.
5. The more subtle and elegant you are in hiding your plot points, the better you are as a writer.
6. If you have a problem with the third act, the real problem is in the first act.
7. A tip from Lubitsch: Let the audience add up two plus two. They'll love you forever.
8. In doing voice-overs, be careful not to describe what the audience already sees. Add to what they're seeing.
9. The event that occurs at the second act curtain triggers the end of the movie.
10. The third act must build, build, build in tempo and action until the last event, and then — that's it. Don't hang around.

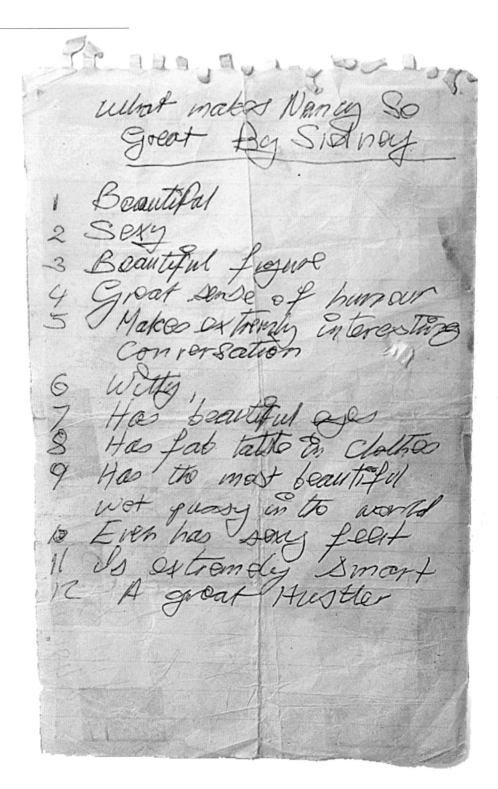

WHAT MAKES NANCY SO GREAT

—

SID VICIOUS
1978

In 1978, iconic and deeply troubled Sex Pistols bassist Sid Vicious hand-wrote a list of things that made his girlfriend of two years, Nancy Spungen, "so great". Tragically, in October of that year, Nancy was found dead in their shared Manhattan hotel room with a stab wound to the abdomen. Four months after that, on February 2nd, 1979, just before he was due to stand trial for her suspected murder, Sid passed away after overdosing on heroin.

smells like
Teen Spirit

needed
1. mercedes benz and a few old cars
2. Access to ^Abandoned a mall, main floor and one Jewelry shop.
3. lots of fake Jewelry
4. school Auditorium (Gym)
5. A cast of hundreds. 1 custodian, students.
6. 6 black cheerleader outfits with Anarchy A's (A)^on chest

'SMELLS LIKE TEEN SPIRIT'

—

KURT COBAIN
1991

Kurt Cobain was 24 years old and on the verge of mainstream stardom when he wrote this – a list of things needed in order to produce a music video for 'Smells Like Teen Spirit', the lead single from his band's second album *Nevermind*. Little did he or his bandmates know, but the single, video and album would all go on to become award-winning and iconic. His band, Nirvana, became one of the most influential of its generation.

I don't [ive readings either unless t'm offered a very large

EDMUND WILSON REGRETS THAT IT IS IMPOSSIBLE FOR HIM TO:

fee.
E·W

READ MANUSCRIPTS,

WRITE ARTICLES OR BOOKS TO ORDER,

WRITE FOREWORDS OR INTRODUCTIONS,

MAKE STATEMENTS FOR PUBLICITY PURPOSES,

DO ANY KIND OF EDITORIAL WORK,

JUDGE LITERARY CONTESTS,

GIVE INTERVIEWS,

CONDUCT EDUCATIONAL COURSES,

DELIVER LECTURES,

GIVE TALKS OR MAKE SPEECHES,

BROADCAST OR APPEAR ON TELEVISION,

TAKE PART IN WRITERS' CONGRESSES,

ANSWER QUESTIONNAIRES,

CONTRIBUTE TO OR TAKE PART IN SYMPOSIUMS OR "PANELS" OF ANY KIND,

CONTRIBUTE MANUSCRIPTS FOR SALES,

DONATE COPIES OF HIS BOOKS TO LIBRARIES,

AUTOGRAPH BOOKS FOR STRANGERS,

ALLOW HIS NAME TO BE USED ON LETTERHEADS,

SUPPLY PERSONAL INFORMATION ABOUT HIMSELF,

SUPPLY PHOTOGRAPHS OF HIMSELF,

SUPPLY OPINIONS ON LITERARY OR OTHER SUBJECTS.

EDMUND WILSON REGRETS

—

EDMUND WILSON
Date Unknown

As his popularity grew, the late literary critic Edmund Wilson found himself forever responding to mail, to the point where he wasn't able to focus on his work. His eventual solution was to send this, a pre-printed list of things it was regretfully impossible for him to do, to all who contacted him with a request he couldn't fulfil. Unluckily for Wilson, news of his unique rejection quickly circulated, and he was soon inundated with requests for the list itself.

SATCHEL'S RULES FOR THE GOOD LIFE

1. Avoid fried foods cause they angers up the blood.

2. If your stomach disputes you, lay down and pacify it with cool thoughts.

3. Keep the juices flowin' by janglin' 'round gently as you move.

4. Go very light on vices such as carryin' on in society. The social ramble just ain't restful.

5. Avoid runnin' at all times.

6. Don't ever look back. Somethin' might be gainin'.

SATCHEL'S RULES FOR THE GOOD LIFE

—

SATCHEL PAIGE
Date Unknown

Satchel Paige was one of the most accomplished and recognised pitchers in Negro League baseball, playing professionally from 20 years of age; he then debuted in the major leagues 22 years later, becoming the oldest person ever to do so. His crowning glory came in 1971, when he was inducted into the Baseball Hall of Fame. Throughout his career, in an effort to pass on his wisdom to as many people as possible, he handed out business cards on which this list of advice was printed on the reverse.

28 12/2/42

γ chamber	#3		#1	#6	
.93 @ 10:55	.87		.01	.08	pause
.925	11.01	.85	.00	.07	
.92	11:03	.84	.00	.065	
.93 -	11:10	.84	.00	.06+	
.925	11.13	.825	.00	.06	
.925	11.14	.815	.00	.06	
.925	11.15	.80	.00	.06	
.92	11.20	.785	.00	.06	
.92	11.23	.78	.00	.06	
	11.26		Rod put in		
.94	11.27	.96	.65	.69	
.94	11.28	.965	.73	.78	
.94	11.30	.965	.75	.81	
.935	11.34	.93	.24	.28	
.93	11.35	.86	.03	.10	
.925	11.37	.84	.00	.06+	
.92	11.39	.80	.00	.06	
.915	11.42	.74	.00	.06	
.91	11.44	.72	.00	.06	
.91	11.45	.70	.00	.06-	
.91	11.49	.67	.00	.06-	
.91	11.52	.66	.00	.06-	
.91	12.00 Noon	.64	✓	✓	
.90	12.02	.63	✓	✓	
.895	12.06	.56	✓	✓	
.89	12.08	.53	✓	✓	
.89	12.09	.50	✓	✓	
	12.16	Rod IN			

WE'RE COOKIN!

—

RICHARD WATTS
December 2nd, 1942

From 1939 until 1945, fearful that the Germans would get there first, an enormous team of scientists led by the US spent billions of dollars in a race to build the first atomic bomb, in a scheme named the Manhattan Project. A major development came in 1942, when physicists successfully orchestrated the first controlled, self-sustaining nuclear chain reaction – an experiment during which Richard Watts listed the on-going results in his notebook. The page seen here shows the very moment when fission occurred, labelled "We're Cookin!"

The project concluded three years after these lists were written, when two atomic bombs were dropped on Japan. Over 200,000 people perished.

12/2/42

γ Chamber	Time	# 3	# 1	# 6
.925	12¹² AM	.95	—	—
.93	12¹³	.965	.73	.78

γ #2(10")	Time	# 3 (10¹⁰)	#1 (10¹⁰)	#6 (10¹⁰)
—	2²⁴ pm	.97	.92	.99
—	2²³	.96	.905	.985
.945	2³⁴	.91	.82	.975
.94	2⁴⁰	.83	.67	.97
.94	248	.81	.62	.975
.935	2⁵⁷	.67	.38	.96
.92	3⁰³	.51	.14	.95⁻
.885	3¹⁵	.20	0	.905
.875	3²⁶	.14	0	.895
.860	3²⁸	.09	0	.88
.850	3²⁹	.06	0	.87
3³⁰ rod in				
.96	3³¹	.95	.9	.99
.96	3³³	.97	.95	.995
.96	3³⁷	.955	.90	.99
.96	3³⁷	.935	.86	.99
.955	3³⁸	.91	.8	.99⁻
.95	3³⁸·⁵	.87	.72	.98⁺
.94	3³⁹	.82	.61	.975
.94	3³⁹·⁵	.74	.46	.97⁻
.93	3⁴⁰	.64	.18	.96⁻
.925	3⁴⁰·²	.55	.16	.95
.92	3⁴¹·²	.48	.10	.94
.90	3⁴²·²	.35	.02	.93⁻

✳ We're cookin!

INDEX

SUBSCRIBERS

Unbound is a new kind of publishing house. Our books are funded directly by readers. This was a very popular idea during the late eighteenth and early nineteenth centuries. Now we have revived it for the internet age. It allows authors to write the books they really want to write and readers to support the writing they would most like to see published.

And now, to the most important list of all. The names listed below are of readers who have pledged their support and made this book happen. If you'd like to join them, visit: www.unbound.co.uk.

Chris Adams
Fiona Adams
Julie Adams
Phil Adams
Gail Affleck Ward
Ann-Maria Ahern
Marcus Ainley
Adrien Albert
Bruce Alcorn
Justine Alderman
Andy Aldridge
Alison Alexander
Robert Alexander-Sinclair
Romjan Ali
Moose Allain
Errol Allcock
Jamie Allen
Damian Amberg
Terje Ruud Andersen
Douglas Anderson
Nicola Anderson
Tom Anderson
Igor Andronov
Angel Of the North
Anonymous
Paul Anson
Sara Appleton
Izzy Appleyard-Yong
Cheryl Arany
Celia Armand Smith
Barbara Arnest
Penny Arrowood
Ara Lucia Ashburne
Sadif Ashraf
Amelia Ashton
Nesher Asner
James Austin
Amal Awad
Bryan Bailey
Susi Bailey
Abbie Baker
Jonathan Ball
Paul Ball
Connor Barclay

Clare Barker
Damon Barker
Leo Barker
Kevin Barrett
Duncan Barrigan
Chris Bartlett
Matt Barton
Isabella Sophia Barzanti Fernandez
Natasha Batsford
Juliet Bawden
Suzanne Bayon
Laura Bayzle
Clive Beautyman
Lynne Bebout
Pete Beck
Tom Beckett
Margaret Bell
Jo Bellamy
Martin Bellamy
Tracey Bellow
Catherine Benson
Howard I. Berrent
Jane Berry
Paula Best
William Bettridge-Radford
Matt, Terri and Joseph Betts
Kieran Binchy
Sally Bindari
Christopher Bishop
Stephen Blackwell
Christopher Blankenship
Robbert Bloem
Nicholas Bond
Nicky Bond
William Bonwitt
BookCunt
Gregory Boone
Ian Botterill
Caroline Bottomley
Wendy Boucek
Karl Bovenizer
Jamie Bowden
Lisa Bowen
Matthew Bowers

Kate Boydell
Geoff Boyle
Carrie Boysun
Geraldine Bradbury
Claire Bradley
Kirstin Bradshaw
Martin Brady
Janey Brant
John Brassey
Richard W H Bray
Leo Breebaart
Ryan Breedon
Sherry Brennan
Stephen Brennan
Sophie Bridge
Rebecca Broadbent
Matt Brockwell
Jane Brookes
Anne & Joe Brophy
Jade Broughton Adams
Claire L Brown
Steven Brown
Sue Brown
Neil Brown and Kristina Dietz
Kala Brownlee
Megan Bryan
Emily Bryce-Perkins
Philip Bryer
Gareth Buchaillard-Davies
Anthony Bunge
Debra Bures
Chris Burns ('Wee Chrissie B')
Kevin Butcher
Marcus Butcher
Fiona Butler
Tom Byrne
Georgina Calder
David Callier
Andrew Campling
Andy & Joy Candler
Stefano Canducci
Alistair Canlin
Xander Cansell
Tony Cantafio

Wharton Caroline
Caroline-Isabelle Caron
Martin Carr
Amy Carroll
Paul Carroll
Melanie Carruthers
Chloe & Greg Carter
Laura Carus
Leslie Casse
Roger Cavanagh
Elizabeth Caygill
Michael Chang
Jeffrey Chase
Andrew Chern
Cheryl Cheryl
Helen Chesshire
James Chilton
Ana Victoria Chiu
Nick Chominski
Tina Chopee
Dr Nicholas Andrew Vance Clarke
Richard Clarke
Elliott Clarkson
Timm & Sam Cleasby
Nic Close
Thom Clutterbuck
Garrett Coakley
Alex Coats
Lorna Anne Coffey and Elizabeth
    Louise Franke
Helen Collard Was Marriott
Pamela Collett
Gavin Collins
Tara Condell
Philip Conner
Edward Cook
Caroline Cookson
Antony Coombs
Glenda Cooper
Tracey Cormack
Elaine Corrington
Alberto Corubolo
Mike Coulter
Robyn Cowan
Amanda Cowlrick
Elizabeth Cox
Joanna Cox
Adrian Crabtree & Debbie Blanchard
Alex Crawford
John Crawford
Victoria Croft
Andrew Croker
Shane Cullinane
Heather Culpin
Bethan Cunnane
Ann Cunningham
Brenda Curin
Cornelia Daheim
Andrew & Antonia Dalmahoy
Felix Da   czak

Alexander Dao
Anne-Marie Dao
Sophia Darlington
Heena Dave
Emma Davies
Harriet Fear Davies
Matt & Owen Davies
Ian Davison
Tom Dawkins
Nelius De Groot
Lindsey Dear
Marjan Debevere
Mary Decious
Benny Declerck
Rachel Deeson
Forrest DeMarcus
Jamie Dempster
Andrew Denton
John Dexter
Nikhil Dhumma
Guy Dickinson
Alistair Dinnie
Ritchie Djamhur
Shereen Docherty
Andrea Dolan
Jacky Dols
Kate Donachie
Julie Donovan
Cressida Downing
Linda Watt Doyle
Liz Drabble
Tracey Drost
Tim Durham
Julie Durkheimer
Dave Dyke
Thom Dyke
Cornelia Eberhardt
Hillary Edwards
Jennie Eggleston
Lisa Elliott
Stefanie Epstein
Karsten Eriksen
Christopher Esposito
Peter Ettedgui
Cath Evans
Charles Evans
Dor Evans
Julie Evans
Jonathan Everall
Pete Faint
Peter Falconer
Jane Farey
Ewan Farry
John Fellows
Gregory Fenby Taylor
Ella Ferdenzi
Melissa Ferreira
Paul Fischer
Susan Foote
Debbie Ford

Doug Forrest
Marco Fossati-Bellani
Clare Fowler
Lynsey Fox
Stephanie Fox
Louise Foxcroft
Stephanie Frackowiak
Ann Frank
Isobel Frankish
Christopher Fretwell
G. Funk
Simon Gadd
Matthew Gallagher
Paul Garbett
Penny Gardiner
Richard Garnett
Annabel Gaskell
Patrick Gatenby
Carl Gaywood
Amro Gebreel
Saunders Gemma
Emma Giacon & Chris Helsen
Jack & Ellie Gibbons
Rob & Joanne Gibbons
Clare Gill
William Gill
Sealy Gilles
Simon Gillis
Matthew Giordano
Dominic Gittins
Tim Godby
Claire Goddard
Daniel Godfrey
Sunita Goli
Philip Goodman
Jim Goody
Bharadwaj Gopinath
Jess Gordon
Peter Gorrie
Jo Gostling
Michele Govier
David Graham
Ritchie Graham
Rebecca Granshaw
Fiona Green
James Green
Jonathan Green
Chris Greenway
Michelle Greenwood
Helen Gregory
Kate Gregory
Peter Griffiths
Frank Guerra
Adam Guest
Rich Gunn
Gwennyth Gwennyth
Sophie H
William Hackett-Jones
Katharine Halcrow
Alfie Hall

Catherine Hamilton
David and Katrina Hancock
John Handley
Lex Hands
Susan Hanlon
Emily Hanson-Coles
Lina Hardenburg
Ruth Ann Harnisch
Jordan Harper
Brian Harrison
A.F. Harrold
Caitlin Harvey
Kate Hawkings
Christina Hawley
Elspeth Head
In memory of my mother, Louise
   Hefter, who left me many beautiful lists.
Helen
Emma Helenius
Brian Henderson
Mark Henderson
Kevlin Henney
Frida Henriquez Kiely
Kirstie Hepburn
Jason Hesse
Robert Hicks
E O Higgins
Davida Highley
ElisabethHill Hill
Alexia Hill-Scott
David Hiltscher
Sigi Hirschbeck
Cheryl Hodgkinson
Joanna Holland
Karen Hollands
Roger Horberry
Bill Horton
Christine Houser
Jenny Howard
Catherine Howard-Dobson
Zoë Howe
Susannah Howell
Matt Huggins
Susan Hughes
Noortje Huisman
Lucy Hunt
Henri Hunter
Giselle, Dan & Maila Huron
Cathy Hurren
Lee Hurst
Mike Hutchinson
Neil Hutchinson
Sylvia Huynh
Malcolm Ingram
Bjarni Ingvarsson
Lori Irving
Alanna Evelyn Irwin
Erin Rachel Irwin
Kaushik Iyer
Madeleine Jackson

Pete Jackson
Michael Jagger
Natalie Jarian
Charlie Järpvall
Karen Jaunzems
Laura Jellicoe
Nimet Johnson
Sandra Johnson
Alex Johnstone
Elspeth Johnstone
Helen Jones
Josie Jones
Karen Jones
Mark Jones
Martin Chad Jones
Meghan Jones
Michelle & Stuart Jordan-Smith
Peter Karpas
Michael Kauffman
Linda Kaye
Deborah Kee Higgins
Steven Kehoe
Andrew Kelly
David Kelly
Alex Kennedy
Mike Kennedy
John Kent
Jennifer Louise Kerr
Rebecca Kerr
Maria Kerschen
Mobeena Khan
Sahira Khwaja
Dan Kieran
Kevin Kieran
Meg Kingston
Katrina Kirkby
Steve Kirtley
Jon Kitto
James Knapman
Peter Knocke
Melanie Knott
Bill Kohn
Matthew Kotok
Gabe Krabbe
Sean Kretz
Stephan Kurz
Nikki Kuyt
Mark Lacey
Mark Lally
Jenny Landreth
Kat Larkin
Jean-Jacques Larrea
Kim Le Patourel
Michael Leader
Johnny Leathers
Anne Frances Leners
Ashley Lewis
Daniel Lewis
Elen Lewis
William Lewis

Lidbert
Claire Liddle
Caroline Lien
Adrian Lightly
Diane Lindquist
Margaret Lindsay
Joonas Linkola
Helen Lippell
Robert Lischke
Tim Litsch
Allen Loades
Eugenia Loh
cmczz London.
Nate Long
Kyle Lonsdale
Isabell Lorenz
Anita Loveland
Dave Loverink
Alison Lowe
Dianne Lowry
Adam Lucas
Magdeline Lum
Bonnie Ma
Sue McAlpine
John MacBrayne
Tara McCausland
Anne Macdonald
Bethany Macdonald
Rob McDonald
Neil Macehiter
Bridget McGing
Helen McGovern
Carole McIntosh
Pete MacIntyre
Gavin McKeown
Maureen Mckerrall
Jonathan Macklin
Elodie Macknay-Swanepoel
Claire McClean
Heather Macleod
Susan McClymont
Kevin McMahon
Debbie McNally
Bryan McNamara
Michelle McNish
Stephen McConnell
Calvin Mcphaul
Helen Macpherson
Gary L. Maddox
Mick Mahoney
Sharoz Makarechi
Lindsey Malcolm
Debra Malouf
Michelle Maltby
Hedy Manders
Rashida Mangera & Hady Bayoumi
Jane Manning
Fabien Marry
Rhodri Marsden
Jane Marshall

Louise Marston
Andrew Martin
Toby Martin
Abigail O. Martone
Alexander Mason
Patrick Mason
Richard Mason
Emma Mathews
Walter Mayes
Sarah Mayfield
Natasha Mayo and David Mayo
Juan Miguel Mazoy
Brian Meacham
Chris Mead
James Medd
Ross Medley
Judith Mellor
Lynne Mendoza
Ann Menke
Doug Merrett
Sarah Merrett
Roger Miles
Tracy Miller and Paul Arnest
Fran Miller-Pezo
Adam Mills
Ruth Mitchell
John Mitchinson
Ronald Mitchinson
James Moakes
Stuart Moffatt
Cameron Moll
Simon Monk
Jim Mooney
Ellen Moore & Paul Arnott
Rose Morley
Helen Morris
Milo F. S. Morris
Nancy Morris
Lucy Moss
Leigh Mower
Niall Muckian
Christopher Mudiappahpillai
Ben Mueller
Nigel Muir
Wesley Mullen
Jane Murison
Brendan Murphy
David Murphy
Ewen Murray
Susie Murray
Nalini Arti Narayan
Stu Nathan
Andrew Neve
Linda Newbown
Andy Nichol
Vic Nicholas
Michelle Nicholson
Chris Niehoff
Stewart Nolan
Greg Norman

B.J. Novak
Peter Nowell
Ethna Nugent
Jim-Robin Nymoen
Neil Oatley
Angela O'Connor
Georgia Odd
Sue Odd
Aude Odeh
Anita Ogilvie
Jenny O'Gorman
Mary O'Malley
Nelleita Omar
Anna O'Neill
Kate Onyett
Susan O'Reilly
Max Orgeldinger
Monica Ormonde
David Overend
Valerie Louise Pace
Asa Packer
Sarah Paley
Shahan Panth
Carol Parker
Luke Parker
Rachel Parker
Richard Parker
Sally Parker Mitchell
James Parsons
Laura Pashby James
S. Pasian
Diana Passy
Martha Patrick
Jonathan Pavey
Noah Payne-Frank
Rachel Peacock
Eric Pearce
Nicholas Pearce
Ben Pearson
Bella Pender
Ben Pert
Kate Pert
Vivien Pert
Mason Petrie
Rose Phillips
Kerry Philpott
Anna Pick
Debra Pickering
Gregory F. Pickersgill
Cynda Pierce
Sarah Pinborough
Marco Piva-Dittrich &
    Solveig Dittrich-Piva
Justin Pollard
Claire Poore
Elspeth Potts
Jenny Pourian
Jean Power
Richard Preston
Neil Pretty

Robert Print
David Pritchett
Emma Probst
Ruth Puttick
Linda Quattrin
Gavin Quinney
Harold Raitt
Rakhi Rajani
Lane Rasberry
Michele Howarth Rashman
Jonathan Ratcliff
Christopher J.R. Ratcliff OBE
Rauf Rawson
Billy, Harry & Wayne Rayner
William Read
Alan Redman
Amy Rees
Guy Reeves
Margaret Reeves
Phillip Reeves
David Reidy
Hugh Richards
Olly Richards
Ali Richardson
Kath Richardson
Terri Richardson
Simon Ricketts
Clare Riding
Phillippa Ritchie
Jeff Robbins
Emma Roberts
Jonny Roberts
Wyn Roberts
Iain Robertson
Andrew Robinson
Clive Robinson
Jayne Robinson
Rachael Robinson
Samantha Rogers
Alison Rogerson
Dr Redentor Rojales
Steve Ronksley
Alison Rooney
Robyn Roscoe
Rebecca Rose
Andrew Rosenberg
Katharine Roseveare &
    Martin Raymond
Catherine Rossi
Laurie Roth
Katharine Rowan
Kirsty Rowan
Allan P Russell
Benjamin Russell
Grant Russell
Ruth & Nigel
Keith Ryan
Mary Saisselin
Adam Sales
Kay Salmon

Christoph Sander
Val Santiago and Marie Chan
Shrikant R Sawant
Neil Sayer
Kim Schilling
Cecilia Schoenbaum
John Schoenbaum
Carl Schwab
Gary Scott
Jillian Scott
Lina Scroggins
James Seabright
Matthew Searle
Will Sefton
Fabio Sensi
Beth Serota
Denise Shanks
Neil Sharma
Dinesh Shenoy
Gary Shewan
Rachael Simmons
Julian Simpson
Bette Sinclair
Mike Singleton
Jan Skakle
Roger Smethurst & Paula Forbes
Christopher Smith
Scott Smith
Simon J Smith
Barbara Snow
Matthew Soar
Todd Solomon
Stuart Southall
James Spackman
Kerri J Spangaro
Joe Sparano
Matthew Spicer
Kylee St George
Kelly Stanford
Pam Stanier
David Stelling
Jim Sterne
Kelly Stevens
LeAnne Stevens
David Stevenson
Lindsay Stewart
Alan Stoll
Julia Stone
Nina Stössinger
Katie Stowell
Michael Strawson
Simon Street
Jessica Stroup
Bob Stuart
Yonga Sun
Ross Sussman
Laura Sykes
Soulla Tantouri Eriksen
Beverley Tarquini
Alison Tarry

Ezra Tassone
Amanda Taylor
Maisie Taylor
Mike Teasdale
Ryan Teel
Melissa Terras
Andrea Thoene
Glenn Thomas
Jayne Thomas
Lynda Thomas
Wayne Thomas
Andrea Thompson
Simon Thompson
Ian Thompson-Corr
Joe Thorley
Amanda Thurman
Denise Tierney
Alice Tjiu
James Tobin
Andy Tootell
John Townley
Catrin Treadwell
Sarah Tregear
Alex Trew
Ma. Angela Tripon
Tjarda Tromp
Shelley Tule
Neil Turton
John and Lindsay Usher
Karen Usher
Ellen Van Gelder
Filip Vandueren
Nikki Vane
Phil Vaughan
Heleen Veerman
David Verey
Linda Verstraten & Pyter Wagenaar
Sarrah Vesselov
Prashanthy Vigneswaran
Thomas Vincent-Townend
Janne von Busse
Jo W
Greg Waddell
Jason Wainwright
Claire Walker
Joel Walker
Sam Walker
Stephen Walker
Steve Walker
Matt Wallace
David Wallman-Durrant
Chelsea Walsh
Rob & Liz Walsh
Josie Ward
Lynne Waters
Richard M. Watt
Catherine Watts
Simon Watts
Tanya Weaver
Rosie Weeks

Andreas Weinberger
Daniel Weir
Annie West
Paul Whelan
Levin Wheller
Rosemary White
Rosemary White
Simon White
Stephen White
Jacob Whitlow
Brenton Whittle
Hayley Wickens
James Wickham
Ali Wiff
Patrick Wilcox
Cary Wilkins
David Wilkinson
Rosie Willescroft
David Williams
Julian Williams
Reshma Williams
Jim Willis
Alexa Wilson
Iain Wilson
Kellie Wilson
Kirsten Wilson
Julie Woodgate
George Woodhouse
Stacey Woods
Ryan Woodward
Ashley Woolf
Anne Wright
Steve Wright
Debbie Wythe
Nicholas Yates
Riana Yeates
Stephen Alan Yorke
Carol Young
Rebecca Young
Simon Young
Jane Zara
Michelle Zitzmann

ACKNOWLEDGEMENTS

Creating a book like this is a mammoth task that requires assistance and guidance from a number of very important people, beginning with – and not just for her help during the often hellish, stress-inducing production of *Lists of Note*, but for her constant support in general – my wife, Karina, someone whose patience has been tested to its fullest since I began writing books but who has somehow managed to stay calm throughout. Special mention must also go to Cathy Hurren, my superhuman production manager, without whom this book literally would have taken a decade to reach the (wrong) printers, no doubt filled to the brim with factual errors, spelling mistakes, and no artwork. Untold thanks also go to the following wonderful people: permissions wizard Fred Courtright; John Mitchinson, Rachael Kerr, Dan Kieran, Isobel Frankish, Caitlin Harvey, Charlie Gleason, Emily Bryce-Perkins, Tim Mahar, Justin Pollard, Xander Cansell, and everyone else at the mighty Unbound; the incomparable Jamie Byng and his brilliant team at Canongate; Natalie Bradbury, who designed this beautiful book, and everyone else at Here Design including Julie Martin and Caz Hildebrand; every single archivist I have had the pleasure of meeting, online and off, all of whom have been more patient than I thought humanly possible; the legend that is Rob 'Scabbs' Gibbons; and, as always, my friends and family.

Finally, a massive, heartfelt thank you to two vitally important sets of people: first, all those who had a hand in writing the lists of note contained in this book; and second, each and every person who made this book a reality by pledging their support via Unbound. I will be eternally grateful.

PERMISSION CREDITS

p.1 Photo copyright © Julien's Auctions; p.1 Reprinted by permission of Lou Robin for the John R. Cash Irrevocable Trust; p.2–3 Reproduced by kind permission of Cambridge University Library; p.4–7 Georges Perec, "An Attempt at an Inventory of the Liquid and the Solid Foodstuffs Ingurgitated by Me in the Course of the Year Nineteen Hundred and Seventy-Four" from Species of Spaces and Other Pieces. Copyright © 1974 by Editions Galilee. Translation copyright © 1997, 1999 by John Sturrock. Reprinted by permission of Penguin Group (UK) Ltd; p.8–9 Photograph copyright © Alexander Autographs; p.10 © Succession Picasso/DACS, London 2014; p.11 A list written by Pablo Picasso of European artists to be included in the 1913 Armory Show, 1912. Walt Kuhn, Kuhn family papers, and Armory Show records, Archives of American Art, Smithsonian Institution; p.15–16 Image copyright © The Royal Society; p.17–18 Translation courtesy of Prods Oktor Skjaervo, Harvard University; p.19 Courtesy of The International Dunhuang Project, The British Library; p.20 Vladyslav Starozhylov/Shutterstock.com; p.28 Edmund Wilson, "The Lexicon of Prohibition" from American Earthquake: A Documentary of the Twenties and Thirties. Copyright © 1958 by Edmund Wilson. Used by permission of Doubleday, a division of Random House, LLC; p.29 © Bettmann/Corbis; p.31 Wellcome Library, London; p.33 Image courtesy of the George Washington Papers, Series 4, General Correspondence, Library of Congress, Washington, D. C.; p.34 © Bettmann/Corbis; p.35 Copyright © Autry Qualified Interest Trust; p.36 Chrissie Hynde, "Advice to Chick Rockers or 'How I Did It'" from Mouth2Mouth (1995). Copyright © 1995. Reprinted with permission; p.37 Fin Costello/Redferns/Getty Images; p.38–9 Courtesy of The Karpeles Library; p.40 Reprinted by permission; p.43–5 © The Trustees of the British Museum; p.46–7 Arts Centre Melbourne, Performing Arts Collection; p.46–7 Reproduced by permission of Nick Cave; p.48 The Walt Disney Company; p.49 Hulton Archive/Stringer/Archive Photos/Getty Images; p.52 George Rose/Hulton Archive/Getty Images; p.53 Susan Sontag, "Rules of Parenting" (September 1959) from Reborn: Journals & Notebooks 1947–1963. Copyright © 2008 by Susan Sontag. Reprinted by permission of Farrar, Straus & Giroux, LLC Hamish Hamilton/Penguin Group (UK) Ltd; p.54 Harry Ransom Center, The University of Texas at Austin; p.54 Courtesy of Daniel Selznick; p.60 By permission of the Estate of Geoffrey Handley-Taylor; p.61 Culture Club/Hulton Archive/Getty Images; p.62 © Bettmann/Corbis; p.64 Reprinted by permission of Ed Gombert; p.65 Courtesy of Morgan Wright; p.65 © Harry Gibson; p.68 Harry Ransom Center, The University of Texas at Austin; p.68 Used by permission of the Julia Child Foundation; p.70–1 Clara Barton, "Register of Missing Men of the Army, No. 2 Miss Clara Barton" (1865). Clara Barton National Historic Site, CLBA 4. National Park Service, Museum Management Program, Carol M. Highsmith, photographer; p.73 Boston Public Library Department of Rare Books and Manuscripts?; p.74 Louis Monier/Gamma-Rapho/Getty Images; p.75 Roland Barthes, "J'aime, je n'aime pas" from A Roland Barthes Reader. Copyright © 1977. Reprinted by permission of Hill & Wang, a division of Farrar, Straus & Giroux LLC and Random House (UK) Ltd; p.76–80 © The Trustees of the British Museum; p.81 Photo copyright © The King Center, Flip Schulke, Benedict Fernandez; p.81 © The Estate of Martin Luther King, Jr.; p.83 © Bettmann/Corbis; p.84–5 Roald Dahl, "The BFG's Vocabulary List" Copyright © RDNL. Reprinted with the permission of David Higham Associates, Ltd., on behalf of The Roald Dahl Museum and Story Centre; The Roald Dahl Museum and Story Centre; p.86–7 Royal Collection Trust / © Her Majesty Queen Elizabeth II 2014; p.89, 93, 95, 97, 99, 101 Courtesy of Folger Shakespeare Library; p.105 Reproduced by kind permission of Cambridge University Library; p.106–7 "New Years Rulin's" by Woody Guthrie. January 1, 1943. New York City, New York. © Woody Guthrie Publications, Inc.; p.106–7 Woody Guthrie, "New Year's Rulin's" (1941) from Woody Guthrie Foundation; p.108 Marilyn Monroe, "Marilyn Monroe's To-Do List" (1955) from Fragments: Poems, Intimate Notes, Letters, edited by Stanley Buchthal and Bernard Comment. Copyright © 2010 by LSAS International, Inc. Reprinted by permission of Farrar, Straus & Giroux, LLC; p.109 Michael Ochs Archives/Stringer/Getty Images; p.110 Noel Coward, "Rules of Palship between Esmé Wynne and Noël Coward" (August 11, 1915) from The Letters of Noel Coward, edited by Barry Day. Copyright © 2007 by N. C. Aventales AG. Used by permission of Alfred A. Knopf, an imprint of the Knopf Doubleday Publishing Group, a division of Random House, LLC. All rights reserved; p.111 © Pictorial Press Ltd/Alamy; p.117 Photo copyright © The Fitzwilliam Museum, Cambridge UK; p.118 Sei Sh nagon, excerpts from The Pillow Book, translated by Meredith McKinney. Copyright © 2006 by Meredith McKinney. Reprinted by permission of Penguin Group (UK) Ltd; p.121, 123 Courtesy of the Library of Congress; p.126 Norman Mailer, "Ten Favorite American Novels" from a letter to Helen Morris (January 16, 1988) in "Norman Mailer: Letters to Jack Abbott" from The New York Review of Books (March 12, 2009). Copyright © 1988 by Norman Mailer. Reprinted by permission of The Wylie Agency, LLC; p.127 Lange Jacques/Paris Match Archive/Getty Images; p.128 Courtesy of Pook & Pook, Inc.; p.129 Courtesy of Dartmouth College Library; p.129 Courtesy of The Robert L. May Co.; p.130–1 Royal Collection Trust / © Her Majesty Queen Elizabeth II 2014; p.132 Library of Congress, Prints & Photographs Division, Exit Art's "Reactions" Exhibition Collection, LC-DIG-ppmsca-01671; p.134–5 Farrell Grehan/National Geographic/Getty Images; p.136 Jack Kerouac, list of "Belief & Technique for Modern Prose" excerpt from a letter to Donald Allen (1958) from Heaven and Other Poems. Copyright © 1959, 1960, 1977 by the Estate of Jack Kerouac. Reprinted by permission of Sterling Lord Literistic LLC; p.137 © Allen Ginsberg/Corbis; p.138 © Bettmann/Corbis; p.139 Sylvia Plath, two lists from December 1952 ["I will not overwhelm him..." and "Back to School Commandments"] from The Unabridged Journals of Sylvia Plath: 1950–1962, edited by Karen V. Kukil. Copyright © 2000 The Estate of Sylvia Plath. Used by permission of Anchor Books, a division of Random House, LLC and Faber and Faber, Ltd; p.141 © Victoria and Albert Museum, London; p.142 Courtesy of the Trustees of the Boston Public Library/Rare Books; p.150–1 © Thelonious Monk; p.153 Courtesy of Biblioteca Nazionale Centrale di Firenze; p.154 Sister Corita Kent, "Immaculate Heart College Art Department Rules" from Jan Steward and Corita Kent, Learning by Heart: Teachings to Free the Creative Spirit. Copyright © 2008 by Jan Steward and Corita Kent. Reprinted with the permission of Skyhorse Publishing, Inc.; p.155 © Hulton-Deutsch Collection/Corbis; p.156–9 Harry S. Truman Presidential Library and Museum; p.160 © Bettmann/Corbis; p.161 David Ogilvy, "How to Write" from The Unpublished David Ogilvy Copyright © 1986, 2012 by The Ogilvy Group. Used by permission of Crown Publishers, a division of Random House LLC; p.162–3 David Markson, list of 54 rejections of Wittgenstein's Mistress. Reprinted by permission of the David Markson Estate; p.164, 166–72 © H.P. Lovecraft; p.165 © Pictorial Press Ltd/Alamy; p.173, 175 William Safire, "Fumblerules of Grammar" from Fumblerules: A Lighthearted Guide to Grammar and Good Usage. Copyright © 1979, 1990 by William Safire. Reprinted with the permission of Janklow & Nesbitt Associates; p.174 Diana Walker/The LIFE Images Collection/Time & Life Pictures/Getty Images; p.176 Christopher Hitchens, excerpt from "The New Commandments" from Vanity Fair (April 2010). Copyright © 2010. Reprinted with permission of the Estate of Christopher Hitchens; p.177 John Donegan/Getty Images Entertainment/Getty Images; p.179 Courtesy of The British Library; p.180, 182–3 Edna Woolman Chase and Ilka Chase, excerpt from Always in Vogue. Copyright 1954 by Edna Woolman Chase and Ilka Chase. Used by permission of Doubleday, a division of Random House LLC; p.181 George Karger/The LIFE Images Collection/Time & Life Pictures/Getty Images; p.184–5 James Agee, "Contempt or hatred for" list (December 26, 1937) from Unclassified: A Walker Evans Anthology (Scalo, 2000). Reprinted with the permission of the James Agee Trust c/o The Wylie Agency, LLC; p.186 The

A NOTE ABOUT THE TYPEFACES

The introductions to the letters are set in DIN, a sans serif font defined in 1931 by the Deutsches Institut fur Normung (the German Institute for Standardization). It is the typeface used on German road signs and on all kinds of technical documents. For a long time it was regarded as the classic example of a corporate typeface (the German Green party rejected its use on a proposed new logo in 2006), but it was clearly influenced by the geometric typeface experiments of the Bauhaus school, and research by the Dutch designer, Albert-Jan Pool, suggests that it wasn't just the work of a committee. He identifies the designer as Siemens engineer Ludwig Goller (1884–1964) who was chairman of the DIN committee for design. Pool himself went on to design a full family of DIN fonts in the mid-1990s. Its clarity and legibility mean it remains one of the most popular sans serif fonts. Type historian Evert Bloemsma attributes its success to the following formula: 80% hi-tech, 10% imperfection (which equates with charm) and 10% static.

The transcripts of the letters are set in Ehrhardt, a typeface developed in 1937 by Stanley Morison while at the Monotype Corporation. Morison was responsible for making modern versions of many antique faces, including Bembo and Baskerville, and designed the now ubiquitous Times New Roman. The creator of the original Ehrhardt typeface is unknown but it is named after the late 17th-century Ehrhardt foundry in Leipzig and is similar to some Dutch typefaces of that period produced by the Amsterdam printer, Anton Janson. The typographical historian Robin Nicholas believes Ehrhardt was Morison's take on Janson, 'made a little heavier and narrower to give improved legibility and economy'.